The Legend of B

Story by
Daniel Bodenstein
Ronald Robrahn

Written by
Daniel Bodenstein

Illustrations by
Ronald Robrahn

Totem Tales Publishing

Royal Palm Beach, Florida

Totem Tales Publishing

www.totemtales.com

Publisher's Note: This is a work of fiction. Names, characters, places, and incidents are a product of the author's imagination. Locales and public names are sometimes used for atmospheric purposes. Any resemblance to actual people, living or dead, or to businesses, companies, events, institutions, or locales is completely coincidental.

Book Layout © 2018 BookDesignTemplates.com

The Legend of Buc Buccaneer/ Daniel Bodenstein & Ronald Robrahn -- 1st ed.
ISBN 978-0-9843228-5-5

Dedication to everyone who inspired us and encouraged us.
Thank you.

The true test of a fowl's merit be not in his acquisition of wealth, but by the means in which it benefits his crew and his family. Although at the end o' the journey, 'tis not hurt to be rich.

- The last written words of Captain Lucky Longfeather

CHAPTER 1

The ocean water lapped against the hull of the majestic wooden vessel. The smell of the sea rolled over the deck and the spray leapt up to tickle the faces of anyone aboard. Bound tightly with cord, the mighty sails of the ship hugged the cross members of the stout main mast. The strong scent of linseed oil, mixed with the salt in the air, formed a pungent fog around the deck. Standing at the helm was a tall and proud rooster, his feathered hands wrapped around the wheel and the maroon tails of his long bandana flapping in the breeze. His eyes narrowed as he surveyed the scene.

"Stow the guns!" the rooster bellowed. "Hoist anchor! Set the main sail! Move like yer lives depend on it ya scurvy buzzards!" He looked over the empty deck of the ship with a critical eye. "Mister Ayg!" he cried. From behind him came the soft patter of bare feet, and the captain looked to see his first mate.

Mister Ayg was, in fact, a fully-grown fowl still trapped within his egg. Cracks had been formed to allow his legs and wings to move freely. For a trapped bird, he got on surprisingly well. Watching him operate in society was a surprising thing and seeing him bobble about the deck of a ship was hypnotic. He was able to perform any task the captain put forth, so long as you didn't mind the way he bumped around and occasionally knocked something over inadvertently. He was also a very expressive bird, who loved to draw faces on his shell. Today, Mister Ayg was all smiles.

The captain sneered down at his first mate and snapped, "Is that the face of a seasoned seaman?"

Mister Ayg shook his egg.

"Wipe that silly grin off your face!" the rooster ordered.

Mister Ayg dragged his sleeve across his front, literally wiping the smile from his face. He produced his coal stick and replaced the grin with a sneer.

"Better," the rooster crowed, though his tone suggested dissatisfaction.

The rooster standing at the helm, barking orders, was Buckley Smythe, a local, yet sometimes misguided, captain of a cargo vessel. Buc, as he was often referred to, drew a deep breath and exhaled loudly. "Is this not the way it should be, Mister Ayg? Sailing the wild sea? Braving danger? Living as free birds?"

Mister Ayg pulled on the coat of his captain and pointed over the starboard side.

The two turned to see the dock and the vessel still safely tied up.

"You know what I mean," the captain muttered, "besides, we have work to do." Buc turned the helm wheel looking at each of the posts as they passed his eye. "Find the knot then seven count to the left," he mumbled, finding the post bearing the knot. He then turned the wheel slowly to the left, allowing the posts to brush against his feathered fingers. Once he reached the count of seven, he stopped the wheel.

A tall gangly stork stepped from the main cabin and approached the two birds. His face had a wide smile, formed shamelessly by a twitch of his lower beak. "Well, Captain Smith?" he asked pleasantly, startling the rooster at the helm. "She be the finest galleon the Caribbean ever set eyes upon. What do you think?"

"Smythe," Buc corrected.

"What?" asked the apparent owner of the ship.

"The name, mate. Pronounced Sm - eye – th," Buc explained, drawing the words out into long notes.

"My apologies, Captain Smythe," said the stork, carefully pronouncing each syllable and bowing his head in apology. From his humbled position, he was unable to see Buc remove the wooden spindle post from the ship's helm, and discreetly slide it into his inner jacket pocket.

"Apology accepted," he replied. Buc turned to Mister Ayg. "Got it, mate," he whispered, "Now let us end this farcical fantasy." Buc turned his attention back to the ship's owner.

Slowly, the owner straightened himself, moaning a little as his back popped and cracked. He placed a hand upon the small of his back and stretched, generating one last pop and a long sigh. "She be shy of a little work," the owner announced.

"Apparently, she's not alone, mate," Buc mumbled.

"But I assure you she'll hold true at sea," the stork promised with a large grin.

The captain turned in a circle, scrutinizing his surroundings with a narrow, suspicious gaze. He strolled to a rail and rested a feathered hand on the beam. "She's a beast of a ship," he announced, turning his gaze to the owner. "She's run down, full of rot, leaks, and she smells funny." He tilted his head close to the rail and began rapping upon its wooden surface vigorously. He closed his eyes and shook his head as though he were a doctor who had just made a hopeless prognosis.

The stork stared in disbelief as Buc moved down the rail, talking to the wood and apologizing that he was too late to save the ship. He looked back at the other bird with an angry expression as the owner scratched his head vigorously. Small, white feathers floated from his head as the stork scratched away, completely dumbfounded by Buc's actions. This ship was just as stout and clean a vessel as any that had sailed the sea. The owner raised a finger in protest but Captain Buc broke in.

"Alas," Buc declared, "I can see you are a man with deep passion for her." He dragged a loving hand over the rail. "So I tell you this: give me the next two days to ponder the offer. I'll meet you back here with my decision, and if luck is on your side, a pouch full of coin."

The ship's owner stood speechless. He remained dead still for a moment, a look of confusion still painted across his brow. Then, as though a light had been shone upon him, his face broke into a wide smile and he chuckled as feathers drifted about the stork's head.

"Right then," said the Buc, strolling past the owner with long, confident strides. "Come, Mister Ayg," he cried out. Merrily whistling a tune as he left, leaving the owner standing by the rail, completely unaware that his potential buyer was walking away with a piece of his ship.

CHAPTER 2

The marketplace of Port Royal sang a chorus of haggling, laughing, sales pitches and the jingling of coins. Birds flapped their feathers and clicked their beaks over baskets and barrels, cups and crates, spools and sacks. Some chicks ran through a maze of booths and carts, laughing and yelling to one another while aged birds looked on with disapproving scowls. In the heart of all the noise and hurry, Buc strolled casually with his hands in his pockets. He deeply pulled in the rich air and sighed a long blast.

"The sea, Ayg!" he cried to his companion toddling along beside him. "It's the spray in the air and the salt in the wind. The tranquil rocking of a deck under your feet and a wide horizon in every direction. The ships and the ports and the men who give up a life upon land for the promise of adventure and the chance at a few gold pieces. Ahh!" he exclaimed. "This, I know, is what I am meant for!"

Looking over the masses moving about the market, Buc threw an arm over Mister Ayg and smiled broadly. His eyes dropped to the egg beside him and the smile faded.

"Mister Ayg?" Buc prompted.

Ayg looked back up with a fierce scowl still drawn upon his shell.

"Fix your face," Buc advised.

Ayg jumped anxiously and wiped his expression clean. When he looked back at Buc's face, it was with a contended expression.

"Much better, mate," Buc said in an approving tone. He looked back over the scene, as happy as he had ever been. He patted the

wooden post, tucked safely in his jacket, and wondered why his friend, Thomas, had asked him to retrieve it, even more to the point, why he needed to be so discreet about it. Thomas Willoughby was the owner of the only bookshop in all of Port Royal. He had befriended Buc when he was but a wee lad. Other than Mister Ayg, Thomas was, perhaps, Buc's only other true friend in all the world.

The only life Buc had ever known, and the only one he could ever imagine living, was his life upon the sea. From his hatching day, the salt of the oceans had been in his blood, coursing through his every fiber. It drove Buc to some far-off greatness as well. He'd been told that his father, the owner of a successful fishing fleet, had always said, "The sea gives us life, and turns a fuzzy little chick to a long-feathered fowl. Treat her with respect, and she will make you the bird you were born to be. Treat her unkindly, and she'll swallow you whole."

The words echoed in Buc's ears. Remembering those words prompted a deeply buried memory. He sadly strained back to the day he was told those words and told of the day his village was attacked by marauders.

The houses and buildings of Kismet Key were put to the torch, and the birds who were not killed were hauled away like cattle to be sold or forced to work upon the ships. Buc was too young to remember the sight of his parents murdered before his very eyes, but somehow, he carried that emotional scar with him.

Alone and frightened, the young chick cried out instinctively for his mother. Not long after the pirates left, a squat captain by the name of Vientre Rojo poked his head into a battered home and found a little tuft of soft feathers around a pair of keen dark eyes. The chick trembled as the captain approached and Rojo hushed him gently.

"There there," the captain cooed. "It's alright." His relatively thick Spanish accent was new to young Buc. He stared in silent wonder, grasping tightly to a small toy rooster with his name written across it.

"My name be Vientre Rojo, but you can call me Rojo," he said quietly.

"Rojo," squeaked the tiny beak.

"I'm going to take you out of here."

The chick was slow to respond, nervous and skeptical of anyone strange to him, but Rojo soon won him over. The captain took the chick upon his ship and set a course for home.

"I will look after you, little master," he promised the chick, standing at the stern of the ship and looking over the deck. "Life is never as you plan for it to be," the captain continued. "But that not always be a bad thing."

The young Buc looked up, face feathers damp with tears.

"It must be hard to see now," Rojo admitted, "but someday you may see this as the greatest turning point in your life. Wait and see, little master. Destiny awaits you."

Rojo took the chick home to his wife. He spent the next two years with the captain as family—until the day came when Rojo's wife demanded that Buc be removed from their home. Buc was told that, with Rojo at sea most of the time, the responsibility of raising a chick was too much for the bewildered hen. He was taken to Madame Hensworth's Orphanage and left there with only Madame Hensworth and the nuns to care for him. Rojo made a promise to the juvenile rooster. He would search the seven seas for any family that Buc may have. The good captain visited the young rooster at regular intervals. Buc was grateful for the visits at first, but, as he grew older, he began to quietly pull away from the captain. He had become friends with another orphan who shared dreams of freedom and adventure. It was an unhatched chick that Buc took to calling Mister Ayg. Buc was a confident young rooster while Mister Ayg, being unhatched, remained shy and withdrawn. Buc took him under his proverbial wing, and they created a spirited friendship.

Capitán Rojo worked hard searching for any of Buc's surviving relatives. Every port he landed upon and every village he passed through, Rojo would call upon the local leaders and tell them the story of the little orphan chick at Madame Hensworth's. Days turned to weeks, weeks into months, and months into years, until one day while Buc was in his early teens, Rojo's searching paid off. With good news in hand, Rojo made an unscheduled visit to the orphanage.

"You have an aunt and uncle, Buc," Rojo explained with glee.

"Mister Ayg?" Buc cried, turning to ignore his benefactor. "What does the sea look like today?"

The egg took out a coal stick and drew a crude face upon his shell. The eyes were mismatched, and the mouth was open and lopsided, as though he was scared and excited all at once.

"My thoughts exactly," Buc said with a nod. "She's a crafty demon, the sea."

"Your relatives are expecting you," Rojo continued. "I have made arrangements for the sisters to allow me to escort you to them tomorrow. They live right here in Port Royal."

"Strange wind a'blowing, Mister Ayg," Buc said through a pinched expression. The young bird ruffled his neck feathers and turned his back upon the captain.

"Buc!" Rojo said with a sharp edge in his voice.

"I'm not going!" the proud young rooster declared. "I'm not living with people I don't know. Mister Ayg and I have plans. Big plans. Our future is on the sea, and I will not let you send me off to some landlubber's cottage, trapped in and cut off from the rest of the world."

"Since when did you want to be a seaman?" Buc turned his head away, but the captain saw enough in his expression to know what was going through the little one's head.

"You said my father loved the sea," Buc answered.

"Yes. He was a fisherman."

"Mister Ayg and I," Buc began, "we are going to be the greatest birds upon the ocean. Everyone everywhere will know our names." His face scowled, "But we can't achieve greatness caged up in some cottage off a cobblestone path."

"You cannot do that from within the gates of an orphanage either," the captain said delicately.

Buc mulled the idea over and looked to Ayg, who wore the same expression as before. The egg shrugged, and Buc returned the gesture.

"You can have both, boy. This is Port Royal!" Rojo announced, eager to fill the young fowl with excitement.

Buc's head snapped round, and he stared in shock at the captain.

Rojo gently shook his head as he looked up at the walls of the orphanage. "This place has been a fortress for you, hiding you from the world for far too long." He focused his attention on the young bird. "Buc, you live in the largest port in all the Caribbean," he said with a knowing smile. "More ships pass through there every day than most landings see in a year." Rojo stood and brushed the front of his coat. "You cannot learn to sail by sitting around here dreaming with your friends."

Buc stared at Ayg then turned to face Rojo. "Why did you leave me here?" he muttered, slack faced and eyes wet with forced back tears.

Rojo let out a deep sigh. "I know it is difficult to understand, but I had no choice." He placed a hand on Buc's shoulder. "But now you have a real family to go to. Blood relatives."

"What if later they decide they do not want me either?" asked Buc, sniffling hard.

"Because, young Buc, you did not see their faces when I told them of you." He lifted Buc head by his lower beak and looked deep into his tear-soaked eyes.

Once again, Buc sniffled. "What of Ayg?" He looked over at his oblong friend. "I cannot leave him here. He is my friend. My only friend."

"Now Buc," said Rojo, again looking deep into the young fowl's eyes, "Do you think I would forget about your first mate?"

Buc seemed to cheer up, awaiting the rest of Rojo's explanation.

"You aunt and uncle have agreed to take him in as well." Rojo stood tall. "It will be as if you are brothers."

Buc smiled, looked over at Ayg, and giggled once he saw Ayg had drawn his own tears on his shell.

"Tomorrow?" asked Buc.

"Tomorrow!" confirmed Rojo.

Never in the history of the orphanage had there been a more sleepless night. The eager anticipation of meeting his new guardian, coupled with Ayg and him now becoming full-fledged brothers kept the two awake all night. The morning dawned quickly as Rojo walked up to the gates of the orphanage. Silhouetted in the early fog stood a young rooster and an egg.

"Our adventure begins!" Buc proclaimed.

Years would pass as Buc and Mister Ayg learned to work the docks. They served as deckhands and scullions and took upon themselves any other odd jobs they could find. The pair could be seen painting the rails of some fishing vessel just as often as they were found hanging from the mizzen of a merchant clipper. Day in and day out, the pair were upon the docks, dreaming of the day when they would be famous sailors with their own ship. Eventually, they gained a regular position with a local shipper, Mr. Torn, who would spend the next five years teaching the duo everything from charts and logs to waves and weapons. The pair could often be found hauling cargo around the docks or repairing the hull of a ship from sun up to sundown. There was no task too small or too great for them.

"The sea is like a woman," Torn once said. "She'll toss you here and there, and damn near kill ye, but she'll love you nonetheless and bring you home safe in the end if you mind her."

"I thought you said your pistol was like a woman?" Buc asked with a confused expression.

"You'll find that most dangerous things are like women," the old shipper replied with a smile. "But don't be tellin' your aunt I said as much. Ye hear?"

"Yes, sir," Buc promised, returning the smile.

With the history of the fate of Kismet Key often weighing heavy on his mind, Buc finally built up the courage to convince his uncle to permit him to travel to the village of his birth. As he stood on its shores he could still make out structures, buildings and docks, all still abandoned after all this time. Buc slowly wandered the wreckage of the bay, sadly passing between the pieces of broken and battered ships, until an idea struck him.

"Uncle, who owns these ships?"

"These?" the old bird asked, nodding at the bones of vessels resting around them. "No one, as far as I can tell. Been abandoned they have."

"Might I have one?" Buc inquired.

"Now why would you want that?"

"To build a ship of my own," said Buc, riddled with excitement. "I shall take to the sea just as my father." He looked around the desolate shipyard. "Just look," he pointed out, extending a feathered hand toward the nearest craft. "This one here has a broken foremast, but a perfectly sound main. And the outer hull is battered, but the riders are all intact. And this one over here," the teenage rooster said excitedly, "this one has all of the planks I would need to fix the other."

"You mean to rebuild a ship?" his uncle asked dubiously.

"Aye, I mean to rebuild a ship," Buc agreed. "I can pay for supplies with my earnings from Mr. Torn, and Ayg can help me."

The older bird hummed his concern. "It will be a lot of work," he pointed out. "And you would be a way from home while you were here. What if the boat is stolen or damaged?"

"Then I shall build another!" Buc said confidently.

His uncle scratched his head.

"Uncle," Buc said, with admiration in his eyes, "what better way to honor where I come from?"

He looked down at his stubborn nephew and knew there was no point in telling him not to do something he would just do anyway. "Fine. I shall talk to your aunt."

Weeks rolled past as the pair spent all their free time rebuilding and restoring the remains of the ship. The two would return home after dark smelling of sweat, tar, linseed oil, and stagnant remains of old, rotted cargo. His aunt would fluff her feathers and comment on the pair's foul stench.

"You two smell like the bowels of a fishing galleon," she would announce. The words would be harsh, but the smile hiding in the corner of her beak would betray her real feelings.

When the vessel was finally ready for Buc to sail it home, it was christened after his aunt's favorite complaint: The Fowl Stench. Now, with a ship at his command, Buc was ready to start a business of his own.

As one of the youngest captains of a merchant vessel, Buc struggled to earn the respect of the larger shipping magnates. His time on the sea was spent ferrying petty goods and passengers across the crystal blue waters of the Caribbean. His pay was not as lavish as those having a constant flow of cargo from a larger exporter, but by sailing off the beaten path, Buc and Ayg were able to meet some colorful and interesting people. His crew was varied and often was poached by the more established captains on the sea, but Buc did not let this discourage him. He offered a job to any fowl willing to sail with him and offer him a strong back.

As he grew beyond his teenage years toward adulthood, Buc was hardly content ferrying goods between the islands with Mister Ayg as his first mate. Something was lacking in his life. There was a piece missing, like a mast that was short a sail. As he dwelled on the feeling, Buc's mind was taken back to when he first met the booksmith, and how he would spend his lunches hunched in Thomas' chair, listening to the tales of pirates, brave captains and battles upon the open water. Thomas would entertain the young rooster with stories of bravery and courage, rage and jealousy, love and hatred; tales of daring captains like Black Bart, Jaques Sparrow, and his favorite, the mysterious pirate Lucky Longfeather. Tales of Lucky's adventures on the high seas always had young Buc on the edge of his seat. "No one knows what happened to old Lucky," Thomas would say, waving his wing in the air to add to the mystery. "He just disappeared. Faded into legend." Buc often dreamed of being the fowl that discovered what truly happened to old Lucky. After the stories, he would head back to the harbor, swinging a stick sword, pretending it was Lucky's sword, Tempest, the rage of the sea, promising to capsize the world in order to find Lucky and share in his wealth.

Today, with the piece of a mysterious vessel hidden in his jacket, Buc strolled the cobbled streets of the local marketplace he had known since childhood. He instinctively turned his feet towards Mr. Willoughby's door. As he drew close, a ruckus was brewing in the street. A small flock had gathered outside the bookshop and, as Buc pushed his way through, he was able to make out a figure lying on the cobblestones.

"Thomas!" Buc crowed. He shouldered his way through the crowd, pushing birds aside if they were too slow to move on their own. "Thomas!" he cried out again. Reaching his friend, Buc fell to his knees and laid his wings over the booksmith's chest. "Who did this?" Buc roared into the crowd. "Who was it? Who?" Waves of anger rolled off him and crashed, hot and suffocating, into those standing closest. A few of the spectators backed up involuntarily. ❷

"Buc?" asked a weak voice.

Buc looked down into the eyes of the booksmith and gasped. "Thomas?" he whimpered. "Thomas, my good friend." Buc pressed the aged fowl's feathers flat and gave a weak smile.

"Buc," Thomas sighed, letting his eyes close again. "Oh, thank heavens."

Buc leaned himself against Thomas' body and cradled his head. "I'm here," he cooed. "I'm here. What happened?"

"Never mind you what happened," the old bird wheezed. He dug in the pocket of his vest and pulled out a small scrap of parchment. "Here," he said, straining every sound past his shivering beak. Thomas pushed the paper into Buc's hand then he lay back and puffed hard, as though trying desperately to catch his breath.

Buc barely glanced at the scrap as he scowled at Thomas. "Who did this to you?" he demanded. "Who?"

"You shall know soon enough," the booksmith muttered, not lifting his head. "You need ... Buc ... you need to..." His thought was cut off by a long string of coughs, raspy and cutting and wet. "You need to ask your uncle," the bird finally managed, "to tell you the truth."

"The truth?" Buc repeated.

"The truth about everything," Thomas continued. "About all of it. Tell him he must. Tell him, 'Thomas said it is time.'"

"The truth?" Buc wondered aloud. "What do you mean?"

"It not be my place to say, lad," Thomas assured him. "He will know."

"So, you dare not tell me who did this," Buc complained softly, "and you refuse tell me what this secret is. You are gambling on a lot of knowing happening later, aren't you?"

"Aren't we all?" the booksmith replied with a fragile smile. "Did you get the spindle? The post. Did you get it?"

"I did," he replied. "But I still don't understand. What is its purpose?"

Thomas smiled then fell into another fit of coughing. Buc waited politely, ignoring the gawkers and the curious birds who were still milling about uncomfortably. "Soon..." he sputtered, clearing his throat. Thomas tried to speak again but the words wouldn't form.

Buc's mind was reeling from Thomas' last sputtered words. All the rooster could think about was how there were secrets being kept from him. Thomas knew and apparently, his uncle did as well. If they were withholding information about Buc, information that seemed important enough to take to the grave, then it was time he knew what was being kept from him.

The door to the cottage blasted open as though it had been shot with a canon. Buc stomped inside and quickly looked about.

"Come out!" the furious bird crowed. "Come on now! Where are you?"

The modest cottage came alive with the flapping of feathers and a great string of incredulous huffs from an unseen host. "Who's there?" a voice demanded from another room. "What's the meaning of this?" The chubby old carpenter came out from around a corner brandishing a large, wooden mallet and wearing an angry scowl. His expression melted, and the mallet went limp when he saw his intruder. "Buc?" the rooster asked in a shocked tone. "What…" He leaned to get a clear glimpse of his front door, now hanging sadly to one side.

"Hello, Uncle," Buc growled.

"My door," the carpenter whined. "What has gotten into you, lad?"

"Thomas is dead," Buc announced in a cool, even voice. His eyes narrowed as he studied his Uncle Robert's reaction.

The portly rooster rocked on his heels and silently mouthed his disbelief. "What?" he asked, unable to process the news. "What do you mean?"

"I mean he is dead," Buc repeated.

The mallet slipped from his hand and fell to the floor beside Robert. From around the corner, sobbing and gasping could be heard.

"Fanny!" Robert cried, and Buc's aunt appeared, her beak hidden behind a wall of trembling feathers. "Did you hear?" the carpenter asked his wife.

Fanny nodded and sobbed into her hand. "How?" she asked. "How could this have happened?"

"Someone killed him," Buc declared. "In his store, today. I arrived just in time to catch his final breath."

"Did they catch him?" his aunt demanded in an angry rush. "Did the guards arrest the scoundrel who did this?"

"It seems the bystanders were tight beaked about it," Buc confessed then added, "But Thomas seemed to think you might have a notion."

Fanny and Robert exchanged a knowing look before they both their heads slowly dropped, facing the floor.

"You are keeping something from me," Buc grumbled. "There is something you need to reveal to me … now." His voice was filled with the anger and rage of a thousand disappointments.

"Buc," his uncle began, but the younger rooster cut him off.

"No more secrets," Buc said decisively. "Whatever tidbit of knowledge you have must be important. Thomas knew it and I believe he was trying to warn me. If you know it," he continued in a stern manner, "and if you have ever had an inkling of care for me, then you will no longer withhold the truth."

"Buc," his aunt said softly, "please. Come and sit down." Buc's aunt had always been the voice of reason in the household. Even as a young rooster appearing on their doorstep so many years ago, the sight of the hen's ocean blue eyes would portray an air of serenity. Buc, still influenced by her loving manner, attempted to fight his heart in favor of his head.

He stood, rigid for a moment, then made his way to the nearest chair. Fanny and Robert took a spot on the sofa while Ayg pushed the door back into the frame.

His aunt and uncle looked at each other for a moment as both decided wordlessly who should be the first to speak. Robert nodded at their unspoken agreement and turned to his nephew.

"For years now," he began in a small, strained voice, "we have struggled to find the right moment to tell you, lad."

"It is true," Fanny insisted, now on the verge of tears.

"We never thought…" Robert started, bowing his head as he paused. "Well … that may be the problem at hand. We never thought." Fanny reached out and took her husband's hand. The old rooster bobbed his head and stuck out his lower beak. "I'm fine," he assured her. "I'm fine." Robert then turned back to Buc and took a deep breath. "When you were young," he began again, "we told you that Rojo rescued you from the village of Kismet Key."

"Yes," Buc agreed nervously. "He arrived with the relief boats after the attack. He found me and took me under his care. I know all this."

Robert stared at the floor and ground his beak, and Buc had a sudden twisting sensation in his gut.

"That may not…" Robert strained then choked on his own words. He made a low hum in his throat then spat out all at once, "That may not be entirely factual."

Buc's mouth sagged, and his brow pinched in befuddlement. The scrape of coal on eggshell was loud in the sudden silence and Buc turned to see a horrified expression scribbled on Ayg's face.

"Rojo did seek us out," Fanny explained.

"And we took you in of our own free will," Robert reassured him.

"We wanted you to be part of our home, Buc. You are, after all, family," Fanny added through tearful eyes.

"I do not understand," Buc admitted. "If Rojo did not rescue me then who did?"

"Oh, Rojo saved you from the aftermath of the destruction," Robert answered quickly.

"Then what is it? Out with it!" Buc demanded impatiently, losing his love for elongated story telling.

"Rojo did not stumble upon you by chance, my boy," the old rooster disclosed. "Buc..." Robert swallowed hard and looked at the floor. "Rojo was the same scoundrel who attacked the village."

Shivers ran over Buc and pierced his bones. The weight of a hundred timbers fell upon his shoulders. "He..."

"Aye, boy. It was Rojo who dispatched your parents," his uncle continued warily. "His ship bore the marauders that attacked Kismet Key. He stormed your house. Your father resisted with every ounce of his being, and he was put to the sword for it." Robert looked over at his wife. "He and your mother. His actions did not end there. Rojo turned on the rest of the village. He gave no quarter. When Rojo found you, Buc, you were little more than a squeaking chick."

Buc rushed from his seat and loomed over the pair of them. "You knew," he raged. "You two knew all along and you never thought it necessary? You knew the identity of the savage that killed my parents?"

"No!" Robert cried. "We didn't. Thomas," the carpenter said, panting. "Thomas knew, and he confided to us what really happened."

"And how did Thomas know?" Buc snapped.

"Because he was there, my boy," Fanny wept. "Thomas had returned from a—" Fanny paused and looked over at her husband "—fishing trip," she concluded. "He saw the carnage that transpired but, sadly, was helpless against such a band of cutthroats."

The room felt very small in that moment, and Buc felt confined, as if in a coffin of his own design. "Thomas." Buc had the sensation of drowning in realization. "He knew my father?"

"Buc," his aunt softly begged. "Please sit. Here," she said, gesturing with a hand toward the chair.

"Aunt Fanny," Buc replied in a forced manner, "you will understand if I am unwilling to sit at present." Every word from his beak was a quiet stab with a knife and a silent report of a pistol; such was the energy welling behind each letter. "But I will hear what you must say," he said. "I will have the entire tale."

Robert wiped his beak and blinked hard. "Rojo," he began, soaking in Buc's response to the name, "he wanted you for himself, to raise you as his own. He and his wife—"

"The witch," Fanny interrupted, spitting the curse and curling the edge of her beak.

Robert scowled at her and she fell into silence.

"They could have no children of their own, you see," the uncle continued. "They kept you for two years until one day she ordered him to be rid of you."

"Be rid of me?" Buc wondered aloud. "But why?"

"She had a vision," Fanny offered as Buc squinted at her in confusion.

"A vision of you, lad," Robert explained.

"A vision? What sort of vision would cause a woman to abandon an adopted child? Was I stealing from the pantry? Was I soiling proper linens? Tracking mud across the floor?" Buc asked heatedly.

"The vision was of you killing Rojo," Robert declared, drawing Buc's complete attention. "She insisted that you were to be his undoing, and that is why you ended up in the orphanage."

Ayg positioned himself beside his friend, his brother, his captain.

"Apparently, Rojo did care for you. Instead of allowing you to be adopted by anyone, he sought us out," Robert shared reluctantly, filling in details Buc never knew existed. "Thomas knew where to find us. Rojo paid for us to relocate here, to Port Royal. He paid for this home for us to raise you in. Apparently, he felt the need to keep an eye on you."

"And Thomas," Buc asked, guessing, "was he part of Rojo's lies?"

"Thomas was no friend of Rojo's. No," Robert insisted. "Thomas was a faithful fowl and cared for you very much. As the only other survivor, he felt a strong connection to you."

Buc began to pace about the room, tugging on his feathers and growling words no one could understand.

"You have every right to be mighty angry, lad," Robert observed, "and sorry I am that the truth has been revealed in this manner."

Buc pressed his eyes closed and pictured the sea captain who he had regarded as a dear friend. His heart twisted and grew hard, burning with hatred and pulsing with rage. "He will pay," Buc swore. "That fat robin will pay for his dastardly deeds." He clenched his feathers into fists and laughed darkly. "His witch was right to warn him, and she was wise to fear me."

"Buc," Robert began in a warning tone, but was cut off by his nephew.

"Mark my words, Uncle. I will not rest until I avenge the death of my parents and my good friend Thomas." He grasped the handle of his sword tightly. "When Rojo and I next meet," the rooster vowed, "my sword will be bathed red with his blood."

Robert stared at the rooster he had raised. He saw the young chick playing with sticks and climbing the shed. He saw the little one with the scraped knees and the penchant for trouble. He saw the rooster that had grown strong and proud, and he prayed that the bird he knew and loved wasn't lost. "Vengeance," he said, picturing the little bird he once knew, "is not the way to adventure, my boy."

Buc's eyes twinkled with purpose and mischief. He reached in his pocket and clutched the note given to him by Thomas. "Adventure?" he asked. "That may have been the desire belonging to the captain of a shipping vessel." He explained. "Have I not made myself clear, Uncle? My story has changed. I'm no longer an adventurer at heart. I'm a pirate."

Chapter 3

The Wooden Stork pub was nearly empty that night, with only a
handful of sailors scattered around the room. There were a couple of
lonesome birds, sitting alone and drowning their sorrows at the bottom
of a mug of hard cider. Crowded about one corner of the bar was a
feisty gang of young roosters, crowing loudly in celebration. On the
other side of the bar, sitting at a small table with his head hung over a
drink and an egg perched at his side, Buc contemplated his glass in the
dim light. He slowly shook his head then raised his glass to the sky.
"To one of my best mates," Buc cried out. "To Thomas. I swear on
pain of death, I shall hunt down the buzzard that did you in and hold
him accountable."

Mister Ayg lifted his own glass and nodded silently. Drawn upon
his shell was a miserably depressed expression, mixed with the
occasional drawn, and erased, tear.

Buc held his glass high for a moment then tipped the drink down
his throat. He slid a piece of paper from his coat pocket and set it upon
the table. Ayg moved closer to get a better view of the note. Thomas
had given him the scrap and written upon it were three names. Each
name, save one, had numbers alongside it. Under the name it simply
read, "Three pouches make one."

"First my parents," Buc mumbled into his empty glass. "Now Thomas." He looked robustly at the piece of parchment. "What is this, old friend? Was this why you were taken from us?" He turned to Ayg. "I fancy it too much of a coincidence. My parents and Thomas were from Kismet Key. It is only safe to assume that Rojo be behind BOTH bits of carnage."

Ayg nodded vigorously, gently patting Buc's arm, trying to console his friend.

Buc stared once again at the piece of crumpled parchment that Thomas had given him. "Dear Thomas. If only you could bestow on me the meaning of these numbers. Are they street numbers? Measurements?" Buc asked.

Ayg tugged on Buc's coat and tapped the top of his shell.

"No, my friend", muttered Buc, "I doubt they are hat sizes." He read the names on the list in silence. "And who are these blokes he listed?"

Buc shook his head slowly from side to side. "I cannot remain my meager self no more Ayg." He exhaled heavily. "It is far time to shed this weak skin mate," he announced, sitting up straight and staring into the distance. "For too long I've teetered on the boundaries of adventurer or pirate. Well, no more. Tonight, I make my stand. Tonight, I become the rooster I was hatched to be." Buc's chest heaved, and his eyes narrowed. A small, sad smile curled one corner of his mouth like a glimmer of hope fighting against the pain in his heart. He breathed deep and let his eyes fall shut. His head was still tipped up and he had begun to raise his glass as a silent promise to the birds in his life that had been taken from him too soon. Such a moment was taking place that, if a painter was present, Buc was certain this pose would have been immortalized forever as the artist's greatest work.

"How are we doing here, gents?" a voice asked, interrupting the scene and forcing Buc to peak from one eye. Penelope, the hard-working serving girl, stood over them with a pitcher of cider in one hand and a face like someone trying to suppress a laugh. "Need a top up?" she asked.

She was a songbird, one of millions that had soared out into the world in search of love, adventure and fame. Yet, like so many birds before her, Penelope had traded the dream for a steady income and a little place to call her own.

Buc did not reply but closed his eyes again and held his pose.

Penelope shifted in her spot for a moment, unsure what to do next. "Sorry to hear about your mate," she said quietly. "Thomas was a good one. Always liked seeing that one come in. He'll be missed by many." She smiled daintily. "I cannot recall 'ow many times good Thomas would come to my aid whenever some wayward gent would give me a hasslin'." She chuckled. "Probably as many times as you had love." She fluffed the feathers on her head, "You two chaps been my knights in armor." Spying the note upon the table, Penelope turned her head to get a proper look at the piece of parchment. "What'cha have there, sweetie?"

Buc sighed and lowered his glass. "To be honest, Penny, I'm not entirely sure. Thomas gave it to me, and I cannot fathom why."

Penny looked over the paper. "That's funny," she said.

Buc turned toward Ayg and gazed upon his drawn face. "That's not funny. That's depression," Buc replied. Mister Ayg leaned in close to his captain's elbow.

"No, silly." Penelope pointed to one of the sets of numbers and declared, "That there is the date me fiancé arrives here from Havana. He's aboard the King's Nugget."

"Another round!" shouted a patron from the other side of the bar. The roosters about him roared their approval and began pounding feathered fists atop the counter.

"Dates?" Buc hissed. He crumpled the list and jammed it into his pocket. Once again, the fire burned in his belly. Anger replaced sorrow and began to rise. "If Rojo wanted this, he knows its value." He looked up at Penny. "I must beat him to the punch."

"How ya gonna do that?" she asked.

"I need to become feared," Buc muttered.

"What's that sweetie?" Penelope asked, a concerned look spreading across her face.

"I need to become feared," Buc proclaimed more loudly. "I need people to fear me. I need a reputation so bad that birds from all around will refrain from looking me in the eye. I must become the most feared pirate in all the Caribbean. Like Lucky Longfeather. Fearsome and ruthless!" Without looking at the girl, Buc waggled his empty cup at Penelope, who promptly topped it off. "Yes," the rooster sang. "The most feared pirate upon the water. I need to rise from these ashes, not unlike the mighty phoenix. Only then will Thomas' killer realize the misfortune they have brought upon themselves. But," he added, holding up a cautionary hand, "the only way to do that is to pillage, plunder, rifle and loot. And yet, even though I would turn the world over to repay the debt owed to Thomas, I fear that I, Buckley Smythe, do not have it in me to set the world on fire."

"Well sweetie," Penelope said with a mischievous look, "if it's rumors of legends ya want, then there be no better place to spread the tales of piracy than a musty old tavern." Penelope blew out the table lantern. "Come with me love," she said, extending her hand to Buc.

The two walked along the outer edge of the tavern, sticking to the shadows until they reached the counter. They passed through the doorway to the back room, and Penny led Buc to a small dark closet. Once inside, she swiftly closed the curtains to the room and lit a nearby candle. The small closet began to glow, making crates, cans and barrels visible to the pair.

"Is there a reason we are in this closet?" asked Buc; his question went unanswered.

Penny rummaged through a series of crates, removing a long, brown coat and giving it a once over. "That might do," she whispered, tossing the coat to Buc. "Put that on," she added.

Buc pawed the coat unenthusiastically, scowling at the dingy, brown fabric and metal tabs. He looked back toward Penny, her arms folded as she waited for Buc to adorn himself with his new attire.

Hesitantly, he put on the coat. He brushed the sleeves and admired himself in a small hanging mirror. *Well done,* he thought.

"Somethin's still a bit off," said Penny, looking over the tall rooster in the long coat. She stepped out through the curtain, and quickly returned carrying a bucket by the handle.

"What's that?" asked Buc.

"Soot, from the fireplace," she replied.

"And what do you have planned for that?" he asked as Penny threw a handful of soot at Buc and on his newfound coat.

Within the dust of airborne grit, Buc simply replied, "Sorry I asked."

As the dust cleared, he could see a smile on Penny's face. "There," she proclaimed, "now you look like a proper pirate."

Buc looked over his new coat and palmed off some of the excess soot. "Was that absolutely necessary?" he asked, examining the grime on his feathered fingertips.

Penny stepped close to him and began to intertwine trinkets into his facial feathers, adding to his now exotic look. "If you long to become a fearless pirate, then ya gonna have'ta get a bit dirty," she explained kindly.

She stared at Buc, a proud pirate rooster standing before her, and, with a twinkle in her eye, she smiled. She looked about, shaking off the uncomfortable feeling. "Now then," she started, "head back to your table, an' don't say a word." She nodded. "Leave the rest to me."

"What are you going to do?" asked Buc, now literally in the dark as Penny blew out the candle.

As the final glow of the candle faded, Penny replied, "I'm gonna change your destiny." She then gestured for him to go.

Buc slowly and quietly returned to his table in the darkened corner. He could tell Ayg was eyeing his new attire. His suspicion was confirmed when Ayg gave him a playful thumbs-up. He then turned his attention to Penny who was making her way to a table across the tavern.

She casually strolled over to the loud group of roosters at the other end of the bar. "It would do you well to keep your celebration to a whisper," she explained.

"What for?" one of them cried as the others laughed loudly at such a ridiculous notion.

"There just so happens to be a fowl here tonight that you would really rather not cross."

"I've not had a pint at a proper table in months, lass," another explained. "Been riding the sea since near this time last year without a room to myself or a voice of my own. I naught but take orders an' bob about like some bloody servant, and I'm in no mood for caterin' to the needs of some bird longing for peace and quiet in a port tavern such as the likes of this. Tell him to take a walk off a pier, if you so wish."

Penelope leaned in close and smiled wickedly. "It not be my wishes that should concern you, love," she said in an even tone. Her arm raised and subtly pointed toward the corner of the bar where Buc and Ayg resided. "It be his."

The sailors strained to look in the corner.

"Who's he?" whispered one of the sailors.

"Who's he?" she repeated in a patronizing and disbelieving tone. "Who's he? You don't recognize one of the most feared pirates in all the Spanish Main?"

"Him?" asked one of the men with a surprised laugh. "The one with the pet egg?"

"Oh, sweetie," Penelope replied in a voice dripping in sadness. "Best ya not let him hear you talk that way, or you'll be swapping stories with old Davy Jones himself."

They all looked at her with dumbfounded expressions.

"You've been away a while," she continued in an understanding manner. "That there is Captain Buc Buccaneer."

"Who?"

"You mean to tell me that strong, smart, seafaring fowls such as yourselves have never heard of the dreaded pirate Buc Buccaneer?"

Again, they looked at each other with lost expressions. "He couldn't be much to talk of if we've never even heard of him," the first rooster commented.

"I think I have," a third rooster offered weakly. "I mean," he hurriedly added, shrinking from the scrutinizing stares of his companions, "I'm not sure what he done, but I do believe that name sounds something familiar."

"'Course you have," Penelope said, clapping the bird on the shoulder. "Why just last week a fancy French pirate came in here. Biggest plume you ever saw spillin' from his hat. Dang near dragged the floor when he walked it did. Captain Pierre Foof was his name," she insisted, making up the story as she went. "He came in spouting nonsense about being the toughest pirate in all the Caribbean. Well, that didn't sit well with Captain Buc over there."

"What did he do?" the second rooster asked quickly. He then drew back and said in a nonchalant manner, "I mean, if he did anything at all that is."

"Anything at all?" Penelope piped, making a disgusted face. "Well I'll tell ya what he did," she declared in an offended tone. "He challenged the Frenchman to a sword fight. Right here. In this very tavern."

"Who won?"

"Who do ya think?" she demanded of the table. "Do you see any fancy feathered Frenchmen here tonight?"

Two of the roosters looked about, but the first just stared at Penelope.

"Captain Buc I tell ya," she cried. "Why it only took him four moves an' he sliced off the right wing of the Frenchman then went back to his drink like nuthin' happened."

The mouths of the sailors hung open, and their eyes all drifted toward Buc.

"The Frenchman swore revenge on Buc and stormed out of the tavern, all hot and flustered as any bird has ever been."

The sailors leaned in, now listening intently.

"Well, Captain Buc won't be standin' for threats, unless of course he be the one bestowin' the threat." The serving girl rested her hands upon the edge of the table and lowered her voice. "He and the merciless crew of The Fowl Stench located and scuttled the Frenchman's ship. He gave no quarter. There were no survivors. Didn't even bother to pillage their ship. Said 'twern't worthy of his effort."

The men were locked in silent awe.

"It's too much to be believed," one said.

"Miss," said another, "I believe I'd like to buy Captain Buc a drink."

"Now why would you do that?" Penelope asked, offended. "Did he ask ya to?"

"Uh, no. I was just offering to, um... "

"Captain Buc killed the last fowl that bought him a drink," Penelope said in a grave voice.

"What? Why?" asked the sailor.

"Why?" She laughed sadly. "Why? Because he wasn't thirsty."

The three roosters all leaned to get a better look at the deadliest bird on the sea. "Really?" one of them asked.

Penelope simply nodded her head and gave them a thoughtful look. She righted herself, brushed her front, and wished the sailors a pleasant rest of their stay. "I'm going to make sure everything is alright with the captain over there. Make sure he's taken no offense to your racket and gawking. You holler if you need anything." She then strolled away to Buc's table.

"What did you tell them?" asked Buc, eager to learn if his name had grown.

"Don't worry 'bout that now," Penelope instructed. "An' stop making that worried face. Look mad as hell, slam your fist on the table as hard as you can, then look over at them."

Buc's expression flashed. He scowled and hammered the table like a barbarian. The sailors, still watching him carefully, nearly jumped right out of their chairs. Buc then slowly turned his head until he was staring the trio in the eye.

The roosters' eyes grew wide and they all looked down at their drinks.

"What did you tell them?" asked Buc again, slowly pulling his stare back to his own table.

"That you are Buc Buccaneer, the fiercest pirate in all the Caribbean," Penelope answered with a hidden smile.

"Really?" Buc replied, the possibilities of such a reputation busily racing through his mind. *"Buc Buccaneer"* he thought, *"Not as fear inspiring as Lucky Longfeather, but it just might do."*

"I'll spin some more tales," whispered Penny, "and you see your reputation in public." she continued, "No lollygagging about. No sulking."

Buc smiled. His first real smile since poor Thomas' demise. "My dear Penny," he sang, reaching into his pouch and dropping an extra silver piece on her tray. "You are a rose among the thorns, love."

"Story of my life, sweetie. Story of my life." With a wink, Penelope walked away, resuming her duties.

Buc strained to keep from smiling. He glanced over at the table of sailors then moved his gaze to the front door. In staggered a man, feet heavy and head wobbly from drink. He was a fine dressed bird; a magistrate to be exact. His air was lofty, and his powdered wig was slightly askew. Buc looked at Thomas' list and recognized the magistrate, Christian Howard.

That's why his name had no date, Buc silently reasoned. *Howard was already here in Port Royal. The numbers were arrival dates.* As the magistrate moved to grasp his coin pouch, Buc was afforded a glimpse of the magistrate's belt and what adorned it.

"Ayg," the captain announced in a low voice. "Finish your drink. We're leaving."

Ayg held the full glass of cider before his shell, shrugged, then set the glass upon the table. The two then rose and made their way toward the door. As they walked through the Wooden Stork, the noise level lowered. When the pair walked past the table of sailors, the roosters desperately tried to avoid eye contact. Just as he passed them, Buc stopped then backed up to their table. All the sailors stood up in haste as though their own captain had just appeared on the deck. Buc's hand fell to the grip of his sword, and he wrapped his fingers tightly around the handle. Two of the roosters shook visibly and the third fainted. He paused for what seemed to the sailors an eternity, and finally said the words, "Let it be known that your measly lives were spared today by the kind gesture of that bonnie lass." He narrowed his eyes deeply. "Feel free to show your appreciation within her gratuity this evening."

Buc nodded to the sailors and left the tavern with long, intentional strides as the tavern air filled with the fumbling and jingling of coin.

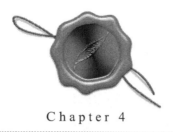

Chapter 4

There is a rhythm to the sea. The tide goes in, the tide goes out, and no matter how violent the storm, it will always be followed by the sun. Such is true with the residents of Port Royal who operate upon their own rhythm. The sailors and pirates who make land at the port rise in the wee hours of the afternoon, typically around suppertime. They begin to drink immediately, washing away the cares of life and fueling a desire for pleasure and distraction. They fight, curse, sing, and dance well into the darkest hours of the night, until, eventually, they either stumble home or pass out where they land. Tomorrow the sun will rise over their sleeping bodies, tucked safely beneath a tavern table or wedged happily beside a shrubbery, waiting until they wake from their stupors. Then the whole process begins again.

It was at this hour, just before the sun was climbing into the air and the port was still heaving from a long and unruly night, that an owl calmly turned from the main street along the docks and headed down a darkened alley. If one of the pirates sleeping on a bench had opened their eyes, just a crack, they would have seen the mysterious owl.

Some citizens of wealth consider these times of night to be the safest to travel along the dark, murky streets of Port Royal. To wander about at the wrong time could be fatal, especially for those of the wealthier class. They rarely travel without a guard, and most never go out alone. On this night, it was a regal owl who had decided to brave the odds. Perhaps it was the luck he found at the card table or the courage he drank from in celebration, but the magistrate moved with a self-assured manner, sneaking into the darkness and strolling about as though he were the king of the city. He passed a cloaked beggar who was seated against a damp, aged wall. The owl paused, tipped his beak at the stranger and pulled at his belt in an exaggerated manner before moseying deeper into the alley. The beggar took note of the magistrate's drunken condition and smiled in delight.

The gold in his pocket jingled loudly as the owl staggered down the narrow path. His toe caught on a loose paving stone and the wealthy bird stumbled a bit. He stood proud, adjusted his white wig back into its proper place, and made a satisfied expression. He continued on his path only stopped by Mister Ayg. The owl giggled at the sight of the sword wielding egg. An angry scowl was drawn upon the surface of the shell.

"Well, bless me," the magistrate gushed. "Are you not the dearest little thing?"

Ayg quickly erased his face, drawing on an even angrier version.

"That is precious," said the owl, slurring his words and dragging out the sentence.

Mister Ayg pointed his sword at the magistrate.

"And look!" the owl panted happily. "It has a sword! You are just adorable. Come now! Let me draw a mustache on you." Ayg swiped high with his weapon, ripping the wig clean off the owl's head. The magistrate became suddenly rigid and confused. He slowly reached up to touch his head and found that his wig was missing, and his balding crown left utterly exposed. Embarrassed, the owl huffed and puffed furiously. "Now see here, you little freak."

"I'd be careful with that one, mate." The voice came from behind, and the magistrate whipped about to find the cloaked beggar. "That egg is more than he appears. He's one of the finest swordsmen in all the Caribbean. I should know," the beggar confessed, tipping his head and smiling broadly. "I trained him."

"And who might you be?" asked the magistrate in a drunken drawl.

"The answer to who I am is not nearly as important as the answer to why I am here," the beggar replied coolly.

"Fine," the owl huffed. "Why are you here?"

"To free you from such a weighty and laborious burden," he replied.

Instinctively, the magistrate dropped a hand to his coin pouch. "Excuse me?"

"Hand over the pouch, kind sir," the beggar demanded.

The owl puffed with pride and looked down his beak at the grimy bird before him. "And if I refuse?"

"May I remind his regalness that there is a rather large egg with a rather large sword pointed at his nether regions?" A smile flashed from under the beggar's hood. "If I were you, mate, I'd hand over the goods and be done with all this un-pleasantry."

The owl glowered at the beggar until the egg bounced angrily and jabbed him in the buttock with the tip of his sword. Carefully, the magistrate reached beneath his coat and removed a coin pouch then tossed it to the cloaked figure.

The magistrate complied far too easily for an object that seemed to hold such importance on the list. "Many thanks, mate, and I admire your enthusiasm," the beggar replied, "but I'll be having the other pouch as well."

"Whatever are you talking about?" the owl snorted. His feathers bristled, and his posture became rigid.

Mister Ayg raised his weapon and tapped the blade upon the owl's chest.

"Willfully or not," the beggar explained, "I'll be having that pouch. The only real question is whether or not feathers fly over it. Yours being the feathers which will take flight, of course."

"Do you know who I am?" asked the owl.

"Does it really matter?" the beggar answered.

"I am Christian Howard!" he bellowed. "Magistrate of the High Courts of Port Royal! Fellow of the Society of Law! I am an advisor to the Royal Court and here by personal invitation of the governor himself!"

The beggar peered at Mister Ayg who shrugged and jabbed the magistrate again.

"Very impressive," the cloaked bird responded in a flat tone. "And do you know who I am?" he asked.

Howard sniffed and rolled his eyes. "I assume you are a pirate," he said, hazarding a guess. "You appear to be some lowly and impoverished scourge of the Caribbean who is no more than a soiled blight on the backside of our otherwise promising society."

"Really?" the cloaked bird replied with a grin. "A soiled blight on the backside of society? Well, that's funny, mate. If asked, I'd have to say the same about you, Magistrate."

Howard narrowed his eyes and held resolute.

"The pouch," pressed the pirate, "if you please."

Begrudgingly, the magistrate stuck his hand down the front of his shirt and drew out a velvety pouch. "You should know it is empty. Void of contents. It is merely a family heirloom, retrieved at the governor's request I might add." He tossed the pouch to the beggar and added, "I assure you, fiend, that this will not go unnoticed."

A wicked smile spread across the face of the cloaked bird. "What will not go unnoticed, most respected of sirs, is the sight of his legalness wandering the streets without his attire."

Color faded from the cheeks of the owl and his eyes popped. "What?" sputtered the magistrate. In a shocked tone, he added, "You would not dare."

"Your clothes," the beggar stated plainly, "remove them."

"Now see here," Howard sputtered. "Dear sir, I do believe you should reconsider the consequences of—"

"Now, Magistrate," the beggar interrupted, in an evenly angered tone.

"No," Howard announced, crossing his large arms over his barrel-like chest. He set his features obstinately and shook his beak. "I will not."

"Oh really?" the beggar sneered, inching closer.

"Now see here, pirate," Howard sputtered, raising his hands before him but trying to sound bolder than he felt. I will not—" Ayg's sword flashed like a streak of lightning across the front of the magistrate whose belt fell limp, causing his pants to fall to the street.

"Either you remove your attire, or he will," the cloaked bird promised. "The choice is, of course, all yours." He took another step closer, raised a hand to the side of his mouth and whispered, "I'd recommend self-removal of the clothing." The cloaked bird veered his head towards the egg. "Swordsman he is, tailor he not be."

The magistrate growled in frustration, unbuttoning his shirt and muttering the whole time, "This is unheard of. Even from a pirate. Unbelievable. Completely beyond decency."

The beggar could not help but snicker. The sight of a magistrate from His Majesty's High Court standing in his underwear in the middle of Port Royal was a joy that was too much to contain.

"Now be gone with you!" the beggar ordered.

Devoid of his clothing, the portly magistrate retreated into the night.

The beggar removed his cloak. "Do you think he knew who I was?" he asked Ayg.

Ayg shrugged then wiped his face clean. Brandishing his coal stick, Mister Ayg drew a neutral face across his shell.

"How can I induce fear into the hearts of men if they don't know the name of Buc Buccaneer?"

Ayg shrugged again.

"Take this, mate," Buc commanded, tossing the pouches to Ayg, "and keep them safe."

"While you're at it," he added, drawing the ship's post from a deep coat pocket, "stow this as well. We still have two more pieces to this puzzle."

Mister Ayg held the pouches and the post in his hand. He turned and studied himself for a moment, unsure what he should do with his burdens. Without a coat, or pants for that matter, Ayg juggled the items for a few beats until he gave an exaggerated and confused shrug.

"Today, Mister Ayg!" Buc cried, pivoting on his heel and taking a step up the alley.

The first mate turned the post sideways then contracted his wings into his shell. Seconds later, his wings reappeared minus the post and pouches. He jingled merrily as he jogged to meet his captain.

Buc hadn't made it far though before he stopped abruptly and cocked his head to the side. Caught by surprise, Ayg bumped gently into the rooster's tail feathers, earning a menacing scowl from the captain. "Is it my imagination," Buc asked in long, suspicious tones, "or are we being watched?" He drew his sword and pointed it into a darkened side alley. Ayg followed suit and looked to his captain for approval. Buc made a gesture, waving his hand over his beak. Ayg hopped and wiped away his neutral expression in favor of a more pirate-like sneer. Buc nodded his approval then turned his attention back to the darkened corner. Nothing could be seen, save for several tall stacks of packing crates and a few loose bottles strewn about. Mister Ayg neither heard nor saw anything strange, but that did not deter Buc.

"Out!" he demanded. "Come out ya filthy buzzards or I'll run ya through!"

Quiet prevailed in the passageway. Light was just beginning to illuminate the furthest end of the space but most of the alley was still shrouded in mist and gloom. Mister Ayg shifted uncomfortably and turned to Buc. Ayg erased one eyebrow and re-drew it up high. The captain never took his eyes off the corner. Instead, he bent forward like a bloodhound on the scent and made a few steps toward the blackened space.

"I've no desire to kill a coward," the rooster warned, "though I will not hesitate to give you a taste of my blade." He took another small step, sucking air through his nostrils and grinding his beak.

The darkness replied with the step of a boot, and several packing crates tumbled from their neatly stacked pile.

"Show yourself," the rooster crowed, "before I step in after you." Beside him, Mister Ayg trembled slightly and a muted tinkling could be heard emitting from the shivering egg.

A dark figure shuffled off to one side and Buc was on him. The figure dove the opposite way, kicking a bottle and causing another pile of crates to tumble, but Mister Ayg cut him off with a swipe of his sword.

"There will be no running," the rooster announced confidently. "You will surrender and live or fight and die, but one way or another we shall meet eye to eye."

Ayg gently elbowed his captain and bounced happily.

"Like the rhyme, did you?" Buc asked proudly, earning another bounce from the egg. "Good. I feel that, even in cutting down those who would stand in our way, it's important to remember that nothing need be done if it is not done well. Don't you agree?"

Mister Ayg nodded his approval and drew a small smile in the corner of his mouth.

"Lower that eyebrow, mate," the captain ordered, "you look bewildered."

In the darkness, the shadowy figure cleared his throat.

"Yes, Yes," Buc answered with a wave. "Just a moment," he assured the figure with a hint of dissatisfaction. He then turned to Ayg and continued, "You can't go about looking confused and angry. No one will take you seriously."

Again, the figure in the shadows cleared his throat.

"I heard you!" Buc snapped before proceeding with Ayg. "You can either be angry or confused, but one surely will cancel out the other. You really can't be both. Not in a practical sense."

The figure stepped from the shadows and said, "Ahem!"

"Why so eager to die all of a sudden?" Buc wondered aloud, but, turning his eyes from Mister Ayg, he lost his breath. Standing before the pirates was a young sparrow dressed in rags and standing with his chest puffed out. "What a ... a child?"

The sparrow huffed and snorted at the pair.

"Who are you, lad?" Buc demanded in a more delicate tone. "And what are you doing sneaking about this time of night?"

"I wasn't sneaking," the young bird answered.

"Well, you weren't exactly making yourself known now, were you?" the rooster pointed out.

"I'm not afraid of you, pirate!" snapped the sparrow.

"Oh, I'm quite certain on that point," Buc replied directly, "but that's not really an answer to my inquiry now, is it, boy?" The two stared in silence for a moment. "Who are you, child?" Buc asked softly, lowering his weapon. Mister Ayg followed suit and sheathed his own sword. "Why are you out here and not at home?"

The sparrow stared at the captain in silent defiance.

"Fine," Buc answered with a wave. "I've no time for games, little bird. Best run off to your mommy and try not to get killed along the way, hmm?"

Another young sparrow slunk from the shadows. She was smaller than her companion, though she had a more intense look about her.

"Ah," Buc said with a smile. "I see. Aren't you a little young to be skulking around the alleys of Port Royal with a lass?" he asked the boy with a wink.

"She's my sister," the boy announced heatedly.

Mister Ayg and Buc shared a look before allowing the birds to explain.

"My brother and I are..." she began, looking about begrudgingly. "We're orphans," she finally managed. "We're orphans, and we're running away."

"Orphans, eh?" the rooster mused.

"Yeah?" the boy snarled. "So?"

"Would it be that you're running from Madame Hensworth's Orphanage?"

"You know it?" the girl asked with a surprised expression.

"Far too well," Buc confessed. "Does the good madam still have ah … that thing growing on her face?"

"Yes," replied the girl, curling her beak and scrunching her nose.

Both Buc and the boy shuddered at the visualization of Madame Hensworth's hideous birthmark.

"Looks like some sort of cursed sea urchin latched itself upon her," Buc explained to Mister Ayg.

The boy laughed, though kept his distance.

"Are you a real pirate?" the girl asked.

"I am Buc Buccaneer," the rooster declared, "and there is no greater pirate on the seas."

"Then let us come with you," she demanded.

"What?" Buc and the boy blurted.

"I want out," she pressed, "and we would make excellent pirates. Promise."

"Sorry lass, but there be no room on the Fowl Stench for children." Buc sighed. "Fancied a pirate ship you know, and it be a veritable nesting ground of filthy behavior, what with all the pillaging, plundering, swearing, and terrible hygiene."

"But Captain," she insisted, flattering Buc with his preferred title, "you can't ask us to go back there."

"Lass, our next port of call be Tortuga, in the hopes of gathering a crew. I can spare no more time dawdling on your problems." Buc looked into their eyes and sheathed his sword. He saw the desperation he once felt being locked up in the orphanage himself. The rooster crossed his arms and lowered his beak over his chest. "Mister Ayg," he said, "give 'em the magistrate's little purse." The egg stood there for a moment, frozen in place, staring at the children.

"Now, Mister Ayg!" Buc snapped, sending Ayg into shivers. The first mate once again, contracted a wing, and wiggled rhythmically His wing then reappeared, clutching the coin filled pouch. He tossed the pouch to Buc who then tossed it to the girl. "Here lass," he said. "Now take this coin and purchase passage on a vessel going anywhere."

"Sir?" the girl muttered, staring wide-eyed at the pouch.

"Anywhere but Tortuga," Buc instructed, turning to leave. "It be no place for wee ones."

Chapter 5

Light rose across the docks as figures slowly began to emerge. In the haze of the morning fog, thick with the rich smells of salt and fish, men silently moved along the wooden planks. Great crates rattled down the bay front of Pelican's Wharf in the backs of wagons and carts on their way to boarding a ship and then out to sea. Workers grumbled and glared through tired eyes as they pulled their loads aboard. The work was difficult, and the days were long for a deckhand, but it was one of the last places a fowl could go and always find a job.

Hollers rolled over the docks as commands echoed in the ears of the birds. Muscles strained, and winches sang as the sounds of ropes and pulleys hoisting products made their way across the sea. Tonight, would bring a new wave of ships bearing loads from as far off as India and China; but in the small hours of the morning, the feathered workers of the dock were busy loading up and preparing to sail all over the Americas. Pelican's Wharf was seen by many as the gateway between east and west and standing at that gate was the Governor of Jamaica.

Now, the trading market of Port Royal was one of the governor's proudest accomplishments, and the fact that it was also one of his greatest revenue generators didn't hurt either. Inbound and outbound, unique taxes were levied by ship and by load. Wandering up and down the dock, with their bright coats and jingling pockets, were the Dock Authority. They were a group of birds who were looked upon with a mix of respect, fear, and loathing. If a bird decided to cross one of them, he could find his ship anchored for a month. And the poor birds who were caught underpaying? Many lost all of their cargo, and some even lost the ship itself. The Dock Authority reveled in their power, but none more than the dock master himself, Winslow Featherby. Featherby strode about the dock, barking orders and verbally abusing the workers. Like the King of the Wharf, everything he saw was under his control, and his rule was absolute. Though powerful, Featherby didn't exactly look the part. He was a stork, a kind of

bird with those comically stretched legs, long, awkward beak, and a nasally voice, which men had to strain to hear. Some felt that they were unable to take such a bird seriously, and that mockery was the game. One such bird, a macaw from the lower Americas, laughed at the dock master and mocked his voice.

"You will submit your vessel to inspection," Featherby had ordered.

"Oh, I'm sorry," the macaw had replied, holding his wing to his ear, "I'm having trouble understanding you." Then, changing his voice to a buzzing whisper, he asked, "You want to do what to my ship?" His crew had laughed, but everyone else knew better.

"You will want to order all of your crew off your vessel," Featherby replied coolly.

"Will I?" the macaw answered.

"Unless you want them at the bottom of the bay as well," Featherby said quietly with a long smile.

"What?" the macaw blurted.

"Arrest him," the dock master ordered, "then sail his boat out and sink it in the bay."

"What?" the unfortunate captain bellowed. "You can't! No!"

"Oh yes I can," Featherby barked. "Or was my voice not clear enough?" he added with a grin.

This morning, the Dock Authority was on the prowl before the sun was high enough to draw a single shadow. Buc and Ayg walked confidently past the ships and crates; one with his beak slightly in the air and the other with a stoic expression drawn upon his shell. All about them, sailors and seamen paused as the two walked past, giving worried looks and muttering in hushed tones.

"You hear that, mate?" Buc asked without looking. "The birth of a legend, that is. I'm not sure what that lass said, or whom she said it to, but our little Penelope is a right proper genius. A few well seeded words and look," he said with a nod. "The people fear us. We'll be the talk of the island in no time."

Ayg nodded thoughtfully and peered about the docks. He spied a galleon displaying the colors of England tied off to the nearest pier. Between rows of crates, a rooster moved about in a gruff manner. His head was down, and his large, tattooed arms strained as he picked up one box after the next and set them upon a small platform, from which they would be hoisted to the deck.

"Hurry up!" barked a crane with a pinched voice. "I haven't got all day to waste watching you move at half-speed."

Mister Ayg pulled at his captain's sleeve and pointed to the laborer. Buc smiled and pulled Ayg off to the side.

Silently, the tattooed rooster snatched another crate from the dock and set it upon the first. The frame of the box creaked and complained under the weight of its contents, though the task didn't seem to slow the rooster at all. He kept moving along at the same steady pace, which was still far too slow for the crane.

"You must move more quickly," he snapped. "Do you hear me?"

"Aye, Mr. Featherby," the rooster answered. "I hear ye well."

"Then pick up your pace, you worthless vagabond," he cawed at the tattooed man. The dock master puffed out his thin chest and tucked his clipboard under a wing. "I've no plans to let my dock fall into disarray," he declared, as though he were the governor himself.

Another crate creaked and slammed down into position.

"Be careful!" shouted Featherby. "Use the block and tackle if you must, but nothing is to arrive damaged from my port." He slammed his clipboard onto the stack of crates and glared at the rooster. "You commoners make me ill. I expect all these crates loaded and ready for sea by the time I return from the lading office." He picked up his clipboard and stomped off, eyes wide and busy scrutinizing the next ship and crew.

The tattooed rooster sighed then proceeded to lift the next crate with an audible grunt. He set the crate upon the platform and turned back to find himself eye to cye with Buc. "Well, well, well," he moaned. "Behold the fearsome pirate, Buc Buccaneer." Buc smiled and gave a little bow. When he straightened, the captain was met with a fist in his beak.

Buc doubled over and crowed loudly.

"Whatever lies you be holding," the large rooster declared calmly, "I'll want nothin' of 'em." Buc began to speak, but the tattooed rooster blasted him in the face again.

Buc spun and fell flat.

The rooster then turned to the egg who quickly wiped off his expression and drew a sheepish grin. "You be too good an egg to still be traveling with this sorry excuse for a captain, Ayg."

Buc climbed to his feet and rubbed his jaw. "He travels with me, Master Chumlee," he proclaimed, "because I am the most fearsome pirate in all the Caribbean."

Chumlee stared at Buc through his brow and raised a pointed finger at the captain. "I know who you are, Captain Buc," the seaman proclaimed. "I know better than most the truth about you."

"Truth is based on perceptions in time, mate," Buc said, still flexing his beak. "And I plan to change your perception of me," he added. "In time."

"You are a liar, a scoundrel, and you still owe me money."

Chumlee grabbed at another crate and dropped it violently atop the others, causing the captain to flinch and reply, "Sounds 'bout right, I suppose." He pondered his reply, "But it is not unheard of—a captain losing one's cargo to the sea."

Chumlee slammed another crate down. "What kind of daft buzzard sails through a hurricane?" he shouted.

"Any captain worth his salt knows that the shortest distance between two points is a straight line," replied Buc.

Chumlee snorted. "A year and a half I sailed with you serving as quartermaster to your cargo ship." He slammed another crate down. "Our biggest haul and you risk it all to save half a day's time." He grabbed yet another crate. "How many people lost their shipments that day? Martin? The Lavershaws? Ez? They all trusted you."

"I'll admit I made some mistakes"—Buc rolled his eyes— "if it makes you feel better."

He approached Chumlee once again, who swung around another crate, forcing Buc to duck quickly.

"Master Chumlee," he said cautiously, "I come to you with information about a journey that you won't… Nay. A journey you cannot refuse." Another crate cracked down into position. Buc leaned on the freshly placed box and began whispering, "Whether you believe the tales or not, you now have a unique fortuity to be part of a legend. You are granted the privilege of being the quartermaster for the most feared pirate in all the Caribbean, mate." Buc stepped back, arms crossed, and throbbing chin held high, silently allowing his words to sink in.

"And?" asked Chumlee in an unimpressed tone.

"And what?" Buc asked, staggering a bit. "That … that was it." He looked at Ayg wondering if he had left something out.

"And you need my help," Chumlee said.

"That goes without saying. So why bother?" Buc asked happily. "What do you say, mate? You have nothing to lose, since nothing begets nothing, and yet you have the world to gain."

Chumlee stood speechless for a few moments, still as a statue and with just as much emotion as one.

"Hey! You there!" shouted a nasally voice from down the docks.

The birds looked to the sound of the voice and found the dock master stomping toward them.

"The terms of your employment do not include lollygagging," Featherby snapped. "You are here to stack crates," he said in a patronizing tone, wagging a finger at Chumlee. "There are a dozen other fowls lined up for this job. If you can't—"

Buc stepped forward, "Pardon me, most respected master of the docks, but do you by chance know who I am?" he asked in a pleasant voice.

Featherby balked at the interruption and frowned at the captain. "I have never seen you before this very moment," he growled, stuffing his clipboard under a wing, and taking another step forward. "For all I can see, you appear to be some unemployed nutter whose only function is interrupting my workers." An assistant to Featherby quickly stepped up and whispered in his ear. Featherby's expression changed from anger to one of concern, and he took a small step back.

Buc smiled. "Apparently, he knows," he said, pointing to Featherby's assistant. Buc saw his opportunity and seized the moment.

"Right about now," the captain replied in a low, smooth voice, "your gut instinct is telling you to run. Am I right?"

Featherby merely stared back, frustration and fear dancing in his eyes.

"In my profession," Buc continued lazily, "it's often encouraged to go with your gut feeling. Unless, of course, you've eaten too much stale seed, in which case your gut may be telling you something completely different."

Featherby stood silent and knit his brow at the strange performance playing before him.

"I see you're having difficulty, so I'll just say it." Buc leaned in toward the bird and, in a gentle whisper, he said, "Run away."

Featherby gripped his clipboard and took a step back. "This is not over," he warned. Buc narrowed his eyes at the dock master and Featherby turned and scurried off.

"I care little for you much as a fowl, much less a captain," Chumlee admitted, watching with pleasure as the dock master was put in his place. "Truth be told I care about that poor sap even less." He crossed his massive arms over his wide chest and looked down at the rooster.

"So, you'll sail with the most notorious captain on the sea?" Buc asked hopefully.

Chumlee chuckled and shook his head. "Don't matter to me whether the stories are true or not since I know what kind of a bird you really are, Buc."

The captain smiled and rested a hand on the hilt of his sword.

"And seeing how you are the lesser of my two evils at this crossroads, I'll choose to sail with you over working for him."

"I'll take it," Buc proclaimed happily.

Ayg pulled out his coal stick and added a satisfied curl to the corner of his mouth.

The three shipmates nodded to one another then proceeded down the docks. Work in the shipyard pulled to a full stop as the small crew made its way past. Birds stood in awe as Chumlee strode off with Buc, who was now the talk of the island. Chumlee did not respond, but once the trio was out of sight of any wandering eyes, he slammed Captain Buc against a stack of crates and laid his forearm against the captain's neck.

"The problem with telling tall tales and spreading false rumors," the quartermaster hissed, "is that the moment will come when the liar will have to live up to them. When that day arrives, will you turn tail feather and run, or will you stand your ground and live up to the legend?" Chumlee leaned in dangerously close, their beaks only having a breath between them. "And don't fool yourself," the quartermaster continued. "That day will come, Buc. When it does, will you be ready?" He released Buc without waiting for a reply and turned to continue down their path.

Buc massaged his neck, pondering whether or not he had it in him to be the pirate he wanted others to think he was.

Chapter 6

Across the island, the Government house stood out from its
surrounding dwellings. Inside, it was surprisingly gloomy, considering
how long the sun had been up. Dark furniture lined the walls, bearing
scrolls and chests and weapons on display. The hardwood floor was
impeccably clean, adorned with a colorful rug, no doubt imported
from the East India Trading Company. The solid mahogany desk in
the middle of the room was twice as wide as any other on the island,
and twice as lavish. Windows that normally gave a panoramic view of
the port were hidden behind thick, red velvet curtains. Behind the desk
was a steely-eyed hawk, pristinely dressed and sipping a goblet of
wine. Fortune had made the predator robust and far rounder than is
normal for such a bird, though he was no less deadly. A long wing
reached across the desk and captured a wooden box. The hawk lifted
the lid and drew out a massive cigar. He snipped one end with his very
own beak and spit the nub into a can beside his chair. Wordlessly, he
pulled a match from a little cup beside the humidor and snapped it
alight on the edge of the desk. He was illuminated clearly for a
moment in the flickering light and several scars could be traced across
the old hawk's face. He took a slow, deep draw from the cigar and let
the smoke billow and roll in his mouth before sighing it into the room.

He was the governor of the island, and no one arrived, thrived, or died without his permission, and the quivering owl in the chair across from him knew it.

The magistrate chuckled nervously, hoping that his life wasn't about to dissipate like the cloud of smoke puffing from the governor. "I uh … I know how all this must sound, Governor Legget."

The hawk didn't reply or even bother to look at the owl. He raised the cigar again to his beak and made the cherry glow wildly.

"It really was outside of my control," the owl blubbered.

"Howard." The hawk sighed around his cigar.

"Yes, Governor?"

"Shut your beak."

"Yes, Governor," the bird answered meekly.

"Just the sound of your voice," the hawk growled, clicking the end of his beak at his magistrate, "is enough to make a bird pluck himself clean."

The magistrate, Christian Howard, sat in obedient silence, counting down the seconds until he was permitted to leave.

The governor plucked his cigar from his beak and perched it on the edge of a large glass ashtray. A thin rope of smoke straightened itself and quickly climbed to the ceiling. Still refusing to look his magistrate in the eye, he folded his hands and asked, "What exactly did you lose?"

The answer was muttered so quietly that the governor had to lean forward and ask for it again.

"Everything," Howard confessed, knowing that his days were about to be significantly shortened.

"Everything?" the hawk repeated, earning a jittery nod from the owl. The governor spat out a sudden string of laughter. It was a vile, deadly maniacal laugh that caused Howard to squirm in his seat and force a smile across his own shocked face. "Everything?" the governor verified through the laughter.

"I…" the owl answered, making sputtering laughing noises of his own. "I am afraid so, your honor."

"Your honor?" the hawk crowed. "I'm not a judge, Howard."

"Yes, your grace," the owl sputtered.

"Please," the governor said, controlling his laughter, "call me Detrick."

Howard looked at his employer skeptically. He had suddenly found himself struck dumb and fought to make any noise at all. "Yes, Detrick," he finally managed, though the words had to be forced out.

"Good," the hawk answered. "Now, tell me about this mugging you suffered." While he spoke, the governor spun in his chair and lifted a tea kettle and a cup from a small table under the window. He spun back to face the owl and poured himself a cup without offering any to the magistrate.

"Well," Howard began, "I was traveling home."

"From?"

"I uh…" Howard said, pulling at his cheek feathers. The magistrate was slow to admit that he had just finished a night of drunken card-playing, though he feared the governor already knew. The old hawk had developed a reputation for knowing more than any one bird had the right to. "I had come from a social event," the owl answered cautiously.

"And did you do well at the card tables?" Detrick inquired.

Caught red feathered, the owl hung his head. "I did, sir. Yes."

"And then?" the governor encouraged.

"And then I decided to walk back to my home," Howard continued. "While on my way back, I came across an egg."

"An egg?"

"Yes, sir," Howard confirmed. "An egg with a sword."

"An armed egg?"

"Yes, sir. He had a face drawn upon his shell and was preventing me from passing along my way."

"You were robbed by an unhatched chick?" Detrick asked.

The pirate rose from his chair and crossed the room until he was standing before the governor.

"Leave him to me, Detrick …" Rojo advised. "Leave him to me."

Chapter 7

"You're a right bloomin' fool." The pigeon laughed.

"I'm tellin' you true, Morgan," his companion cooed in a nervous tone. "He was all alone! Fifty to one!" The bird stuck close to his friend, eyes narrowed and constantly searching as they walked down the narrow street.

"No bird can stand at such odds and live to see the sun rise," the first declared. "It's not a task that can be done."

The second pigeon made a trembling sound in his throat. "You say that," he muttered, "but the bird's still alive, isn't he?"

"For all you say." His friend smiled, laying a hand on the door of The Wooden Stork. He gave a swift yank, and the air was suddenly filled with the sound of laughing, yelling, talking and the clink of glass. A fat owl roared with laughter at the bar while a pretty little pheasant bopped between tables, batting her eyes, and making the old sailors blush. "Ask me," the first pigeon continued, "and I'll tell you it's all a jumble of poppycock."

"But that's not all," the second sputtered. "He took a ship."

"Oh, a pirate takin' a ship." Sarcasm soaked his reply. "Plenty a pirate has taken a ship."

"All by his lonesome," the bird finished. "Single-handedly commandeered a naval vessel."

"You're off it, you are," his friend declared.

The two moved inside and found a table near the door. A skinny hen with a keen eye walked up and put a hand on her hip. "What'll it be, boys?" she demanded in an even tone.

"I'll have a pint o' cider," the first replied.

"Same," cooed his friend.

"Two pints," the server answered before trotting off to the bar.

"I tell you this," the second pigeon insisted, "he's alive, and I hear he's right here in Port Royal."

"The most dangerous rooster alive?" the first spat doubtfully.

"The most dangerous rooster alive," was the passionate response.

"Here? In Port Royal? Bah!" cried the first.

The door to the tavern opened, but neither of the pigeons bothered to look up. All around them, the chatter died off and the laughter faded. Glasses clinked against the tables and the room fell silent. The pigeons looked about at the shocked and nervous faces, all looking at their tables and searching the corners of the tavern.

"What the…" started the first pigeon, turning to the door. There he found the silhouette of a rooster in the doorway. All over the room a name was whispered carefully and quietly.

"That's him."

"That be Buc Buccaneer."

"Deadliest pirate on the sea."

"It's Buc."

"That there is Buc Buccaneer."

Buc took a step inside and let the door fall closed behind him. He was preceded by Mister Ayg and Chumlee who wasted no time crossing the room and claiming a table in the back corner. Buc moved slowly through, stretching the moment as birds of all kinds shifted uncomfortably in their seats, working hard to avoid the eye of the notorious killer.

As he strolled past a table with two pigeons, Buc could clearly hear the words, "I told you!" being hissed. "I told you he was real!"

A smile grew on his face, but he shook it off and tried to look impassive. When he finally reached the corner table, he pulled out a chair and paused. He suddenly turned his face back to the other patrons with a scowl. The room crawled as though it were filled with ants. Everyone tried to look natural and pretend that they didn't see him. Buc snorted and took a seat.

Penelope strolled up and dropped three pints at the table.

"Thank ye, Penny," Buc said in a gravelly voice.

The server stifled a giggle and nodded before strolling away.

"You done with yer little show, then?" Chumlee asked in a voice that was far too loud for Buc's comfort.

"Keep it down, will ya?" the captain asked. "Leave the mystique intact, eh?"

"Aye," Chumlee agreed, his voice lowering to a patronizing level. "Not wantin' the whole of the island to know the real you, are we?"

"For all you know, mate," Buc answered in a crafty tone, "this is the real me."

Chumlee looked on in disbelief.

"Perhaps the Buc you knew was just stuck inside a shell," whispered Buc.

Ayg nodded his approval and stared at Chumlee.

The big rooster crossed his arms and rested them upon the table. He leaned in and shook his head. "Yer right," he admitted.

"I am?" Buc asked, confused.

"Aye," Chumlee continued. "An' it's time to reveal the truth, eh?" Chumlee suggested. "Time I knew the whole story, savvy? What be the reason for all the rumors and tales?"

"Artistic expressions of my adventures," Buc answered in an airy voice.

"So, a load o' rubbish," Chumlee decided. "Do they have anything to do with poor Thomas?"

Buc looked around nervously and bobbed his hand in the air, motioning for Chumlee to keep a hushed tone. "Yes and no, mate," he whispered. "A few days past, Thomas asked me to visit a ship. That ship, The Flair Lady, arrived at the docks yesterday for sale. I was to pretend to be an interested buyer. Indiscreetly I was to obtain, by any means, a post from the helm wheel. Naturally, I inquired as to the reasoning behind it but he told me 'twasn't the time." Buc glanced around to make sure no one was attempting to listen in. "Upon returning to the book smith's shop, I found him stabbed and hanging on for dear life on the cobblestone street. Before he passed on, he bestowed this upon me." He drew out the scrap of parchment from the inside pocket of his coat and slid it across the table. "He also informed me that my entire past had been nothing but a lie."

Chumlee glanced at the list. "Do ye know who ran him through?" Chumlee asked, sounding slightly bored.

"Aye. The same scallywag that done in my parents," Buc declared. "Vientre Rojo."

Chumlee pulled back from the table. "Rojo?" he whispered, suddenly interested. "I thought him a friend? Your childhood samaritan of sorts. I thought he the one who saved you, aye? Back when the village was pillaged?"

"As did I. But seems it 'twas only a tale, an' nothing more. My aunt and uncle told me the truth about how I came to their care."

"But why did he skewer poor Thomas?" asked Chumlee.

"For this," Buc answered, putting a finger upon the list. "Three names," he said in a voice Chumlee could barely hear. "Two with numbers aligned to them." He pointed to the first name, "Do ya recognize this name?"

Chumlee looked at the name. "Aye," he said with a nod. "The crooked magistrate."

"Aye," Buc replied. "Last night, Ayg and I confronted the good magistrate. He was acting upon orders from the governor himself to convey this item to him." Buc produced the pouch he took from the magistrate.

Chumlee took the pouch from him. "An empty coin pouch? What use would the governor have for a dusty old bag?" he asked, holding it up to the light.

"I know not why," Buc confessed, looking at the way the light hit the pouch. He plucked it from Chumlee's grip and slowly unthreaded the drawstring, allowing the fabric to unfurl. He then laid the fabric upon the table in front of them and flipped it over to reveal a portion of a drawing.

"A map?" Chumlee breathed, looking about to be sure no one heard him.

"Aye, it would appear so, leastwise part of one." Buc ran his fingers over the corner of the fabric, when something caught his eye. He held the fabric up near the flickering light of the candle. His eyes went wide with excitement as he made a startling revelation.

"Double L," he muttered, still staring wide-eyed at the fabric.

Chumlee, gulping his ale, lowered his mug and wiped his sleeve across his face. 'What?"

Buc leaned forward with the fabric in his hand. "The double letter L on the map." He looked up and into the eyes of Chumlee. "Lucky Longfeather."

Chumlee looked at the map then back at Buc.

Buc shook his head at Chumlee's lack of understanding. "This must be a map to the whereabouts of Lucky Longfeather."

"How can you be sure?" asked Chumlee.

Buc looked around once again, securing his location. "There be no fowl that know more about Longfeather than Thomas. It only be natural that he be keen on his whereabouts." Buc looked over the cloth. "This must have something to do with Lucky Longfeather."

Chumlee took another long gulp of his ale. "For once you seem to be makin' a lick of sense," he said, once again dragging his sleeve across his beak. "So, what be our next move?"

Buc looked once again at the list given to him by Thomas. "According to the tavern's bonnie lass, this here be the day her fiancé be arrivin' in Port Royal aboard the King's Nugget. This bloke," he said, pointing to the name next to the date, "likely to be a passenger on that ship. I'd wager my sword he's carrying another crumb of the map. That's why Rojo skewered Thomas. Thomas was privy as to who had the pieces."

Chumlee took another swig of his ale. "What's the plan, say ya?"

"The plan," Buc mused, rubbing his chin. "In three days' time, that ship is to arrive here. The plan, Master Chumlee, is for the fierce pirate Buc Buccaneer to sail to Tortuga, pick up a crew, and acquire the remaining pieces of the map at all costs."

Chumlee sat back and gave a small chuckle. "So," he said, quickly changing the subject. "Buc Buccaneer? That be the name you be taking to?"

"Well, the lass had more say in it than I," Buc revealed, nodding at Penelope. "Besides, mate, Buckley Smythe lacks the ability to strike fear into people, savvy?"

Chumlee made a little grunt and dropped his eyes back to the list. "And the last name on your list?" he asked. "D'ye know it?"

"That has an air of uncertainty to it," Buc replied.

"How uncertain?"

"Completely and utterly uncertain," responded Buc.

"Well," he answered, with a grin, "perhaps an old acquaintance of mine may shed some light." With a tip of his glass, Chumlee finished his cider and wiped his chin with his sleeve.

Buc and Chumlee strolled quietly along the all too familiar docks, ducking and hiding behind stacks of crates. Buc had been hoping for a grander appearance, like his previous visit, but Chumlee insisted on stealth. The only bird who would know what ships were arriving and departing would be the dock master himself, Featherby. As they darted in and out of sight, Chumlee's size was seemingly more difficult to conceal.

"You there!" shouted Featherby, his old boss. "You no longer work here. You ran off with that vagabond—"

Buc emerged from behind Chumlee. "Vagabond? I rather like the sound of that. Actually"—he approached the dock master—"vagabond may be the wrong nomenclature. It implies that I have no home. But the truth is my home is the sea." He placed a wing over Featherby's shoulder. "And the sea is what I am here to see you about."

He reached for Featherby's log book. "Might I relieve you of this burden for a spell?" He slid the log book out from Featherby's hands and handed it to Chumlee in one fluid motion. "Now, sir. Remember our first encounter when I bestowed on you a valuable lesson about running away?" Featherby's eyes widened, and he dipped down, slipping Buc's grasp, and ran off.

Chumlee fumbled through the log book, looking for the date. "Aye, here it is. The Lucinda Marie." His brow lowered, "Lucinda Marie? That's no name for a ship."

Buc grabbed the log book from Chumlee's grasp. "Let me see that." He looked over the entry and confirmed. "Aye. The Lucinda Marie." He stroked his chin. "Perhaps the ship we are to meet is, in fact, a woman?" Curious, he raised a brow. "Nonetheless," he snapped as he tossed the log book aside. "Time to prep the ship." The two shipmates headed down the dock, ready to make sail, unaware of prying eyes.

Chapter 8

The East Down docks were not as meticulous as the Port Royal main docks. East Down had a reputation for being rather relaxed when it came to laws and regulations. If you needed bits of cargo to arrive unnoticed, these docks would serve a captain well. But the docks were also safe harbor for merchant captains on tight budgets. A ship could dock here for a month for the same price as a week at the Port Royal docks.

The weather was fair and the docks aflutter with sailors and salesmen alike. Standing on the docks before the Fowl Stench, Buc held a deep sense of pride. He had a ship. He had a quest, and soon he would have a crew. "Master at arms!" he cried aloud, "the sea is willing, and she calls my name. Are we at the ready?"

"Aye, Captain," Chumlee barked. "Bob's your uncle," he added with an understanding nod.

"Beg pardon?" the captain answered. Buc furrowed his brow and his slightly opened beak made him look lost in that moment. "I do not believe you are using that expression properly, Master Chumlee."

The sailor pointed to the dock and Buc turned to find his Uncle Robert and his Aunt Fanny making their way along the docks.

"Well I'll be…" Buc declared. "Bob's my uncle."

"We be here to see you off, lad!" Robert called. Fanny held on to her husband tightly, clearly upset by the proceedings, though Robert had a wide smile painted across his face.

Buc flashed a smile of his own then said quietly, "Mister Ayg?"

Ayg stood tall and moved in close to his captain.

"You're with me," Buc finished, moving toward his relatives. Ayg moved quickly, drawing a welcoming smile to greet them.

"We wouldn't miss our favorite nephew's departure," Robert announced with a strange look in his eye.

"'Twould be true if I were not your only nephew," Buc answered, forcing a smile of his own. "Hello Uncle Robert. Aunt Fanny."

"Oh, Buc," Fanny spewed suddenly. "Why? Why do you do this?"

"Now, Aunt Fanny, really," Buc replied. "There is no reason to be overdramatic."

"You are sailing off to take revenge upon the fowl responsible for the death of your parents." She wept.

"There's more to it than that, but that's still no reason to overreact," Buc said with a forced smile.

"Revenge, Buc?" Robert asked, his own smile fading. "I can say with a touch of certainty revenge is not what your parents would have wished for you."

"Well, they're not here to contradict you, are they?" the captain replied.

"They are not here because of violence," Fanny declared.

"No, Aunt Fanny, they are not present because they were murdered," Buc corrected. "You say you know my father's mind, but we can't exactly go ask him, can we, Uncle? You say they fought to protect me? Well then, allow me to fight to protect their memory."

"You want justice, lad?" Robert sighed. "And right you should, but revenge is a different beast altogether."

"Revenge is justice gone wild, Uncle," Buc answered softly. "Justice? Justice is corrupt. If I must go vigilante," he said, his ire rising, "if I must go pirate to exact my revenge, then so be it. You tell me not to go rushing off. If not now, Uncle, then when?"

"But he is a murderer," Fanny heaved.

"You cannot go pullin' the dog's tail now, my boy," Robert added.

"I believe I have something he wants," Buc reminded him. "It only be a matter of time before he comes after me and everything I hold dear. Thomas already paid that price. I must stop him before anyone else suffers the same fate."

"Then give him what he wants!" Fanny cried. "End this now."

"If we give in to corruption then our voices mean nothing," Buc said firmly. "I will find what he desires most, and I will use it to avenge my parents."

"So, there be no talking you out of this?" Robert accepted in a sad tone.

"Sorry, Uncle," Buc said, not sounding sorry at all. "If I am a disappointment then so be it. I will not stand by and let others be bullied by the corrupt."

"So, you be the hero now?" the older bird asked.

"I am merely a fowl that has the ability to protect the ones I love," Buc professed to his only living family.

Robert nodded and smiled as Fanny wiped away fresh tears. His uncle pulled Buc in close, squishing him at his side. Looking up at the mast of the ship, he pointed and said, "She's a fine vessel, boy." He looked at Buc eye to eye and added, "Treat her right and she'll always bring you home."

"But we first must leave in order to return and enjoy the aforementioned memory of the right treatment," Buc said with a crooked grin.

His remark went unheard.

Robert handed him a pouch of coin and said, "Take this. You'll need a bit of coin to ready the ship for battle."

Battle? thought Buc anxiously. Never thought I'd be taking the Stench into battle.

"You'll soon find there is much you don't know about the path you are about to undertake. You'll be needin' a crew, lad, and some armament," Robert continued, unaware of his nephew's silent struggle. "The Stench isn't a fighting ship, but she'll be needin' to be, won't she?"

"Aye," Buc agreed, sounding more confident than he felt.

"You can do it, lad." The old rooster voiced his decision. "Despite my disapproval, my heart is pleased you have decided to honor those who have passed."

"Thank you, Uncle." Buc smiled.

Fanny approached him with a face of bitter resignation. "If you're to go pirate," she said quietly, "then you'll be needing a proper flag." She handed him a bundle of heavy material, as black as anything Buc had ever seen. "Don't go raising it unless you are certain this is the path you wish to take." The tears in her eyes began to pour in earnest, and sobs bounced in her beak. Her blubbering drew curious eyes, but at that point Buc didn't care who saw.

"Well, come on," his uncle said at last. "Give your Aunt Fanny a kiss goodbye, boy," Robert commanded.

Suddenly, Buc became rigid and looked about. He was now all too aware of the eyes around the dock and of his position as captain.

"Well?" the uncle pressed.

"If it's all the same," Buc whispered, "I'd prefer to limit signs of affection while in public."

"Now really, Buc," Robert spat. "You haven't become as hardened as that. Doesn't your aunt deserve a kiss before you sail?"

The rooster stood tall. "You know what? You're right. Mister Ayg," Buc barked, turning and walking up the plank, "kiss my Aunt Fanny."

Robert tightly embraced his wife, whispering to her so that only she could hear. She nodded slightly and wiped newly formed tears

from her eyes. After sharing a kiss, Robert followed Captain Buc up
the gangplank of the ship. As the older rooster stepped onto the deck,
Buc stopped him.

"Where might you be going, Uncle?" he inquired.

"Barnacle Bob reporting for duty, Captain!" Robert answered.

"The humor is lost on me, Uncle," Buc assured him. "I've no
intention of taking you into harm's way."

"I wasn't always a landlubber carpenter," Robert reminded his
nephew. "And if it's revenge you're after," he said, stepping closer,
"well, it would beseech you to remember that dastardly fowl Rojo
killed my brother."

"Uncle", Buc whispered, "I don't..."

"I know my way around a ship, lad. You're gonna need all the help
ye can getting the Stench into port."

"I shall not endanger you as well," Buc swore, struggling with
emotion.

"Buc, whether you realize it or not, you've already endangered us,"
Robert answered merrily. "But if things go south, I'll jump ship in
Tortuga and catch a vessel back to Port Royal."

"In the meantime?" Buc asked.

"In the meantime," Robert answered, "it looks as though you could
use a good carpenter in your crew."

Buc never agreed, but neither did he tell his uncle to leave. "Master
Chumlee?" he called.

"Aye, Captain?" came the reply.

"Weigh anchor. Release the mooring lines. Prepare to drop
canvas."

"Aye, Captain!"

"Mr Ayg! Take the helm," Buc said, turning to face his friend.
"Let's go get us a crew."

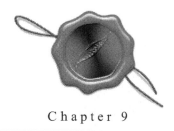

Chapter 9

Behind his handcrafted wooden desk, the Governor of Port Royal sat and hummed a quiet tune. He had spent the morning signing orders for the execution of a variety of citizens, all of whom had violated the law according to his rule. As the chief authority on the island, he was the only one who could sign such a judgment, and he reveled in the task. A gentle knock at the door interrupted him but didn't break his mood.

"Enter," he barked, not bothering to look up from his task.

A servant entered. "Capitán Vientre Rojo to see you, sir."

"Send him in."

Rojo entered the office and the servant closed the door behind him. He took a step forward and stopped, staring fervently at a spot on the floor. On the previously pristine wooden floor was a spot that had been recently scrubbed clean.

"Ah, justice," the governor sang. "Is there anything as satisfactory as that moment when the world is set right and the guilty receive their due?" He placed his quill back into its holder with a deft motion and looked up to his guest. "Tell me, Rojo"—he beamed—"do I have reason to rejoice?"

"Detrick," the captain answered in a tone that set the governor on edge. "I suppose that would depend on your expectations."

The governor rose from his desk, tension working into his muscles. "My expectations, *Capitán*?" he asked. The way the governor said his title sent a clear message to Rojo, reminding him that a word so easily spoken could also be easily taken away. "Let us see," he continued darkly, stroking his feathery chin. "What I expect is for you to deliver what you promised. What I expect is for you to tell me you have retrieved the item you failed to recover from the book smith. What I expect is nothing less than complete and utter satisfaction."

Rojo stared at the governor, beak set and unfazed by the hostile demeanor of his host. The pirate captain lolled his head to one side and remained silent.

"Rojo," the governor said, adopting a more cordial tone. "Come. Sit. Share what you have come to say."

Rojo blinked at the governor then stepped up to the desk and took a seat.

"Capitán Rojo," the governor began smugly, "I believe you can understand my frustration. Each day I am confronted with another inquiry as to your … actions." He waited for Rojo to reply, but when one did not come he continued. "Do you have the list?" he asked.

"No," replied Rojo evenly.

The governor tensed, his eyes fluttering and his hands balling into tight fists.

"But I know who has it," Rojo announced calmly, "and where it is."

The governor glared at the round robin before him. "Then what are you waiting for?" he cried. "It's obviously this Buc fellow. You have a history with him. Go to him and get the list."

"My dear Governor," Rojo said, leaning back in his chair. "Yes, the lad has the list."

"Well?" the Governor demanded.

"Even with the list, we would still be at odds with finding the location. Longfeather was no fool. In addition to the items on the list, there could be more intricate obstacles to it."

"What are you saying?" snapped the Governor.

"The lad, Buc, has a fortuitous nature to him," Rojo explained. "He is clever. I say allow him to solve the problem for us. Let him do the work and locate the treasure. I'll remain in the wings. When he succeeds, we take the treasure and dispatch our little problem."

The governor eyed Rojo apprehensively. "Do not fail me, Capitán. I would hate for all your past regressions to suddenly come to light."

Rojo smirked, tipped his head, and then rose from his seat. "Good day, Governor," he offered, brushing his front. Without another word, the Spaniard turned to the door and left.

The governor huffed and rose from his seat. He moved to his balcony and opened the door. From the balcony entered a tall rooster, dressed in his finest navy attire.

"Your orders, sir?" the commodore asked.

"I no longer have need of the Spaniard," the governor said evenly. "Ready the Triumph. No doubt this Buc character will head to Tortuga to acquire a crew. We will wait for him offshore. Perhaps we can appeal to his fortuitous nature in other ways."

"We, sir?"

"Yes, Commodore Paddington," the governor said with a smile. "I will be aboard the Triumph." His grin faded to a snarl. "Is there a problem with that?"

"None, sir," the officer said casually.

"Good man." The governor strode to his cabinet and selected a bottle from the shelf. "Ready the ship," he commanded. "We leave at first light."

"Aye, sir." With a tip of his head, the commodore headed toward the office door. Before leaving he turned back toward the governor and asked, "Is it true, sir?"

"Is what true, Commodore?"

"What the Spaniard said?" he asked confidently. "Is it a map that belonged to the pirate Lucky Longfeather?"

The governor poured his drink and corked the bottle. "You keep your eyes on your task, Paddington. The prize is not the treasure itself but the reward it brings us," he warned.

"Aye, sir," the officer replied and stepped into the hall.

Chapter 10

The sea rolled gently as the Fowl Stench slipped over the water. Buc stood tall and proud at the helm of his pirate ship, guiding the vessel with smooth confidence. He inhaled the ocean air with his chin high and Ayg standing at his elbow. They were still hours from Tortuga and the pair was beginning to get excited for their new crew.

"Tortuga, Mister Ayg!" Buc cried out. "Tortuga possesses everything that is unsound in the world. But"—he raised a feathery finger—"it also embodies everything that is sound as well. Freedom. Friendship. Laughter and fun. It can all be found in Tortuga."

Buc took a deep breath. "Smell that, Mister Ayg?" he asked, his own eyes half closed in ecstasy.

Ayg leaned back so that the face of his shell was pointing upward.

"That right there," Buc continued, "the salt in the air. The planks under our feet. Is this not what we dream of, Mister Ayg? Our great adventure begins now. You and me against the world. The sky above and the sea, stretched out—"

Buc paused as a long string of crashing noises erupted from the deck below. When it stopped, the captain cleared his throat and continued.

"The sky abo—"

More crashing, as boxes tipped and clacked on floor and thudded against the bulkhead.

"The sky above," Buc said quickly, "and the sea below, stretched out as far as the—"

The sound of Chumlee's hollering sounded over a new string of crashing noises. The noises persisted, but Buc pressed on.

"The Stench…"

Roaring and crashing continued.

"…cuts over…"

A crate sounded as though it had broken, and Chumlee let loose with a terrifying string of laughter.

"…sea of possibility…"

The ruckus pressed on until Buc could no longer take it. "Mister Ayg, you have the wheel."

Ayg gave a nod and stepped up to the helm. Buc growled and made his way to the stairs. From the top, he scowled at the level below and blared, "Master Chumlee!" The noise rolled up the stairs once again and Buc raised his voice. "Master Chumlee!" he shouted. "What in the depths of Davy Jones' locker is transpiring below? You sound as though you are wrangling wild horses and it is interrupting a rather elegant monologue!"

Chumlee appeared in the shadows at the bottom of the stairs, an awkward load weighing each hand. His feet clumped loudly as he dredged his way up the steps, and his expression reeked of frustration. "I'll tell ye what, Captain," the large rooster huffed, making the top of the stairs.

With a grunt Chumlee forced his burdens before the captain and announced, "Stowaways!"

Struggling at the end of each arm were two children, a boy and a girl, and the pair had determination written all over their faces. The chicks struggled in vain to break free from Chumlee, who now rolled his eyes and dangled the kids as though they were a pair of baby mice.

"Let us go, you ogre!" shouted the girl.

Buc slowly lowered himself to their level and knit his brow as the memory came back to him. "You?" he asked, and the children stopped fidgeting.

"You know them, Captain?" Chumlee asked, suspicious.

Buc righted himself and donned a determined face. "Master Chumlee, release them. They be discovered, and presently have nowhere for them to run."

The young boy shook off his captor, and Chumlee released the girl.

"I've seen you two before, haven't I?" asked Buc. He scratched his chin and narrowed his eyes at his guests. "The back alley of Port Royal, right? I gave you coin and told you to seek passage on a vessel."

"Right sir," spoke the girl in a soft, almost timid voice.

"I distinctly recall telling you to seek a vessel not journeying to Tortuga, right?" Buc clarified.

She nodded gently.

"Let me throw them to the sharks, sir. It's been a spell since I've seen a rightful shark frenzy," begged Chumlee.

Buc stood a moment and glared at the children who at first shrank under the suggestion before they both stuck their chins in the air. Buc let slip a small laugh and said, "Not quite yet, Master Chumlee."

"We can pay you," the girl declared. She reached in her pocket and retrieved the same pouch Buc had given her.

"Sorry lass, not enough to earn passage to where we're going," he replied.

The girl's face darkened, and she stared at the ship rocking beneath her feet. She gave a long, miserable sigh and reached around to the back of her neck. Her brother blurted, "Ava! No!"

The girl unclasped her necklace and presented it to Buc. At the end of a weathered gold chain was a golden locket.

Despite the persistent pleas of the boy, Buc gently accepted the locket. He held up the piece, letting the sun dance over the engraved face. "An odd trinket for an orphan," Buc considered. He opened the locket and found the image of a fresh-faced song bird. Her radiant smile gave off an air of pure happiness.

"That is our mother," Ava explained. "I know it is not much, but it is the most precious thing we own. It is the only portrait we have of her," she added sadly.

Buc raised a curious eyebrow. "Your mother you say?"

"Yes sir," Ava replied. "She died shortly after we hatched. So, we were told."

Buc closed the locket and handed it back to the girl. "Sorry lass," he answered loudly, "but I have to refuse."

"What?" the pair sounded.

"I have no need of your trinket," he explained.

"Please sir," Ava begged. "We have nothing else in the world."

"Settle down, lass," Buc cooed. He looked at the boy and said, "You lad. What's your name?"

"Edward, sir," the boy replied, clearly relieved that the captain had refused the locket but still profoundly defiant.

"Edward and Ava," Buc said, looking each child in the eye. "As captain of this vessel," he continued, "and by the law of the sea, I hereby place you under arrest. The pair of you are now my prisoners."

The twins gasped.

"That being said," the captain added quickly, "it is up to me to decide upon your treatment. I could, as Master Chumlee suggested, feed you to the sharks"— Buc paced slowly before the two young birds, his eyes on the clouds—"or I could throw you in the brig and leave you to rot until we see fit to return to Port Royal."

The siblings looked on with anxiety, impatient for the captain's decision.

"Or," Buc announced, turning his eyes back to the stowaways and leaning in close, "I can make some use of the two of ye. So," he said loudly, resuming his full height, "until I see otherwise fit, the two of you will become indentured crew to this ship. You will follow orders given to you by myself and Master Chumlee. As deckhands you will perform whatever task we assign; you know, the cooking, cleaning, and bits 'n' bobs that no one else on-board cares to partake in."

"No," Edward replied sternly, "I will not be a slave for you!"

"Allow me to finish, young master Edward," Buc continued in a serious tone. "If you see fit not to agree to the terms set herein"—the captain threatened him in a quiet voice, leaning in so close Edward could feel the breath of each word against his own beak—"then, Master Chumlee," Buc explained, "will have my full blessing to toss your chubby little self over the gunwale and feed you to the sharks."

The twins grew rigid and they struggled against showing their fear.

Buc stood back up and gave the pair a hard look. "Do we have an accord then?"

The twins looked at each other, confusion written over their faces.

Buc bent over toward them and whispered, "It means do we have an agreement?" He snapped back upright and repeated his question. "I'll ask again, do we have an accord?"

"Yes," Ava answered then scowled at her brother.

Edward ground his beak before replying, "Yes."

"Yes what?" asked Master Chumlee.

"Yes, Captain," the two said in unison.

"Now, off to the galley," Buc ordered. "Find a bit of food and drink."

The two children gave the captain surprised expressions.

"It's down the stairs and to the left," he explained.

Their eyes grew wide and excited before they turned and raced down the stairs.

"Stay clear of the cider!" shouted Buc as they scurried off.

Chumlee watched them go with an apprehensive look on his face. He approached his captain, shaking his head. "Wicked bad luck it be to have children on board, Captain."

"Luck, Master Chumlee," came the reply, "is what we make of it."

Chumlee grumbled quietly but said nothing.

Buc looked out over the sea ahead of him, thinking of the portrait in the locket and how, like the orphans, he too grew up without parents. He breathed in the salt air as if it was the breath of life, filling his lungs with hope, determination, and strength.

Robert crept up alongside Buc and placed his hands upon the wooden railing. He tightened his grip on the rail as he spoke. "Might I have a word with you Buc … err … Captain?" Robert corrected himself.

Pivoting on his heel, Buc leaned back against the rail to face his uncle. "Back in Port Royal," began Robert, "you stated that you had something Rojo wanted?" Buc flashed a small secret smile, his brow raised high. "I did, and I do." Robert's beak curled as he struggled to find the words to loosen his nephew's beak. "Would you be willing to share a wee bit of clarity?" Buc's hand slipped into his pocket, retrieving the parchment list of names. "Before he died, Thomas bestowed this upon me." He presented the list to Robert. "Even in his weakened state, he was persistent that I take on this mysterious task." He inhaled deeply and confidently. "Together, Ayg and I have acquired the first pouch from the first gent on the list. The pouch revealed part of a map. Once we leave Tortuga, we shall locate the other two pieces and put together Thomas' puzzle."

Robert returned the list to Buc. He stroked his feathery chin. "What is the map to?" he asked.

Buc rested his wings upon the railing of the ship, his mind filled with horrible delight. "I believe it holds the location of the pirate Lucky Longfeather."

"Longfeather?" replied Robert in pure disbelief. "Lad, no one has heard a flutter of him in ages." He shook his head. "I hope yer not letting Thomas' stories still fill your head."

"Nonetheless"—he spun once again to face his uncle— "what I do know is that Rojo killed Thomas for it. For that reason alone, I must find the pieces and, per Thomas' instruction, beat him to whatever lies at the end."

Robert's brow wrinkled; his face filled with worry. "This mystery of yours, lad, you be up to the task?" he asked.

Buc's head bobbed up and down in acceptance of the challenge. "To quote Lucky Longfeather, if a mystery were known it would not be a mystery."

Unseen by Buc, a prideful smile fell upon Robert's face as he headed off across the deck.

Buc strolled along the rail and looked on as the port known as Tortuga grew in sight. He thought of what waited upon the docks and smiled knowingly.

Chapter 11

Rojo moved steadily along the quiet alley. Few ever came this way, and the rare vagrant who spied the captain knew better than to maintain eye contact for long. He didn't waste time looking about, but walked up to a thick, wooden door in a plain stone wall and inserted a key. The lock snapped free, and with a shove he was inside. He moved inside and slipped out of his sword belt. It clattered atop a side table and he stepped into the dining hall.

The home was large and spacious, having previously belonged to a Port Royal magistrate. Rojo and his wife, Catalina, arrived on the island one day, and the next they found, and took over the residence. Rumors swirled around the incident, claiming that the newcomers had murdered the magistrate who had disappeared so suddenly. The women of the town claimed that Catalina was a witch and had turned the former owners into toads. Others said that Rojo was a vicious killer who had cut them down on the street. No one knew the truth and, if Rojo had any say, they never would.

In the dining hall, the captain found his wife at the large table. There were no chairs left and no cups or plates. Instead there was an extensive collection of glass jars, beakers, and pots. There were bowls filled with herbs, spices, and strange plants, and cups filled with odd fluid. Smoke billowed happily from a small fire at the center of the table, but Rojo didn't care to know what his dear wife was cooking.

Catalina was standing to one end, hunched over a collection of tarot cards and a tray of bird bones.

"The governor is going to betray you," she announced, studying the tray.

"I do not need those fool bones to tell me that," Rojo snapped.

His wife's gaze rose to meet him, and a smile blossomed. She sauntered over to him, drawing a smile from her sour husband. She leaned in close and slapped his face. "Did you get the list of names from the book smith?"

"Working for the governor, eh?" he answered, flexing his beak. "He asked me the same thing."

"And?" she asked impatiently.

"And I'll tell you what I told him," Rojo replied. "I know where the list is and who has it. I also know that little fowl will collect all the pieces. Then, and only then, shall I swoop in and take them."

Catalina's feathered hand flashed toward her husband's cheek, but he grabbed her wrist before it could land. "I let you get away with that once, dear," he said darkly. "It won't happen again." He tossed her wrist away and cocked his head to one side.

"None of this would have happened if you had just done what I told you!" she shouted angrily, stomping over to her crucible. She grabbed a pestle and began grinding and stamping the herbs at the bottom of a mortar.

"You said to get rid of him." Rojo recalled an earlier conversation. "You never mentioned killing him."

"Don't mince words with me," she snarled. "You knew exactly what I meant. Why you decided to keep that boy alive is beyond me." Catalina continued working at the herbs, grinding harder and faster as the seconds ticked by.

"You've been wrong before," Rojo said with a sigh, still very much in control. "You told me that he would be my end, and nothing could change that. You couldn't tell me when and you couldn't tell me where. That means the vision was clouded. Does it not?"

Catalina slammed her pestle down and signed deeply. She turned to her husband, not needing to acknowledge his inquiry.

He approached his wife, his wings spread wide, and hugged her. "Fortune, my love," he reminded her, "it's in our reach, but I will have to confront him in order to attain it." She pushed away from the embrace and he released her. "I know your worries," Rojo continued, "but even you have said if one knows their destiny they then have the power to change it."

Catalina narrowed her eyes at her husband's stubbornness and returned to her work at the table.

"Do not turn your back on me, woman!" hollered Rojo.

Catalina turned around, her cheeks flaming in anger. Her fingers twitched as their eyes met once again.

Rojo approached his wife and held her gently. "Fear not for me, my love. For no one shapes my destiny but me." He kissed her. A kiss she feared would be their last.

Chapter 12

Tortuga. The name alone brought forth visions of a desperate and lonely place, full of scoundrels of the most despicable nature. Name any crime at random and chances are it is happening right now in Tortuga. The small island stood as an oasis of thieves, murderers, and the lowest forms of life on the sea.

Buc figured this would be the perfect place to recruit the rest of his crew.

On approach, Buc turned to his current crew and frowned. "Mister Ayg!" he bellowed. "You are to remain here with Barnacle Bob to watch over the ship and the twins, in that order."

Ayg snapped into a salute from his position behind the wheel.

"Master Chumlee," the captain continued, "you will escort me into town and assist in gathering a crew."

"And to prevent your inevitable kidnapping," Robert whispered to Mister Ayg, who quickly covered the smile drawn upon his front.

"Beg pardon?" Buc asked, leaning toward the pair and glaring suspiciously.

"I said aye, Captain," Robert lied.

"Good," Buc snapped, not believing his uncle for a moment. "Keep watch of my ship. Feathers will fly if anything happens to her in my absence."

"Aye, Captain," his uncle answered.

"Master Chumlee?!" Buc cried, turning to find a scowling face staring over the gunwale. "Ready?"

"Aye," he answered in a low voice, "as ready as any bird can be in Tortuga."

"Good," Buc piped back, moving over the side of the ship. "Oy, twins!" he added, calling out over his shoulder as he descended the gangplank. The pair looked up at him from beside Ayg with concerned expressions. "Don't touch my stuff," Buc demanded, not bothering to look back.

The streets and back alleys of Tortuga made Port Royal seem like a king's private isle. Everywhere Buc and Chumlee looked there was filth. From trash piled in the gutters and corners to the muck smeared across the faces of the desperate birds asleep in the street, everything was dirty and worn. Buildings in desperate need of maintenance stood watch over roads riddled with potholes. Vagrants and vagabonds, sailors, and pirates; all of them had come here to outrun their old lives and find fortune in a new one.

At least, that's what Buc was hoping to find.

Chumlee strode alongside him, silently eyeing the surroundings. He was not a rooster to trust others easily, and he saw nothing to convince him to change his mind now.

"Looks like this be the place to go for a hardened crew," Buc commented quietly.

His burly quartermaster scowled at a pair of ancient birds bickering over the last few dregs in the bottom of a rum bottle and snorted loudly.

Buc ignored the reply. "The streets are lined with brave souls, no doubt."

"The streets are littered with scavengers," Chumlee corrected. "I've not seen a fit sailor since laying a boot on this grimy old rock."

"Then maybe," Buc suggested with a smile, pulling up to a stop outside a noisy doorway, "we need to seek a new place to look."

Leaning around his captain, Chumlee grunted distrustfully at the dark room overflowing with yells, laughter, and the continuous sound of clinking glass. "You thinkin' this be the place?" he asked warily, eyeing the faded wooden sign naming the tavern as The Down Anchor.

A window behind the pair erupted in screams and broken glass. Buc and Chumlee spun just in time to see a goose fall onto his face in the street as a shower of window bits fell around him. From inside The Down Anchor, roars of rolling laughter could be heard as birds pointed and laughed at the goose who was wobbling to his feet.

"Oh yes," Buc said confidently. "This is the place for certain."

Chumlee gave his captain a doubtful look but followed him into the tavern nonetheless.

Inside the door, the pair paused to take in the surroundings. Small, rickety tables were scattered indiscriminately around the floor in strange groups. Birds stumbled between tables, making their way to and from the bar or floundering off to the toilet. Messy hens with feathers falling out bounced amongst the patrons in bright dresses and bold makeup, making sure everyone's glasses were kept full. The bar was long and narrow, with an old African Grey parrot behind the counter, frowning at the noisy drinkers. Two birds popped out of their seats and began to fight, swearing proudly that they would sooner kill than be insulted for another moment. The fight tripped past Chumlee and Buc before spilling into the street.

"Those two might do," Buc muttered quietly.

"Those two? The blokes are tryin' to kill each other," Chumlee pointed out.

"That just means they ought not work next to each other," Buc replied, as though telling his quartermaster what he didn't already know. "You must learn to broaden your horizons."

Chumlee shook his head and moved toward the bar with Buc following closely behind.

"Two ciders," Buc ordered, nodding to Chumlee.

The barkeep poured two glasses and demanded payment in a dry voice. "Two pence."

Buc dropped a shilling on the counter, catching the attention of the server. He pushed the coin at the bird and asked, "If a bird were to be in search of a crew, where might he begin in these parts?"

"A crew?" the barkeep mused, plucking the shilling from the counter, and dropping it in his coat pocket. "An' what 'appened to your last?"

"My last?" Buc asked, a little surprised.

"Aye," the barkeep said, leaning on the bar. "I've heard of you." He continued, in a hushed tone, "Birds been talking about you. You're Captain Buc Buccaneer, ain't ya?"

Buc made himself tall and stuck out his chest. "Aye," he replied arrogantly.

"I have heard tall stories, Captain," the bartender confessed. "I never expected to see you lookin' for a crew here on this old rock, 'less some misfortune may have fell to them."

Panic raced through Buc's stomach, but he swallowed it down hard. He was elated that the tales of his pirate nature had already travelled to Tortuga, but he was surprised to find that he would have to so strongly support them. He had to find a reason for requiring a new crew before his reputation expired without him. "Can you keep a secret, mate?" he asked the bartender, knowing that gossip was a form of currency in Tortuga.

The old parrot's eyes twinkled, and he gave a little nod.

"Every few years I favor my crew an extended leave," Buc explained. "During said leave, I recruit new members. When the duration of the leave has expired, I weed out the weak and undesirable." Buc watched the barkeep's eyes carefully for signs that his story was failing. The captain didn't dare look at Chumlee for fear that his crewman would give it away.

"What for?" the bartender wondered.

"Keep the crew fresh," Buc said easily. "Savvy?"

"Ah," the parrot said with a knowing nod. "Fresh meat for the fight."

Buc smiled. "Too right," he agreed.

"And it's fighters ya seek?" he verified.

"The filthiest," Buc confirmed.

❸ "Well, Captain," the bartender said, standing to his full height, "the best way to find a fighter is to start yourself a brawl."

Buc stroked his chin then reached into a pocket and retrieved two more shillings. "In advance of the damages," he explained, pushing the coins at the parrot who slipped them into his pocket with the first. Buc then turned from the bar and said to his companion, "Master Chumlee, would you be so kind as to start a brawl? From said brawl, you shall select an assortment of potential crew members."

"You can't be serious," the bigger rooster questioned.

"I could not be more so," the captain replied. Chumlee shrugged, smiled, and grabbed the shirt back of a passing sailor. Before the hopeless victim could sound a protest, Chumlee hurled the sailor into a table of other birds, spilling their drinks and knocking one to the ground.

That bird quickly stood and punched the sailor square in the face, causing him to fall into another table. Again, another bird rose and began throwing punches. Moments later, the violence spread like fire in a hayfield.

There was screaming and cursing, and punches were being thrown everywhere. The entire tavern quickly erupted in a brawl. Buc and

Chumlee took their cider, gave a nod to the barkeep, and made their way throughout the flying and flailing bodies towards a table in the corner. As the pair made their way, a lone sailor prepared to punch Buc. The captain merely held up one feathered finger and shook his head no. Realization flashed in the eyes of the sailor when he recognized his target. His beak dropped open and his balled fist fell to his side. The shock was so complete that the sailor failed to notice the chair swung at his face until it made port between his eyes. Buc and Chumlee winced at the sight of the bird folding to the ground.

"Not that one," Buc advised.

Chumlee didn't bother to respond but silently continued to move toward their table.

Once seated, Buc quickly downed his cider. He slammed the cup on the table and wiped his beak with a sleeve. "Pick ten to twelve souls," he instructed Master Chumlee. "Promise them the standard wage and meet me back on the ship."

"Aye sir," Chumlee replied, watching Buc carefully as the captain rose and dusted himself. "Might I inquire, Captain, as to where you be headed?"

"To acquire armament for the Stench," Buc announced. "We cannot strike fear into the hearts of fowl by throwing rocks and shouting obscenities, can we now?"

"I could," Chumlee muttered, sipping his cider.

"Aye," Buc agreed, still scanning the crowd. "But not all of us are … um—" Buc turned his eyes to the massive frame of Chumlee and smiled, fighting for the right word "—gifted with size. You may be able to turn a pear red, but I could make it dance. Find me a rowdy group of pears, Master Chumlee. I aim to get them some toys."

As Buc left the table, a tall, gangly bird fell upon it. Chumlee poked the bird in the arm before giving him a shake. He lifted the head of the semiconscious bird who looked back with a slack jaw and a pair of starry eyes. "Oye," Chumlee asked, "you wanna be a pirate?"

Buc strolled down the creaking, and rotting, docks of Tortuga. Behind him was a large cart pulled by an ox and driven by a salty sea dog of a parrot. His torn and stained clothes, poor hygiene and cracked beak made him look more like a pirate than a merchant. But it was Tortuga, so there was a strong chance he was both.

He stopped once he saw his new crew standing at attention before his ship.

"Here you are, Captain," Chumlee announced. "Your men." The quartermaster extended a feathered hand to an odd assortment of birds.

Buc took one look at the motley bunch before leaning into Chumlee, hiding his beak behind a hand, and asking, "These were the winners?"

"Not exactly," the other admitted.

Buc blanched at the answer. "They weren't the losers, were they?" he asked, slightly horrified.

"No, Captain," Chumlee answered with a smile.

"Well then," Buc asked, cocking an eyebrow at the ragamuffin band, "what are they?"

"These, sir," Chumlee announced proudly, "are the ones who performed the noblest of tasks in order to avoid confrontation."

Buc narrowed his eyes at the quartermaster then scrutinized the new crew. "So," he began slowly, "they are the survivors?"

"Aye, Captain," Chumlee replied happily.

"And they all have that rare and special fortitude," Buc continued, "to know when to turn tail feather and live to fight—" Buc cleared his throat in the face of the unimpressive crew "—or rather to live and run away another day."

"Aye, sir," Chumlee agreed. "I watched carefully and each one demonstrated a caution and sense of self-preservation that will be invaluable on a trip such as ours."

"I see," Buc answered, not sounding convinced. He leaned in to Chumlee and muttered, "The ancient bird delivering the arsenal would strike more fear than these."

Chumlee made a confused face and Buc shook a crazy idea out of his head. He approached the first sailor and looked him over warily. "You, sir," the captain snapped, "what's your name?"

Buc had approached the red bearded pelican with the intention to look him directly in the eye, but the task proved more difficult than he assumed. The bird's left eye veered off toward the left and his right eye toward the right, both displaying a slightly upward bend. Buc waved a feathered hand in front of the sailor who responded with two slow blinks.

"Pugwald, sir," the quartermaster announced.

"Master Chumlee," Buc began carefully, "is this bird visually impaired?"

"Aye, sir," Chumlee answered in a voice of confusion.

"And why would I want a blind bird on my ship?" the captain asked.

"Oh!" Chumlee sounded as though suddenly remembering something. "Pugwald!" he bellowed. "Put yer patch on."

The pelican hurriedly pulled an eye patch from his satchel and slapped it over his left eye. Once in place, the right eye corrected itself, slowly rotating until Pugwald was looking straight at Buc.

The entire routine gave Buc a case of the shivers and he pulled back a bit. Curiosity won over though, and he gingerly reached out and lifted the eye patch. The pelican's eyes rotated and wandered unnaturally. Buc made a sound of disgust and replaced the patch.

"He be a deck hand," Chumlee shared. "And our lookout."

Buc's face contorted with skepticism. He turned to Chumlee to make sure he had heard correctly. "Lookout?"

"Aye, sir," the reply came. "I figures if he's only got the one good eye then he be blind to distractions."

Buc took a moment to allow the logic to settle in. "Blind indeed," he said at last, feeling a little doubtful. "Quite the differentia." He turned to the pelican and smiled. "Welcome aboard, sailor."

The rest of the crew did little to instill confidence in their new captain. Twelve were gathered in all, and none of them seemed like the crew in Buc's imagination.

Buc counted, and realized there was a thirteenth seaman in the row, standing silent, his face hidden by the hood of a well-worn cloak.

"Who are ye?" shouted Chumlee, not recognizing the bird as one he had chosen. "Remove your hood in the presence of a captain!" he snapped.

The figure slowly removed his hood to reveal his face. The fowl's appearance was that of a variety of different birds. As he lowered his hood, he revealed his burnt and singed feathers, along with distinguished coloring and markings. Chumlee gasped and reached for his sword, preparing to lunge at the meek fowl.

"Stand down, Master Chumlee," barked Buc.

"But Captain!" answered Chumlee.

The captain's eye pierced Chumlee's own. Knowing his place in the crew, Chumlee sheathed his weapon.

The skinny wannabe crewman continued to look downward, daring not to make eye contact with his would-be captain.

"You there!" spoke Buc.

The fowl looked upward reluctantly to meet eyes with the captain. "You turducken?"

With great hesitation, and a strong urge to flee, the bird replied, "Aye."

Once again, with falcon speed, Chumlee grabbed for his sword.

"I said stand down, Master Chumlee," barked Buc once again. Again, Chumlee obliged his captain.

"I take it you have a name?" asked Buc.

"Twitch, sir. They call me Twitch."

"Well, Mister Twitch, if it is true what they say of your kind, I must inquire. What is your affliction?" Buc knew the stories of the turducken, a wild crossbreed of multiple birds. Considered a distortion of nature, many people believed they were cursed. Turducken were a nomadic species, untrusted by many due to their freakish appearance and oddly supernatural afflictions.

"Speak up, freak! Name your curse!" yelled Chumlee.

"Lightning sir," mumbled Twitch.

Again, Chumlee gasped. "Lightning," he muttered, looking up with deep concern.

Twitch continued, "I have been stuck by lightning over one hundred and forty-two times in my life."

Chumlee turned to his captain. "Captain, we cannot have a creature like this around our powder or armament. Let me put the freak out of his misery."

The captain looked at the slim, meager sailor before him. "I am sorry, Mister Twitch. As much as I regret, I have to agree with my quartermaster. For these scales, the risk outweighs compassion."

Buc began walking away. "Captain!" Twitch called out.

The captain pivoted on his heel and turned back toward the lad.

"I have no family. My kind is scattered to the wind. Not seen another like me since I was a wee lad. All I ask … all I wish for is to be part of a crew." He stepped towards the captain, alarming Chumlee.

"I will do any task. I will do any favor. All I ask is ... for the chance to be part of something rather than an outcast."

Buc peered deeply into Twitch's eyes. In them, he saw his own reflection, taking him back to when he begged his uncle to build the Stench. He saw a vision of himself sitting wide-eyed on the edge of a seat as Thomas spun tales of crews gathered together in celebration, united as one.

Buc smiled briefly then stood tall, clearing his throat as he spoke. "Welcome aboard, Mister Twitch."

"Captain?" inquired Chumlee, "what about all that about scales and risk?"

"Sometimes, Master Chumlee, we must tip the scales in favor of what be right rather than what keeps us safe."

He whispered to Twitch, "Be a good lad, and stay clear of any combustibles, flammables or valuables."

"Aye sir," replied Twitch. He smiled as his eyes teared up. His tears of joy were quickly vanquished as Chumlee approached him with anger in his eyes. "Hear me, freak." His voice was a hard whisper. "Keep your distance from me"—he poked Twitch hard in the chest— "or I will personally throw you down to the locker."

Buc looked to Chumlee who was tall and powerful. He might have been a little foolish now and again—not to mention being prone to violent outbursts—but, all in all, he was a model fowl of fortune. *Even Mister Ayg,* Buc argued silently, *with his ... well ... condition... Even Ayg knows how to draw a sword when the time comes.* Buc worked to get rid of the image of his crew abandoning ship at the first sign of a storm and waved for Chumlee to continue. "Master Chumlee," he said in a surprisingly tired voice, "if you would be so kind as to read the articles of conduct for our new crew."

"Aye, sir," was the reply. Chumlee pulled out a roll of parchment and positioned himself before the would-be crew. He cleared his throat and began with a booming voice, which echoed over the old Tortuga docks. "The captain reserves the right to take action for the good of all. Every fowl aboard shall obey all orders given to them by officers, and any fowl whosoever disobeys the command shall lose their share or receive punishment as the captain or the quartermaster deem fit. Any fowl that breeds a mutiny or riot on board the ship shall forfeit his shares and receive punishment as the captain or quartermaster deem fit."

"If you choose that one," Buc interrupted, "plan on it ending poorly for you, lads."

From the top of the gangplank came a series of clanging noises. Everyone looked up to see Mister Ayg punishing the rail with the flat of his sword. The face drawn upon his shell was threatening and angry. The egg pointed his sword at the crew and then mimed dragging it across a throat.

"Exactly, Mister Ayg," Buc agreed. "Master Chumlee, you may continue."

"If a fowl conceals or hides any treasure captured," the quartermaster pressed on, "or fails to place it into the general fund, he shall be marooned and sent ashore on a deserted island. Any fowl turning chicken, or presenting cowardice in time of engagement, shall lose his shares."

Several of the potential crew members went rigid and white.

"That doesn't apply if you are literally a chicken," Buc explained with a moan.

There was an audible sigh of relief from half of the birds, and Buc began to seriously worry for his own safety.

Chumlee snorted as though someone had just told a joke and then looked back to the article. "He that shall have the misfortune of losing an eye, leg or arm, shall receive six hundred pieces of eight."

Slowly, Twitch raised his hand. "So if I were to lose a leg, or perhaps my arm, I would get six hundred pieces of eight?"

"Aye," replied the Captain warily.

Another hand shot up. "What if I just lose a foot," the bird asked, "and not a whole leg?"

Chumlee rolled his eyes as the captain spoke up. "You err … you would receive—" Buc paused, looking at his quartermaster "—two hundred pieces of eight?"

Upon hearing the captain's response, others spoke up.

"What if I lose a toe?"

"If I get rope burn, can I get a hundred pieces of eight?"

"What about splinters? If I get a splinter can I get some silver?"

"I have a headache. Can I get twenty pieces of eight for that? It is such a burden."

"I have sea spray in my eyes," another whined. "Might I have a shilling?"

The shouting was abruptly interrupted by a pistol shot. Instinctively, the entire collection of potential crew members ducked and cowered at the sound. "Enough!" Chumlee bellowed. His voice reverberated over the docks and carried well out into the sea. "Shut yer beaks ya bloomin' scavengers," he shouted. Humored by their responses, Chumlee tried not to laugh. Buc was crouched with a hand over his beak, trying himself not to laugh.

Buc quickly stood and brushed himself off. "Continue," he said in a loud voice, hoping none of the crew had seen his reaction.

"The captain has addressed the Company Articles," Chumlee snapped. "Now be the time to agree." The quartermaster held out the articles and continued reading. "We the crew are now birds of the company herein known as the Crew of The Fowl Stench. We do here and now band ourselves together into a brotherhood of fortune seekers. We will stand by our brothers, protecting them and fighting side by side. Let no fowl flounder or stand alone." Looking up to the hopefuls, Chumlee demanded, "Do ye agree to the articles presented before you?"

The crew answered in unison. "Aye!"

"Splendid," Buc decided, looking up at the sky. "It be past time we shove off, Master Chumlee. Load the cargo and let us take the Stench to sea."

"Aye, sir," Chumlee replied. "Alright ya buzzards! Unload the goods and get 'em stowed. Man the lines and ready the ship for departure. Move like yer lives are in peril!" Chumlee turned toward Twitch. "You there, stay clear of the powder."

"Aye, sir," was the shivering response.

As Buc walked up the gangplank, he noticed his uncle talking to the ox cart driver. The odd pair seemed to be in the midst of a slightly heated discussion. His gaze did not go unnoticed. His uncle ended his discussion and approached the gangplank. "What was all that about?" asked Buc.

"Just thanking him for delivering off the beaten path," replied Robert.

Buc scratched his chin in disbelief. "Be that as it may, the entire island is 'off the beaten path'," he jested. "So," he continued, "what do you think of our new crew?"

"The crew is only as good as their captain," Robert answered.

As Buc stood in front of his uncle he muttered, "Well, the disposition of the captain is still in flux."

"No worry, lad. You'll do fine." His uncle's vote of confidence raised Buc's hopes.

Buc smiled at his uncle then cleared his throat. "Barnacle Bob, see to the fitting and fabrication needed for our new arsenal."

Robert watched as the crew carried cargo aboard. "What be the cargo, sir?"

"Four cannons—only three functional—five swivel cannons, twenty-four kegs of powder, an assortment of pistols, ammunition, and a quaternary of harpoons."

"Harpoons?" inquired Robert.

"Aye, harpoons," confirmed Buc.

"Are ya planning on doing battle with a beastie?" asked Robert with a chuckle.

"In fact, Uncle, I am. And that beast's name is Rojo."

The Wooden Stork was aflutter with salty fowl ending their day with story and drink. An alley tavern is the place where rumors spread, and tales are given flight. Port Royal was often the hub for the wheel that spun ships out and across the Spanish main. The ever-present barmaid danced between tables as if she was performing a choreographed routine for the patrons to see. She made her way behind the bar to restock her tray for the flock of parched fowl. As she turned back toward the main room, her exit was blocked by another bird.

"I am looking for a particular sailor," the fowl announced, his tone menacing and rugged.

Penelope smiled genuinely at the gentleman. "I know who you be lookin' for, and I know who you are, Rojo." She elongated his name, mocking his desire to remain anonymous.

Rojo's beak snarled as he moved closer to Penny, "Where is Buc?" he asked angrily, his hot breath flashing across her face.

"'Ow should I know?" she snapped. "So, if ye don't mind, I need to be getting back to me duties." Her strong sense of responsibility to her patrons, smothered in arrogance, filled her every word.

Rojo did mind. He stood his ground, projecting his own arrogant nature back at her with every breath.

"I see," said Penelope. "I guess I should ask again." She pulled out a small knife from within her dress and pressed the tip under Rojo's chest plate and against his feathery skin. His eyes widened, confirming to Penelope that he got the point.

"I understand now what Buc sees in you," he said, his beak almost touching hers. "But do you have the courage to use it?" he asked in a huffed, rushed tone.

"I do not have to," she said smugly. She continued to stare him down, her eyes not blinking for a moment. Slowly, she removed the blade from Rojo's side.

"You are a weak little thing," he said, wrinkling his beak in disgust. "I've killed women for less." He looked her up and down. "I would have no reservations about dispensing a tavern wench," he snarled in anger.

"I'm sorry, sir," Penny said aloud, "we're all out of sarsaparilla." She smiled at Rojo as he continued to glare at her in anger.

Rojo's brow slowly dropped low, not understanding her comment. He had not asked her for anything, much less sarsaparilla. Turning his head slowly to the left and then to the right, he finally understood that her statement was not meant for him.

Pointed at him from behind was an assortment of blades and pistols, held by the patrons of the tavern. Her statement was code.

Penny leaned in toward Rojo. "They get a bit miffed if something comes between them and their drinks, sweetie," she whispered.

Rojo backed away from Penny slowly as the collection of weapons followed his every footstep until he exited the tavern.

The patrons cheered and went back to their tables as Penny began to fill mugs behind the bar. Amidst the celebration of intoxicated bird, a strong sense of worry flowed over her as her mind wandered to Buc's safety.

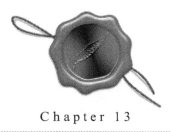

Chapter 13

"Oye!" Edward bellowed. "I want to see!" The young bird pushed and hopped, trying to see over the shoulders of the adult fowl gathered around the captain's desk.

With the officers of the Stench gathered in his cabin, Buc reviewed his charts of the Caribbean. From the corner of his eye, he saw the little bird vigorously bouncing and pulling on the shirts of the rest of the crew and took pity on the lad. Lifting young Edward up, and sitting him on the edge of the table, Buc waved a warning finger at him to stay quiet. Edward nodded and strained to see the entire chart. Every island of the Caribbean, along with the coast of Florida and the Gulf of Mexico, was visible. Cuba, Jamaica, and the Hispaniola port of Tortuga were all clearly marked. Edward didn't realize the ocean was so vast or so populated with islands.

"The King's Nugget is due to arrive at Port Royal in two days," Buc continued. "That means she'd have to be making way south of the Bahama islands, between Cuba and Hispaniola." He looked up from the map with a wide grin. "That is where she'll be so that's where we'll be."

From outside the cabin came a bellowing cry. "Ship off the port side!"

Buc looked at Chumlee then toward Robert. Both frowned and headed toward the door. Buc stomped after them and the rest of the crew followed.

"Mr. Pugwald!" Buc shouted. "Report."

"Captain," the pelican panted, "there be a ship off the port side."

Buc rolled his eyes at the pelican's lack of detail.

He approached the rail and extended his spyglass. Carefully scanning the horizon, Buc's gaze fell upon the vessel in the distance.

"Beastie's bones," Buc spat, pulling his eye out of the glass to scowl at Chumlee. "The bird's near blind. How does he do that without a spyglass?"

"No distractions," the quartermaster reminded him, pointing at one eye.

"Right," he replied, looking back to the craft. Aboard the distant ship were a variety of fowl running about, waving their wings frantically.

"Shall I run out the cannons, Captain?" Chumlee asked.

Continuing to look at the distant ship, Buc shook his head and said, "No mate. No cause for alarm. It's a ship of fools."

"Even more reason to attack," Chumlee argued. "We send a clear message to the other ships that be in the area. Let them know we are a fearsome crew."

Buc lowered his glass and gave the quartermaster a look. "Master Chumlee," he began patiently, "I applaud your enthusiasm to extend my reputation and that of this ship, but only a fool attacks a ship of fools. For the fools, doing foolish things comes natural. So the foolish fools who attack the fools foolishly fall folly to the fools floundering foolishly. So, it's best not to be fooled by their foolish facade, savvy?"

Chumlee's beak hung open slightly and his eye glazed over a bit. "Did you just make that up or did you read it in one of your learning books?"

Buc took that as an affirmative and closed his scope. "Set our course, Master Chumlee," he commanded. "I wish to see if Cuba is beautiful this time of year."

All through the night, the crew kept watch. Two more ships came within range, though neither bore the name of The King's Nugget. The dawning sun began its journey from the amber horizon to the deep blue sky, creating an array of multicolored rays that danced over the rippling sea. Climbing the stairs from the lower deck, young Edward blinked as the light exposed itself to the darkness. Looking around, he realized he was the only crew member awake. Even his sister, still tightly wrapped in a blanket, slept silently as dawn blossomed. As he turned his gaze skyward, he saw the dimly lit silhouette of a lone crewman sitting in the crow's nest. Edward climbed the rigging to find Buc silently staring out into the distance. His face was drawn and serious, with a hard edge the boy was unfamiliar with seeing on the usually animated captain. It was a little unsettling, and caused the lad to pause before climbing in.

Buc looked over at sea and sky that seemed equally vast in a way only sailors would understand. It was the sensation that the world had been cleaved in two with half of existence being given to air, half to water, and the ship riding the knife's edge in between. He studied the horizon, soaking in a color that was reminiscent of a young cardinal's plumage. He thought about an old saying that his Uncle Robert used to share. "Red sky at dawn, sailors be warned." The magenta hues crawling across the morning sky and staining the sea gave him a new appreciation of the phrase.

"Hello, Edward," the captain said without warning.

"You knew it was me?" Edward said in a shocked tone.

"My ship, mate," Buc explained, still studying the sunrise, "a captain always knows what happens on his ship."

"What are you doing up here?" the boy asked after a moment.

Buc pointed at the horizon. "Watching the rising sun, mate."

Edward clambered into the nest with the captain and struggled to make himself at home. The boy then looked out at the sun, pushing its way past the edge of the ocean. "So," he asked at length, "what's so special about the sun?"

Buc moved aside to make room for the boy and replied, "Every morning, the sun rises. No matter what yesterday brought, calm seas or Poseidon's wrath, the sun always knows to rise. The sun knows where it belongs. It has a defined place in this world."

Edward stared out over the sea and nodded thoughtfully then admitted, "I don't understand."

"No worries, mate," Buc consoled. "You've got time to make your mark in this world." He lifted his spyglass to his eye and smiled. "But, to do that, one must be willing to do something remarkable." He pressed the glass closed and turned to the lad. "Time to wake the crew, boy."

Below deck, the crew enjoyed a morning meal of fruits, grains, and cider. The mood was reserved, and the men ate in relative silence.

Twitch sat alone, preferring to sit along the wall so he could see everyone rather than along the mess table with the rest of the crew— that and quite a few members of the crew had asked if he were to be struck by lightning that he do it away from them. Pugwald kept moving his patch from one side to the other so as to see up and down the table clearly. A few of the birds smacked their beaks sleepily, still groggy from a night in their hammocks. Chumlee strolled the length of the room, plucking food from trays as he went.

"Eat up, ya dogs," the quartermaster barked. "You'll not be gettin' much time to sit on yer tail feathers once we spot the King's Nugget, so get what ya can now. Every hand will be on deck when the captain calls."

On the bow of the Fowl Stench, Buc stood perched on the rail taking long pulls of the rich, briny air. The ship rolled gently upon an even sea, like a chick tucked into a hen's wing. The wind was light and cool, and the sun was warm and bright. The planks smelled of oil and the sound of the rousing crew was growing to a dull roar. The course was known, and adventure awaited them. At that very moment, the captain was surrounded by everything he prized about being on the water and everything he believed a pirate to be. Holding tightly to the rigging and leaning over the bow, he sang, "With the wind in our feathers, we all flock together. Yo, ho! Is a pirate so lucky?"

"On our way we set sail," answered Robert in a deep voice, "with the wind at our tail. Yo, ho! Is a pirate so lucky?"

Buc turned to see his uncle standing behind him. He smiled at the old bird, gratified that his uncle knew the words.

"Excuse me, captain," Ava asked timidly, "what's that ya singin'?"

"That there's a pirate song, isn't it, Captain?" answered Edward, coiling rope on the deck.

Buc jumped down from the railing with a smile. "It is, lad", he said. "It be a little shanty sung by a famous pirate. Perchance the greatest pirate of all. Lucky Longfeather."

"Lucky Longfeather?" asked Edward.

"Aye lad," Buc answered reverentially. "Categorically the most feared pirate in all the Spanish Main."

"Possibly the world," added Robert.

"Well then, how come I never heard of him?" asked Edward.

"Well, he's long gone now, lad," Buc replied with a hint of sadness in his voice.

"Gone where?" Ava wondered aloud.

"Just gone," Buc replied. "Some say he died battling ferocious creatures of the deep. Others say he sailed clean off the edge of the map. No one really knows, but he vanished years ago." He knelt down to the level of the young birds and said, "There are a few that gather he went down to meet old Hobb." Buc made horns with his fingers and grinned wickedly. "Personally, I like to think the old pirate has gone and retired to some tropical paradise, surrounded by sun, sand, and the treasure of a lifetime."

"Wow," Edward breathed. "What was he like then?"

Buc strolled to a nearby barrel and plucked out an apple. He thought back to when he was Edward's age and Thomas used to tell him stories of Lucky Longfeather. He smiled knowing that Thomas' stories would live on, certain that the book smith would have been pleased. "I'll tell you, lad," Buc said, rolling the apple in his hand. "Lucky was the crow's nose. He was a bona fide pirate in every sense. While other pirates would pillage and plunder any ship they chanced upon, Lucky concentrated his endeavors on the greedily wealthy. He made subject of his wrath any who amassed their great wealth at the expense of the weak and unremarkable—dock owners who treated their men like slaves and factory managers who worked birds to death, hardly paying a wage they could live on. Lucky aimed to put the wealth into the pockets of the less fortunate, leaving them as empty-handed as possible. He would clean a ship out bow to stern, and, oh, did he have a nose for gold. No hidden stash was safe from old Lucky. He would tear a ship apart before he left the greedy with but a single coin to their name."

"Did he give all the treasure to the poor?" Ava asked excitedly.

"He's a pirate, lass," Buc laughed. "Not a priest."

The little lady pulled in her bottom beak and looked at Robert who shrugged and smiled at her.

"His crew," Buc continued, biting into his apple, "was as loyal as the sea is wide. Seven years. Seven years is what old Captain Longfeather demanded from each of his crew. And when their time of indentured servitude was expired, he levied upon them the option to stay on or take their cut and depart." He took another bite and savored it slowly. "But to ol' Captain Longfeather, his crew was his family, and ya take care of family. Legend says he built a commune of pirates."

"Like Tortuga?" Edward interrupted.

"Gah!" Robert spat. "I hope not."

"No, lad," Buc answered. "This be a place where the old pirates could live out the rest of their days with Lucky taking care of 'em all till the day they die." Buc looked back at Ava, 'That be what most of the treasure was for." Taking a final bite of his apple and tossed the core overboard. "Nope. The way I see, Old Longfeather is living fancy on a beach in parts unknown, all tickety-boo," he sang, mussing the feathers on Edward's head. "Yo ho! Is a pirate so lucky?"

"Captain!" shouted a bird from the crow's nest. Pugwald leaned over the edge of his perch and yelled down to Buc, "Ship off the starboard side, sir!"

"Can you identify her, Mr. Pugwald?" Buc answered.

"Aye sir," the pelican replied, beaming back at him. "It be the King's Nugget, sir!"

Buc smiled at Robert and gave him a nod. "Yo ho! Is a pirate so lucky."

Chapter 14

The senior officers stood around the large table in the captain's cabin. The room was sparsely furnished, save for a pair of chairs set to one side, a small writing desk under a window, and a modest bed with a fiery red satin cover. The windows were draped with the same material as the bed cover, and someone had painted the image of a large feather over the doorpost.

Buc looked around the table at his men, one hand on the hilt of his sword and the other holding to the edge of the table. Robert and Chumlee stood silent with their arms crossed over their chests, and Ayg was cleaning a pistol, settling for something less than a spit-shine. "Pugwald has confirmed she be the Nugget," Buc informed the men.

"How shall we go about takin' her, Captain?" Chumlee asked.

"I recommend raisin' the colors an' firing a shot across her bow," Robert advised. It had taken the better part of the day to chase the Nugget down, and the sky had grown dark and cold. Lightning zigzagged outside the window and the wind could be heard whipping the Stench's mighty sails.

Buc scratched his chin and narrowed his eyes. "And if she runs?"

"Then we pursue," Chumlee snapped eagerly, a wishful grin flashing across his face.

"Most likely, if not armed, they will drop sail and negotiate," Robert shared.

"Negotiate?" questioned Buc. "I never fathomed negotiations would be a tool aboard this ship."

"Aye," Robert said firmly. "It's little known that most pirates prefer negotiation to attack. Attacks are messy and costly. They waste resources and damage the potential prize." Barnacle Bob rested his hands upon the table and leaned in. "Best to give a show of force an' just ask nicely, aye?"

Buc stared at his uncle in wonder. "And how do you know so much about pirating?" he asked, genuinely concerned about his uncle's unforeseen knowledge.

"Sometimes, carpentry takes you to the sea," the older bird said with a grin. "An' sometimes those vessels are pirate ships."

Thunder rumbled and rattled the contents of the cabin as the men spoke. Buc thought he heard the cry of Mister Twitch somewhere off in the distance. "Master Chumlee," he barked, pushing aside the mental image of his feathered barometer cowering in a barrel. "Prepare the warning shot and make ready the crew."

"Aye, sir," the bird replied then stomped out of the cabin, wringing his hands in delight.

As the sea tossed the Stench about, rolling with the building storm, Buc swaggered over to his desk and opened the top drawer. Inside was a tightly bound bundle of black cloth. He pulled it out carefully and held in in his hands for a moment, admiring the dark color and weight of it in his feathery hands.

"I know that flag," Robert admitted, recognizing it as the one Fanny had given his nephew.

"She told me not to fly it unless I was absolutely sure," Buc recalled.

"And?" Robert asked.

Buc gave the older bird a definite look. "It was Thomas' dying wish for me to find these pieces. I do it for him. So right now, Uncle,

I've never been so sure of anything in my life." Buc tucked the flag under a wing and exited his cabin. "Mr. Pugwald!" he crowed over the deck. "Mr. Marley!"

"Aye sir," they answered in unison.

Buc presented them with the black, folded cloth and proudly announced, "Hoist the colors!"

"Aye sir!" the men replied.

The birds attached the flag to the ship's rigging with the speed of seasoned sailors. Pulling upon the halyard line, they hoisted the flag into the air. The wind blew hard and strong against the flag, which stretched out like a dark wing across a swirling, grey sky. Upon it was the skull of a bird and two crossed feathers. Its tattered edges told the story of its early wear and tear. Perhaps it was used in battle or merely as a decoration for a local tavern. It did not matter. It now represented the fearsome pirate Buc Buccaneer and his mighty ship, the Fowl Stench.

"How did Aunt Fanny acquire such a magnificent article?" Buc asked his uncle.

"She told me she found it in a box stacked three deep from a marketplace merchant in Port Royal." Robert hummed, eyeing the flag with a look of pride.

Buc watched as the flag reached the top of the mast, waving and snapping majestically. Its bold design and unmistakable coloring loudly told the world that he was, in fact, a pirate. "I cannot imagine anyone parting with such an impressive declaration."

"Nor can I," Robert agreed.

With a smile across his face, Buc shouted over a shoulder, "Master Chumlee!"

"Aye, Captain?" the quartermaster replied.

"Ready a single shot," Buc commanded. "Let it fly across her bow."

"Aye, Captain," Chumlee answered, turning to go below. The crew gathered on deck to watch the ordeal as it unfolded.

Buc looked through his spyglass at the ship as they approached, but something was amiss. He looked at his crew, all silent and intent with their hands folded and their mouths closed. "Ahem," he cleared his throat to gain the attention of his crew, "it be best not to forget we're pirates. Perhaps we could sound the part? Hmm?"

The crew looked at one another for a moment then shrugged. The birds broke into a torrent of yelling and crowing. Deep growls and loud bellows drifted over the waters as the men waved swords and stomped their boots.

"Better, lads," Buc praised, returning to his spyglass. "Better."

The clamor was momentarily drowned by the sound of canon fire as Chumlee let loose the first shot.

Buc watched intently as the ball ripped across the waves and burst

through the Nugget's figurehead. He gingerly lowered his spyglass and stared in shock. "He hit the ship," he mumbled. "He hit the ship."

Ayg drew an impassive expression upon his shell and shrugged, quickly wiping it clean and drawing a more surprised face.

Buc raced to the stairs and called for Chumlee who soon

appeared from around the corner. "You hit the ship," he announced in a strained tone.

"Aye," the quartermaster sighed sheepishly. "Sorry 'bout that, Captain. I was aiming for—"

"But you hit the ship."

"Aye, Captain. I knows," Chumlee answered, irritation growing in his tone. "An' I'm sorry."

"You were supposed to warn them," Buc reminded him.

"Indeed, Captain, they are now well warned now, aye?" Chumlee answered with a weak grin.

"Captain!" rang the hollers from the deck.

Buc ran back to the rail to find several birds of the crew pointing at the King's Nugget. Her captain and crew had gathered to look at the damage done by the Stench.

"They look mad," Edward pointed out.

Buc extended his spyglass once again and gazed upon the ship. "Oh, crawfish and pickles," he mumbled.

Robert approached Buc. "Captain," he said quietly, "perhaps to arms?"

Buc nodded, his head still in a fog. "Mister Ayg," he said dreamily, "call the men to arms."

Ayg drew a confused expression upon his shell and looked to Robert.

The captain turned angrily to his crewman before choking on his own words. "Right," Buc said, shaking his head clear. He stepped to the center of the deck and cried, "Avast, ye dullards, to arms! To arms!"

Pugwald set a course for the Nugget as the crew erupted in a roar, firing pistols into the air and waving their swords over their heads. Once they were broadsided, Buc grabbed a line from the Stench and swung across to the Nugget. At his immediate side, were Chumlee, Ayg, Twitch, Pugwald, and Marley. The boarding party crossed the gap, their boots landing heavily upon the deck of the Nugget.

"You there," Buc called out, pointing to a shivering crow. "Call out your Captain."

There proved to be no need for the order. A tall stork approached Buc with grace and dignity. His head was held high and he looked down upon Buc and his men. "I am Captain Finnegan. Why have you fired upon my ship? What gives you the right?"

Buc took a step back and pointed at himself. "Um, pirate," he said, referencing his attire and demeanor. "Was that not apparent to all present?" He leaned in toward his opposite. "Did you not see the flag? It's rather impressive if you don't mind my saying so."

The captain continued, "You have no right to—"

He was interrupted by Buc, holding up a feathery finger. "My dear fellow captain," he began. "I would like to apologize for the egregious actions of my crew. The impact upon your ship was purely accidental, I promise. That being said, it would be in your best interest that we dispose with conversation and get right to the action at hand."

The Nugget's captain puffed out his chest and released a slow sigh. His eyes scanned the deck of the Stench and her rowdy crew then reviewed the missing figurehead. "Very well," he said at last. "What is it you want?"

The sky flashed white through the tightly knitted, ash colored clouds and Twitch gave a small squeak.

"I seek one of your passengers," Buc declared, "solely to discuss a mutually beneficial arrangement." As he spoke, one of the deck hands began moving toward him. Buc, without turning his eye from the captain, raised his flintlock and pointed it at the approaching deck hand. "No need for bravery, lad," he warned. He turned to face the energetic young bird. "No need to start troubles, mate. We've stated our business. Once done, we'll be on our merry way. No harm, no foul."

"You expect us to trust the word of a pirate?" the crewman snapped.

"No," Buc answered calmly, "and thank you for recognizing that I am, in fact, a pirate."

The deckhand straightened in surprise.

"Trust is a commodity that is earned," Buc explained, "not bestowed. Do what you will, lad. But I shall complete my transaction. The only question that remains is whether or not you have a hole in your chest when I sail away."

The deckhand balled a fist then backed down.

Buc returned his attention to Captain Finnegan and continued. "With your permission, Captain, I would like to speak to the passenger Bently Montigue. I'd also kindly appreciate the use of your cabin."

The stork stroked his long beak and said, "I have your word then, you will do no further harm to me, my crew or my ship?"

Buc nodded. "Aye." He was curious as to why the good captain neglected to include passengers in his caveat.

"Then I'll show you to my cabin," the stork offered, extending a hand toward the stern.

Buc waited inside the large cabin for the passenger to arrive. The room was indeed much grander than Buc's own space, and far more richly furnished. He bounced in the lavish chair several times and stroked the fine fabric. The furniture was all of the finest quality, but what else would one expect on a ship called the King's Nugget?

Over and over again, he repeated in his head what he was going to say. He knew he had to be strong and fierce, like one of the pirates of old. He was grimacing and snarling his demands in a silent display when the door swung open and an elderly heron stood before him.

"Please," said Buc in a soft tone. "Come in. Sit down."

That was not exactly how he had rehearsed it.

The elderly bird hesitantly approached the chair and sat down.

"It has come to my attention that you have been summoned to Port Royal," Buc began. "Is this true?"

"Yes," the bird replied evenly.

"By the governor himself?"

"Aye," was the reply. The old bird shifted nervously in his seat.

"And you carry with you an item," Buc stated. "An heirloom of some sort? A pouch perhaps?"

The bird's eyes showed surprise and he fidgeted with his jacket. "Aye. But how did you—"

"That's not the most important thing at this moment," Buc reminded him. The captain dramatically drew his cutlass in a large arc. "I must insist you hand the pouch over to me." He pointed his cutlass at the old bird's heart and maintained a severe face. A resounding clap of thunder added to the ominous request.

"But..." The heron faltered. "But it was my son's. He told me to hold on to it and never to relinquish it."

"That be all well and good, mate," Buc assured him, "and I am sorry to have to do this, but the situation has changed. The governor must not lay hands on your possession."

The bird looked distraught. "My son," he sputtered, looking at Buc, "he told me it would bring me luck."

Buc chuckled to himself and thought of something Thomas told him. "Foolish men believe in luck," Buc informed the old bird. "Strong fowl believe in themselves."

The heron furled his brow. "What did you say?"

Buc blinked and looked back to the elderly bird. "Sorry mate," he offered, still leveling the sword at Bently. "It's something from another time. Something another pirate once said."

The bird looked at Buc with a new degree of surprise and wonder in his eyes. "I know," he said in an airy voice. "Lucky Longfeather. It was often spoken by him. Are you..." he began, drawing away from Buc.

"Longfeather?" Buc asked in a started tone. "No, but," he asked, lowering the sword a notch, and staring into the older bird's eyes, "What do you know of him?"

"My son," the man announced, smiling widely, "he sailed with Longfeather, aboard the Fortunada. My boy was at hand when..." Bently covered his beak with a feathered hand and his expression became guilty. "Forgive me," he muttered, staring at the floor. "I cannot speak of this."

Buc grabbed Bently with his free hand and shook the bird violently. "Your son," he yelled, adjusting the grip he held on the sword, "was he at Kismet Key?"

The bird's eyes grew wide and his mouth fell open.

"I'll take that as a yes," Buc decided, still holding Bently by the jacket.

"I," the old bird stuttered, trying to find the courage to say the words burning in his chest. "I ... should not ... be..." He reached into his pocket and pulled out the pouch. "Please." The word came out like a wretched prayer. "Please just take it. It pains me to relive those stories. Take it and go, sir. Leave an old bird in peace." Bently peeled Buc's hand off his jacket and filled it with the pouch. The motion reminded Buc of how Thomas forced the list into his hand not so long ago.

Buc stood and let the point of his sword drop to the floor. Staring at the pouch in his hand, he gestured with a tip of his head for Bently to get lost. The bird rose hastily and stumbled to the exit, running out the cabin door with a loud crash. The Nugget's crew looked on with anxious stares as the old passenger made a commotion of fleeing from the pirate.

Buc stood for a moment and stared at the pouch in his hand. It seemed such a small thing to cause so much trouble.

A plank beyond the open door squeaked and the corner of Buc's beak flashed in a momentary smile. "Might I have a word with you, Captain?" he asked, not bothering to look up.

From his hiding place beyond the open door, the captain of the Nugget entered with a slow stride. Lightning reflected in the glass panes of the double doors and more thunder reverberated through the small space, adding to the tension that was already building between them.

Buc bounced the old pouch in an open hand before slipping it into his coat pocket. Outside, the storm rolled and crashed against the side of the ship. Buc knew he needed to get back to the Stench soon, but there was something he had to resolve first.

Turning to the captain, he couldn't help but be touched by the bird's defeated appearance. His drawn-out expression, so horrendously exaggerated by the stork's beak, made Buc want to quip, "Hey, Cap. Why the long face?" He chose instead to hold his peace. This was a moment that could not be wasted.

"Captain," Buc began in a cool and steady tone. "When you arrive in Port Royal, you will hear stories about the atrocities I have performed on land and at sea." He watched calmly as the captain of the Golden Nugget shifted his stance and swallowed hard. Buc took a few steps, letting his boots thump a slow rhythm while he circled the captain. "I have shown you and your men great mercy compared to other vessels I have encountered."

The captain stood tall and strained to keep himself from trembling too greatly. "Aye," he admitted. "That you have."

"And it is will be great respect that I ask you to return that kindness in a rather unconventional manner."

The stork's head turned to watch Buc cross in front of him and stop. "Name your terms," he said, trying to sound brave.

Buc took a step, drawing himself so close he could smell the captain's breath and see the tremble in his feathers. "When you arrive in Port Royal," he said with quiet menace, "you must not allow my act of kindness to be known. Savvy?"

The captain's eyes moved to one side and Buc could see the wheel in his mind turning over. The stork rubbed his chin and mused quietly, "The way I see it, Captain, you fired upon my vessel, boarded it and threatened our lives if we did not meet your demands, as atypical as they might have been. We have only barely escaped."

Buc nodded in appreciation. As he turned to leave, the Nugget's captain called out, "But…"

Buc froze, and his eyes rose to meet his fellow captain's nervous gaze.

"If it were known by those of my employ that I merely yielded," the stork worried, "and offered no resistance at all…"

"Ah," Buc sighed knowingly. "Your contractual obligation contains a caveat for cowardice?"

"Aye," the captain confessed, hanging his head.

A slow smile spread across Buc's face.

Outside the cabin door, Chumlee stood with his great arms strapped over his wide chest. The crew of the Nugget watched him with a fearful reverence, none daring to speak but none willing to take their eyes off him. Occasionally, Chumlee would snort at the cowering flock and laugh to himself as they all chirped and shivered. It was a simple way to entertain himself as the quiet moments ticked by, waiting for Buc to emerge and lead them back to the Stench, which should have been happening at any moment. With the thunder rolling overhead and the waves gaining steam, Buc would either have to come out soon or Chumlee would have to go in after him.

Lightning flashed in the clouds above and the roar of thunder sounded over the sea, though this time there was something in the sound that was different.

It seemed louder.

And closer.

Glass shattered and Chumlee jumped. The noise had come from the captain's cabin. More crashing noises followed, and the quartermaster drew his sword and spun toward the door. "Captain!" he cried, grasping the handle. "Captain Buc!" He twisted the knob but found it seized tight. The sound of breaking wood echoed through the door followed by more shattering glass. "Captain!" Chumlee shouted again, pressing against the door. He sheathed his sword, stepped back, and braced himself to crash in the door. He let out a ferocious cry and the door promptly popped open. He looked quizzically at the Nugget's captain who was now blocking the doorway.

The stork was tattered, bruised, and bleeding from his beak. He fell forward when Buc gave him a shove, his long legs skittering to keep him from falling onto his face. An ominous silence fell over the crew, and it appeared to Buc that a few were struggling to muster enough courage to fight back.

"Baaah!" Buc roared loudly, pushing the captain, and sending him tripping into the arms of his crewmen. "Never again attempt to interfere with my affairs," he warned.

The crew member who earlier tried to rush Buc shouted, "I knew he couldn't be trusted!"

Chumlee stepped in and grasped the bold crewman by the shirt. The quartermaster sneered and ground his beak until the much smaller bird was smiling sheepishly and muttering a weak apology.

Buc pointed an angry finger at the captain and said, "I shall return to my vessel. Then, and only then, will I decide whether I will scuttle your ship to the locker!"

Chumlee dropped the crewman from his grasp and moved to the rail. Buc pivoted toward his own men then had a change of heart.

He looked over the crew and passengers of the Nugget standing on the deck before him. They shook collectively as though in a harsh winter storm. "What fowl among you is betrothed to one Penelope of Port Royal?" he demanded.

The passengers looked at one another, as well as around, eager to find who the pirate had called out.

"Come now, speak up!" Buc called. "No harm shall come to you," he promised, though several of the Nugget's crewmen looked dubiously over their own captain. The roaring thunder and flashes that filled the sky over the ships did not make Buc's tone seem any less threatening either.

"Here, sir," called a well-dressed rooster at long last. Stepping forward from the press of nervous travelers, it was clear he was from a wealthy family. The rooster's attire was impeccable, as were his general speech and manner.

Buc approached the aristocratic rooster. "I care not what your name is, lad, but heed this warning. Your Penelope is a rare gem. It would do you well to treat her as such."

The rooster conveyed a confused face but nodded obediently.

Buc stared back then took a deep breath and moved closer to the lad. "For if I was to hear that she has been treated less than admirably," he added in a tone that could not be mistaken, "or that she had been driven to an unhappy state, I would be forced to hunt down the source of her depression and dispatch it with great vengeance."

The young bird swallowed hard, creating an audible gulp.

Buc brushed the front of the lad's jacket like a valet and smiled menacingly. "Do I make myself clear?"

The rooster blinked nervously. "Unmistakably clear, sir," he stammered.

"Perfect." As Buc stepped back, thunder rumbled through the air, and lightning crackled above. Beyond the sound of the booming sky, he heard another voice. He turned to look back toward the Stench and saw Robert waving his arms and pointing into the distance.

Buc pulled out his spy scope and began scanning in the direction Robert was frantically pointing. It was another ship, a ship Buc recognized from the docks of Port Royal. It was the H.M.S. Triumph.

"Men," Buc said with reserved tension, "get back to the Stench." He swiftly drew up alongside the captain of the Nugget. "Weigh anchor," the pirate commanded. "Drop sail and head for open sea."

The stork stood frozen for a moment as though unsure whether the warning was sincere. It wasn't until Buc leaned in and screamed, "Now!" that Captain Finnegan gave his crew the order to make way.

The deck became alive with the stomping of feet and the barking of commands. As Buc cut a path to the side rail, he looked back over his shoulder at the Nugget's captain, now barking orders to his crew with the confidence of a seasoned shipman. The main sails snapped and unfurled in the building wind while the crew of the Nugget hurried to secure the sail before the storm made it no longer possible. They all became so engaged that no one saw Buc and his men swing to the Stench and move to slip into the growing darkness.

Chapter 15

The sky deepened and grew thick as the Stench turned and pulled away. Black clouds like the hearts of devils formed overhead, thrumming, and beating with thunder and cracking with lighting. The raven's sky blew a stale wind and Buc flared his nostrils into the breeze. The crew of the Stench tightened the lines and secured the rigging. As the captain and his senior crew made their way to the captain's quarters, the deck echoed with the vibration of wood as Pugwald landed face first on the decking. Buc leapt back and looked up at the crow's nest then back at Pugwald rising to compose himself.

"Mister Pugwald, as I applaud your visual acuity, I must say that you possess the grace of a well drenched tar mop."

"Sir." Pugwald continued to compose himself from his unconventional free-fall. "The governor," he puffed.

Buc's eyes grew wide.

draw the bow of a ship. "If we can contrive ta wallop a hole in the side of their vessel—" he began.

"You're drawing on my map," Buc interrupted tersely.

"—just a wee bit shy of the first cannon port, it will fracture a lintel and bring down a vertical support."

"Ahem," Buc growled. "You are drawing on my map."

"Yes," Robert replied like an irritated parent. "Very sorry," he said in a tone that implied the opposite. He tossed the coal stick back to Ayg and smiled at Chumlee. "And without a vertical support?" he prompted.

Edward and Ava approached the table and eyed the rough drawing.

A smile flashed over Chumlee's face. "Her very ribs would go and the whole side'd cave in," he said brightly.

"With that storm churnin' outside," Robert agreed, "that hole'll fill an' buckle the forward decking. The wretched vessel'll sink bow first into the briny deep before they are even aware, poor fools." He turned his eyes to Buc and waited for the captain's response.

Buc adjusted his hat and stared at the drawing. "We've only three working cannons," he reminded his uncle. "Should not we employ them in defense?"

"Well lad," Robert sighed, "this be the part you're not gonna favor. We give them all guns at the mark," he said quickly before taking a long breath. "An' we raise a white flag."

"What?" Buc shouted. The outburst was so sudden and violent that Ava and Edward jumped back several paces each. "Surrender?" the captain spat. "Never." Buc pushed himself away from the table and shook his head.

"It be only a ruse, lad," Robert said, approaching Buc and placing a hand on his shoulder. "Fighting fair is no longer in our favor, boy. The time's come to be cunning and clever if we mean to seize the day." He pulled Buc closer and whispered in his ear, "Your advantage holds that they be required to adhere to their laws. Once the flag be flying, they be required to cease fire. We conjure that to our advantage."

"That be very pirate-like of you, Uncle," Buc whispered back.

"We are who we are," the bird replied softly.

A dark look washed over his face and Buc sighed deeply. "Everyone out!" he snapped. When his crew only looked about confused and perplexed, the captain railed all the more loudly. "Avast, ye buzzards! Out!" he barked. Buc turned to Ayg and leveled a finger at him. "Save you, Mister Ayg. The rest of you get out, now!"

One by one they moved to the exit. As the last crew member standing in the doorway, Robert turned back to his nephew and gave a look before latching the door shut behind him.

A sharp sigh poured out of Buc as he turned his eyes to Ayg. "I'm not sure I can go through with this, mate," he confessed. "It's been a nice show and all, but the tide is rolling in and the bay is about to become very deep indeed."

Ayg wiped his face clean and drew a concerned look upon his shell.

The captain smiled sadly and laid a feathery hand upon his friend's wing. "Perhaps Chumlee was right," he offered. "You are too good an egg for the likes of me." He stroked Ayg's shell and looked to the drawing his uncle had left on the map. "We're not two young lads playing pirate on the docks anymore, mate. We've gone and crossed that line, haven't we?"

Ayg drew an eye patch on his shell.

"Aye," Buc replied steadily. "We be pirates now."

He smiled at his friend and patted him on the back. The two had dreamed of adventures on the high seas since Buc was a chick and Ayg was … well … a smaller egg. And now those dreams had come to life before their eyes, and the adventures were upon them. Yet, as excited as he was, Buc's head was growing light with the thoughts of fighting off a ship of the royal fleet, and his stomach tumbled within him while he considered the fate of himself and his men if should he fail. Ayg seemed to sense his captain's thoughts and grasped him on the shoulder.

"Thank you, my friend," the rooster said softly.

Their somber moment was interrupted by a pounding at the door.

"I do not wish to be disturbed!" Buc shouted, and when the door opened anyway he thought he would lose his mind with rage. "Blasted seed-brained idiot!" he roared.

"Begging the captain's pardon," Robert said from behind the half-opened hatch, "but I thought perhaps you'd favor some counsel."

Buc closed his eyes and reluctantly waved his uncle into the cabin. Robert closed the door behind him and suddenly Buc felt trapped in a fate he couldn't avoid. The captain walked toward the aft windows and gazed at the sky above, wringing his feathered hands and muttering, "I do not believe I can do this, Uncle."

"Codswallop," Robert retorted.

"I wish I had half your confidence, Uncle," Buc confessed, "because I see only a loud beginning and a very sad end to this storm-raged night."

"You're wrong, boy," Robert assured him. "You're dead wrong to a level the likes you have never fathomed. You are a ship's captain, and you can fight the fight." He stood beside his nephew and stared him in the eye. "Your crew believes in you," he said in a voice that was both soft and firm. "I believe in you."

Buc looked into the face of his uncle and shook his head. "My crew believes a silly story," he reminded the older bird. "They follow the lies and gossip of a pirate that never was. Buc Buccaneer is just a tale spun by a barmaid."

"Lies," Robert said gently, "or merely exaggerations?" He placed his two winged hands on Buc's shoulders and held him in his stare. "Are these not exaggerations 'bout a rooster who holds within him the courage to break out of his shell or of a rooster that be more than what others see? Are you not a fowl made solid enough to bring them stories to life?" Robert thought momentarily before he added, "Hopefully without all the grisly parts." A smile threatened at the corner of Buc's beak, and Robert knew he was getting through to the nervous captain. "The stories are about you, lad. Whether they be of physical actions or actions of the heart. It is all you." He reminded his nephew, "Your aunt gave you the warning. 'Don't raise the flag until you be certain this be the path you wish to take,' she said. Remember?"

"I raised the flag to strike fear into the hearts of simpletons on a meager ship, not to go into battle," Buc replied quickly. Ayg nodded vigorously.

"But what did that flag mean to you? Was it not the call you have been listenin' for your whole life? Deep down, lad, you chose this path long ago; ever since you were a squeaking' chick you were held with a fascination for Longfeather's adventures." Robert smiled and looked for the old twinkle in his nephew's eye. "What was it Longfeather always said? 'Adventure,' he said, 'be but the next journey away.' Buc. My boy. This is your day. This is your journey. This is the adventure you've longed for. All you have to do is ta step out this cabin and seize it."

"But what if I fail?" asked Buc, venting his greatest fear. "What if I hoist the sword and we fall all the same?"

"Ya think Longfeather never failed, eh?" Robert slapped the air and blurted, "Bah! Malarkey and poppycock. No pirate won every fight, but no fight is ever won from behind a cabin door."

Buc shook his head slowly. "Chumlee warned me," he lamented. "He warned me about not living up to the tales."

Robert took his nephew by the shoulders. "It be time to prove the tattooed oaf wrong then, won't it?" He smiled again at Buc and steadied his tone. "Remember lad. They make the rules. We just be usin' them to our advantage is all." He released his nephew and stepped back to look over him properly. "Now, Captain," he said sharply. "Fix your coat. Take a deep lungful of the salty air. Then go out there and command yer crew. They'll follow yer lead, I promise it. Be strong. Be confident, and they will fight like devils for ye."

Buc paused, but Ayg wiped his face clean and drew on a fierce pirate grimace. The expression stirred something within Buc, and he adjusted his coat with a snapping noise. The captain headed to the door with Ayg and laid his hand upon the handle. "Uncle," he said quietly. "I just want to say—"

"Shut yer gob already!" Robert shouted roughly, having exhausted all his patience. "Yer a pirate, not a nursemaid. There be no time for sentimental hogwash. Buck up and sound the call to arms, ya babblin' fool!" A shot of lighting flashed in Buc's eyes, and the old bird knew he was ready.

"We have a ship to sink," Buc announced.

"Aye!" Robert called loudly.

The cabin door whipped open and Buc stomped onto the deck and into the staring eyes of his crew. They stood before him, each one primed and ready to do his bidding. Buc looked into the eyes of Master Chumlee and gave a little nod. "Master Chumlee," the captain barked, "ready my ship for battle."

A dark smile spread over Chumlee's face as he replied, "Aye, aye, Captain."

"Robert!" Buc shouted into the night. The sounds of boots behind him were the emboldening beats of the drums of war. "Ready the weapons!" Buc cried. "We run your plan of attack."

"Aye," Robert answered, darting off with Ayg at his heels.

Buc turned his attention next to young Edward and Ava. "You two," he snapped, "assist Robert and stay in the shadows. I want you out of sight." Ava scurried after Robert and Ayg, but Edward looked around nervously. Seeing himself in the boy, Buc asked, "Are you scared, lad?"

Edward looked back with wide eyes and a shivering expression. "Are you mad?"

Buc spied his uncle slipping down the main stair and turned back to the youngster. "No, lad," he replied. "What you are feeling is right, but don't let it stop you from doing what you have to do. Being scared doesn't mean you are weak, lad. It means you're not stupid."

The HMS Triumph was the pride of the Royal Navy. As powerful as it was lavish, the grand architecture and extravagant details made the vessel as beautiful as it was deadly. Intricate carvings of angels promised protection for her crew and offered to serve as a guide into the void for anyone who stood against the mighty ship. Within the captain's cabin, framed in velvet curtains and seated behind a wide and polished desk, sat Governor Legget. A small teacup and saucer of the finest china was cradled in his long and confident fingers, and the spiced steam rose and circled around his narrow beak.

The governor lifted the cup and sipped, humming in appreciation of the flavorful blend. "How long until we intercept?" he asked, returning the cup to the saucer.

The commodore straightened himself and inclined his head toward his commander. "Not long, sir," he replied. "They have made no attempt to run."

"And why would they?" the governor chortled. "The Triumph dominates these waters, my dear man, and that sniveling little rooster knows it."

The commodore nodded his agreement but hesitated before returning to the deck. "Sir," he began carefully, "if they should choose to resist?"

The governor's eye sparkled devilishly in the bright light of the cabin. "Oh, they will resist." His words were seasoned with anticipation and his grin became an arrogant sneer. "And we will let them, Commodore, for they will have no choice but to yield in the end. I did not achieve this position in life by cowering before a fight." He placed his cup and saucer upon the desk and flattened his hands to either side of the steaming brew. "No. The very future of the Caribbean is at stake here. I shall not stand by while a few ruffians wishing to play pirate work to take away everything I have achieved. Am I clear, Commodore?"

"Perfectly, sir," the other reported. The sailor stomped a boot and snapped his hand into a salute. Once answered, the commodore spun and marched toward the cabin door. As the brass clasp clicked shut behind the officer, the governor slipped a hand around the teacup and hoisted it to his nose. He drew a long breath and exhaled with strong and resolute satisfaction.

Buc paused for a moment in the gloom of the Stench's belly. The room was damp, and the very walls and floor creaked lightly with every roll of the sea around them. For any who were watching, the captain appeared to be staring at the wall as a man would study arithmetic. In truth, Buc was looking beyond the wall, imagining the colossal vessel cutting through the waves and circling around his modest ship. "I've no intention of falling to you this day or any other," he whispered to the wall.

"Captain?"

Buc turned to find Edward standing close by. All around the pair, the crew scrambled to prepare for the coming encounter. Cannons were fastened, and bags of powder were set in a tray to protect them from any incoming sea spray from ports that were soon to be opened.

"Oye!" Robert barked at Edward. "Move yer legs! Get them powder bags here and cover them up, boy! Damp powder does us no good at all! Hear?"

"Aye, sir!" Edward answered, spinning from his place, and grabbing a large pouch of gunpowder and struggling to drag it to a large box behind the line of cannons.

"What can I do ta help, Mister Robert?" Ava called over the din.

"Fetch the rammer, lass," he said pointing to the pole hung on the wall. Robert looked at the two children and grunted disapprovingly. A pirate ship, he knew, was no place for the likes of them, but the captain deemed they were crew and crew must pull their weight. "Either of you ever ready a cannon for firin' before?" he asked, knowing full well the answer before they gave it.

The twins shook their heads.

"Right then," he huffed. "Pay attention now. It takes weeks for a full-grown bird to learn this properly and be deadly with it, and we only have a few minutes. But no fear," he said with a reassuring smile that he hoped hid his reservations. "First you pull the cannon back and make sure ya sponge her insides good." He placed the sponge pole inside the cannon and removed the excess waste and grit. "Get it all, hear?"

"Aye, sir," the young birds replied.

"Hand me a bag o' powder, lad," he ordered. Edward lifted a bag and took it to Robert. "Now go ahead my boy an' slip the bag into the cannon." Edward did as he was told and tried to look brave while he worked. "Now lass," Robert continued, "grab that rammer pole an' push it in there real good. As far as you can," he instructed. "That's it. All the way in 'til you're packing the powder in there nice and tight. Good." Robert smiled as he watched the petite bird loading a cannon that was longer than she was tall. "Now, lad," he continued. "Think you can muscle up a cannon ball?" he asked Edward.

Edward's eyes grew wide. Excitedly, he smiled and nodded, running to the stockpile, and wrapping his hands around a shot. The small bird tried to pluck one from the pile, but it slipped from his grasp and fell to the deck. Edward gasped and jumped back, covering his face behind a wing.

Robert let out a big, bellowing laugh and shook his head. "Don't fret, boy," he advised. "'Tis not the ball ya need to worry 'bout. That's just a hunk of iron."

Ava giggled at her brother.

"Don't just stand there snickering, you," the older bird snapped. "Go and help your shipmate. Now!"

Together Ava and Edward hoisted the ball and carried it to the cannon.

"Now, together," Robert barked. "Lift!"

The two struggled and grunted loudly, but eventually managed to get the twelve-pound cannonball into the mouth of the gun. "Now let her roll back gracefully," Robert said calmly with a stroke of his hand. "Now, kiddos. When your captain tells ya to ready the cannon, each of ya grabs a rope and you pull, hard. Them pulleys there'll drag the cannon forward."

"How do we fire it?"

"You see that there pole with the split ends? That there is a linstock. It holds a piece of match rope. Once it's lit, you can tap it to the touchhole and BOOM!" he cried, waving his feathers and making the young birds jump.

The kids smiled at Robert's re-enactment.

"Now you, young miss," he instructed, "go grab some blankets for the pair of ya. You'll want to be safe if any splinters start flying."

"Aye sir," replied Ava energetically as she ran off.

"When she gets back, it be up to you, Master Edward, to make sure the two of ya stay outta harm's way. Aye?"

"Aye sir!" replied Edward.

The boy's voice was filled with excitement and his eyes danced with visions of cannon fire and great victories. Robert couldn't help be see the likeness of a young rooster he used to know, and feared for the child's safety all the more for it.

He left the lower deck and emerged into the chill sea air. The old bird winced when he saw how close the Triumph had become while he was below deck. He turned his eyes to the upper deck and the captain appearing steady and in control.

Buc held his chin high from his place at the helm, hands firm upon the wheel as he watched his crew readying themselves for their first battle. At least, they believed it would be their first battle. Buc looked on as the Triumph began its approach, steadily cutting through the waves like the very scythe of death herself. The knots in his stomach grew tighter but the resolution upon his brow became more dominant. He called out instructions and Robert watched as the crew scrambled to ready the ship, following the orders of their fearless captain. The old bird watched his nephew at the wheel and smiled genuinely.

Twitch stumbled up the forecastle stairs and approached the helm. Just as he began to speak, a streak of lightning flashed above, causing him to duck slightly. "Captain," he said from his hunched position as thunder filled his ears, "do we have a plan?"

"Of course we do, Mister Twitch," Buc replied evenly, his eyes locked on the Triumph. The sound of shivering brought his eyes down to his nervous crewman and Buc smirked. "Trust me. It's always darkest before the storm."

"I thought it was darkest before the dawn?" Twitch inquired.

"Either way," Buc answered, looking over the head of the shivering rooster. The winds rose and took hold of the sails as the last bit of blue sky faded from sight. "Mister Pugwald! Mister Marley!"

the captain called. "Trim the lines. We've got 'er on the weather side!"

"Captain!" shouted Chumlee, rising from the lower deck. "Cannons are ready. Pistols are primed."

"Good work, Master Chumlee," Buc replied. "And our stowaways?"

"I've stashed them below sir," Robert answered. "Told them to stay low."

Chumlee stood on the first two steps of the stairs heading to the helm and stared at his commander. "Captain." Chumlee paused to grind his beak and measure his words. "They're going to hit us with everything they've got," he decided. "You may wager whatever you like, but on that first pass she'll be giving it all."

"I'm well aware of that," Buc reported.

"But can the ship take it?" Chumlee worried.

"It's not the ship that concerns me, mate," the captain confided, looking over his scrambling crew.

Chumlee climbed two more steps and cleared his throat. "Perhaps then an utterance from you?" the quartermaster recommended. "A word to your crew to boost morale?"

Buc breathed in the cool, salted air and looked out over the deck of the Stench. Scrambling over the planks was a ragged crew made up of cast-outs and ruffians, each of them with a vexed mark on their brow and a jittering in their feathers. For all they knew, death was waiting on the other side of a few waves and the last sunrise they ever saw was already gone. Battle was coming, and it was the second time since her christening that Buc had decided to steer his vessel into such waters as these. For a moment, the captain could almost hear the sounds of nails being driven as he and Ayg worked shoulder to shell, building their dream one board after the next. Now in a state as dark as the clouds gathering above, the possibility still weighed heavily that this ship could see her last night and be dragged down to the deep to the song of cannon fire.

"Master Chumlee," Buc cried out, "take the helm. Keep her on a parallel course, mind, and distant from the long guns of the Triumph." He scurried down the steps and Chumlee nodded approvingly until the captain turned sharp and disappeared into his quarters, that is.

The quartermaster scowled down the stairs as the captain's cabin door slammed shut and wondered what the rooster had up his sleeve. Thunder rolled, and lightning cracked above the ships, stealing Chumlee's attention. When his eyes retuned to the water he saw his encmy, outlined against a dim horizon. Like a shadow on the sea, the HMS Triumph moved over the water in a cloak of deepening black.

"Oye!"

Chumlee turned his eyes to the lower deck as the captain returned to his men.

"Every man aboard who think he brave, settle before me here," Buc shouted, his arms raised and his features resolute.

Chumlee looked on and shook his head as the crew exchanged looks and wondered what they were to do. "Ye heard the captain!" he cried. "All hands on deck!"

Buc nodded to the quartermaster and made a wide sweeping gesture with his hand. The crew scurried to form a crooked line on the deck before him and Buc tipped his hat approvingly. "Fowl," he began in a deep and commanding tone, "the burden laid before us be a grand, daring, and daunting endeavor. "He looked over the crew with a confident expression. "The sailors there be true to the flag, regardless whether the flag be honest or forthright. But we too have a flag," he reminded them, pointing to the top of the main mast. "An' it be a flag that embodies freedom. Our flag carries more than just a wag and a flutter. Our flag speaks. It tells all that behold that we decline rules an' laws governed by those holdin' themselves above 'em. Now there be those among you with a shiver of fear." Buc looked at his uncle. "It doesn't make you weak for shaking," the captain recited. "It jus' means you lot not be stupid." He smiled and laughed as his own statement. "Aye, the Triumph be armed well, but it takes more than a cadre of cannons to defeat a foe." Buc looked each of his men in the face. "I say to you, bold and sure, are you ready to fight? What say ye?"

"Aye!" shouted the crew collectively.

"Are ye ready to win?" shouted Buc.

The roar from the crew was loud enough to drown away the sounds of the sea and the rowdy sky above.

Buc became drunk on the cheers of his men. He could see in their faces that they felt a new height of energy and sureness. There was a stronger disposition painted in their eyes and, once again, Buc smiled.

"Crew!" he shouted. "To your stations!" Filled with a new-found sense of courage, the crew fluttered to their posts. Ayg approached Buc and saluted. Buc knelt down to Ayg's level. "We may have fantasized about taking the Stench into battle," he whispered, "but I never thought it would actually be." He put a feathered hand on Ayg's shell. "We dreamed of adventure, sailing off into the blue and pretending to be Ol' Lucky Longfeather. We overlooked the fact that they had to fight to keep their adventure alive. The Triumph wishes to put an end to our adventure. For Thomas, for my parents, my friend, we must prevail, and there be no other creature upon the deep that I'd rather have at my side." Buc clasped his hand over the side of his friend's shell and the two shared a look. Ayg took his charcoal and added a little smirk to the corner of his pirate's sneer. "Good man," Buc praised, sending Mister Ayg to his station.

"Captain!" Chumlee shouted from the helm.

Buc climbed the steps to the helm and took his place beside the quartermaster.

"If yer done with yer rallying," Chumlee growled. He tilted his head in the direction of the Triumph and snorted. "We have a real threat to contend to."

Buc looked over at the approaching ship. "Aye," the rooster agreed.

He took over the helm. "Avast, ya lazy scallywags! Ready the starboard guns! Man the swivels! There's no death today for the bird ready to spit in the eye of fate and receive the devil himself!" The thunder rumbled above, and the sky broke into an honest downpour. The Triumph would intercept them shortly and Buc could see the ship's bow pushing whitecaps over the black water. Its speed mimicked that of the clouds above and the dark color of both was a collection of every tint of grey. Buc squinted into the thickening rain as the Triumph approached their starboard side. "Hold fast, men! And keep that powder dry!"

Buc looked on as the Triumph rocked and dipped on a sea that looked like the robes of death himself. Across the deck of the naval ship hustled a blur of redcoats and upon the upper deck stood Buc's adversary, the commodore himself.

4 Sweat and rain gathered on his brow and Buc's heart rate pounded against his ribs. The captain swore he could see a smile on the face of the commodore in the flash of the lightning.

"A little more," Buc muttered. "A little more. A little closer." The cannon ports were all pulled open on the side of the Triumph and a dozen black eyes peered out at the Foul Stench. "Almost there." As the forward cannon port of the Triumph approached the first swivel, the captain finally gave the order. "Fire!"

The air exploded with a fog of smoke and flame. Cannon balls jumped over the waves and buried themselves into the hull of the Triumph. No sooner had the first shot from the Stench let loose than their enemy returned fire. The first shot took out a portion of the railing and skipped over the water on the far side of the ship. Pain ripped through Buc as the ship he built with his own two feathered hands became wounded. Thunderous blasts continued as the Triumph moved in to overtake the Stench. Shards of wood filled the air, tumbling in the smoke of the cannons.

"Keep firing!" Chumlee screamed from behind his scrambling crewmates. Birds wheezed behind terrified eyes, but the cannons were loaded, and they traded shot for show with the king's pride of the Caribbean. Cannonballs were sent through the ports as quickly as the men could take aim, and Chumlee was there with Robert, shouting commands and ordering the crew to hold their ground. "I'll not die today by the hand of such a pretty ship!" Chumlee complained. "I'll be an old bird, withered and dusty and sour, staring down the face of the Dutchman and the nastiest pirates the water has ever known. I'll not go to the deep by the doings of such clean hands! So, fire on, lads! Let them have it! Tear a hole in that ship's belly so wide the captain can dock in it!" The men worked the cannons and the quartermaster continued. "Keep firing, you scabby sea bass, or you'll hang by the gizzards!" he shouted.

The Stench's cannons continued to fire as Buc finished his pass and veered his ship away from the Triumph. "Ha ha!" the lucky captain cried out.

So, this is what it be like, Buc thought. This is what it's like to be a pirate. To fight against odds. To take on the world. To—

A wave of nausea twisted Buc's stomach as he looked over the Triumph's forward section. There was hardly a mark to her, and the hole they hoped would send the ship spiraling into the void was nowhere near large enough. He rotated the helm to pull the Stench further away from the Triumph. As he did so, he called out, "Ayg! Take the helm!" Buc released the wheel and raced down the stairs to the entrance of the gun deck. "Robert! Chumlee!" he screamed down the hatch. "My quarters. Now!"

Buc then stumbled into his cabin and pulled at his feathers with trembling hands. The door wasn't even shut behind his senior crew members when he bellowed, "The plan failed. The hole's too small."

"We've taken a beating of our own," Chumlee reported. "Another pass and they'll have us."

"We're one pass from joining the sharks," Buc moaned.

"Calm down," Robert snapped. "Take a moment, Captain. Explore the circumstances."

"The circumstances!" Buc's voice squealed. "The circumstances! We failed. The plan failed. If we stand they will come about and fire upon us again and we will be done." He turned away and huffed before turning back. "I will not lose my ship!" he shouted. He threw the contents of his desk off with one swoop of his wing and roared in fear and anger. "I never thought the white flag would be truthful," he muttered.

"Captain," Chumlee reasoned, "we still have weapons. We can still give them the fight we intended."

"To what end?" Buc panted. "I apologize. I promised you I could do this but I regret that I cannot."

"No," the quartermaster answered. "Not good enough!"

Buc looked scornfully at his quartermaster.

Chumlee pointed an angry finger at his captain and bared his teeth. "I forewarned you, did I not? An' I did not agree to this venture so you could turn tail like some sniveling coward at the first sign of a fight."

"If we fight, we die," Buc swore.

"Enough!" Robert bellowed, stepping between the men. "The plan may not be fulfilled in the manner we planned," he explained, "but there is still hope."

"Hope?" Buc laughed sadly. "They will be back upon us; they will fire again, and we will sink."

"Hoist the flag of truce," Robert ordered.

"Surrender?" Buc chortled. "That be your grandiose plan?"

"Dammit, Buc," Robert snapped. "I tire of your relentless mannerisms." He raised a finger to his nephew and narrowed his eyes. "You wanted to be a pirate. You sought revenge, aye? Well, you got what you wanted now. An' now be the time to battle with wits not cannon fire."

His uncle's demeanor unsettled Buc and he spoke softly in return. "What's in yer' head?"

"Hoist the white flag and bring the Stench in for a broadside. With the Triumph in close, and the storm brewing, waves will build between the hulls of the two vessels." The words triggered a connection in Buc's mind. Robert saw the light go on and smiled. "Right, lad. It be a longshot, but we may still have a chance."

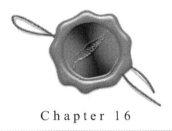

Chapter 16

Darkness prevailed as the storm clouds thickened and the sky disappeared behind them. The wind whipped across the water, pushing the still waters into a choppy frenzy that morphed into mountains of angry waves. The wind slammed rain onto the faces of the crew on the deck of the Fowl Stench like tiny stones. They held tightly on to the mast, on to ropes, on to anything to keep from blowing over the side into the angry ocean as the waves lapped harder and higher against the hull of the Fowl Stench. The H.M.S. Triumph danced with the same windy fate as it brazenly pulled alongside the Foul Stench. The first of four soldiers climbed the rope ladder from the longboat and pulled himself aboard the Stench. The four soldiers secured the lines as the Triumph was pulled side by side with the Fowl Stench. Commodore Paddington crossed the gangplank and was closely followed by the governor himself.

The governor nodded to the commodore, who retrieved a

rolled parchment from his inner jacket pocket.

"Captain Buc Buccaneer, you are hereby charged with piracy, treason, and the murder of one Thomas Willoughby."

The governor smirked as he looked upon Buc's scowling face. "How do you plead?" he asked smugly.

Buc's stomach twisted. Aside from his delight at being recognized by his pirate name, he scowled at the thought that he was a suspect in Thomas' demise. Lightning flashed, sending streaks of pure white crackling across the overhead blanket of grey. Buc watched closely, anticipating a rise in the water that would flood the hull of the Triumph as waves crashed with increasing violence against it.

"What be the options for my plea?" he asked, stalling for time, hoping the storm would maintain its intensity.

"The way I see it, you have no options. The only plea I shall accept is one of guilty."

"Rather less of a choice than an actual demand, I fancy." Buc continued to look beyond the naval men toward the rocking Triumph.

The governor approached him closely. "I could have easily ordered the commodore here to sink your vessel. But you and I both know there is something much more valuable on board than mere ego."

The governor smiled and placed his arm around Buc. Leading him toward the captain's cabin, he whispered, "Captain, I think it best that we not speak in the presence of your crew, or mine for that matter." He gently opened the door to the cabin and gestured for Buc to enter before him.

Buc, leery of the governor's good will, poured a goblet of cider, and offered it to the governor who accepted it politely.

Buc began to drink as the governor continued, "One year ago, a little bird whispered in my ear a tidbit of knowledge that represented information regarding the whereabouts of a lost treasure, the main trove belonging to the pirate known as Lucky Longfeather."

Buc paused mid drink.

"Ah, I see," sneered the governor sensing his interest.

Buc placed the goblet down and wiped his mouth with his sleeve.

The governor laughed maniacally. "I assumed that you were aware whose treasure it was. But I can see by your expression that you are as unaware as you are powerless."

He placed his feathery hands on Buc's table. "I am willing to extend the same arrangement with you as I did with your friend, Capitán Rojo."

Buc's face flushed red and he slammed his tightly wound fists on the table. "Rojo is not my friend!" he shouted.

The roaring thunder above bellowed loud and rocked the rolling waves of the ocean as it agreed with the captain's heartfelt claim.

In the damp, smoldering hull of the Stench, Ava and Edward emerged from the smoky shadows. They peered out the canon port to see the Triumph gently rocking alongside their ship. Their confused expressions changed quickly to worry as they realized that things up on deck were going very wrong.

"The ship. It's not sinking," whispered Ava, in a low, shaky voice. "Listen," she continued, "there are soldiers on our deck."

"We have to do something," snapped Edward.

"What can we do?" asked Ava, worried. "The captain ordered us to stay hidden."

"If we do nuthin' then it's back to the orphanage for us, and short drop and a quick stop for the crew."

Ava's head jerked back, and she glared at Edward. "You sound like a pirate."

Edward covered his beak and giggled quietly. He gazed out the cannon port once again. "Look, Ava, the hole."

Ava steadied herself against the rocking ship and glanced out. "What about it?"

"It's too small. Mister Robert said the hole would have to be big enough to flood the ship…"

"So?"

"So, it's too small."

"So?"

Edward threw his hands in the air and puffed a frustrated sigh. "If the ship doesn't sink, they will take us all back to Port Royal. The captain and crew will be hung, and we will have to go back to—"

"Ack!" cried Ava. "Don't say it again." She looked at the hole. "So, what do we do?"

Edward looked at the canon still positioned in front of the porthole. A devious and wicked smiled filled his face. He wasn't only starting to sound like a pirate, he was thinking doggedly like one.

He didn't need to say anything to Ava. He tiptoed briskly to the stack of cannon balls and exchanged remote glances with her. He could hear the rush of air sucked into his sister's beak when she gasped, realizing what he had in mind.

Buc ground the edges of his beak. Was the governor being truthful? Was the list made up of clues to the whereabouts of the lost treasure of Lucky Longfeather? He glared angrily at the smug falcon. If he was being truthful, Buc had a duty to his friend Thomas to protect the map and the list with the final name. Could the map lead to clues that would reveal what happened to Longfeather? His disappearance had been one of the great mysteries of the Caribbean.

"Have you spoken to your …" The governor trailed off, correcting his words. "Have you spoken to Capitán Rojo as of late?"

"No," Buc replied, his tone filled with crisp anger.

"Did it ever occur to you why I enlisted him to assist me in the acquisition of this treasure?"

"I assumed greed. It seems to be what you relish." Buc's words were filled with disgust for the bird.

"Perhaps greed, but I hold something greater in mind." The governor's tone shifted to a friendlier melody. "Of late, I have been enlightened by a glimpse of the future regarding our little island of Jamaica. You see, the king is secretly contemplating parting with our little island and handing it to Spain."

"What?" Buc felt as if his heart skipped a beat and a shiver ran up his spine.

"Imagine the island of Jamaica no longer under the rule of England, but under the rule of the Spanish monarchy."

The pieces began to fall into place for Buc as he listened to the governor. This wasn't about the treasure as much as it was about the governors' need to finance his dark quest for power. Buc took another sip of cider as he stared out the window at the relentless waves that continued to batter the Triumph.

He turned back to the governor. "You plan to use the treasure to swindle the island out from under the Spanish King?"

The governor shook his head gently. "I wish to purpose the wealth to influence the king to leave the island under his rule."

Buc's chest tightened. He felt as if he might suffocate on the lies that swirled around the governor like flies on a corpse. Governor Legget was interested only in his own self-gain. The people who suffered under his rule were only as important as long as he could use them to serve his own twisted agendas. No. Buc was not going to allow the governor to believe that he, Buc Buccaneer, Captain of the Fowl Stench, was buying into his deception.

"Twaddle speak!" Buc screeched. "I have lived in Port Royal for the better part of my life. Your rule upon that island gem has been through fear, torment, and greed. Now you wish me to believe that you hold a desire to protect those who live under your tyranny from others who might do us harm? Again, sir, I call twaddle speak. If you were merely interested in protecting the innocent, you'd be allowing your commodore to play out this task. But here you are, standing before me. That, my dear Governor, can only mean one thing. You wish to purchase the island from the king, and rule Jamaica for yourself."

The governor smirked and nodded to the side gently. "Rojo was right. You are an intuitive one." He brushed the sleeves of his jacket. "I will rescind all the charges against you, Buc. And, as it be, I will also concede to give you a small portion of the treasure. You can continue on as captain of your ship and I will not arrest your drab crew."

Buc snickered. "You plan to arrest my crew, do you?"

"Your bedraggled pirates won't stand a chance against my soldiers. You would be a fool not to give my offer the consideration it deserves." Buc's arrogance was starting to weigh heavy on the governor's shoulders. "I assure you, Captain, refusal of my offer will invoke grave and deadly consequences upon you and your crew—"

He was cut short by an immediate noise, so loud and deafening that it seemed to herald death and destruction. It cracked through the air, rattling the decking below their feet. Through a small window, the governor and Buc could see the smoke and fire billowing from the direction of the canon fire. The pair were frozen in place ... but only for a fraction of a second before looking at each other and heading towards the cabin door.

On deck, they found the commodore and his men looking over the wooden railing at a single smoking canon port. A mixture of white and black smoke swirled fiercely upward like the gray clouds already dotting the sky above. Buc didn't waste any time signaling to his crew with a nod. That was all they needed. Robert and Chumlee kicked

their swords from the deck to their hands. Before the soldiers could realize what was happening, they whipped around to clash steel. The pirates held their blades even at a perfect, undaunted horizon as the soldiers finally caught up and brandished their own swords. Blades flashed as they were brought overhead, and the swords cut through the air.

The governor cowered behind the commodore who had turned to face Buc with his sword drawn and at the ready. Ayg heard the fighting taking place and he grabbed his own sword, running up to join in. The governor was sneaking away, heading towards the ladder to the longboat that had been used by his soldiers.

Ava and Edward looked at the other ship through the canon port. Ava had gripped her brother's feathers when the booming sound had rocketed through the whole hull. Their beaks, pointed at the Triumph that had welcomed the hit of the canon with a shattering response, were open wide.

"Oh my goodness, Edward! It shot clear through," bellowed Ava.

Edward gazed at the large hole in the side of the Triumph. "I think you may have been right, Ava. Too much powder."

"Look!" shouted Ava, alarmed. The sea began to pour into the newly formed gaping hole in the side of the mighty Triumph. The water took over everything in its path as the sea streamed in. With each new wave, water shattered wood with the angry colors of the lightning and stormy sky above. The storm aggravated the way the water flooded into the Triumph.

Edward looked over at the ship. "Like I said. Just the right amount of powder."

The turbulent waves of the ocean continued to tease and toss the sinking ship, pitching it around like a child's rag doll. The wind mocked the crew of the Triumph that tried to jump across to the longboat or swing away from their ship. They were trying desperately to escape the hunger of the ocean as the weight of the water filled the ship and pulled it down rapidly.

Ava smiled at her brother. "You should say something pirate-like now."

Edward wasted no time, remembering something his captain had said. He grinned. "Yo, ho! Is a pirate so lucky!" he screamed at the top of his bird lungs to the sinking ship.

Buc and the commodore were locked in a steel blade battle. After knocking the commodore off himself with a kick to the stomach, Buc looked over the rail to see the governor climbing down the ladder towards a longboat. He shouted at the only sailor near enough to stop him. "Twitch stop him!" The captain blocked the next attack of the commodore and pushed him off with a heavy-handed shove of his sword.

Twitch ran across the wet, slippery deck and sliced the ropes supporting the ladder. The governor, still grasping the rungs of the rope ladder, fell into the longboat with a crash. Buc glanced over the side and rolled his eyes. "I said stop him, not help him."

The commodore lunged at Buc while he was distracted. Buc caught the movement out of the corner of his eye and shoved the commodore back once again. Buc swiped his steel blade at the medals adorning the commodore's chest. Both birds watched as two of the medals flew off and landed with a splash in the water.

The commodore looked back at Buc. Buc had his hand over his beak, suppressing a laugh. "I am laughing with you mate, not at you."

The commodore lunged at him in anger. Buc deflected the blow and touched the tip of his sword to the commodore's throat.

"I lied," Buc said, "I was laughing at you." The tip of his sword pressed into the commodore's flesh just enough to draw a trickle of blood. The commodore felt the nick and dropped his sword to the deck.

As the commodore was submitting, Ayg was fighting off one of the stouter soldiers. Ayg's oblong nature made it difficult for close quarters fighting. With his limited room to move, and inability to duck and cover, the soldier easily struck him in the top of his shell. The blow cracked Ayg's shell, and the shock sent him stumbling backward Buc who, seeing Ayg stumble back, shoved the commodore out of the way to engage Ayg's attacker. He pushed the stout soldier to the railing and then, using the soldier's own knife, he stabbed through the soldier's coat into the wooden rail. Once secure, he flipped the soldier over the railing, leaving him dangling by his own jacket sleeve.

Buc dashed to Ayg's side. "Ayg, are you alright, mate?" Buc was down on his knees, helping his friend. Seeing that the captain's back was turned, the commodore approached from behind and grabbed him swiftly. He placed his wing around Buc's neck and dragged him back.

"Call your men off!" he demanded.

"Why?" asked Buc in an amused voice. "We're winning." He threw his elbow back and knocked the commodore off of him, turning the tables.

At the same time, Twitch was humorously helping the governor to his feet. He may have helped the governor down into the longboat, but he had immediately followed. Before the governor had regained his composure, Twitch had him at laid out at knifepoint. "Back to the Stench we go, Governor," he demanded, forcing him back onto the ship at knifepoint. The governor looked on in awe as his soldiers did their best to fight off the pirates, but they were losing. Buc quickly faced him and held his cutlass outward in a confident stance. There was no use threatening the governor or overstating the obvious. Buc sincerely wanted everything to end now, and the governor and his crew off his ship.

"Now, Governor, as captain of this vessel, I order you and your men to drop your weapons or suffer grave and permanent consequences."

The commodore looked about and saw that Buc's ragtag crew had his trained seamen in their midst. The proud bird sighed deeply and threw his sword to the deck. Bayonets rattled on impact as each of his crew followed his lead.

Buc wasted no time in asserting the glory of his leadership and apparent triumph. This time, he leaned in toward the governor so close that the governor could feel hot breath against his face. "The way I see it, you have two options. One, you sign a statement pardoning me for said crimes, and then I place you and your crew in a longboat with provisions and you row your fluffy-feathered selves back to Port Royal."

"What, pray tell, is the other option?" the governor asked, his words dripping with sarcasm.

"I return you and your crew to your ship."

The governor looked to his side and saw the last visible aspect of the Triumph floundering down into the sea. His crew were still clamoring to reach the lifeboats. "Not much of a choice in those options," he muttered.

"Perhaps not as clever as guilty and not guilty, but I have found, when faced with multiple unflattering options, one will often say, 'It's not much of a choice,' in lieu of selecting the logical, yet still unflattering, option."

The commodore grunted; his eyes darkened with anger.

"So, what say you?" asked Buc.

As the governor and his crew boarded the longboat, he paused. "Captain!" he barked. Buc looked over the railing, down toward the governor. "It will only be one day's journey back to Port Royal. At that time, I will triple the bounty on your head, and you will have nowhere in the Caribbean to hide."

Buc only paused for a second to think about the governor's words before pulling out his pistol, aiming it at the governor. The governor and his battered crew already in the longboat flinched and covered their heads. Buc fired a single shot into the hull of the longboat and water immediately began flowing into it.

"That ought to delay your journey a tad." Buc flashed a smug smirk across his beak.

He nodded to Chumlee and his men, who all shot holes in the other longboats that the soldiers were gathered in.

Buc smiled and turned to Chumlee. "With that being done, let us go below and rustle up our loose cannons."

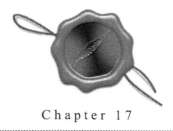

Chapter 17

The thunderous pounding of galloping hoofs on cobblestones resonated through the sound of the falling rain. The raindrops fell on the earth's crust with inexplicable angered revenge as it penetrated the soil and formed large holes, big enough to be home to beetles and crickets. The two steeds pulling the carriage seemed less affected by the inclement weather than the damp, yet determined, carriage driver. Down passages and backstreets the carriage raced on, indifferent towards the dangers of the slippery road. Only a fool would be out in such intolerable weather—a fool or perhaps someone with determination and a lot of need in their heart.

The carriage came to a halt in front of a small, quaint, rundown cottage. Its broken gate slammed with each passing gust of tropical air. The driver placed the reins to the side and jumped from his perch to the street below, adding further insult to injury by landing in a puddle. Opening the carriage door, the hooded passenger glanced at the falling rain then stepped out of the carriage. Mysteriously, the passenger slowly looked about before settling eyes on the driver. If not for the concealing hood, there surely would have been a serious expression and a fearsome nonchalant squeeze that would have followed the face that quietly focused on the driver.

"Remain here," the passenger instructed.

The mysterious cloaked figure walked briskly through the cascading rain to the cottage's front porch. The poorly patched porch roof afforded little protection from the continuous downpour. The stranger slowly glanced at the surroundings of the cottage again before a glistening wing extended from beneath the cloak. The stranger knocked briskly three times and showed no movement to indicate that another attempt would be forthcoming.

The door creaked as it opened slowly. An elderly rooster peered around the corner of the door through his cracked spectacles. "Yes, who is it?"

"Are you Peter Furlong?" asked the cloaked figure.

"Aye" said the old bird. "And who might you be?"

"I have in my possession an urgent message for you. Might I come in?"

The old rooster slowly opened the door. His skinny, grey-feathered body lacked plumage all about. His back cracked as he strained to stand fully upright.

If the stranger noticed the old rooster's aging discomfort, they were quick to wave it off by advancing forward. The stranger stepped inside and closed the door.

After shaking away the remnants of the storm outside, the guest's hand reached for the hood to reveal a round, feathered face, typical of a young female bird. "My name be Fanny Smythe," she hurriedly announced.

The bird squinted. "Do I know you?"

"No." She retrieved a folded piece of parchment from her inner pocket and stared long at the old rooster.

"I have been led to believe you can assist me. You *are* the pirate known as Parlay Pete, are you not?"

His eyes widened, and he spat out a dry cough. "Ma'am, it be in excess of two decades since I laid ears upon that moniker. Who are ye? What do ya want?"

Her unflinching stare was still coldly fixed on the rooster as she handed him the note. "This note will explain all. We have no time to delay."

"Delay? Delay what?" The man took the note and looked at the emblem embedded in the wax seal. His neck cracked as his head snapped back up at the woman. "This ... this cannot be."

It was as if the female bird expected the shocked response that the old rooster forcibly let out of his tired lungs. "The fact you are holding it in yer hands means it be. Now read it." Her desperate need for haste was apparent in her tone.

The wax seal crumbled as he snapped it to open the note. His shoulders hunched, and his eyes widened as he read the note. The female bird settled into patience. Her eyes remained on the rooster the entire time he focused his beak on the letters that were scribbled on the note.

"No. No. This ... you are mistaken." His hands were suddenly shaking; he desperately tried to hand the letter back to her. It was as if the letter held messages that would burn his hands and blind him if he refused to let go of it before the passage of time. He was already pacing on the spot and was stretching the letter towards his guest. His head was turned towards the other direction as he tried uncontrollably to let go of the note in his hand.

His guest responded by drawing the pistol concealed under her cloak and pointing it at him. He must have been unsettled by the ruffling of clothes behind him for the rooster finally turned his head, settling it on the pistol that was already positioned to fire at the middle of his head, a little above his beak. He stammered back, let out a moan, and fell backward into an old chair.

She pressed on. "You are bound by oath, Peter Furlong. That oath requires you to follow those instructions regardless of the circumstances. You have an unsettled debt to pay!"

"Belay yer threats, woman," he snapped. "The oath is void. He's dead. They all are!" he shouted.

"The oath is binding until your death, not his. It be valid until the reaper sees fit to take you. You have laid eyes upon the seal. The note is authentic."

"How? How can this be?" he asked, begging.

"Mind you not the manner of its being." Shaking her head, as if to jolt out of the awkwardness of the situation, Fanny holstered her pistol and extended a damp, feathered hand to help the frazzled rooster to his feet. "Peter, I am in desperate need'a yer help." Her tone shifted to one of concern and desperation, but there was still that gruesome haste in her movement and speech.

Parlay Pete removed his glasses, and, using a corner of his shirt, began to clean them. His hands were beginning to get ahold of things as he steadily placed them back on his face, and he began to cry. "I am an old bird. Surely there be someone younger, 'n' more capable to help you with this." He referenced the folded note.

"Perhaps. But there be no one recommended more highly or more trustworthy than you," she replied, smiling.

The rooster sighed deeply. He hobbled slowly over to his closet and asked, "How many years have you been holdin' that note, lass?"

"As long as it was necessary," she replied, listening to the sound of things falling to the fragile hard wood floor of the rooster's closet. The rooster had suddenly donned the kind of urgency that his guest had come in with. Objects started rounding up on the floor as he went through his closet. Fanny had to quickly dodge to the right corner of the room as an unidentified object flew towards the center of the room.

The elderly, grey rooster finally emerged from his closet. Around his head was a red bandana. His new attire was adorned with a pistol and cutlass. "Parlay Pete reporting for duty, Ma'am." The smile on his beak was nothing compared to the large grin that spread magnanimously across Fanny's feathered face.

The sun had risen and set twice since they set the governor and his crew adrift at sea. Still there was no sign of the Lucinda Marie. The Stench had circled the waters between Hispaniola and Cuba, awaiting any sight of the ship, yet there was no luck in getting hold of even the shadow of the ship on the horizon of the still waters. Captain Buc sat behind his desk, over and over second guessing himself and his motives. He and his crew barely survived their encounter with the Triumph and they were no closer to locating the treasure. He shuttered at the thought of his beloved Jamaica coming under the malicious and absolute rule of Governor Legget. There was no stopping the exploitation and other evils that would be wrought on the island if the governor were to finally own it. Buc cursed under his breath and spat at the thin air as his tongue waggled at the despicable thought of the governor's rule.

His thoughts were soon disrupted by a shout from the deck.

"Ship off the port side!"

Finally, thought Buc, snapping to his feet. He exited his cabin and approached the port side of the ship. He looked out over the vast sea but could not see any ship. He extended his spy scope and scanned the horizon. Lowering his scope, he turned back and upward toward the crow's nest. "Might you be mistaken, Mister Pugwald?"

"Take a gander overboard sir," shouted Pugwald.

Buc moved closer to the rail and looked over it. Alongside the Stench was a small dinghy. Its small sail was torn and lying across the front of the tiny boat. Spread across the back of the boat was a disheveled flamingo. He was unconscious, and his body echoed the symptoms of dehydration and hunger.

"Master Chumlee, retrieve that sailor. Mister Twitch, please see to his immediate medical needs." Buc noticed Ava peeking around a corner. "Miss Ava, please assist Mister Twitch. That soul may be in need of a gentle touch." Young Ava emerged from the shadows and walked on deck. She looked excitedly back and forth at the sailors and watched as Chumlee climbed a ladder with the flamingo draped over his shoulder.

"Miss Ava, fetch water and some rags," he demanded.

Chumlee sat the flamingo up on a barrel, leaning him back on the mast. He shook the bird to awaken him. "Oye!" he shouted.

Ava hurriedly carried over a bucket of water and handed a mug of water to Chumlee who proceeded to splash the water into the flamingo's face. He handed the mug back to the girl indicating that she refill it. Ava's curious gaze didn't leave the unconscious flamingo as she rushed back and forth. She was back in time to see the thin, pink bird's eyes flutter awake. Quickly hurrying to his side, she handed him the mug of water in her hands. The bird took it and began drinking rapidly.

"Slow down," Chumlee instructed. With the way the flamingo gulped the water in the mug, it was as if the thirsty bird would soon drown himself with the rush of fresh water.

The bird gasped when the last drop reached his throat, finally having the time to glance at the worried faces around him. His eyes looked over everyone at the same time. "Thank you," he finally said in a whisper; he had obviously lost his voice to the currents of the sea since he been adrift on it. He turned to Ava and stretched the mug towards her. "Might I bother you for another?"

Bewildered, Ava looked at Chumlee who nodded at her. She refilled the mug and returned it to the bird.

"Indebted to ye I am," he said, tilting his head back to drink again. From that position, he was able to get a look at the dark flag waving high in the wind. He dropped the mug. "Pirates!" He struggled to stand up, his face suddenly squeezed with tension and a need for survival as he reached for his knife, but it was missing.

"Looking for this?" chuckled Chumlee, holding up the bird's knife.

"Chumlee," snapped the captain, "stop frightening the bird," fully realizing that Chumlee's sheer size alone was frightening enough to cause the wits of an average fowl to waver. But there was no need to torment the poor flamingo; he looked helpless and fragile enough, though the captain knew well enough that appearance wasn't everything in judging a bird.

Buc approached the flamingo, now pressed against the rail in a panicked state. "There be no danger here for you, mate. If we had wished you harm, we would have left ye adrift and at the mercy of the currents."

Buc slowly extended his feathered hand to gain the bird's trust. "What be your name?"

The frightened flamingo took the captain's hand slowly too. "Sparkles, sir." His voice was starting to regain its croaking sound.

"Sparkles?" repeated the captain.

"Aye, Sparkles."

"Odd name for a flashy fowl," said the captain.

"I like it," said Ava, smiling at Sparkles who returned the gesture. Sparkles was starting to gain his composure as he stared trustingly at the young bird. "I'm Ava." She introduced herself as she mimicked her captain with a slow stretch of her feathered fingers towards the flamingo. Sparkles, getting the joke, purposefully took her hand and introduced himself again. "Aye, Ava. Such dear name be for such a fine youngling as y'self. Sparkles." He pointed a finger at his chest as he uttered his name.

As this went on, Robert approached Buc and whispered in his ear. "Aye," replied the captain with a nod of his head. He his shoulders shuddered, and he approached Sparkles. "How is it you come to this impasse?"

"Our ship," Sparkles explained, "the Condor, was attacked. It was downright brutal." He shook his feathers as if he was reliving the horrible tale he told everyone. "I awoke adrift, clinging to a shattered piece of decking. That's when I eyed the longboat. I shouted but there was no answer to be found. I paddled my way to the boat to find its lone passenger dead. Tuddles was his name. He was also crew on the Condor. I took the longboat and, after a day in the warmth of the sun, I had to cut loose poor Tuddles." A depressed look came over the flamingo's face, expressing how sorry he was for having to toss his shipmate overboard.

"Who attacked your ship?" ask Buc.

The flamingo cleared his throat. "Spanish colors, sir. 'Tis all I know."

"And what was your purpose on the ship? What were your duties on board?" asked Buc.

"Deck hand, sir," he replied.

Buc smiled. "Well, Mister Sparkles, take ye some rest, you be in safe hands now."

"Many thanks to you, Captain."

"Miss Ava," called Buc, "please take our guest below and show him a place to rest."

Ava guided the guest happily below by the hand. She quickly started a conversation with him and their soft chirps could be heard as both descended down the stairs. Sparkles' eyes, though, seemed to be focused everywhere on the ship as he descended the stairs.

"Master Chumlee, Ayg, Robert. Come with me," ordered Buc as he headed for his cabin.

The two fowl and the egg entered Buc's cabin and closed the doors behind them. Buc circled around his desk to face his men. "First, I believe we may have missed our opportunity with the Lucinda Marie. She's meant to be in port on the morrow. We must return to Port Royal." He sat down and sighed. Then he raised his head to the men. "Second, as for our guest, make it known to all not to reveal anything of our plans."

Chumlee leered at Robert. "Aye, sir. Are ye thinkin' it was Rojo?" asked Robert.

"I perceived that as well," replied Buc. "It be possible Rojo is attacking ships at random in hopes of finding the pieces of the map."

Mister Ayg wrapped a bandana around his shell where he would normally have drawn eyes and began to stammer around.

"Ayg's right. Rojo be usin' blind luck to find what he wants," chirped in Chumlee.

"The foul fowl knows nothing about luck," mumbled Robert.

Buc looked at his uncle then turned his attention to Mister Ayg.

"Mister Ayg"—Buc looked over at his long-time friend— "after removing your blindfold and fixing your face, set a course for Port Royal. Be mindful of the currents and tide, I do not want to arrive before nightfall," he announced.

"Sir?" asked Chumlee, confused. Ayg didn't bother to draw anything on his shell. He just kept staring at the captain. The whole room went rigid, unsure whether they understood the message in the captain's tone.

Buc's beak twitched to the left as he smirked. "If by chance our governor has made it back, I'd rather not arrive with a cadre of bayonets pointed at me."

"Aye." Chumlee finally nodded. "Port Royal it is."

The misty air held heavy with a briny scent. It was one of those mysterious night as the fog shielded the light from the crescent moon. This made slipping in and out of the shadows virtually effortless for Buc as he advanced towards his favored night tavern. Dodging a few locals who has had a little too much hard cider, he made his way to the back door of The Wooden Stork. He lowered the hood of his cloak, and silently entered the tavern. Quickly dashing into an alcove near the end of the bar, he managed to avoid being seen as a patron stumbled past him. As usual, the young serving girl was attending to the host of drunken birds that wanted a gulp of the drinks she carried on the tray in her hands. After serving every filled cup, she collected the empty ones and called out to the grumbling that greeted her from another round of birds. "I'll be back with ya drinks in a flash lads." Penelope twirled around the tables of the Wooden Stork, balancing an empty tray in her hand. As she passed the alcove, she squeaked as a feathery hand covered her beak and pulled her into the shadows.

Penelope struggled to break free and was about to scream beneath the tight hand on her beak when Buc's familiar voice calmed her. "Hold fast" whispered Buc, "'Tis I, Buc."

She stopped struggling, and Buc removed his hand. She regained the breaths she lost when he held her by inhaling short steady breaths.

"What are ya doing scarin' a lady like 'dat?" she finally said in a hushed voice.

"Well, I just …" Buc's reply was interrupted by a slap to the face by Penelope. Before he could compose himself, she pressed her beak to his, and kissed him. Both happened so fast, that Buc had to handle short steady breaths himself.

Buc paused, then hesitantly spoke up, "I am a bit confused?"

"You attacked the ship my fiancé' was aboard?" she explained, in a hurried, heated tone.

"Aye. But I have good reason." Replied Buc.

Penelope slapped him across the face, and once again kissed him. She did not give him a chance to recover, "You should o'heard him and the crew. Ramblin' on about a dreaded pirate attacking their ship and beating upon their Captain." She protested, shaking her fist in anger.

Buc held up his own finger, still maintaining the short steady breaths. It was the only thing to do with the tense situation "I can explain." He attempted once again to explain his side of the story.

Penelope's feathery palm landed across his face, and as before, she kissed him. "You threatened my fiancé'." She spat., "He broke off our engagement. He said he had a scare put into him by the same dreaded pirate."

Buc tried to be heard, "All I said…"

Again, she slapped him, and kissed him. Buc totally lost count of the kisses and the slaps. He wondered what had gotten over Penelope as he silently cursed under the short breaths he took. He held up a feathered finger, and took one step back, bewildered from the sting of her latest whop. "My dear Penny … pick an emotion. The sudden extreme changability is starting to ruffle feathers." He demanded, quietly.

"He told me, after we were to be married, he had planned to take me back to England where I were to become a house maid, servin' him and his five brothers. If it weren't for the fright put into him by you, I'd be on me way to live a life of unpleasant servitude." Penelope finally twittered.

"Instead your here, serving cider to the vagrants and underbellies of society. Clearly I cannot infer a difference."

Buc prepared to be slapped again, but instead Penelope enveloped him in her arms and kissed him. Foregoing the slap that he had become accustom to, the kiss was longer and emotional, as it seemed to last from low to high tide.

"You saved me life, Captain Buc. You saved me life!" Her smile suddenly faded to scorn, "And as for this establishment, you should know I have an agreement with old Gus there. As soon as I can afford it, I plan to buy the Stork as my own." She whispered in his ear, "You're not the only bird with dreams." She smiled, and just as before, her smile faded as she came to a painful realization, "Oye! You cannot be here! Back in Port Royal. Rojo be lookin' for ya and the Governor's put out a warrant for your arrest!" She exclaimed. "He's blaming' you for Thomas' death. Along with the sinking of a ship of the fleet. Is it true?" she asked in a panic.

"No and Yes." Replied Buc.

"Well which is it?"

"No, I didn't kill poor Thomas, and Yes, I did sink their ship."

"You have to leave. If he finds you here. ..." She held his hand and wanted to drag him towards the back door of the tavern.

"I need to find a man named William Beakman." interrupted Buc. He held her steady within the shadows of their darkened alcove.

Penelope paused, "Beakman?" She looked about the tavern. "There's a lad over yonder whose name is Bill Beakman. Would that be him?"

"That's the lad." Buc suddenly made a startling realization. He turned back to face Penny, "Wait, you said Rojo was looking for me. Was he here?" he asked hastily.

"Aye, came in all threatening like." She replied.

Buc looked her over, "Are you hurt? Did he hurt you? Did you order sarsaparilla?" His questions and concern flew fast.

"Well now," replied Penny with a smile, "Aren't we all Prince Charming-like" She continued to smile in delight from Buc's worrisome outburst.

Like a bumbling schoolboy, Buc tried to avoid answering, and shook off his genuine concern. He turned away, awkwardly, "I'll have words with Beakman now." Buc began to exit the shadows and make his way through the tavern.

"Oye!" Penelope snapped. "You cannot just go wondering about likes of them. Not with a bounty upon you. Do ye have any money on ya?" She asked.

"Aye" Buc raised a brow.

"Well I suggest the next round is on you love." Penelope leaned towards him and wiggled her face mischievously.

Buc handed over a pouch of coin to Penelope, trusting her to get things done. He seriously still owed his dreaded pirate personality to her witty tavern rumor, and her ability to spin false tales.

"It's a good 'ting I'm in yer debt Buc Buccaneer." She said as she began walking away, mumbling, "Draggin' me into yer pirate fantasies."

Buc watched from the shadows as Penelope made her announcement. The entire tavern erupted in cheers. Music and cider flowed freely as Buc raised his cloak, smiling and making his way through the tavern. Penelope strolled from table to table. Once she reached the table where Buc could find William Beakman, she signaled him with a gentle nod. Beakman had passed out and was lying face down on the table. Buc laughed and cheered, carrying a mug of cider as he approached the table. He lifted the Beakman's head, but he was indeed too intoxicated for conversation. Buc sat next to the man spoke into the air, "Old Billy boy ya cannot hold yer cider."

When his comment went unnoticed by all the celebrating tavern patrons, Buc took this as a good sign. He reached into the man's pockets and searched for a pouch similar to the one's carried by the others. When his fingers fell on a familiar feel in one of the deep pockets, Buc knew luck was on his side again as he found it in the man's inside coat pocket. Buc stood up, preparing to leave. He reached into his own pocket and retrieved two shillings. As he left, he passed Penelope and placed the two shillings on her tray, "For his tab love." He whispered without stopping.

"Will I see you again?" she asked.

Buc stopped and turned back toward her. He smiled and returned the hood over his head, "Unquestionably," He said as he strolled into the darkness of the fog once again.

The purple and yellowish glow of the approaching dawn spread across the distant darkened horizon. Through the still water, the mirror-like reflection of the curved banana-shaped crescent moon faded, signifying the coming end of the night. On this vast ocean of water, a lone longboat skated gently, without fuss, until it broadsided the deeply darkened wooded sideboards of the Fowl Stench. Chumlee's crowned head popped out from the deck of the Stench, straining to see the sailor of the longboat. Moments later, a rope ladder clattered against the side of the ship as it unfurled into the longboat below. Buc, still having his face concealed by his hooded cloak, carefully climbed the ladder. As he reached the top, Chumlee offered him a hand up, getting the captain onboard the deck of his ship.

"Do ye have it?" asked Chumlee. His eyes swept across his Captain to see if he held in his hand the pouch which held the perceived final clue to what they all waited for.

"Aye." smiled Buc. He glanced about at the anxious faces that fell on him and motioned towards his quarters. "Chumlee, Robert, Ayg, y'all with me, now."

The crewmates entered his quarters like patient hounds expecting a table scrap from their compassionate master, as they arranged themselves to form a small circle in front of Buc's desk. Immediately after Robert closed the door behind them, Buc stared at the map that had been sprawled strategically atop his wooden desk. He moved the pouches about until the edges of the drawings on the maps matched. Looking over the map again, he frowned. The patient crewmates exchanged glances, expecting that Buc would share his worries soon enough. His frown become more burrowed before he finally said to the large room "There be no references, no names, no bearings."

Everyone kept silent as Buc ran his fingers over the map, obviously searching for something, until he came to a small oval shape on the maps edge. He leaned towards the map to have a better look as his eyes wavered towards the opposite side of the map and saw a familiar mark.

"The post!" he exclaimed with a whisper.

He flashed at Mister Ayg, still whispering, "Ayg, the post."

Ayg reached inside his shell and retrieved a wooden spindle post. It was the same post Buc had removed from a ship's wheel at Thomas' request. When he gave it to the captain, Chumlee shook his head compassionately.

"That had to be uncomfortable mate." muttered Chumlee, nodding at Ayg.

Ayg replied with a mere bob of his shell and focused his attention back on what the captain was up to.

Buc examined the post and turned it slowly to reveal a similar marking on the end of it. When he turned it against the light in the room again, a faint and raised X shape appeared along its edge. The suspense in the room was entirely suffocating, as everyone silently expected the captain to be through with his examination. It was the only word that could describe the whole process as it unfurled before them. Ayg was prepared to draw a confused face on his shell when Buc snatched the coal stick from Ayg's feathery grip. Ignoring Ayg's shuddering protest, Buc ran the coal over the wooden post. Carefully darkening the raised X, he lined up the end markers and rolled the post over the map. As the coal stained embossment made contact with the parchment, an X appeared.

This brought a temporal smile to the captain's face, but it soon faded as he realized there was still no navigational information on the map at all. Suddenly breathing fast and hard, Buc pulled at the charts and threw them about, trying to match the shape of the island to shapes on the maps. At a point, Ayg attempted to join the captain in his futile effort but was discouraged by Robert, who shook his head sparingly as if to say 'it was better to allow the captain figure this one out himself'. Buc was totally lost in his quest to find meanings to all the location markings with no specific direction, he wasn't thinking to glance at the confusion that had enveloped the whole crew in front of his desk. When he finally raised his head, his bird's eyes reeked of a sailor that was altogether frustrated with an unyielding storm.

He fought with the post and the map and shoved them off the table with a single swipe of his feathered hand. His harsh, uncustomary actions sent the group into a confusion, as everyone stepped away from the desk in unison. Chumlee shuddered as he, and Mister Ayg, unable to display their concern for their friend and captain, retreated slowly towards a far corner of the room. Buc raised his beak at everyone and let it all out. "Get out! Get out I say." When Ayg and Chumlee exchanged worried glances, Buc became more agitated and reached for his pistol, "Get out!" He needn't say it thrice, the crew rushed out, totally perplexed at the reason behind Buc's fowl reaction.

Robert slowly walked after Ayg and Chumlee who had hurriedly scattered out of the room and closed the door, still inside the captain's quarters. For a long time, he stared at Buc scornfully before approaching Buc and landed a steel blow across the captain's beak,

sending him a few feet away from his desk. Wide eyed, Buc
responded by standing fast and angry, drawing his pistol at his uncle.

"Ye dare point ye pistol at me boy!" shouted Robert, apparently
angry as well.

"Aye!" shouted Buc.

"Ye good an angry lad! Wanna tear me limb from limb?" Robert's
brimful expression
outwardly mocked Buc.

"Aye!" shouted Buc
again. His hand
reaching for his beak,
rubbing the spot that
had received Robert's
blow.

"Good." Robert
muttered.

In a flash, Robert
rushed to Buc and
grabbed his pistol
wielding hand, helping
him to position the
small weapon exactly
in front of his aging
feathered skull, "Hold
on to that feeling boy. Brand it deep in ye mind." He was no longer
angry at everything. A new feeling of unease washed over him,
obviously towards himself for his haughty reaction at failure.
Eventually, Buc's eyes filled with a new determination.

"That pulsatin' emotion ye need to muster to be a captain of a
vessel such as this. Yer gonna need that fire in yer belly to figure out
this puzzle. No pirate worth his salt would give up a treasure so
easily." Robert said as he guided Buc's hand down towards the floor
of the room. He released Buc and stared hard into his eyes.

"Now think boy! Who is it that told ye of the map pieces?"

"Thomas. You know that."

"Aye Thomas." He turned his back to Buc and stared into an unknown distance.

"But Thomas is dead." Buc announced to his uncle's back, willing to explain the complicated condition, assuming that Robert hadn't thought of it. But surprisingly, Robert coughed and turned again, making sure he was face to face with his discouraged captain.

"Contrary to popular belief lad, dead men do tell tales." He said, one of his fingers pointing to the wooden roof.

"Even the dead tell tales." mumbled Buc. His eyes suddenly sparkled with a glimmer of a new thought.

"What's that boy? Speak yer mind. Enough of this mumbling' about." Robert sincerely was curious. A few seconds ago, he had thought that his fowl standing before him had lost all hope in his quest for revenge.

"Something Thomas said." Buc started, "'even the dead tell tales." He continued.

"And what be his thinking about that?"

Buc looked at his Uncle, "The dead leave clues."

"Aye. And where do ye think them clues may be?" Robert obviously was starting to follow in Buc's sudden idea.

"His bookshop!" Buc exclaimed, holstering his pistol. "We have to return to Port Royal!" His shoulder had resumed their fine stand as he advanced towards his uncle.

"Now you're thinking like a pirate boy." Robert smiled, nodding encouragingly at Buc.

"I'll have Ayg reverse course." Buc announced as he hurried toward the door. His hand on the knob, he paused, and turned to his uncle. "Uncle, perhaps you'd fancy a visit with Aunt Fanny during our return."

Robert smiled, "My dear boy, when we first departed Port Royal, I expressed to your aunt my desire for her to visit friends in Barbados."

Buc looked puzzled, "Barbados?"

"Aye. Rojo knows of yer aunt. It wouldn't be beneath him to use her to get to you." Robert smiled. When Buc's hand tilted around the knob, Robert smiled at him and said, "Yer aunt is safe. There be no need to worry."

Buc sighed and smiled at his uncle, who responded in kind. But as Buc turned and opened the door, stepping out into the already glaring dawn of the new day to change course for home, Robert's smile faded. There was a sudden blankness to the old bird's face as he sighed deeply and fell into one of the chairs in the captain's quarters. He looked at the floor next to the chair, leaned down and picked up the pieced together map. His gaze shifted back to the door Buc just left, and once again, he sighed.

Chapter 18

The stray beams of light bleeding through the downtown marketplace of Port Royal meant only one thing. *Dawn was approaching.* Buc decided he had to move fast. It wouldn't be long before shop owners arrived to begin setting up their outdoor stands and displays. Getting to the corner that housed Thomas' small bookshop, he looked up at the sign hanging above the door. It wasn't as lavish as other establishments, and it only had one word on it: "Books." Buc hurriedly glanced back and forth to be certain no one was about. The door of the shop was plastered with a sign permitting no entrance "by order of the King's Guard of Port Royal." Not expecting it to be open, he tried the door latch anyway. When it didn't budge, he nodded his head to tell himself that he was right.

Once again, he took a gander about, being watchful for prying eyes. Tapping a few cobblestones in front of the store with his foot, he stopped at the one that made a hollower sound. He lifted the stone and, also as expected, a key lay under it. He held the key firmly in his hand, remembering all the times Thomas let him close the shop late while reading a newfound adventure book. Getting back to the latch, a smile crossed Buc's beak as he unlocked the door. The memories of Thomas would forever bring a sweet taste to his mouth.

When he got in, the store was in a shamble. Books were tossed about, maps askew, and papers were everywhere. Thomas would have hated to see his shop in such disarray and for a moment Buc was glad Thomas wasn't around to see it. Behind the disheveled desk, there was a map on the wall that reminded him of his childhood with Thomas. He smiled as he looked at all the markings on it that he had made as a child. Then, dreaming of adventure, Buc had marked places on the map he would visit when he was older. He quickly shoved this thought aside as he reminded himself he was back here for a purpose. He glanced around the shop again and saw that the bookcases stood facing forward, rather than the side by side arrangement of a typical bookstore. Thomas once told Buc he set his store up to provide his patrons with a way to browse books discreetly. Buc didn't understand when he was younger, but now, as he stepped in and out of the rows, he understood. He was about to reach for one of the books when a familiar voice broke into the silence of the dusty bookshop.

"That old bird truly cared about you."

The voice broke through the shadows between the standing bookcases, reminding Buc of his earlier years with a different bird. He grasped his sword handle and turned to face the voice. From within the shadows emerged a figure Buc had known his whole life. A fowl he had recently grown to despise. "Rojo," he grumbled.

"Hello Buc," said Rojo, stepping into the newly formed daylight that was already peering through the store's mud stained windows.

Buc withdrew his sword. "I should do the island a service and run you through right here," he said.

Rojo only smiled wickedly and said nothing, bringing an angry snicker to Buc's face.

"You killed Thomas, you mongrel." Buc leered at him. "And you killed my parents," he added.

Rojo's eyes narrowed. "Told you, did he?"

Buc frowned for a while then shot his next words at the despicable bird. "No. It was not Thomas. It was my aunt and uncle," he replied, waving his sword in the air.

"Did they happen to divulge to you the entire story?" asked Rojo. "Did they tell you everything?" He kicked some books lying on the floor in front of him. Seeing someone so recklessly care not for books, would have made Thomas red with anger.

"Aye. They told me of the massacre at Kismet Key. They made it known to me how you and your crew of cutthroats killed every soul save me." Buc's beak tightened, and his eyes glared with hatred.

"But did they tell you everything?" asked Rojo, kicking more books out of the way and advancing towards Buc.

Buc gripped his sword tightly, fronting its sharp point at Rojo. "I have no patience for mincing words with you, Rojo. If you wish to say something, out with it."

Rojo slowly approached Buc and the tip of the blade followed his every move.

"The island and village of Kismet Key was not selected on a random whim, lad. I was an ambitious sailor on a mission of my own. Months prior, I came across a vessel and, upon the painful and prolonged interrogation of the crew, I learned of an island—an island that was home to a particular fowl." He walked slowly among the scattered books lying about the floor. "After the untimely demise of my captain, I persuaded the crew to name me as captain." He continued to stroll about the room then snapped back at Buc. "My first order of business upon arriving at Kismet Key was to make haste an' locate this special fowl. It didn't take long. My new crew was loyal and rather determined. Once in my custody, I pleaded with the pathetic bird to provide me with the information I requested, but he refused me repeatedly. With my patience at a low, I ran him through."

"Ye dancing about with words, Rojo. My father! You're speaking of my father, you scalawag."

"The fowl I killed was best known by the name Lucky Longfeather," Rojo provided.

Buc's face turned long and hard. "No. You are twisting words and spinning yarns. If Lucky Longfeather was killed, it would be noted in journals. Word would have carried across the Spanish Main!" he snapped.

"History is written by the victors, Buc." Rojo's smug smirk was a slap to Buc's face.

"Why?" asked Buc.

"You know of the tales, boy. Thomas made sure of it. Tales gleaming with rumbles of a great wealth amassed by Longfeather. 'Twas that wealth that I sought to make my own."

"Then why did you kill everyone? Why did you kill my parents?" shouted Buc.

"After I rid the world of Longfeather, it was my hopes that his demise would motivate others to come forth and reveal the location of his cache. But, sadly, no one stepped forth." He shook his head and tried to sound sympathetic, but arrogance filled his words. "His followers were most loyal."

Buc only looked at him, despair, and irritation all over his frown. "So that's when you killed my father, my mother and all those other villagers."

"Those villagers were his crew, not the innocent souls of which Thomas spoke. Your father was the first to give his life in protection of that cursed treasure." Rojo's eyes gleamed with delight.

"My father was not a member of any pirate crew," Buc barked.

"You are correct, boy," replied Rojo. A mischievous smile was written across his face.

Buc's brow furled. "What are you saying?"

"Your father was not a member of the crew. Your father was that special fowl I sought. Your father was Lucky Longfeather."

Color rushed from Buc's face. Pale and dumbfounded, he stumbled backward, almost losing the sword in his hand. "No. My father was a fisherman, he wasn't a…" he stammered.

"A pirate?" snapped Rojo.

Buck stood straight and pointed his sword back at Rojo. "My aunt and uncle—"

"Lies!" Rojo cut him off quickly. "Just another one of their lies." His face filled with content. "You, my boy, are the only living heir of the notorious pirate Lucky Longfeather."

Buc wanted to believe Rojo was spouting nothing but lies, but the seriousness in the bird's tone told him otherwise. Fighting the flood of emotions that were brewing in his churning stomach, he pressed forward, his sword raised and poised at Rojo again. Anger took hold of him and he was ready to lunge at Rojo and tear his beating heart from his chest.

"Help me find the treasure, lad." Rojo wasn't making any move to protect himself.

Buc's mind was a whirling tempest of thoughts. The scared child in him longed to run away as fast as he could; but from within his core, deep in his belly, a fire grew. *Is that why Rojo spared me? Has my entire life been a lie? What did Thomas know, and how long did he know it?* Thoughts flooded Buc's mind. *My entire life, as told to me by Rojo, has been one lie after another. But what if it be true? What if I am the only descendant of Lucky Longfeather?* His eyes narrowed with determination and ferocity as his thoughts echoed about his skull.

"If what you say is true, then it is my duty — nay, my birthright — to ensure you and the governor never set an eye or feather on that treasure." Buc finally allowed himself to think of the advantage his new knowledge awarded him.

Rojo laughed. "Do you assume I care for what the governor wishes? He is merely a means to an end." He had stopped moving. His eyes wandered around the bookshop and settled on Buc with a piercing stare.

"Then what purpose do you have for the treasure? What end could possibly justify killing poor Thomas and threatening me?" *Get the truth out of him,* Buc devised.

"The end is simple, my boy, to rule Jamaica!" Rojo closed his fist. "And poor Thomas, as you so warily stated, was a key member of Longfeather's crew. How else would he have amassed so much knowledge of Longfeather's ventures?" Rojo smiled. "I knew Thomas would lead me to the treasure if I leaned on him long enough."

Buc drew in a deep breath. "What did you do to him?" he demanded.

"I simply let him know that I had discovered his secret, and that I would soon learn the location of the treasure." His eyes narrowed. "Even if I had to kill you to convince him," he sneered.

In a flash, Buc realized that Thomas had given his life to protect him. His breathing quickened as the anger grew within him.

"Once left with no option, Thomas set out to warn those who held the pieces of the map. One such fellow was the father of the local magistrate. I believe you are acquainted with him?" Rojo was now playing with Buc, trying to trigger an emotional response. Buc held fast to keep his focus as Rojo pressed on. "As fate would have it, Thomas fought me at every turn." Again, Rojo smiled, kicking books about the floor. "When he refused to turn over the list of names, we took up weapons." He turned and looked at Buc over his shoulder. "I killed him."

Buc, eyes bloodshot and flooded with determination, ground his beak.

"And I will dispose of anyone who stands in my way." The last words were said between clenched teeth as Rojo advanced towards Buc. Buc continued to stare into Rojo's eyes, gripping his sword tightly as the scrape of metal on metal revealed Rojo's own sword. Rojo lunged first, allowing Buc to counter this move easily. Buc adjusted his footing. Stepping on pages torn from books made the floor slippery and unforgiving as both pirates swiped back at each other. Buc kept switching direction and swiping again to keep his attack afloat but Rojo kept up. Still maintaining a solid footing, Buc continued to block Rojo's advances, throwing his at a calculated pace.

"You're better than I expected, boy," muttered Rojo as he bent to evade one of Buc's swipes.

"You'll be finding I'm full of surprises," replied Buc, swiping at Rojo repeatedly with a newfound force. Rojo moved backward, quickly changing hands and getting prepared to lunge again.

"You're no longer that little lad playing pirate with a wooden sword." Rojo was trying to antagonize Buc, building up a method to get him to lose concentration, but his methods were not working.

Buc slashed and stabbed toward Rojo with an angry rage. Rojo, sensing that Buc might take a sudden turn, began a full front attack, backing Buc against Thomas' desk. As Rojo retracted his blade, preparing to strike forcefully, Buc rolled back up onto the desk causing Rojo to miss. Rojo, shocked and impressed, looked up at Buc standing on the desk. Buc smirked and kicked Rojo square in the beak, sending him backward into one of the bookcases.

"I am no longer that little bird you so easily discarded!" declared Buc, standing tall and proud.

Rojo, bewildered, quickly scrambled back to his feet and questioned, "Discarded? I never discarded you, Buc. I merely placed you in more capable hands. I knew one day you'd lead me to the treasure."

Buc felt as if the weight of the whole vast ocean had been deposited on his shoulders. Rojo's words irritated him to no end. "You will be betrayed by the very words spewing forth from your beak, for I will NEVER lead you to the treasure!" he shouted, lunging at Rojo once again.

Rojo, totally prepared for Buc's fast strike, flicked a book and it flew at Buc's knee. Off his footing, Buc stepped, landing hard and knocking over the next bookshelf as he fell. His sword had scrambled from his hand as well. The sudden blunder gave Rojo the perfect advantage to position the tip of his sword at Buc's back as he fell. But Buc wasn't giving up that easily. Continuing off the momentum of his fall to the ground, he grabbed a heavy book and quickly turned to have it forcefully broadside Rojo on the side of the head, rendering him unconscious. Rojo fell to the floor with a last thud, the metal of his sword reverberating as it joined him on the floor.

The noise created while they fought drew too much attention; Buc could hear sounds of guards trying brazenly to get through the locked door. He was about to toss the book aside when he noticed its title. The words, "*The Legend of Lucky Longfeather* by Thomas Willoughby" were etched on the cover of the book. Buc smiled.

Quickly holstering his sword, he went for the only available escape route. As the front door of the shop was forced open, no one noticed a lonely bird silently letting himself out of the bookshop through the backdoor. He briskly cut across the street, carrying an average-sized book tucked under his velvet V-neck coat. Buc whistled gently as he made his way steadily back to the Fowl Stench.

Chapter 19

It was fast becoming the norm that every crew member should await the arrival of the ship's captain. They would sometimes form a straight line on deck, expecting him to give news or new instructions after his endeavors as to where next the ship would sail to. This time around, they all stood, anxious and alert, as Buc climbed on board the Stench. He was indifferent as his face fell on expectant faces. The captain merely nodded to every bird before giving a very large book to Ava. "Here, little one, see what you can make of this," he said, without looking at her.

Ava, always curious, went about opening the book immediately after it reached her hands.

"Ayg, set sail," the captain commanded.

Ayg's coal drawn eyes shot up as he shrugged, wondering what their destination was.

"Set course for the Black River," the captain eventually added.

"Sir?" inquired Chumlee, concerned. Chumlee had been watching the captain since he had been back on deck. He appeared both totally distracted and determined. It was as if Buc was considering a lot of things in his head at the same time.

Buc, sensing the concern in his crew member's voice, looked over at Ava and Edward who already had their heads buried in the book, and then rested his brows back at Chumlee. "It's possible we might be over the moon on this one. The bookshop was a dead end." He stepped forward, staring at the far sea horizon for a while before he looked up towards the sky, an unreadable expression coursing through his feathered face. "Sorry, Thomas," he whispered.

He looked back at Chumlee. "We need her help."

Chumlee looked worried, "But sir. You've heard the stories. Perhaps she won't be willing—"

Buc, impatient, held up a feathery hand to silence Chumlee. "We will walk off that plank when and if we come to it. But, until then, that—" Buc paused as if he was considering the possibility itself "—woman may be our best chance of decoding Thomas' map."

The whole time, Robert was absent. As he ascended the stairs from below deck, obviously willing to add to the conversation, Buc turned to him, stopping him with a wave of his hand. "I have no need of council, Uncle," he said in hushed tones. "When this all be said and done, you and I shall have a steadfast talk about my father and Lucky Longfeather." Without further words or a shred of willingness to receive a reply from Robert, Buc turned his back on his uncle and proceeded to the helm.

Robert, initially astounded, made notion to follow but, instead, turned and returned to his duties. Ayg and Chumlee could only exchange glances, hoping that the captain knew exactly what he was doing.

The peaceful Jamaican weather layered a moist flow of humid air over the ship like a blanket of fog. The waters, in harmony with the Caribbean breeze, gently rocked the Foul Stench as it circumvented the island towards the deep shadow that many called the "Mouth of the Black River". The shadow, at the moment, was created by the rising sun that fell on two rocks that guided the large waters into a lonely river, which streamed along a single channel into what was known as the Black River. The sun wasn't at its height yet, but orange and yellow rays had taken over the whole sea horizon, suggesting that it was almost the complete break of dawn. Aboard the Fowl Stench, Chumlee started to reiterate his concern about their destination while Buc, at the helm, continued to scan the waters, apparently taken by the natural shape it took as it responded to the movement of the ship.

"Captain, what is it yer thinking that would guide you to the river?" Chumlee asked.

Buc's head snapped up from the water, his beak twitched to a curve as he looked at Chumlee. "She is still a friend, Master Chumlee. Favors owed; bargains to be made."

"You lost her cargo; it is you who owes the favors. And the tales, Captain," Chumlee complained.

"Aye."

"You tell me yer not the least concerned?"

"Aye." Buc lied. He was concerned. Rumors had spread far and wide about the woman they planned to visit. But Buc was gambling with the hopes that she still favored him as a friend. The possibility still held that she was too far gone for that. Over the edge, their soon-to-be guest was a very difficult woman. She was once a good woman, Buc thought to himself, and a very good friend. He finally decided that he had to trust his own decision to meet with her and hope that his luck hadn't finally run out. He returned to the view of the waters and ignored the tattooed bird's further concerns.

As both sailors concentrated on the task ahead, the sky was starting a new task itself. The clear sky began to gather untraceable dark clouds that took over the brownish-yellow rays of the sun. The dark shadows of the rocks were no longer the only shadows in the large waters as shadows began to consume the sky and the water below. There were no loud bangs in the sky to suggest the coming of a heavy downpour or a storm, yet the currents of the gentle breeze yielded into a constant heavy flap of wind. Buc, mystified, gripped the helm tightly as he stared into the ever-changing sky. Swirling gray clouds began to converge to obscure the hitherto cobalt blue sky. The air around suddenly became heavy and thick with precipitation as the damp air filled his nostrils. As the air pressure began to change, Buc plucked a single feather from his chest and tossed it into the air. Carefully watching it dance in the accumulating breeze, his eyes widened.

"Master Chumlee!" he barked.

Chumlee looked up from the main deck, just noticing the changed weather himself. "Aye, sir?"

"Batten down the hatches. Prepare the crew. We're in for a bad blow."

"You thinking a storm, sir?" asked Chumlee.

"Worse," replied Buc.

Chumlee quickly approached Buc. "A tempest? This time o' year? 'Tain't natural." His eyes had gone wide at the view that greeted the ship.

Buc looked upward and gritted his teeth. "There'll be nothing natural about this blast," he said before rushing to take control of the wheel. Everyone was about to witness a tempest that might send the ship tumbling and shriveling around the deep waters in seconds.

The whole crew on deck were already alerted by the sudden weather and Chumlee's directions as he screamed the captain's commands from the wheel. Everyone scrambled to ready the ship for the storm, picking up fast paces to batten down the hatches and get the ship's wings ready for heavy wind. Captain Buc insisted that the sails remain full mast, despite the prevailing gale, and that the children stay below, along with Mister Ayg. The rolling deck of a ship had proven no place for a crewman so oblong, he insisted.

Ava looked worried as Ayg began to escort her and Edward below.

"Do not worry, Ava," said Twitch, looking up at the sky. "This will be a light storm, nothing to fret about."

The dark clouds were starting to roar thunders as the air became thicker. No crew member could say where the only source of light in the sky came from, but despite the overshadowing clouds, the deep waters were partially visible. Master Chumlee and Thomas were at the main sail rigging, securing it as lightning flashed above, sometimes giving a full view of the fog that was building at the end of the sea. Mister Twitch flinched as the glow of the lightning lit up the storm-darkened sky. Pugwald, shivering, climbed down the rigging from the crow's nest, flailing about in the wind. The crew held on tightly to ropes as the storm' intensity grew. Marley tied himself and Pugwald to the side railing, in hopes of not getting swept overboard by the raging sea. Thick drops of heavy rain were already pouring from the dark clouds, lashing at the rough wood of the ship. The rain collided with the angry wind, making it into a terrible blow of water on everyone's faces. The waves of the water, supported by the wind, also crashed into the sides of the ship, sometimes almost tripping it over. But the captain took over the wheel with utmost superiority. He was expertly driving the ship against the waves of the water and the agony of the downpour that wished to see the ship at the bottom of the sea.

"I know what you are doing. Do you have no dignity at all?" Buc's voice boomed over the crashing waves, catching the attention of his quartermaster. Chumlee stared back, leering through the pounding rain, uncertain to whom the captain was speaking. Waves crashed over the sides and onto the deck, drenching Marley and Pugwald. Robert and Twitch scrambled to secure additional lines and tighten down the deck's side cargo. It wasn't long before Chumlee felt it necessary to confront his captain.

"Captain, you think it be time to drop sail and ride her out below?"

The captain stared back at Chumlee. Rainwater already poured off every feather on his body. He gritted his teeth. "Any man not worth his salt ought not to be aboard. The exits are all around ya. But a true pirate stands his ground."

Chumlee was prepared to argue in favor of the crew when Buc turned his attention back to the sky.

"You concocted the potential for redemption. Can it be you are afraid?" he shouted, quickly turning the wheel to avoid a coursing wave that wanted to splash across the sides of the ship.

Lightning lit up the coal-black sky, creating shapes and forms along the outlines of the clouds. A single bolt distracted the heat between Chumlee and Buc as it lashed downward toward the ship, striking Mister Twitch. Both Buc and Chumlee looked over at Twitch, still smoldering from the blast. Wobbly and off balance, Twitch mumbled, "Just a light storm. Nothing to fret about."

Buc smiled as the torrential rain lashed down at his grinning face. *Tough little bird,* he thought. He gripped the helm tightly and lashed out at the storm once more. "Is that all you got?"

Chumlee, fighting to gain balance on the rolling deck, approached the helm. "Captain," he shouted, "it be bad luck to taunt the storm!"

"Bad luck?" The captain laughed. "Master Chumlee, any fool can have bad luck; it be a better man that knows how to capitalize on it." His eyes were wide, and his brow furrowed. Chumlee was starting to think that Buc had lost it. It was the first time since boarding the vessel that he thought the captain might actually be going mad. *Has the quest gotten to him? Has the truth now just set in?* Chumlee stared at his captain, wondering if it might be time for him to step in.

"Did you not hear me? Is that all you have to offer? I'm Captain Buc Buccaneer, and I can stomach anything the sea can throw at me!" Buc continued to curse at the angry clouds.

Again, lightning flashed above, illuminating the captain's daring face. Chumlee became more deeply concerned. As he approached the helm once more, the sails began to go slack, and the wind began dying down. He looked up at the sky and reveled in the sight of parting clouds as the rain began to subside.

Chumlee made his way up to face Buc.

"There, Master Chumlee." The captain suddenly shouted, pointing ahead to an opening near the beach-lined jungle. "The Mouth of the Black River!" He smiled, raising his chest to showcase how proud he was of his feat.

Chumlee turned to face where the captain had pointed. The captain indeed had driven the ship towards their destination, and Chumlee felt ashamed for doubting his capability. He cleared his throat and faced the captain once more. "Captain—" he paused "—for a time there, I thought..." Again, he paused.

"Thought what, Master Chumlee? Thought I was mad?

Thought I had gone off the map?"

"No, sir. For a moment I were thinking you were talkin' to the storm."

Buc let out a laugh. Chumlee joined in realizing how silly his comment actually sounded.

Buc left the wheel and placed a hand on Chumlee's shoulder, "My dear Master Chumlee." He leaned in close to Chumlee and whispered, "I was."

Wooden oars slapped against the dark water at the mouth of the Black River. The large vegetation and foliage that adorned the river entrance glistened with morning dew. As the longboat entered the river, the long shadows faded, and reflections vanished while the buzzing and chirping of insects filled the air. The Black River was indeed named well. Its lack of penetrating sunlight and musty air would send chills up the spine of any seasoned sailor. Beams of sunlight disappeared quickly again, making the entire river dark and ominous. Buc lit a lantern and hung it on the end of the longboat hook, desperately trying to illuminate the passage ahead. Hot, damp air filled his lungs as he strained to see what the river had in store for them. He turned to look back, watching the final glimpse of sunlight fade away as if the jungle had swallowed them whole.

"Why isn't Robert here?" Twitch whispered to Chumlee.

"Because I have no need for him at this time," Buc replied, knowing full well why he did not invite his uncle. Rojo's words still echoed in Buc's head and he was not ready to discuss them.

As if a candle was suddenly blown out, the river went silent. The continuous drone of chirps and clicks from the insects that greeted them at the mouth of the river disappeared as the longboat jostled, catching the attention of young Edward. "What was that?" he asked.

Buc held the lantern over the edge of the boat, looking to the dark, murky water of the river. He moved to the opposite side of the boat and again observed the water. "You can take in the oars, mates, not much need for them now."

As Chumlee and Twitch pulled in the oars, Edward looked over the edge. "We're still moving forward," he said, confused.

Chumlee quickly looked over the edge. "The river. The current."

Buc cut off his quartermaster. "I know, mate. It's flowing upstream." Buc tried to disguise his concern with an air of confidence.

Chumlee looked on in confusion. "It's unnatural that's what that is."

❺ "The spider draws the flies to her," mumbled Buc, wondering if his decision to journey up the Black River was in fact a wise one.

The current increased, causing him to sit quickly. "Hold on, mates. No telling what she's up to."

"The woman?" asked Twitch.

"No, mate. The river," Buc replied.

The longboat's speed increased, in harmony with the violent nature of the dark waters. Through the darkness, barely visible by the light of the lantern, water splashed about as the boat was dragged deeper into the dark recesses of the Black River. Buc continued to strain to look ahead, fearful of what might lie ahead. This was not his first venture down these dark waters, but his past journeys were never this violent. He feared the manner of the waters might reflect the misfortune that fell to the woman he sought for aid. With a flicker of luck, he saw what lay ahead. "Rocks," he said. He grabbed an oar and plunged it into the water. "Keep us off the rocks!" he shouted, his voice muffled by the raging waters. Chumlee grabbed the other oar and helped steer the longboat clear of the rocks. The boat shuddered as it hurled them through the frothing waters and across the outer edge of the jagged rocks. Edward fell backwards into Twitch's arms as the boat was shaken and tossed, as if an unseeing hand was toying with them. Buc's oar snapped in two as he strained to push the boat out of the path of the toothed and serrated rocks lining the river. He looked at his broken oar then to the river ahead, hoping the frenzy would end soon. Once again, he strained his eyes into the darkness. The glimmer of light reflected upon the river just enough for him to see the water stirring violently ahead. "Hold on tight, mates!" The water ahead spun in a tight circle forming a dangerous and deadly whirlpool within the center of the murky river.

"It's unnatural I tell you!" shouted Chumlee.

"You keep saying that, but it won't make it any more natural," replied Buc, holding tight to the sides of the longboat.

The boat swiftly spun clockwise, held tightly by the grasp of the mysterious whirlpool. Buc, Edward, Twitch and Chumlee crouched down, screaming as they held on for dear life. The flowing waters of the Black River merged and spun intensely as if some mysterious force was spinning a bottle to decide their next direction.

Then, as quickly as the river demonstrated its rage, it showed compassion. The roar of the river subsided, and the air was once again filled with the sounds of insects. The longboat, no longer spinning out of control, drifted slowly towards an old, wooden dock. The bow of the boat gently kissed the edge of the dock and came to a halt.

Buc stood and steadied himself then turned to his crew. "That t'werent so bad now, was it?"

Wood creaked as Buc and his crewmates slowly walked along the dock. On dry land, a well-worn path led deeper into the moss-covered canopy of the jungle. Buc held out his lantern in hopes that it would help illuminate the otherwise dark, algae-covered path. Brackish water was at either side of the path, streaming through the area towards an unending stagnant flow upward. The darkness above gave the trees that surrounded the unmoving stream creepy shapes as many either joined branches or shared roots that spread from the neighboring marshes down to the shorelines of the brackish water. The bayou stream was a jungle itself. Tall trees spread across from one side of the stream to the other, wrapping the stream in a cocoon.

"Where are we going?" whispered Edward, staring at the creepy figures of the trees.

"To see a woman about a location. Well, more of a witch than a woman, and more of an island than a location," explained Buc. "Actually", he continued, "I seem to remember she prefers enchantress to witch."

"What's her name?" asked Edward.

Buc stopped in his path, leering through the blackness at a figure in the distance. His eyes narrowed as it seemingly faded into the darkness of the lush foliage.

"Esmerelda," he whispered, cautious as she possibly already knew they were coming.

"Is she a good witch?" Edward's questions began to weigh on Buc.

Buc turned toward him, extending his wings wide. "Would a good witch choose to live in a place such as this, lad?" Buc's sarcastic response was interrupted by the snap of a branch in the distance. He spun and held out his lantern to witness a slow-moving shadow figure moving through the nearby forest.

"What's that?" asked Edward, clinging closer to Buc. "Are they zombies?" he asked.

Buc's beak wrinkled. "No lad. They're half-zombies."

Edward tried to get a better look. "Half-zombies?" he muttered. "How can you tell?"

Buc looked down at Edward and tapped his own beak. "Because they only smell half as bad."

"Captain? Weren't there a cabin here on our last visit?" asked Chumlee nervously.

"Aye," replied Buc, wondering if the absence of a dwelling meant she was no longer there. "We move on."

Holding up the flickering lantern, Buc barely had time to finish his reply when the crackle of flames filled the air. Around them, torches became lit, and the darkness that enveloped the crew now became visible. Buc spun round looking for who or what was lighting the torches, but no one was to be found. The torches continued to light and illuminate a previously unseen path leading to a large banyan tree, its branches spread out as if it were waiting to grasp at unwanted visitors.

As the travelers reached the tree, they discovered an entrance formed within its massive trunk. Buc held up his lantern, shedding light on the giant knot opening. Inside he could see tree roots twisted and curled, forming a set of living stairs that led deep under the tree.

"Captain," Chumlee called out, "I have a bad feeling about this."

Buc didn't bother to look back at his nerve-stricken quartermaster. "I'd be more worried if you had a good feeling about this, mate." Buc took his first step onto the sketchy stairs, starting his journey down into the musty depths of the old tree. The stairs led the travelers into a large underground opening. Entering the hollow cavity, the air was filled with the aroma of decayed and decomposing foliage. The disagreeable scent forced most of the crew to cover their noses while Edward, affected by the dusty air, sneezed repeatedly. The floor was covered with decomposing leaves and plants. It crackled under their feet as their weight snapped the twigs and branches scattered about. If Esmerelda didn't already know she had guests, she would definitely know now.

"My dearest Esmerelda," Buc graciously announced as the others caught sight of the shadowy figure standing at the far end of the cavern. Just as before, candles and lanterns instantly ignited, adding the flickering glow of flame to the less than desirable environment. The cloaked figure sat behind a wooden table, staring at the intruders. "I see the rumors are true?" Buc continued as the figure glanced at the crew, moving her head from one single bird to the next, until it rested on the captain. Buc looked around the dimly lit room. "And I see you relocated," he added.

The dark figure stood and slowly stepped toward her unwanted guests. Her appearance caused an audible gasp from several others as her full profile came into view. Esmerelda glistened in the flickering light, her body covered with reptilian scales, oozing a thick, transparent slime. The lights in the room reflected off her eyes that seemed to pop out of the hooded cloak she was wearing. She moved into full view, and Buc smirked as his crew instinctively stepped backward, reacting unconsciously to the creature that stood before them. When she stopped, her hand reached out from her cloak toward Buc. Her reptilian claw stopped just shy of touching his face.

"My dear old friend Buc Smythe." Her gravelly voice sent chills down Buc's spine. "Or do you prefer Buc Buccaneer now?" she hissed, he large tail waving behind her.

"It seems the tales of my courage have spread deep into your jungle," Buc managed to say.

"Yes, dey have." She smiled, revealing a rattling, fork-like tongue. Then her smile froze, contracting her scaly face into shuddering anger and despair. "What do you want?" she asked, whipping her tail about, and snarling at the other intruders in her home.

"The tales of your—" Buc paused "—transformation were apparently true." He tried to be polite, avoiding adding insult to the fact she was no longer a fowl, and was more reptilian in nature. "I have to say I was not expecting the new voice." he added.

Esmerelda sneered at Buc, showing off more of her hideous nature. "It came with de face." She said, gesturing with her claw at her own face. "Now, I ask again. What is it you want?"

She faced Buc with piercing eyes, uninterested in games.

"I am looking for an island and I need your help," Buc started. "There, are you happy? Pleasantries are over." He turned toward Chumlee. "She used to thrive on small talk."

Chumlee just nodded softly, still mesmerized by the transformation of the woman he once knew.

"And what do you have to bargain wit'?" She grinned casually.

"Ez? Do you not trust me, love? I was hoping you'd allow me to compensate you after we'd found the island and the—" He paused, hesitating to provide any further details of their quest "—thing we seek upon aforementioned island."

Leaning towards Buc, Esmerelda spoke in a low, rattling tone, her tongue meeting her lips at every turn. "T'ings have changed, Buc Buccaneer."

Her enunciation of Buc's name sent a shiver down his spine. "That is visually apparent," Buc replied, getting a better look at her conical eyes.

"If you are still upset about your cargo and that hurricane, I've had every intention of—" Buc was quickly cut off.

"Only a fool try to sail through a hurricane!" shouted Esmerelda, her voice echoing through the hollow tree.

"Told you," whispered Chumlee to Buc.

"But"—Buc held up a feathery finger— "if I had succeeded, I would have become famous as the first merchant sailor to traverse a hurricane." Buc looked back toward his crew as Chumlee shook his head slowly in disapproval.

"You think dis is the result of cargo gone missing?" She waved her claw in front of her body. "The sea took from me what was mine." She looked upward to where the sky would have been if they were not deep among the roots of a tree. "De gods cursed me, and now dis be my time here." She reached out with her claw and closed it quickly. "Now I take from those what they hold dear." She growled, taking her eyes off the confused captain.

"If I gather correctly, you are saying I can pay you later. Savvy?" Buc smiled and looked around at his crew.

"You know what happened to de last fowl who said, 'I pay you later'?" she hissed, walking past Buc.

He shook his head, knowing full well her next statement wouldn't be pleasing to the ears at all.

Esmerelda pointed to a bird cage with the skeletal remains of an owl still wearing a powdered wig and filled the room with cracking laughter.

"I don't trust her," whispered a voice from behind Buc and Chumlee.

Esmerelda stopped smiling, smirked at Buc, and shifted her view to see the boy cowering behind Chumlee. She grinned wickedly, showing off her stained, sharp teeth. "I will help you, Captain Buc Buccaneer, in trade for de boy."

Buc looked down at the boy, but before he could protest, Edward's voice rang out. "Never! I don't care what you do. I'll never leave my sister."

Esmerelda's smile widened, becoming more hideous. "And his sister," she added.

"No!" shouted the boy.

Chumlee, sensing that the boy was adding fuel to the fire by shouting, quickly grabbed the boy and covered his beak.

Buc looked at Esmerelda and back at the boy. He pulled Edward away from Chumlee and lifted him up in front of Esmerelda, staring at her inquisitively. "Put me down!" shouted Edward. But it seemed Buc was trying to provoke a reaction as he said nothing, he only stared at the reptilian woman. Buc lowered the boy and pushed him back towards Chumlee. Chumlee wasted no time pulling him close and covering his beak once again.

"What would you want with such a boy?" Buc returned to Esmerelda. "You're not going to eat him, are you? That would just be wrong. He's skinny, talks too much, and his sister? She whines all the time."

"De boy just lacks the right discipline," she grumbled. "Besides, there be plenty o' chores to be done about here for de two. I not be one for de housekeepin'," Esmerelda replied, hissing, and swinging her tail up high.

"That tidbit is rather apparent," Buc said as he leaned across the table, closer to Esmerelda. "Give me your word you shan't harm them, and you may have them … after our little venture is over."

Esmerelda stared back into Buc's eyes. Each waited for the other to flinch and back down. When neither did, the old witch smiled wide; her now fully visible stained and rotten teeth made her appear even beastlier. "You have my word, Buc Buccaneer, but there is one caveat."

"No, that was it," Buc protested. "The deal is done. No more caveats, provisos, conditions or stipulations."

Esmerelda sat down, grabbed her walking stick, and slowly lifted it, tapping gently on the cage containing the skeletal corpse.

Buc quickly gathered her meaning. He leaned forward towards her. "What did you have in mind?"

"That I accompany you on your voyage to watch over that which will be mine."

Edward, upon hearing this, struggled to break free of Chumlee's grip, fully aware that he and his sister were about to be traded.

Buc continued to stare into the dark eyes of the disturbed creature, but she paid no heed to his piercing glance.

"Since we are in a state of amendment," he said, "I have but one caveat of my own." His eyes tightened, filling them with a sense of threatening enforcement. "No harm shall ever come to the two, whether under my protection or yours."

Trying to be indifferent, he stood up straight. "Do we have an accord?"

Esmerelda flashed her rotten teeth again, stood upright, and removed her hood. Her ghastly figure was now even more grotesque in the flickering candlelight. "Aye," she said, nodding her head gently to support her word.

Buc wasted no time after her agreement. He reached into his coat pocket and retrieved the pieced together map. Slamming it on the table, he peered actively into Esmerelda's eyes. "We're lookin' for an island."

Esmerelda looked at the map then looked up at Buc. She quickly spun around, her tail whipping about, missing Buc by mere inches. The reptilian woman began to pack a bag, pulling jars and vials from her broken down shelf and placing them in a satchel. Once the bag was full, she spun back around. "We must hurry if we are to make de tide." She hissed and growled as she strolled past Buc and his crew, avoiding the stairs, and clawing her way to the surface.

"Wait?" shouted Buc. "That's it? We're leaving?"

Chapter 20

With her walking stick continually tapping the wooden ship,
Esmerelda walked on board the Fowl Stench steadily as if the deck
was normal everyday ground for her. Her cloak covered most of her
hands and legs, so it would seem to some of the ship mates as if she
was floating ghost-like across the deck as she moved. She had taken
off the hood and there was enough daylight left to showcase her full
grotesque features.

When Buc and the others returned with her, Ava and Robert stared
at the creature, constantly glancing back at something else whenever
her glass-like eyes moved to settle on theirs. Esmerelda took note of

everyone's stare and would sometime meet a member of the crew eye to eye, suddenly flicking her rattling tongue out to scare the poor bird. She hissed and snarled at those staring at her. Ava, startled by the lady-lizard, ran to a far corner of the boat. Esmerelda cackled hard, the sky's lightning colliding with her loud, gargling laugh. The truth was that Esmerelda's presence was unsettling; having an unnatural creature on deck could make even the best of sailors tremble in his pants. But Buc was with Esmerelda, calm and resolute, relying on the old witch to keep to their agreement.

"So, as we have come to an accord, it's time that you provide us with the location," Buc insisted.

"True, we do have an accord, but I cannot tell what I do not know," replied Ez.

Buc's eyes filled with anger. He approached the old woman and got as close as he could tolerate to question her. "We had an accord, woman. You said you would tell us where to find the island."

"No!" she shouted, following her denial with a loud growl, causing Buc to flinch. She whipped her tail about and smiled, once again showing off her stained, decaying teeth. "I said I would he'p you find de island. I neva' promised to know de way." Esmerelda's emotion was like the moving sea; calm one moment and unsteady the other. She moved from calm and smiling to aggravation and rage within a twitch of time.

Chumlee, irritated by the witch's arrogance, reached for his sword, and began to move forward. His eyes met Buc's, and he knew that look. "Stand down."

"Esmerelda, we go way, way back." Buc returned his gaze to her and glanced upward. "Well, maybe just way back. I knew you long before you became all … scaley and drooly. Do you take me for a fool?"

"Always," she responded, her reptilian tongue extending the S sound as it wiggled in the air. "But," she added, "not today. I made you a promise, and I intend to keep dat promise." She glanced over at the boy who had found his sister in the corner. His hand cupped her ear, as he told her what had happened inland. Esmerelda glanced back at Buc and, once again, grinned wickedly.

Her glance did not go unnoticed as Buc wondered what she was up to and what she intended with the children. He shuddered to think of her throwing them in some sort of voodoo stew, his tongue went bitter at the thought. He stood upright, adjusted his jacket, and fixed his eyes on Esmerelda. "Well then—" he cocked his head "—where to?"

Esmerelda's smile froze and was later replaced with a furrow as she strolled toward the edge of the ship, grabbing hold of one of the main lines. "Der is only one creature alive who 'as soared over every ocean, every island, and every scrap o' land that exists." She turned back towards Buc and his company. "Dat is who we seek and must find."

Chumlee's chuckle followed Esmerelda's advice. This drew the attention of Esmerelda and the others. His chuckle continued until it grew into an outburst of laughter. He held his stomach, still laughing as he gestured toward Esmerelda and looked at Buc. "She talkin' about the falcon. The old hag is talking about the thousand-year-old falcon." He looked towards her again. "It's a legend, you daft witch. He doesn't exist."

Buc huffed and approached Chumlee. "It only be a legend until someone discovers it, mate."

Chumlee, defiant, leaned into Buc's face. "She be leading ya on a wild goose chase."

"I dated a wild goose once. Don't recommend it." Buc tapped Chumlee on the beak. "My boat; my chase, mate." Chumlee only stared on, gritting his beak at the confident captain. Buc stepped away and stared at the rest of his crew members, commanding everyone with his best ordering tone."Mr. Pugwald, please escort Miss Esmerelda to the helm and have her give you course and bearing."

"Aye, sir!" shouted Pugwald from the crow's nest.

"Then escort her to the galley," Buc added. "That woman makes a mean jambalaya."

"Aye, sir!" Pugwald shouted again as he landed gullet first on the deck. He stood up, gained his bearing, and secretly clutched his lucky clover. Esmerelda, seeing the bird's desire for superstitious protection, smirked as she strolled alongside him toward the helm.

The captain, grinning as Pugwald and Esmerelda passed by, was initially unaware of Ava's approach. The young girl approached Buc with an angry expression burning through her feathered face. "How could you!" she shouted.

Buc turned to her and smiled. "Hello love." The pleasantry was ignored and swiftly amended by Ava kicking Buc in the leg.

"Ouch!" he shouted, confused at the girl's action. "If you were only two inches taller, throw you in the brig I would," he said, looking down at his young attacker.

"You're trading us!" she shouted.

"I could stick you in a barrel," he muttered, "you are the right height for that." He held his hand up to her head, measuring her height.

"We came to you for help to get away from one mean woman, and you are going to trade us to another!"

Buc bent down, his eyes peering into her young eyes with utmost sincerity. "Lass, you are a stowaway. By the code, you are my prisoner. The fact that I allowed you and your overly rambunctious brother to remain was out of pity. I have not allowed any harm to come to you, agreed?" he asked.

"Well, yes," she replied.

"Then there be no sense worrying about things that haven't happened." He stood up. "My word is my bond."

"But—" she hesitated "—your word is nothing. You're a pirate."

Buc rolled his eyes and gestured for Edward to come close. The three huddled together as Buc whispered, "I promise under pain of death never to turn you over to that evil woman. Savvy?"

Ava, still suspicious, sighed deeply and nodded.

"Now", Buc added, standing upright, "make yourself useful, lass; join Miss Esmerelda in the galley." He looked proudly around his ship. "Everyone on this ship pulls their weight." He looked at Chumlee and stared hard at the tattooed bird. "Some pull more than others." Chumlee grunted, and walked away mumbling, "Stupid legend."

The ear rattling, reverberating tone of the clattering of pots and pans forced Ava to cover her ears. Esmerelda was coursing through the utensils, searching for something, and it seemed she was getting aggravated with every item in the galley. "'How am I to create anyt'ing in dis jumble of a galley?" She continued to muddle through the makeshift kitchen as if on a scavenger hunt.

Esmerelda bent down, and her lizard tail wiggled behind her. She peered under the table, behind a cloth, for pots. "Ahh," she sighed.

As she stood up, her back cracked. "You there … girl. A proper pot!" Her smile revealed her discolored, blackened teeth.

"My name is Ava," snapped the little fowl.

Esmerelda hissed and leaned down toward Ava. "Me don't care if ya name is Billy Bones." She slammed the pot onto the stovetop. "Find me a ladle!" she barked then continued to mumble, "One decent pot, and I is supposed ta make a decent meal?" She turned back toward Ava. "Fetch me some onions, ears of corn, okra, and some peppas. We gonna make a good gumbo for dis here crew." She stretched out the word good as if she was howling at the moon. While Ava fetched the vegetables, Esmerelda dragged a sack of rice over toward the stove. She strained over the weight, her back cracked and popped.

"I thought the captain said you were making jumbo liar?"

Esmerelda slammed her utensil down. "You can't make it rain if der no clouds in da sky."

Ava remained silent, confused by the answer, and still wondering what 'jumbo liar' was. She slowly headed back toward Esmerelda, carrying a crate with the vegetables she was requested to pick out. "Dat's good." Esmerelda's tone changed. "Where's d'ladle?" she barked.

"I still haven't found it," replied Ava.

"Well ya not gonna find it standin' here talkin' to me all lazy-like," she snarled. "One pot. No ladle. I be living in the bowels of Hades."

Ava rolled her eyes and went in search of the ladle, wondering if she would have been better off at Madame Hensworth's Orphanage than stuck here with a crazy lizard woman.

Esmerelda began to chop the onions, humming a song. She chopped quickly, like a seasoned chef at a fancy London restaurant. Onions rolled back and forth on the table as the ship gently rocked upon the ocean. In the midst of her chopping, she would occasional slam the knife on the table to prevent an onion from rolling off.

"I found it!" shouted Ava, excited that she'd found the ladle Esmerelda so desperately needed.

"Dat's good. I'll alert da crew. We all t'join hands and sing a song 'bout de ladle you found." Her words dripped with sarcasm. "Bring it here," she growled, disappointing Ava with her mocking tone.

As quickly as Esmerelda took the ladle from Ava, she placed several ears of corn in her hands. "Shuck de corn."

Ava looked at the corn and back toward Esmerelda, confused. "What?"

"Shuck de corn," Esmerelda repeated, waving the corn in front of her.

"I don't know what that means," muttered Ava.

"Didn't ya momma eva' teach you how to shuck corn?" she huffed.

Ava looked down, wondering if she should tell Esmerelda that she and Edward were orphans. Not to mention stowaways. She decided to simply reply, "No."

"I suppose she never teach you how to cook either, eh?"

"No." Ava lowered her head. "I don't remember my mom."

Esmerelda rubbed her scaly chin then laughed loudly. Her laugh resembled the sound of someone choking on a piece of hardtack.

"It's not funny," grunted Ava.

"Everyt'ing is funny till it's not," replied Esmerelda. "But don't you fret, I don't rememba my family either." She paused. "But I don't know if der was anything to remember about eitha.'" She shrugged. "Oh well." Turning her attention back to Ava, she said, "Now, grab me an ear, and I'll show ya how to shuck."

Ava placed an ear of corn in Esmerelda's reptilian hand and cringed as her scaly fingers wrapped around the vegetable.

"Before d'day's over, little one, you gonna be able to cook de best gumbo dis side of ... wherever we are." She cackled aloud, amusing herself.

Ava gave a small smile and watched as Esmerelda showed her how to shuck corn. Ava mimicked Esmerelda's movements, removing the husk from the corn, and cleaning off all the fibers.

The deck of the Fowl Stench was a flutter of whispers and murmurs as crew members scurried about speaking in hushed tones. Sometimes, glancing toward the stairs that advanced to the lower part of the ship, they would return, head to head, whispering until the name Esmerelda hung in the dry air. Chumlee walked on deck, watching the crew intently, and his eyes narrowed as he noticed their behavior and actions.

Twitch, glancing up and seeing the tattooed bird, walked over to Chumlee slowly. "Master Chumlee, sir?"

Chumlee glared down at him.

"Is it wise to have that—" he paused mid-sentence "—woman aboard?"

Chumlee sighed deeply and spoke softly. "I fathom for the captain one freak on this ship was not enough." He paused, his eyes burning into Twitch's own with a long stare. "Although I share your concern, we are to do as the captain says."

"Aye, sir," replied Twitch, reluctant to leave.

"Is there something else, freak?" asked Chumlee, irritated.

Twitch looked down at the decking. "I was wondering if there was anything you could tell us about her." He looked up, worried and afraid. "If it be no trouble."

Chumlee looked across the deck, checking through the faces of the rest. They all carried the same look of concern. All the whispering had stopped, and all eyes were on him. Again, he sighed deeply. "All hands," he called, "gather round."

The crew gathered swiftly around Chumlee with expectant faces.

"I gather all yea have reservations about our captain's latest guest," he started.

The crew members nodded.

"Her name be Esmerelda, and she weren't always what you see," he began. "Years back, the captain an' I met her as she once was, a young, beautiful song bird."

The crew's eyes widened, obviously not expecting the tale to start from such angle.

"She sold various trinkets and herbs in a local marketplace. Aye, she dabbled a bit in the mystic arts, but she be no witch. She limited her witchery to healing and helping those in need. A kindly woman." Chumlee ran his hand through his comb. "Be not too long till she fell in love and started a family of her own. But fate had a different destiny for her. On a voyage across the Caribbean, the ship she and her family be traveling on ran into a beastly tempest. The ship was ripped from stem to stern. After days at sea, she washed up on the shore of a wee bit o' land, barely a sandbar, much less an island. She searched the horizon for any signs of her family, but no luck was to be found. After many a day, her luck had changed with the passing of a merchant ship, but she still lost those nearest to her heart. Every day she'd spend at the shore waiting for any sign of her family's survival and as each day passed her heart turned blacker and blacker."

Chumlee held the crew's attention, sometimes waving his feathers to enact the tale he retold. "She turned dark and angry. Some would go as far as to say evil." From the shadows below, Edward was listening in closely as well. "Till one day she could no longer contain her rage. She cursed at Poseidon, damning his name, and blaming him for the loss of her husband and children. But one does not simply curse the sea god and get away with it." He peered deeply into the eyes of his crewmates. "It is said that Poseidon placed upon her a curse, making her as hideous on the outside as she had become on the inside."

"Is that why she's all scaley and icky, snake-like?" asked Marley.

"Aye. It is," a voice responded from a near end of the deck. The captain's answer startled the crew, including Chumlee who turned, startled, with his beak slightly open.

"Sorry, sir. I was just—" Chumlee tried to explain but was aptly interrupted by the captain.

"Entertaining the crew with stories, legends and falsehoods?" Buc replied.

"Aye sir," Chumlee confessed, disconcerted.

"Well, fear not, men, Esmerelda, despite her deformities, is a guest on board and we have an agreement as to the conditions of her cooperation." Buc's tone was gentle, but the message was clear enough as everyone nodded in accord with his words. No one was to make the guest uncomfortable, and no one was to further argue about her stay on the ship. The silent instruction was as simple as that.

Edward, seeing everything from the dark corner below, retreated back into the shadows.

Chapter 21

The galley below seemed to have come to life as the sweet aroma of home cooking and white steam filled the air. The sound of clattering pots was replaced with the churning and bubbling of water. Ava and Esmerelda worked on the gumbo for almost two hours. Ava, smiling triumphantly, chopped vegetables and spooned rice into the pot. All the while, she carefully listened to Esmerelda's instructions, adding more and more ingredients into the pot as she was told. Standing on the now-empty vegetable crate, she continued to stir the pot while Esmerelda hummed and sprinkled seasonings into the gumbo. Ava looked into the pot, grinning as the mixture of vegetables danced within while the steam rose to fill her nostrils with an exotic aroma. "This shall be much better than hardtack," she said aloud to the ears of the silent room.

Esmerelda snarled at the young girl. "Hardtack. Bah! Better to eat the wood off the ship." Ava laughed as she continued to stir the pot. Esmerelda stepped towards the pot and sniffed the aroma, her reptilian nostrils flaring overly wide. She grasped a spoon and dipped it into the pot. She opened her mouth and her long, pointy tongue emerged and snatched the contents off the spoon in an instant, startling Ava. "Ah," she said, "time to add some special seasoning."

Ava, still startled, looked up at her waiting to hear what it was.

"Go get me dat bag over there." Esmerelda pointed to her satchel in the corner with her scaled fingers. Ava's eyes followed the claw-like fingernails as they pointed the way. "Grab da jar with de red liquid," the witch hissed.

Ava, obeying, jumped down and scurried over to the bag. She dug through it and removed a tightly corked jar containing a thick, red fluid.

"Dat's it. Bring it here girl … err … Ava."

"What is it?" asked Ava.

"What is it? I tell you what it is." She leaned into Ava. "On de far side of de mountain, near the gully, off the Black River, is a field. In de field are vines with thorns so sharp they can cut a fowl to shreds." Ava gasped and handed the jar to Esmerelda as she continued. "In dat field are the most spicy, tasty peppers in all Jamaica." She held up the jar. "Dis be the oil of dem peppas. Very strong. Very potent."

She handed the jar back to Ava with a spoon. "Add two spoonfuls, but no more. Don't be wantin' to burn the crew insides out."

Ava, excited, flashed a smile towards the older woman. "Careful you must be," she warned Ava as she slowly opened the jar. Ava dipped the spoon into the jar twice and poured each spoonful into the pot. Esmerelda only hummed with glee as she stirred the pot. Ava re-corked the jar tightly and watched Esmerelda as she tasted their culinary delight. Esmerelda stirred the pot once more and dipped the spoon in for a taste. She hesitated and looked at Ava, moving the spoon towards Ava instead, and nodded, indicating that she should taste it.

Ava smiled at Esmerelda again then moved in and tasted the gumbo she just helped make.

The shoreline of Falcon Island could be mistaken for the shoreline of every other island in the Caribbean. Lush vegetation blanketed the seashore and white sands kissed the ocean as each wave lapped the shore. The waves, like a pendulum, moved back and forth over the white sands, clamoring loud, flapping sounds as it hit them. The tall trees and grasses, like the waves too, continued to fall prey to the warm island breeze. The breeze, it would seem, blew mostly from the east as most of the island trees were tilted to the west, giving them the shape of a bowing worshipper.

After one of the best meals the crew had eaten in a while, they prepared to journey into the heart the island. Robert spontaneously, and unexpectedly, volunteered to keep watch over the ship as Buc and the others traveled by longboat to the shore of the island. As the boat came into the shallows, Chumlee and Twitch jumped out and pulled their longboat onto the beach with Buc and Esmerelda still seated. As if the island was aware of the new arrival, its palm trees swayed as the salty air blew the tropical winds across the island's surface. Buc stared forward at the vegetation, impressed by the mighty size of the tall trees and distant mountains. There was certainly something mysterious about the island, and he knew he was about to find out what it was as Esmerelda motioned for them to continue on. He focused on her, thinking about the way the scaled creature had changed physically since he asked for her help at her home. Her glass-like eyes had gotten darker and it was as if her scales were gaining more weight and space on her skin.

"So, Ez," asked Buc, glancing at three empty, large sacks that Twitch had taken along at Esmerelda's request. "What, pray tell, is the purpose of those sacks?" Buc could not help but realize that Esmerelda had changed more than just physically. He would like to have thought he trusted Esmerelda, but she had grown darker and more mysterious than the last time they had met. He was not sure of her motives, and that made his distrust of her grow.

"Do not worry about dem sacks. Let me worry 'bout dem," she replied in a disturbing rasp.

Her answer did not reassure Buc in any way. Reminding himself to be wary of the witch, he walked with his crew as they headed toward the lush, tropical landscape, guided by uncertainty. She pawed away the large leaves of the island as they went in deep. Someone gasped when she pawed at an obtrusive plant that revealed a sign that read, "Turn back now if ye value ye life."

Buc turned back towards Chumlee who was scanning his environment cautiously. His fingers had not left the hilt of his sword since they arrived on the island and his beak had formed a sensitive curve revealing how ready he was to be offensive. "Still think this be a good idea?" Chumlee asked, not taking his eyes off the tropical trees that surrounded them. Buc ignored his comments as Esmerelda continued to lead them forward. Chumlee continued to look all about, turning his head and hissing at any noise he heard.

"I'd feel better if we had not brought the freak along," he said to Buc, quickening his step to walk alongside the captain. "There be enough mystery here without the need to worry 'bout lightning," he finished, ignoring the fact that the captain was not responding to his concerns.

As they continued inward, the foliage had become increasingly dense and the canopy above them began to get thicker. Esmerelda, now branding a machete, began chopping away at an unseen path. Insects chattered and bit as the crew made their way through the damp jungle interior. Leading the way, Esmerelda passed a mango tree and turned her head to face Twitch. "Grab dat fruit. Place it in the sack," she instructed. Then she continued down the path and pointed at another tree. "Grab dem bananas," she demanded. She continued to instruct Twitch to pluck, pull and pick a wide variety of fruits, having him fill the three sacks full. With a final slice of the blade, Esmerelda revealed a mountainside cave.

"In der. Dat's where we find him," she said, her boney, clawed finger pointing the way to the cave entrance.

Buc cautiously moved forward. He withdrew his sword and motioned that Chumlee and the rest should engage as well before they entered the large opening of the cave. "Rather large cave for a falcon," he muttered. Sunlight only penetrated the first few feet of the cave and there was barely any sense of life in it.

The dampness of the cave filled his lungs as Buc wandered further, followed by Chumlee. Buc, needing torches to light the way, spun his finger around, signaling to Chumlee in silence the need for them. Chumlee, turning swiftly, held his sword fast as Buc removed three torches from the rucksack, along with a flask of lantern oil. Using a piece of flint and steel, he lit the first torch and in turn lit the others. Chumlee took one and forcefully gave Twitch the other, almost burning him in the process.

As Buc lifted the torch, the light illuminated the cave walls, revealing intricate drawings. Tracing his fingers on the arid walls of the cave, he finally stepped back to get a better view. As he stepped backward, the whole drawing began to take the form of a new shape. It looked like a map, drawn, and wrapped all around the walls of the cave. Spinning around, he quickly found Port Royal and Tortuga on the map. "This is astounding," he mumbled, sharing surprised glances with the rest of the crew that were behind him.

Twitch, stumbling deeper into the cave, suddenly let out a loud cry. "Ahhhh!"

Buc and the others turned toward the direction of the sound and found Twitch standing in front of a pile of bones. On a post in front of him was the skull of a bird, and it still had flesh on it.

"Captain, perhaps it be wise that we retreat to the jungle and wait out our falcon friend?" Chumlee suggested. He held a torch in one hand while his second hand gripped his sword firmly. He still had that offensive look about him.

"I must agree with you, Master Chumlee," mumbled Buc, finally seeing sense in the quartermaster's worry. He looked at the crew and nodded towards the entrance, reiterating Chumlee's advice. As the crew turned to exit the cave, the light previously penetrating the

opening of the cave suddenly went dark and the wind outside picked up fiercely. Dust and sand were being blown around the cave opening and into the cave, causing the crew to struggle to shield their eyes with their feathers. Buc drew his sword and rooted his feet to the ground, ready for attack. "Stand and make yourself known, beastie."

The shadow at the top of the entrance began to take form and a roaring voice inquired, "Beastie?" The voice echoed throughout the cavern. "You invade my home and I am the beast?" Its voice bellowed through the cavern walls, which seemed to shake violently. "Thieves. Outlaws. Pirates. You all be the same."

"We wish you no harm," shouted Buc, his sword still drawn and ready.

"Your aggressive stance says otherwise," replied the figure in a ghostly voice.

"Going to eat us and stack our bones, he is," whimpered Twitch, shaking in his boots.

Buc squinted at him then turned his attention to the shadowy figure. "We seek the advice of the one known as the Thousand-year-old falcon." Buc's voice flowed with confidence, sprinkled with a hint of nervousness. "We have no quarrel with you," he chirped, still raising his sword towards the darkness.

"Enough of this!" growled Esmerelda. "Put down that sword," she demanded. "And you," she said, facing the shadowed figure, "belay your theatrics."

"Esmerelda?" inquired the shadow figure.

"Aye. 'Tis I," she replied in her raspy voice.

The shadow figure stepped into the light, allowing his true nature and size to be known to all.

"Sweet Mother of Pearl!" Chumlee exclaimed.

The figure was in fact a falcon, the largest falcon Buc and his crew had ever seen. The flickering torch flames reflected off of his grey-white feathers, which extended from one edge of the cave to the next as he flung them about. His golden-yellow beak, dulled and chipped from age, was all smiles. "Any friend of Esmerelda be a friend of mine." He extended his large wings again in greeting. "Welcome, friends." The whole crew stood silent in horrified delight at the vision of the large bird of prey. Moments seemed like hours as they stared awkwardly at the magnificent bird, their beaks hung wide.

Buc, recovering from the shock, sheathed his sword and took the falcon's hand. "My name is Buc. Buc Buccaneer."

"A pleasure, Buc. My friends call me Mel," replied the falcon. He then turned his attention to Twitch. "You there!" he bellowed. "You turducken?" he asked genuinely.

Twitch twitched, almost retreating into the darkness behind him. "Aye," he replied nervously.

"Ha! Ha!" laughed Mel. "Been too long since I seen a turducken." He ran up to Twitch and shook his hand vigorously. Twitch's entire body shook as much as his hand.

"And who might this large rooster be?" he asked, looking at Chumlee.

"The name's Chumlee, sir," the quartermaster replied.

"Nice tattoo. From the Tatkret clan no doubt," replied Mel, his demeanor filled with cheerful exhilaration.

"Aye." Chumlee looked at Buc perplexed then back at Mel. "How did you know?"

"Ha! Ha!" His laugh bellowed. "Met many clans in my day, lad."

"Mel? Sir." Buc interrupted as he reached into his pocket, retrieving his map. "We arc looking for an island."

Mel held up his feathered hand. "Stop," he commanded.

Buc looked around, still yet to get a hold of the nature of the large bird.

"It is customary to provide an offering when requesting the wisdom of the falcon," announced Esmerelda as she walked over to Twitch. She signaled for him to bring forth the sack of fruit. "Mel, I offer to you dis sack of fruit from the island of Jamaica."

Buc and Chumlee looked at each other, both knowing that Esmerelda was not telling the truth but not daring to speak up. "Jamaican fruit!" Mel's happy face lit up as he approached the sack and pulled out some fruit, shoving it into his beak without thought.

With bits falling from his chewing mouth, he said, "Fruit from Jamaica tastes so much better than the local fruit." Then he threw another piece into his mouth.

Twitch looked around, still bewildered, then decided to speak up. "But, sir, that fruit is from—" He was quickly silenced by a slap from Esmerelda who concluded for him. "The ripest trees in all Jamaica." She presented the other two sacks.

"Wonderful," proclaimed Mel, looking around. "Let's get out of this cave and head up to my home," he said.

"You mean this isn't your home?" asked Twitch, eyeing the pile of bones.

"Ha! Ha!" laughed Mel. "No mate. I use this place to scare away fowls with no purpose."

"And the—" Twitch gulped loudly "—bones?"

"Merely a deterrent for those who might stumble upon this lair." Mel grinned particularly at Twitch who forced a smiled, grasping the falcon's ruse. The large falcon moved out of the cave and beckoned for the crew to follow him, leading them along the edge of the hillside to another cave near a running stream. The new cave was different and exquisite. Beautiful flowers lined the walls to a small cove, which was formed by cold spring. The spring, like a moving snake, coiled into a tiny river flowing from the cove. It divided the cave into two equal parts; while one part bore more flowers extending into a large garden, the other parts had trees of different kinds, bearing fruits, and reaching the sky of the cave to form a tropical fortress. Inside, every corner of the cave bore sparkling and rare items from all over the world, ranging from trinkets to paintings, sculptures, gold, silver, and diamond jewelry.

"How did you acquire these antiquities?" Chumlee asked, gasping at the falcon's personal treasure trove.

"When you're over a thousand years old," Mel said, following Chumlee's gaze to a particular bronze urn placed beside the wall, "your everyday things become antiques."

Buc gently touched a jade Asian statue.

"A few of my kestrel friends make a run from the Caribbean to the orient," Mel continued, making a big wave with his large wings to demonstrate the distance of the journey.

Buc wished he had time for sightseeing but there was an important task ahead already. Once again, he reached into his inside pocket and stepped towards the falcon. "As I was saying, we are looking for an island."

"For what purpose?" asked Mel without glancing at Buc.

Buc looked at Chumlee then back toward the large falcon. "I do not see why that would matter," he confessed.

At this, Mel just stared at Buc and continued to eat one of the fruits. Neither seemed prepared to budge in a game of will. The silence went on awkwardly for some time, as if one was waiting for the burst of words that would decide if one would get what he wanted and whether the second would be willing to help.

Finally, Buc spoke up. "It is said the island holds a vast treasure," he began.

Mel continued chewing his fruit and mumbled something unintelligible.

"Pardon?" asked Buc.

Mel swallowed hard and stared at the captain again. "What is your claim on this treasure?"

Buc looked at Esmerelda, knowing that she did not know his secret. He was hesitant to speak, wondering if he was ready for her to know the truth. He knew that, if he could not give the falcon good reason to share the location of the island, the trip would be for nothing. He knew there really was no choice as he stood tall and faced the falcon squarely. "The treasure belongs to the pirate known as Lucky Longfeather. And I—" Buc paused "—I am his only living heir."

Esmerelda flinched.

Buc, ignoring her visible outburst, approached Mel. "It is important that we locate this treasure before other parties do. Their intentions with the treasure would send ripples through the Caribbean and cause great unrest to its citizens. I can only hope that you can recognize the island and help us locate it." Buc held out the piece of parchment, saying nothing more.

"Lad," said Mel, eyeing the parchment without taking it, "I have traveled around this world many times. I have seen islands great and small. I've seen creatures that would make you stand in awe and others that would make you cower in your bed. I have seen every scrap of land imaginable."

Buc handed him the parchment. He pored over the map; the crew watched intently, trying frantically to see the emotion on the falcon's face. Mel dropped the map and gave a carefree expression.

"Nope. Never seen it," he said as he handed the map back to Buc.

Buc stood in shock. "What?" he asked, taken aback and off guard by the falcon's tone.

"I have never seen that island," replied Mel, taking in another piece of fruit.

"Do you care to study it? Look over it? Compare it to charts?"

"To what end?" asked Mel. "I can tell you I have never seen that island." He began to walk away.

Buc stood dumbfounded. "Do not turn your back on me!" he shouted, approaching Mel. Chumlee grabbed Buc's arm to prevent confrontation. "I traveled here with great expectations of you," barked Buc. "I was entrusted with this map with an earnest commitment to finding it. I will not deny those who entrusted me to this task." He was trying to break free from Chumlee who held him down with a firm grip of his fingers.

Mel turned back. "Captain Buc, it is not my intent to shatter expectations, you asked me if I had ever seen an island of that shape and the answer is no." He turned away once again. "If the party who entrusted you with the map was steadfast in you finding the island, they would have told you where it was."

Buc broke free of Chumlee's hold. "Do you mock me?" His voice was bathed in desperation.

Mel huffed and walked over to his desk, retrieving a rolled map. He tossed the map to Buc who caught it easily. Mel presented a large piece of blank parchment and a writing quill. He dabbed his quill in ink and began to draw. At his new movement, Buc added confusion to his angry mood. Mel's grey-feathered hands were moving swiftly on the large piece of new parchment. "Jamaica!" he shouted, continuing to draw. "Hispaniola." He dabbed the quill in ink once again. "New Providence." He turned to Buc. "You care for something more

foreign?" He turned his attention back to the parchment. "Madagascar
… the Galapagos." Mel slammed the quill down on his desk and
turned to Buc. He gestured toward the desk. "There. Compare those

drawings to the map in your hand.
You will see every inlet, every
peninsula, and every cove." He
approached Buc. "My dear
captain, I have circumnavigated
this world for over ten centuries. I
know every island, every
continent, every scrap of land.
Mocking you I am not. I care very
little for the reason behind your
journey to this island. But it
simply does not exist."

Buc's brow furled, and he let out a deep, desperate sigh of
disappointment.

"I tell you this, Captain. By my own honor, I swear that island does
not exist. Beyond that, I can do no more." Mel turned his back on Buc,
and leaned on his desk, staring at the empty wall behind him.

Buc closed his eyes. His desire to find the treasure had
overshadowed his compassion; something he knew happened to
sailors too many times from the tales Thomas once told him. He
walked to Mel and placed the rolled map on the desk. He then placed
his hand on the falcon's shoulder. "I apologize. I meant no disrespect,
and certainly did not wish to impugn your honor." Mel continued,
looking down at his desk, "I wish I could do more." He reached over
and patted Buc hand. "You are all welcome to stay the night. The
jungle is no place after dark," he said, glancing back at the rest of the
world.

Buc stepped back and stood silent, Chumlee at his side.

Esmerelda's eyes narrowed, and she nodded at Mel. She had been quiet since Buc had been enraged and, right now, Buc wondered what was going on in her mind.

Buc motioned towards his crew and everyone turned to leave.

"I wish you luck, Buc Buccaneer," Mel said, turning fully to face Buc. "I see in you what I saw in your father."

Buc turned back toward Mel. "You knew him?" A sense of childlike excitement filled his voice.

"Aye." Mel smiled. "A hard time he had, too, balancing desire and compassion." He continued to smile. "But I am sure you will learn to find that balance, as he did." He looked deep into Buc's eyes. "When I said I wish I could do more, it was sincere." He closed his eyes and inhaled deeply before opening them again. "Your father saved my life. When you said you were his son…" His voice trailed off. "I hoped this would be the opportunity for me to repay that debt."

The silence in the room made the sounds of the approaching night apparent.

Mel took another deep breath and waved everyone away. "Now, off to bed, all of you." And, once again, he turned away.

As his crew turned to leave, Buc stopped. He signaled everyone else to continue on and turned back toward Mel. "I just wanted to be honest with you," he started as Mel turned to face him. "The fruit. 'Twas not from Jamaica. It were from your island. There was nothing special about it."

Mel smiled. "I know."

"You knew?"

"Aye. But I pretended to go along with the story."

"Why?"

Mel smiled. "It may not have been fruit from Jamaica, but at least I didn't have to pick it."

Chapter 22

"Dawn came early for ships' captains" was the ancient pirate saying. Perhaps it was the observation of beams of light penetrating the darkness or the beautiful gleam of the revealing lighted clouds that Buc loved. It reminded him that, no matter how dark it may seem, if one was patient, light would find its way to them. He retrieved his spyglass and began scanning the horizon. The falcon was of little help. Buc still had no idea where the island was, and Mel had insisted that it did not exist. *Then what is it? If not an island, then what? The map has no other identifiable markers indicating its location. Maybe its true location is not meant to be known. Or perhaps there is another piece of the puzzle missing.* Buc wondered about this as his eyes watched out across the distant sea.

Master Chumlee was now awake, and he approached his captain, hoping to console him about the difficult mystery that was yet to be unraveled. "Captain, I know you be disappointed but…"

Chumlee was interrupted by the sound of Buc angrily closing his spyglass. "Gather the men," he ordered. "We're leaving."

The captain didn't wait for his order to be followed before he moved towards the shoreline.

back to Sparkles. "Let us get to the bottom of this," Captain Buc said as he stood before the flamingo with Chumlee at his back and at the ready. Edward, who had woken up, was between the two and he tried desperately to peer between them to see what was happening. Sparkles, panicking, knocked the crate off the barrel and flipped the lid off. He reached in with one hand and pulled Ava from the barrel then drew his knife and placed it to her neck. "Ava!" shouted Edward.

"Steady, lad," said Buc. "Let her go and I promise not to kill you."

"He has my family. My children," stuttered Sparkles. He was struggling to keep Ava still. He bobbed slightly in all directions, knowing he was cornered. Again, he poked the knife at her neck.

Buc looked into his adversary's eyes. "Hogwash," he said.

"What?" replied Sparkles.

"A man who values his children's life would not put another in harm's way," said Buc. "So, I say again. Hogwash!"

Sparkles grew angry that Buc had seen through his lie. "He will kill me," he said, holding Ava tightly.

"That I believe. But, if you harm the girl, I will kill you." Buc's voice was now filled with anger and determination. "The choice you hold is whether you prefer my means to his. But"—Buc's tone deepened and his tempo increased—"there is but only one way this ends with you not dying." He stepped forward toward the bird. "Release the girl, traitor."

Sparkles was wise enough to know that he was cornered. There was no other way out. "You won't kill me?" he asked.

"I promise you will not die at my hands," replied Buc.

"Might be by my hands though," remarked Chumlee, grinning.

Buc rolled his eyes. "I promise you will leave this ship alive," he reaffirmed, caring for the child's life.

"Aw," said Chumlee with a sigh, disappointed.

The large, pink bird was breathing and heaving, desperately shifting his weight from leg to leg. He had a dilemma and knew what he stood to lose at every turn. He finally let out a loud cry and released

Ava. She ran to Buc who quickly passed her off to her brother. "You're safe now, love." He spoke softly. Once again, he returned his stern gaze to the fowl before him. "You, on the other hand … what have you told him?" barked Buc.

Sparkles hesitated then began to cry. "Everything," he mumbled. He sat down on a nearby crate and buried his head in his hands. Sobs emitted as the flamingo began to cry.

"Pathetic," muttered Chumlee, spitting at him.

Sparkles sniffled and looked up toward Buc. "Wait, how did you know?" he asked.

Buc reached into his coat and retrieved a bottle, waving it in front of the flamingo, "If you fancy throwing things overboard, make sure you know the tides, mate."

Sparkles continued to cry. "What are you going to do with me?" he asked through his tear-soaked, feathery hands.

Buc stroked his chin and smiled. "You like putting messages in bottles, ay? Well, I have a message of my own for your shepherd."

At his back, Chumlee's wicked grin spoke volumes for the captain's own mischievous plan.

The captain's quarters aboard the Corazón del Mar were lavish with a variety of mismatched items, no doubt collected from his various ventures. Captain Rojo sat as his desk richly while Governor Legget addressed him. "I am concerned that things have not moved more swiftly."

"Things, as you so eloquently put it, are progressing as I have planned," replied Rojo.

"As *you* have planned?" The governor moved closer to Rojo's desk. "Need I remind you, Captain, that this endeavor was a joint venture?" He leaned heavily on the edge of the large desk. "I have overlooked many of your discretions, all of which were noticed by those I report to. I have spent considerable time and effort in distracting their gaze elsewhere." He stood up. "Once this endeavor is over, I will have control over the territory." He wandered about the cabin. "Then, and only then, will your discretions be eliminated." He turned back toward the captain. "Once again, as I stated, I am concerned that things have not moved swifter."

Rojo's gaze was broken by the knock at the door. "Enter," replied Rojo, maintaining his gaze on the governor.

A crewman entered briskly. "Capitán. You're needed on deck, sir."

Rojo stood from behind his desk and broke his gaze from the governor. "We will continue this conversation at a later time."

As he exited and walked on deck, the governor stubbornly followed. He approached the deck railing as a crew member pointed downward into the water. Floating in the water was a wooden barrel. Written on the lid of the barrel were the words, "For Rojo." He nodded towards his crew and three crewmen rushed to retrieve the barrel from the water. They cast a net, snagged the barrel, and gently lowered it onto the deck. The barrel obviously contained heavy material as all three men carried it with much effort before it finally rested on the wooden deck. A crewman opened the barrel, revealing the flamingo, bound, and gagged, with a note tied to his shirt. They lifted him out of the barrel and Rojo, confounded, approached the pink bird. He plucked the note from his chest and frowned at the letters that greeted him.

The note read, "Turn back or die." Reading it again, Rojo laughed deeply and handed the note to Legget.

"This seals it!" barked the governor. "This is a fool's errand. Rojo, you have lost complete control of the situation." He turned about, facing the ship's second in command. "Commander, I demand you return us to Port Royal immediately. Your captain has lost grasp of this situation." His stern demeanor was soiled as he gasped, looking down at the tip of the blade now protruding from his chest.

"How's that for control, Governor?" Rojo pronounced the last word while he spat. He held the grip of his sword tightly as he slowly removed the blade from the governor's back. The governor, feeling life rushing away with his thick blood, fell to the deck. "Would you say I have a firm grasp of the situation now?" Rojo spat again as the governor's body fell lifelessly to the deck.

Capitán Rojo motioned for his men to remove the body from the deck. He produced a handkerchief and proceeded to wipe the governor's blood from his blade. He then turned his blade to Sparkles. "Now," he said sternly, "what can you possibly tell me that would prevent you from joining the governor?" He moved close to the flamingo, virtually beak to beak. "Did you hear where they were going?"

Reluctantly, fearing for his life, the bird mumbled, "No."

Rojo took two steps back. "Kill him," he ordered.

"Wait!" shouted Sparkles.

Rojo raised his hand to belay his crew. "Do you have something to say?"

"Before they caught me, the girl, she was reading a book about Longfeather."

"Go on," said Rojo intently.

"She had marked a page. It had a map of an island on it."

"And what was the name of the island?"

Sparkles struggled to remember. He continued to mutter sounds.

Rojo motioned his men again to kill him.

"Hitchcock!" shouted Sparkles. "Hitchcock Cove."

Rojo smiled before he approached Sparkles. "You see, lad. That was not so hard."

Sparkles forced a smile.

"I strive to be a fair captain. Oh, do I strive. I promise my men a future of wealth and prosperity," he said, strolling around Sparkles. "In return, I ask for loyalty."

"I … I have been loyal, sir," muttered Sparkles.

"That you have"—Rojo bowed slightly—"and I thank you for it."
He rushed in close to Sparkles, "But you were also careless, and
carelessness gets you killed."

Sparkles began to speak but stopped abruptly. His eyes widened as
he felt the blade of Rojo's sword cut him deep.

Rojo removed the blade and wiped the blood clean again then he
motioned to his men to get rid of the body. "The sharks shall feast
tonight," he proclaimed.

Buc strolled across the deck of the Stench toward his cabin
followed by Chumlee. Two disappointments in less than a day had left
him depressed. He seriously wondered if he was ever going to get to
the treasure at all, and he was also beginning to doubt its very
existence. *But it does! It does exist!* he repeated over and over in his
head.

"Captain," called Robert from behind, "might I have a word with
you? You have not spoken a lick to me since we returned from Port
Royal."

Buc closed his eyes. "Uncle, now is not the time." *Was this what it
was like for Lucky Longfeather? How many disappointments preceded
his successes? Was this part of being a pirate? Was this the end of the
adventure?* Buc's head was starting to fill with endless questions. The
falcon was a dead end and he still had no idea where the island was.
He placed his hand on the handle to his door and paused. No, he
thought. This was not time for regrets. It was time to redouble his
efforts.

"Captain." It was Ava this time around.

Buc spun around and looked past Chumlee to see the lass running
across the deck toward him.

"No need for thanks, love," he said. "You're part of the crew and
our crew is family." He hoped to quickly send the girl off.

She struggled to hold up the book she was reading. "I found something in the book," she said.

Buc took the book from her. "What's that, little one?" he asked.

She pushed past the captain and walked into his cabin causing the captain to roll his eyes. Chumlee puffed his chest. He was over having children on board.

"I was reading about Lucky Longfeather and I found something."

"Yes, you said that," replied Buc. He placed the book on his desk.

"In one chapter, Thomas speaks of a place called Hitchcock Cove. It is an island with a volcano," she explained. "Later, he mentions returning to Hitchcock Cove after the volcano erupted. He talks about a vast underground river and massive caverns created by the eruption."

"Read the book I have, love. Cover to cover, several times since I was about your size." He measured her with his hand.

"He was disappointed because it was once a beautiful gem of the Caribbean," Ava continued. "So, It got me curious about Hitchcock Cove."

"Lass, I hate to present this notion, but are you working toward an impending point? I have already had a rather disappointing day and would rather not compound the issue."

"I found a map in the book." She opened the book and fumbled toward the page. "This is a map of the island." She pointed to the map and showed it to Buc and Chumlee.

"I applaud your effort, little one, but that looks nothing like the island we are looking for," explained Buc.

"No," she replied, "but this does." She pointed to a small area of the map.

Buc strained to see the smallish drawing. His eyes widened for a second before he moved to the other side of the desk and opened the drawer to retrieve his magnifier. He turned the book, so he could see it better.

He held it over the map. The area she pointed to was a body of water labeled "Bodego Bay".

"Sweet Mother of Pearl, the lass be right, Captain," muttered Chumlee.

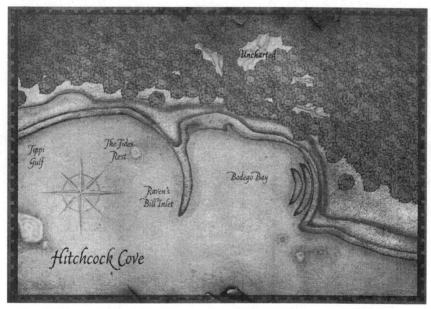

"Incredible." Buc looked up from the book. "It never was an island." He rubbed his chin. "That's why the Falcon didn't recognize it. It's not an island."

He ran over to his chart table and unrolled a map. "Hitchcock Cove," he muttered. He took his compass, measured the distance, and drew a line on the map. Judging by the location of the island in the book, it was at the far end of the Caribbean Sea, behind cloudy waterfalls and hills. Although only a spec of an island, the bay itself pushed deep into its center. Mostly volcano, the island had nothing to offer visitors. He dashed out of his cabin and up the stairs to the helm. Taking the helm, he shouted, "Hoist the anchor!" His crew, who had been waiting patiently for a new course and heading, snapped to attention. Master Chumlee exited the quarters and looked up at Buc then back to the deck. "You heard your captain, bugs! Hoist the anchor!"

Buc continued to shout orders. "Full canvas; prepare to come about!"

Robert approached the helm. "We have a course, Captain?" he asked.

"Aye," replied Buc. "Ayg! Take the helm. We gather 'bout for the Middle Sea!" he barked. Ayg slowly waddled up the stairs and approached the helm. "You alright, mate?" Buc inquired. "You seem a bit sluggish today." Ayg nodded, drew a quick smile, and gave Buc a thumbs up. Buc, semi-convinced, returned his gaze to his crew.

"Robert"—Buc turned to his uncle—" I shall have words with you now."

Inside the captain's quarters, Buc sat down at his desk, looking over the book. He was impressed that Ava had been so quick to piece together the puzzle, and surprised that he hadn't. Across from him stood his uncle, patiently waiting for his nephew to speak. Buc closed his eyes and took a deep breath.

"Buc," interjected Robert, "I just—"

He was quickly interrupted by Buc. "I shall do the talking first, Uncle." Buc gestured for him to sit.

Buc knew there was no other way to go about the discussion. It was finally time to air his concerns about his birthright. "I will not mince words with you. Am I the child of Lucky Longfeather?" he asked.

Robert looked deep into the eyes of the chick he had known virtually his whole life. "Yes," he said softly.

Buc closed his eyes and shook his head. "Why did you not tell me?" he begged.

"How did you find out?" asked Robert.

"Why did you not tell me?" asked Buc more forcefully.

"Was it Rojo? Did he tell you back in Port Royal?"

"Do not avoid the question, Uncle. Why in blue blazes did you not tell me?" Buc barked angrily. Robert was making everything more hurtful by delaying the truth.

"Buc"—Robert's voice was filled with sadness—" I had lost so much." His eyes welled up. "I dare not risk losing you. One day you will understand that there be times when parents do things to protect their children."

"But I am not your child, Uncle. I am the child of notorious pirate Lucky Longfeather. All these years I thought my father a fisherman." He stood up. "All this time, my fascination with Longfeather was justified with blood."

"Buc—"

Again, Buc interrupted his uncle. "I can understand Rojo lying to me; he is who he is." He sat on the edge of his desk. "But you, Uncle…" Buc stared into the distance. "That is the reason the books never speak of his demise. That is why he faded away into legend."

"Buc … we were just trying to protect you." Robert tried to explain, turning away.

Buc stood up. "Look at me, Uncle." Robert did not.

"LOOK AT ME!" Buc shouted, his uncle jumping, forced to look intently at his face. "I am a chick no more. I am a fully-grown fowl. As much as I appreciate what you and Aunt Fanny have done for me my whole life, at some point you need to allow me to live my life."

He leaned closer to his uncle's side. "We are so close now, Uncle. So very, very close." He rested his hand on his uncle shoulder. "I need to know you are with me on this. I need to know that, no matter what happens, you will be here for me. Above all, I need you to be truthful to me."

"What do you mean you are close?" asked Robert, ignoring the rest of Buc's demands.

Buc looked up; excitement filled his face as he too ignored his former line of questioning. "We found it. Hitchcock Cove," he said.

Robert shook his head. "No boy. That map is not of Hitchcock Cove."

Buc stood up. "You are right, Uncle. It is not Hitchcock Cove." He held up the map. "This map is the outline of a body of water hugging the coast. Bodego Bay." He held the map tightly in his palm. "Bodego Bay is on Hitchcock Cove." He handed the map to Robert.

Robert anxiously unscrambled the map and looked at it. Then he smiled gently. "You did it, boy." He looked up at Buc. "You found it." The two were all smiles as they shook hands, proud tears welling up in Robert's eyes at the accomplishment of the young chick he raised. Robert broke the handshake to hug Buc, who accepted a quick embrace, gently patted his uncle's back, and smiled.

"Captain!" Chumlee suddenly called, accompanied by a vigorous knocking at the door.

"Enter!" Buc replied.

Chumlee opened the door and stepped in; his face was flush with worry and anger. He muttered one word, which passed the same emotions to Buc.

"Rojo."

Chapter 23

Dead stop. Off the coast of Falcon Island, the Fowl Stench sat perfectly still, holding full sail. The waveless, glass-like reflection of the sea mimicked the powder-blue sky in every detail. At the helm of the ship, the Stench's captain peered feverishly through his spyglass at another vessel in the distance, dead in the water, deadlocked as they. The focus of his gaze was the fowl he had once trusted but now despised. The captain and crew of the Corazón del Mar seemed just as confused as the crew of the Stench, both vessels in the same race but with no momentum to propel their journey.

At the bow of the Stench, Mister Twitch sat alone, winding twine into neatly coiled stacks. Being alone was something the shrouded bird was used to. His kind stuck mostly to shadows and in some circles were the source of tall tales and tavern stories. He had endured a lifetime of stern remarks and insults pointed toward him and his kind. His people were nomadic, traveling from place to place. In time, traveling together seemed to make them easy targets for those who feared and hated them. They were sometimes attacked, abused, or toyed with for sport. So, with a heavy heart, his people scattered to the wind, taking refuge anywhere the wind would take them. It had been well over a decade since he had laid eyes on another like him.

Twitch made several long glances across the deck and towards the young lass who was reading her book. Twitch thought about meeting with her about what bothered his mind; especially since the object currently in her hands could possibly make it bother him less. He had watched her show compassion towards a stranger in the past, and, in addition, he knew she had read the book on Longfeather from cover to cover. A single question echoed in his mind, a question whose answer he had hoped she would have stumbled upon and brought to his attention. But perhaps she feared him too much to share any newfound knowledge. While attempting to be inconspicuous, he realized he had been staring at her, but only after she glanced back toward him and smiled. Like the twine in his hand, Twitch recoiled within and turned away from her gaze.

Ava approached the odd fowl and spoke softly. "You are not a bad bird," she said.

Twitch looked up toward her. "What?"

"I said you are not a bad bird." She smiled softly. "I know people are afraid of you because of the…" She paused.

Twitch finished her sentence. "Because of my curse," he muttered.

Ava thought of something pirate-like to say and quickly chirped out the first phrase that came to mind. "Belay that, sailor," she snapped. The two looked at each other, both shocked that such a phrase would pierce the beak of such a tiny fowl. Together, they both laughed at it.

"It's only a curse if you let it be," she added.

"Your words are kind, but not everyone thinks as you." Twitch pulled back his hood and boldly addressed Ava. "Might I ask a question of you, young miss?"

Ava smiled. "Mister Twitch, you have nothing to fear from me. You may ask me anything you like," she replied.

Twitch swallowed hard, building up the courage to ask a question that had been burning inside him since he first saw her with the book. He closed his eyes and asked, "In your readings, did ye ever come cross a passage that made mention of…" His voice trailed off.

"Of what, Mister Twitch?"

Twitch opened his eyes and cleared his throat, trying hard to sound less anxious. "When I was a young lad," he began, "no older than yer brother, I remember stories of a brave turducken that served with Captain Longfeather. I be wondering if perhaps…" Twitch's eyes met with the book in the young fowl's hands then rested back on Ava's.

"You want to know if I have encountered any writings about it?" she asked.

Twitch nodded, his eyes wide with expectation.

Ava was hesitant as she tried to find the right words. "I am sorry, Mister Twitch, but I have not read anything about a unique bird such as yourself."

The edges of Twitch's mouth curled as he forced a smile, contrary to the disappointment he felt in his heart. "It was a foolish of me t'—" He cut off mid-sentence as he looked at the small feathers on his wing. They began to stand upright, one by one. Following the direction his

feathers were facing, he looked up at the sky, frenzied.

"Is something wrong, Mister Twitch?" asked Ava. "Are you well?"

Twitch wasn't listening as his eyes grew wide, tensed. He began to spin in every direction, as if he was a mother bird who had lost a child in a busy marketplace. He continued to stare up at the sky with horrid gasps as if some terrible force was prepared to descend upon them.

"I must speak to the captain," he muttered. Darting past young Ava, Twitch headed toward the captain's quarters, head still gazing at the sky and his beak muttering inaudible words. He was almost at the captain's door when he was stopped abruptly by the quartermaster.

"Where are you going, freak?" Chumlee stood, arms bent at his hips, scowling at the agitated bird.

"I have urgent need to see the captain." Twitch puffed the words out between excited breaths.

Chumlee poked at the turducken's chest, irritated. "You are crew, freak. If you have words for the captain, I shall bring them to him." He grunted.

"The pressure be a flutter." Twitch pointed to the sky. "The upper levels are readied to descend. We must warn the captain!" he shouted frantically, trying to escape the quartermaster's heavyset body and meet with the captain as he had planned.

"The only pressure that be in flux is the pressure I plan to exert on you, freak!" bellowed Chumlee. He made no move to allow the bird to escape the block he had created with his body.

Twitch boiled. Perhaps it was the kindness of young Ava or the mere fact that he had his limits and currently felt that the quartermaster had gone beyond them with his hatred. Chumlee's harsh words struck a mighty chord within the core of the meager turducken. That chord began to resonate and build within him the courage to lash out at the burly quartermaster. And he did, unable to control his temper.

"Quit calling me freak, you brainless oaf!" he demanded.

Chumlee pulled back, a mixture of anger and boiling rage on his face. Angered, he grabbed the turducken by his thin, elongated neck and lifted him skyward. Then, pulling him closer, he brought the turducken so close that his face rested on his, eyes peering hard into the bird's very soul. "I hold no reservations about throwing you to the sharks, freak," he hissed.

"There is an irregular excess of persons wanting to throw other persons to the sharks aboard my ship." Buc stood steadfast behind his quartermaster, speaking with an impassive tone.

Chumlee turned to face the approaching captain, still holding the befuddled fowl in his grip. Dropping the bird to the deck, he addressed his captain. "Just maintaining discipline in the ranks, sir."

The captain strolled past Chumlee, eyeing him the whole time, and approached Twitch's position on the deck. He extended his wing, offering the bird a hand up.

Lifting Twitch to his feet, the captain asked, "And what, pray tell, is the cause of this heated disagreement?"

"Captain, I—" Twitch was quickly interrupted by Chumlee who saw fit to speak on his behalf, perhaps only to justify his actions.

"The freak be rambling on about pressure or some other nonsensical barmy. He be a blathering idiot, Captain. Best to be taking anything he be offering with a grain's worth of salt."

Buc looked over at his crew member who was still rubbing his neck from his encounter with Chumlee's powerful grip.

"And what about the pressure, Mister Twitch?" asked Buc.

"Captain!" barked Chumlee. "I protest! Are you going to stand to and listen to the daft ravings of this freak?"

The captain leered intensely at his quartermaster, his impassive tone swiftly changing into a commanding one. "Your prejudice aside, Master Chumlee, interrupt Mister Twitch once again and I shall order you to clap yourself in irons."

Chumlee opened his beak to reciprocate, forcing the captain to fiercely interject. "Do not test me."

Buc turned his attention back to his crewman. "Mister Twitch, please enlighten me as to your discovery."

Twitch blinked nervously, reluctant to say anything at first while he stared at the tattooed bird behind the captain. Then he drew courage from the captain's faithful and encouraging stare, fixing his shoulders to a height before speaking. "Sir, Captain, the air pressure is changing, I can feel it in my feathers." Twitch held up his wing and the small feathers upon it seemed to dance and sway.

"That is a rather peculiar oddity," replied Buc, bending slightly to examine the tiny wiggles of Twitch's feathery wing. The captain stood erect. "But what does this dance ensemble mean for us?" he asked.

Twitch pointed skyward. "The pressure will impact upon the upper winds, sir." The captain and the crew about him stared upward, bewildered, and confused. "Captain, as the pressure changes, those winds will begin to fall."

"Go on," replied Buc, "further enlighten us."

"With Rojo on our tail, those winds will find his sails in advance of our own." Twitch ran portside and pointed to the vessel in the distance. He anxiously trailed his eyes from the captain to the vessel in the distance and then to the sky before resting to examine the ship he was on. "His guns will be on us before the winds descend to punch our sails."

Buc once again examined the clouds and looked at the exasperated Twitch. "Are you certain?" he asked.

"Captain," proclaimed Twitch, "I have had sufficient share of weather oddities to know this to be true."

Buc stroked his chin as he looked over his sails. He stared down at Ava. "And what do you think of all this, little miss?" he asked.

Ava looked at the turducken. She remembered him telling her the last storm would be a light one and nothing to fret about. He had been wrong. What if he was wrong now? She smiled at the strange fowl and presented her answer to the captain. "I believe him, sir."

Buc tousled her feathery head. "Well then, we only have one question left to answer."

"What's that?" she asked.

"'Tis be an age-old question of sailors." He looked young Ava square in the eyes. "How does one catch the wind?"

Ava looked up at the highest point of the Stench's mighty mast. "If only our mast was higher, perhaps we could catch it."

Buc shielded his eyes from the sun above with his palm and looked at the top of the mast. The mast's highest sail sat dormant, yet the clouds above moved swiftly. He looked behind them towards Rojo's ship then back at the mast and smiled. "The mast need not be higher, little miss." He knelt down to her level. "Only the sail need to be high."

Chumlee, still reeling from his captain's tongue-lashing hesitantly spoke out. "You have a plan, sir?" he asked with the respect of a seasoned sailor.

"Aye, matey, we beat him to that punch."

Buc's face was as bright as the morning sun as his beak twitched into a knowing smile, consumed with the conception of a brilliant idea.

Ava looked over at Twitch and smiled, hoping she had made the right decision.

Prepared on the deck of the Corazón del Mar was a lavishly decorated table. The table was being attended by valets, who were carefully preparing an ornate tea service not unlike one that would be expected to be seen every day in the governor's mansion house. No doubt it belonged to the governor, prior to Rojo's disposal of him. The governor's personal valet, concerned for his own wellbeing, took to serving Rojo as a form of self-preservation. At the table before them there sat only one fowl, Capitán Rojo. The Spanish bird stirred his tea and gently placed the spoon on the saucer before him. He lifted the teacup to his beak and sipped gracefully. Staring at an unknown distance, Rojo held on to the saucer for a while, a smile on his beak as if he was temporarily in happy thoughts. When he placed the decorative cup on its saucer, he gingerly looked upward at his sails and shook his head as if to say, "They hang still like the dead. No wind can be found to fill them."

"Captain, sir." His first officer approached him. "There seems to be some sort of activity upon the deck of their ship."

"Mister Merryweather, the English are an odd sort," the captain replied nonchalantly. He sipped his tea once again. "But I have to admire some of their customs. Afternoon tea, for example; it is a simple custom, but the history is in the details." He placed the cup back on the saucer, lifted a cloth napkin to his beak and wiped it gently. Standing up, he asked, "Now, Mister Merryweather, can you be more specific … perhaps add some detail to your disruptive concern?"

"Aye, sir." The fowl cleared his throat, apparently afraid of the captain's penchant for dispatching those who present disappointing news. "It appears they have laid out a piece of sail on their deck. We are unable to determine what their motives are."

Rojo snapped his fingers and gestured an open hand at his first officer. The officer quickly filled the empty, feathery hand with a spy scope. Rojo extended the scope and looked upon the deck of the Fowl Stench. He quickly closed the scope and handed it back to Merryweather.

"Nothing to be concerned with. They, like us, have no wind to carry them. It is likely they are just replacing a damaged sail."

"Aye, sir." Merryweather turned to leave and felt a hand grasp his wing. He turned to face the captain.

"But just to be certain," Rojo added, "keep an active eye on them."

Merryweather smiled. "Aye, sir."

On the deck of the Stench, crewmates had stretched a piece of canvas across the deck. Every hand was on deck—from one of the sides Twitch began unrolling the canvas across the deck while Robert, Pugwald, Marley and Chumlee were attaching rope to the cornered ends of the canvas.

"Make those knots tight!" shouted Buc. "We don't want her breaking loose."

From below deck, young Edward raced up the stairs to the main deck. Peeking only his head out to scan the deck, the young lad inquired about the captain's whereabout. "Captain!" he shouted.

"I'm right here, mate, no need to raise tone," replied Buc, standing only feet away from the lad.

"It's Mister Ayg, sir, I think him unwell," uttered the boy, gasping for breath.

Buc didn't hesitate; he headed below, leaping over stairs as quickly as possible. "Ayg!" he called out.

Edward followed behind pointing to a corner as he leaped beside the captain.

"In here." Edward passed Buc and Buc followed, allowing the boy to lead the way into the darkness. Inside the dark and musty crew quarters, Buc found Ayg lying in a crew hammock next to Ava. His shell had become dingy in color. Patches of grey and pale-yellow splotches covered his once egg-white shell. Buc, concerned for his friend, went weak-kneed and fell slowly to the floor beside him. "Ayg, what's ailing you, mate?"

Ayg's feathered hands shook as he struggled to retrieve his signature coal stick. With great hesitant effort, he simply drew a sad face on his shell. The lines were a bit shaky, reminiscent of his drawing abilities as a younger egg, but it was clear to Buc that he was not at all well.

Buc carefully touched the top of Ayg's shell where it had been cracked in the battle against the governor and his men. The shell was oddly warm to the touch. Buc turned to the young bird. "Edward, Ava, quickly, fetch some rags and water." Edward nodded and darted out of the room.

"I will find a way to make you well, Ayg," Buc said, gently caressing his friend's shell. "We are so close now, mate."

Edward came back into the room carrying a bucket of water and several rags on his shoulder. Behind him was Esmerelda.

Ava ran to Esmerelda. "Is there anything you can do?" she asked.

"Whatever happens, happens," she replied, her tongue elongating the S sound. She flung her claw in the air and turned to walk away.

"Please, Esmerelda," begged Ava.

Esmerelda paused. She looked back over her shoulder to see Ava with her hands folded, begging. Esmerelda's eyes rotated, and she hissed loudly.

"Stand back, give de egg some room," she said, quickly scanning the dark canvas hammock before finally settling in beside the ill egg.

Buc backed away as she knelt down next to Ayg. Her tail whipped around, barely missing him. "Gimme de rags," she hissed as she snatched the rags from Edward and soaked them in water. She dropped the rags all around Ayg's shell, attempting to cool him down. "We must keep de rags cool. Got to bring his temperature down," she said.

"Is he going to pull through?" asked Buc.

Esmerelda turned and eyed Buc. She said nothing before she exited the room, with Buc right behind her. "His shell be cracked." Her whispers sounded more like hisses. "Dere is no tellin' what might be going on inside de shell."

Buc's stomach tightened, and his legs felt as if they were made of timber, unable to move. "There must be something more we can do?" he asked gingerly.

"All we can do is ta' keep him comfy—" she looked back toward Ayg "—and hope for de best."

Buc was lost for words. The room grew silent without the sound of rags being soaked in water to fill the empty space.

The ensuing silence was broken from above deck as Chumlee called down below, "Captain, we are ready."

Buc looked back at Ayg. He felt compelled to stay with his childhood friend, and brother.

"Go Buc. Go do what you do. I stay with him for now. There be no more you can do down here," Esmerelda said, pointing upward. "Go, be de captain." She looked toward Ayg. "And perhaps—" she paused then knelt down once again at Ayg's side. She gently soaked a rag in the bucket of water and wrung it out, placing it across his shell. Ayg slowly retracted his wings and legs into his shell, as if to curl up into a ball. She turned back toward Buc, forgetting about her unfinished sentence. "Just go!"

Buc whirled and strolled towards the stairs that led up deck. He sighed at the circumstances, and quickly adjusted his mood to accommodate the current situation above. As he exited the stairs, he could see his crew hard at work, tugging at lines and lifting the cast iron cannon into place. Guiding the cannon was Buc's uncle, Robert. He held the guide rope tight as they pivoted the cannon above the ship's wooden deck. Along the bow railing rested a single harpoon. Wrapped firmly around the harpoon was the canvas that had previously been set out on the deck. Tied to the harpoon were four

lines of rope, each with their ends tied securely to various strong
points on the ship.

"Careful, mates!" shouted Robert. "One misguided move and
she'll fall through the decking."

He guided the cannon rope to rest it in front of the forward mast.
"Lower it down, mates!" he shouted. The cannon swiftly dropped
about three feet as the three crewmen struggled to hold and support
the full weight of the cast iron cannon. "Easy there! She'll break free
if ya let her!"

Slowly, the cannon was lowered into place. Marley ran and placed
support blocks behind the cannon wheels to prevent it from rolling
into the mast. As Robert prepped the cannon, Chumlee grabbed the
harpoon. Robert signaled Chumlee, who placed it gently into the
barrel of the cannon. Everyone on deck worked as one towards a
single goal, seamless and efficient amidst Buc's shouted orders.

Buc peered around the mast post at his uncle. "Still think those
harpoons be silly, Uncle?"

"What I ponder is what gave you the foresight to purchase them?" He looked over at Buc. "What could have bewitched you to think harpoons be a viable weapon for us?" he asked.

"To be honest, Uncle—" Buc looked around to make sure no one was in range of hearing him "—they were on sale."

Still prepping the cannon, Robert laughed and snorted. "Well lad, if it works, I'll be impressed. If not, well…" He paused. "We best be getting this cannon back where she belongs before Rojo is upon us."

Buc turned toward Twitch, who was working on the roping, double checked the secured ropes as his captain approached. "Any advice on catching the wind, Mister Twitch?"

Twitch looked up at his captain, happy to be of help. "Once the sail takes hold, the ship will jostle. It be best to be prepared for such a jolt," he announced.

"Good advice, mate." Buc turned to the crew and raised his voice. "Men, if we are at the ready, it be time to hold on to something tangible." He turned back toward Twitch. "Would you care to do the honors, Mister Twitch?" he asked.

"Would there be someone more qualified, sir?"

"None I trust," replied Buc.

With no wind, the sailors on board the Corazón del Mar retreated to the shadows and shade to keep cool. The hot Caribbean sun was relentlessly married to the humid air. The sailors longed for a hint of an ocean breeze. There was no need for them to adjust the rigging, tighten the lines or keep a watchful eye. The gentle, almost nonexistent waves lapped against the hull of the ship. There was movement generated by the slightest wind, yet it was not enough to push the sails of the mighty vessel.

Unrolled and held in place by the finest china, Rojo studied the map of the Caribbean, centrally focusing on the area known as

Hitchcock Cove. He removed his previously stained knife from its sheath and plunged it into the map with an aggressive thud. Its tip buried deep into the finely crafted wood table, Rojo rested both hands on the large map, heaving frustrated sighs. His angry action was disrupted by the sound of cannon fire.

Rojo leapt to his feet and looked beyond the bow of his ship toward the Fowl Stench. Merryweather wasted no time as the captain leapt to his feet. He handed the captain his spy scope and, through it, Rojo could see ropes extending upward from the distant ship.

"What the devil?" he muttered.

What happened next, he certainly could not understand, nor had he foreseen or expected it. The Fowl Stench was moving! The ship he so desperately had tried to catch was now moving. He peered away from his spy scope and up at his own sails. Puzzled, he returned his gaze through his spy scope at the Stench. Following  the rope skyward, he looked on in disbelief. Hovering way above the top of their mast was a large piece of canvas, and it was full of wind. The skyward sail was pulling the ship through the dead calm waters. He watched as crewmen manned each of the four ropes tied to the aerial sail.

Rojo slid his spy scope closed and angrily tossed it overboard. He cursed aloud and faced his crew who could see the anger in his crumpled face. Their suspicions were verified as he swept his wings across the table, sending all the fancy tableware crashing to the ship's deck. Slamming his fist on the table he shouted, "Merryweather!"

His first officer nervously appeared quickly at his side. "Aye, sir."

Rojo grabbed his trusted officer by his jacket and then plucked the knife from the table. Merryweather's eyes went wide as Rojo held the knife, preparing to plunge it into the loyal fowl's chest. But then the captain's eyes caught a movement on the ropes. Rojo paused and loosened his tight grip on the jacket of the fowl, slowly walking towards the rope of the ship's sail and dragging Merryweather with him. He looked up toward the highest sail on his vessel and noticed that it had finally begun to waver. He studied and watched it as it soon began to buckle and flutter. *Wind,* he thought. He lowered his arm and finally released Merryweather.

"Mister Merryweather, prepare the ship. Set course for Hitchcock Cove." He brushed off his first officer's jacket and added, "Make haste. I do not care if you have to throw every sailor overboard. We must not lose sight of that vessel."

The Fowl Stench sliced through the blue waters of the Caribbean as if it were riding the edge of a pirate cutlass. Much more mysterious was how the air around the sailing ship seemed as if it were separated from the rest of the Caribbean Sea and more like a gift from Poseidon himself. The excitement on deck was only matched by the pride felt within the heart of the ship's captain.

Buc watched with childish delight as the *Corazón del Mar* fell further behind them, giving them the advantage necessary to arrive at Bodego Bay first. He closed his spyglass and thought back to Thomas' storytelling days. All that time that Thomas was teaching him about Lucky Longfeather, he was actually teaching him about his father. He smiled inwardly knowing that Thomas would have been proud of how far he had come. His inner smile widened as he realized that his father too would be proud. He, like his legendary father, also gathered a rag-tag group of misfits and unwanted pirates to follow in his quest and footsteps. It was a way of pirating that only Longfeather was known for—preventing the powerful from exploiting the weak. This was something Buc always loved about the stories he was told. Now he was on the edge of being one of those stories. Still with a proud grin, he slowly approached his cabin door.

"Have ye conjured a plan, Captain?" asked Robert from behind.

Buc paused before entering. "I have part of a plan, Uncle. But, alas, we must reach the island before we can strategize how to deal with Rojo."

"A half-cracked plan now be better than a scrambled plan later," replied Robert.

"Quoting Longfeather?" Buc chuckled. He thought about how much more weight a quote from Lucky Longfeather now carried since learning that Longfeather was his father. Perhaps all those quotes were words of wisdom meant to be passed down for generations, or perhaps just fatherly advice meant for every Joe bird. Quotation aside, Buc knew his uncle, and Longfeather, were right. Better to have some sort of plan now than to be caught with a sheathed cutlass.

Buc slowly opened the door to his cabin and gave the word. "Call the officers to assemble within."

"Aye, sir," replied Robert.

"Oh, and Uncle," added Buc, "invite Mister Twitch."

One by one, the officers of the Fowl Stench, absent of Mister Ayg, entered the captain's cabin. Buc stood about a table gazing upon the map of the Caribbean with the biography of Longfeather at his side. Robert and Chumlee stood with space between themselves and Mister Twitch, who fidgeted in place, feeling out of sorts in the Captain's quarters.

Chumlee grumbled to himself "*Freak.*", wondering why the captain would invite the turducken to an officer gathering, but he dared not allow the captain to know his disapproval.

"Why are you here?" asked Buc.

Twitch's head tilted in confusion before he quickly stated, "Robert instructed me to join you." Then he turned to leave. "I apologize, Captain."

Buc lowered his gaze to a space behind Chumlee instead. "Not you, mate. Young Edward, you be crew, lad, not an officer aboard my ship, and not here by invite."

Edward peered out from behind Chumlee, who was not too pleased to see the young lad hiding behind him, much less the fact that a stowaway had snuck his way into the captain's quarters. Chumlee grabbed Edward by the back of his shirt. "Out ya go, you little vagabond."

"Belay that, Master Chumlee," barked Buc.

"Sir?" questioned Chumlee, still holding the young fowl by his shirt.

Buc looked at Edward with a certain seriousness. Chumlee raised him to Buc's eye level. "Do ye have somethin' to be sayin', boy?" asked Buc, thinking of all the times Robert had called him "boy" and how the tone instantly sparked a fire in his own belly.

Edward looked down at the decking then back at the captain. "My fate is no different than yours. I deserve to partake," he said, pleased he had thought of something pirate-like to say, but nervous that he may have overstepped his bounds.

Buc signaled for Chumlee to drop the boy. He could tell Chumlee was none-too-pleased. "When you captain your own vessel, Master Chumlee, you can keelhaul your crew and feed them to the sharks to your heart's content; but until that day, mate, my ship, my rules," the captain stated.

Then he looked over at Edward, a corner of his beak curling upward. "Right so," he said. Buc pointed to Hitchcock Cove on the

map. "We shall drop anchor here." He paused then looked up at
Chumlee. "You and the crew will stand ground and defend the Stench.
There be no telling how many men Rojo will have loyal to him. We
must hold them here. Rojo shall not set foot upon that island." The
captain stood upright and faced the men before him, totally confident
that they had all understood the little task he had envisioned.

The distant rumble of thunder was right on cue for the captain.
"Mister Twitch, that is the sound of your destiny calling." Chumlee
and Robert quickly stepped a bit further away.

"I do not understand, Captain," replied the meek bird.

"Why would ya understand, freak?" mumbled Chumlee.

Buc turned to his quartermaster. "Do you understand my
meaning?" he asked, words laced with sarcasm. "Because I have not
yet gotten to that point."

He turned his attention back to Twitch. "Storms a'brewin' out
there, mate. There is no other fowl on these seas that knows the
weather like thee."

"Captain, I am afraid to say I still do not understand."

Buc smiled at the turducken. "When the time comes, you will
know how t'parlay your unique affliction best. Carpe' diem, mate.
Seize the day."

Robert's eyes narrowed, realizing that there was a part of the plan
yet to be mentioned. "And what part of this plan pertains to you,
Captain?" he asked.

Buc exhaled, knowing this next part of his plan would draw
resistance. "I will gather a longboat, travel to the island and locate the
treasure."

"Captain," squawked Robert, "you plan to go ashore alone?"

"That be daft, man!" added Chumlee.

"Aye. We need all hands to defend the Stench. There is no good in
holdin' a treasure if we cannot transport it."

"I do not care for the notion of you going alone," disagreed Robert.
"It's too dangerous."

Buc ran his feathered hand over his maroon cockscomb. "Fine. I shall take Mister Pugwald with me."

Chumlee and Robert looked surprised. "Peg-legged and half blind?" asked Chumlee. "What good would that do for ya?"

Buc eyed Chumlee lavishly before he spoke. "For one, mate, of all the smaller fowl, pelicans are fliers. Not great fliers, but the same cannot be said for roosters and the like. Second..." Buc paused. "Second, I'm the captain so there need not be a second reason."

"Captain, we'll be needin' all hands to fight off the Spaniard's men!" cried Chumlee.

"So ya sayin' he'd be a better fighter than a strong back for rowin'?" asked Buc.

Chumlee and Robert shared a look again.

Buc smiled. "Right then?"

"I can row," added Edward.

Buc shook his head softly and knelt down to Edward's level, "Aye you can, lad. But there's another treasure that needs protectin'. I entrust upon you the most important task on this here journey. You must protect Miss Ava, Miss Esmerelda, and Mister Ayg." He looked over at Robert and Chumlee. "If things go all sixes and sevens out there, to say if things get a bit entangled with soldiers and hostiles, I would rather you all be safe." He placed his hand on Edward's shoulder, "Can ye do that for me, lad?"

Edward nodded. "Aye Captain. But, why do I have to protect that witch? If she fell to the soldiers, you would not be obligated to give us away."

Buc bit his lower beak. "She still be a friend, mate. Besides, never judge your cargo by its crate." He smiled at Edward, "How is my first mate doing?" he asked, trying to hold back his deep concern behind a brave face.

"He pulled his wings and legs into his shell, and there be a weird slime covering the cracks. Miss Esmerelda said not to worry, his body trying to heal itself."

Buc closed his eyes and sighed. When he reopened his eyes, and in a voice that was barely above a whisper he implored the little bird, "Edward, please keep him safe." He inched closer to young lad. "Keep them <u>all</u> safe." He rested his feathered hand on Edward's shoulder for a moment, then stood up to leave. Before exiting, he paused, "and as for your worries about Esmerelda, well, —" Buc's voice was overpowered by a loud shout from outside the cabin.

"Land ho!"

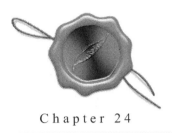

Chapter 24

The Fowl Stench dropped anchor at the center of Hitchcock Cove, its captain stressing a desire to leave enough distance for an escape route if the need arose. The wooden oars of one of the ship's longboats slapped the water surface as Buc and Pugwald set out for the far side of Bodego Bay, the small body of water nestled within the cove. Along the northwest corner of the bay, directly in line with the X found on the map, Buc stared through his spy scope at the opening to a cave. Through the glass he could see vines hanging down, covering the entrance as rushing waters swiftly flowed into the eerily awaiting mouth of the cave. His brow raised in concern. The map of Hitchcock Cove found in Thomas' book labeled the area beyond the X as uncharted territory. There was no telling what awaited them beyond the mouth of the cave. The rush of water could indicate raging rivers or an underground cavern. The uncertainty of those two options would strike fear into the hearts of any normal fowl. But, despite the raging water ahead, Buc was filled with purpose and determination. As they approached the mouth of the cave, the current began to draw them into the darkened cavern, capturing them in its liquid rage.

Buc struggled to light a torch quickly as the longboat took a sharp dive, grasped by the raging waters of the cascading waterfall flowing within. Pugwald tried to control their motion using the oars but couldn't prevail against the turbulent waters holding them firmly.

Unable to break free, the pair were completely without control and at the mercy of the furious current. Swaying side to side with the swift motion of the waters, the longboat glided through the dark cave, guided only by the flickering flame of Buc's lone torch.

"Why is it never just an X in the sand like in all the stories?" he asked aloud as the longboat rocketed through the darkness.

The downward angle of their torrent fall lessened, and Buc could feel the water's fury subsiding. The cave settled them out into a massive cavern deep within the belly of the uncharted interior of the island.

With no reference as to where they were, the two sailors had no choice but to keep moving forward. With the waters speed now more manageable, Pugwald lowered the oars into the water and began to row into the unknown.

"There be no turning back now, eh, mate?" asked Buc, to a relatively nervous Pugwald.

Buc finally had a chance to see what surrounded them in the now calm waterway they traveled. Large stalactites hung from the ceiling, and the water glowed with a turquoise-blue hue. Around them, roots from trees, grown fertile from the volcanic soil, penetrated the cave ceiling and walls and created their own web-like design. Stray strands of light penetrated cracks in the walls, giving the appearance of shimmering veins throughout the cavern. Small pools of heated water created small gurgling springs, filling the air with the faint smell of sulfur, not unlike that of rotting food. Columns of steam rose from the heated water and mixed with the cooler air, creating ghostlike shapes. Large crystal formations buried deep in the rock face produced a spectacle of dancing reflected light.

The ominous glow from the crystals allowed Buc to view a sign that was carefully staked on a nearby stalagmite growing up from the ground. It was a handwritten sign that bore words that appeared almost unintelligible to Buc at first. Its aged wood and partially faded words echoed with years of decay and moisture fueled mold. On second read, he came to realize the words belonged to a particular culture, one he recognized and was reluctant as a youth to learn.

"Tria flumina naviga atque fortunatus es," he read aloud, as if they were magical words meant to open a special doorway directly to Longfeather's legendary treasure trove. "Flumen infortunatum consumet.", he continued.

"What does it mean, Captain?" asked Pugwald, carefully pressing his lucky clover tightly between his feathered fingers.

"My Latin is a bit rusty, as I have not set eyes upon it in a parrot's age." Buc cautiously wondered if this was why Thomas forced him to read and learn the Latin language. Even with his knowledge, the message was shaky. Translating Latin seemed more like a guess or interpretation than a direct meaning.

"Navigate the three rivers and be lucky." Buc pondered its meaning, wondering whether the translation of "lucky" referred to the name "Lucky". He continued, "The river will consume the unlucky."

"Con ... consume?" stammered Pugwald. He began to peer with immense fear at the waters and the walls about them. The air vibrated as a low rumble of thunder filled the empty spaces within the underground river's walls.

"As to say, 'eat'?" Pugwald's feathers shuddered at the thought of being eaten by a river.

Buc stroked his chin again, still rather unsure about the whole interpretation. "I fathom this be some sort of test that perhaps only Longfeather was meant to solve." He was indeed confused, and it didn't take long before the confusion gave way to panic as his sight rested on what lay ahead of them. The massive space they were ejected into now focused into a smaller, more confined area.

Directly in front of the sailors was a physical split in the river, flowing into three different caverns. The single river they had been traveling had given way to three new rivers.

"It would seem we have encountered our first obstacle, Mister Pugwald," Buc announced, staring long at the divided turquoise body of water that flowed ahead.

The three rivers before them were preceded by large, individual stone markers. Each path the river split into was represented by its own marker. Three rivers. Three markers. Upon each of the markers was a symbol chiseled in the stone, like an omen meant to last for all time.

The first cavern river, farthest to the left, had a marker that bore a simple square, the second a diamond shape, and the third a tilted triangle.

"How do we navigate all three rivers at the same time?" asked Pugwald. "That be what the sign said, right, Captain?"

Buc focused hard and studied the symbols, eyeing them as their boat inched forward slowly.

"I do not believe the meaning of the sign referred to these three rivers," Buc finally said. He looked back toward Pugwald. "If so, mate, why not place the sign within view of them?"

When Pugwald refused to reply with nothing more than a dumbfounded face, Buc turned back toward the split river and raised a brow. "I believe we have encountered the first test of three. Three symbols, but which leads us to the treasure?" he asked himself aloud. Thinking back to the stories told him by Thomas in those days, something itched at the back of Buc's mind about the number three. There was something he was desperately trying to remember.

"The diamond," whispered Pugwald, "It be a lucky gem." He pointed toward the river flowing into the cavern with the diamond marker, hoping his suggestion could be of favorable regard.

"Perhaps, Mister Pugwald," pondered Buc, "you may be right. After all—" he paused "—we are looking for treasure." He wagged his finger in the direction of diamond marker.

Oars slapped the water as the duo passed the diamond marker and began to enter the river of their first test. Buc stared over at the last marker. Something about its shape and position seemed to rattle his memory. Just before the marker left his view, Buc's mind snapped, and his eyes lit up.

"Back us off, Mister Pugwald!" he shouted.

"Sir?"

"Back off! Back off!" Buc reached into the water and began to back paddle out of the diamond marked river. The overly warm waters soaked his feathered hands as he frantically struggled to move the longboat backwards.Back at a safe distance, Pugwald held them steady.

"I believe I've made a grave error that could have cost us our lives."

Pugwald swallowed hard and reached for his lucky clover.

"It is not the diamond, it is the triangle," Buc announced, relieved they did not venture too far down the wrong river, subjecting themselves to the river's fury.

"Are you certain?" asked Pugwald.

"Lucky's lucky number was three, a fact Thomas repeatedly made note of

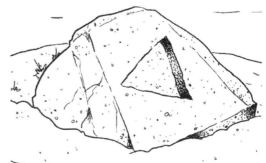

each time the number three came up." Buc began to explain, "Whenever the number three came up, Thomas would say, 'Lucky's lucky.'" Buc hoped his explanation made enough sense to make the Pugwald understand. He waved his hands in the air eccentrically. "Three rivers; three markers." He squinted deep in thought. "I think the key to this puzzle is the number three." Waving a feathery finger, he pointed to the triangle marker. "Three rivers; three sides on a triangle," he explained. "Consequentially, that triangle is also pointing down that river," he said, pointing his soaked wing toward the third river.

Pugwald looked at the river marker then back toward the diamond marker. "If ye are wrong, the river will consume us. The sign. Remember the sign!" His eyes went wide with fright as he spoke and frantically clutched his clover.

Buc flashed a reassuring smile, letting go of his own doubt and fear first. "Let us hope that the sign was being metaphoric," he said, "and not really intended to mean a genuine eating of the unlucky."

He motioned toward the triangle marked river. "Onward, Mister Pugwald," he ordered. "We have treasure to find."

As Mister Pugwald began to row, Buc hid his worry about his decision. What if he was wrong? What if this was the wrong path? If he was to be consumed by the river, what of his friends, his family, his crew?

For the better part of an hour, Buc and Pugwald rowed through the cavern river. The repeated 'drip, drip, drip', of water and humid air became a constant reminder of how deep and gone they were. Steam continued to rise from the water as the temperature in the cave began to increase. Roots from trees several feet above them on dry land grew downward as if trying to reach any weary traveler senseless enough to engage the river. Despite being truly nervous, Buc was growing more confident in his decision as time edged forward. The two pirates had not since been consumed by the river nor encountered any adversities. Yet, the proud rooster's confidence was about to be tested once again as they approached another split in the river. Just as before, each split in the river had a stone marker at the mouth of its cavern entrance. But unlike the previous puzzles, these markers contained an even more strange set of symbols. Although the previous puzzles' markers contained geometric shapes, these seemed to be simple line drawings on the rocks. The symbols were not letters, numbers, or shapes in the English language. And Latin definitely wasn't to be consulted either.

"Are those markings of the devil?" asked Pugwald nervously as he rubbed his clover and spat in the boat.

Buc looked down at where he spat and glared back toward Pugwald.

"Sorry," apologized Pugwald.

Buc chuckled. His snorted laugh was not because of the comment from his crew member, but at the symbols. He was beginning to realize that the ensuing journey kept forcing him to remember events from his past. The first test seemed to be in relation to something Thomas had so desperately tried to teach him in his youth. It seemed the second test would also relate to a past lesson.

"This be bunk," young Buc would proclaim. "For what reason would I need to learn this?" he remembered asking Thomas about odd looking symbols at a time when his young curiosity always got the best of him.

"You never know what knowledge you be needin' in the future," was the standard reply he'd get. Eventually, under the careful schooling of Thomas, Buc had managed to learn them well enough to satisfy the old booksmith.

"Thomas, you crafty devil," Buc said aloud.

"So, they are markings of the devil?" asked Pugwald once again as he inhaled saliva from his mouth.

"First, Mister Pugwald, please refrain from spitting in my boat again," Buc said with a stern look. "And, second, my reference was to something an old friend forced a young headstrong chick to learn." He pointed to the three stones in succession. "Those are runes." The cavern rumbled, and Buc looked upward with his torch, hoping it was just an echo of thunder brewing on the surface.

"Yes. I agree. Those are ruined. If not for those shapes carved in them, they'd be good rocks," Pugwald stated. Humorously, Pugwald only wanted to hear what he wanted to hear.

"No. Not 'ruined', runes! They are ancient Celtic symbols," explained Buc.

"Aye," replied Pugwald, "that be what I meant." His eye looked away from Buc as he added, "But they are ruined as well." He reached into his pocket and threw a pinch of salt over his shoulder.

Buc set his focus on the runes and strained desperately to recall their meanings. Now was not the time for guesswork. He closed his eyes and his head bobbed lightly as he recalled distant memories. He pointed at the second rune symbol. "That," he said, "that is the symbol for 'sun'".

Pugwald looked at the symbol. "Are you certain, Captain? It looks more like a bolt of lightning." Pugwald lit up. "Perhaps it represents Mister Twitch. He be keen on lightning."

Buc rolled his eyes. Pugwald was becoming more ridiculous as every second ticked by. Perhaps it was the fear of being consumed or the storm brewing above that excited his personality. "I should have sailed alone," he muttered to himself.

"And just how, perchance, would Lucky Longfeather know that someone searching for his treasure would not only have a turducken on his ship, but one whose affliction be lightning?" he asked Pugwald, his voice dripping with sarcasm.

Pugwald scratched his head, thinking of an answer. Snapping his feathered fingers, he exclaimed, "Witchcraft!"

Buc shook his head. "As much as I enjoy your enthusiasm, I must ask you to remain quiet while I ponder our latest debacle."

"But sir—" Pugwald was quickly cut off by Buc.

"Shush, Pugwald."

Pugwald removed a string of beads from his pocket and placed them around his neck. He then spun around twice in the boat and prepared to spit before making eye contact with his captain. Pugwald swallowed hard.

As Buc examined the next rune, the boat began to inch closer to the entrance of the far-right river. The motion of the boat didn't fail to reach his attention.

"Mister Pugwald, back us off. I do not wish to find out what may happen if we accidentally enter the wrong river." Buc's mind leapt back to the sign at the entrance to the multitude of rivers. He cared not to find out if the sign was being literal and unlucky travelers would be consumed by the river.

Pugwald began to paddle the boat off as Buc examined the rune directly in front of them.

"Upward line, half an arrow," he mumbled. "Ah!" He snapped his fingers. "That one means 'lake'."

One more, he thought, focusing on the last rune symbol. There was a familiarity about it that he could not recall. His concentration was broken by the echoing sound of a feather-plucking scream deep in the distance.

Pugwald went stiff and began to shiver. Buc, no longer focused on the symbols, realized the scream was coming from within the system of caves. The scream itself carried with it two meanings. First, the warning on the sign, about the unlucky being consumed by the river, was apparently all too real. The river would deal harshly with trespassers who answered incorrectly. Second, there was no doubt in his mind they were being followed. There would be only one fowl who could have possibly found them; only one fowl who would risk everything and everyone to find the treasure. *Rojo*. The thought stung his mind like a swarm of bees.

Above them, in the far distance, the air echoed and rumbled with the sound of cannon fire. The resonating sound gave confirmation that The Stench had engaged the enemy. Not only was Rojo possibly on the river, but his band of pirates were now locked in a battle with Buc's own crew. This sent an invisible shiver down Buc's spine. This was the endgame. The entire quest came to this. There was absolutely, positively, no turning back now.

Pugwald began to turn the boat around with swift, panic laced motions.

"Belay your actions, Mister Pugwald," he said calmly, hiding his own deeply buried desire to turn back as well.

"But, sir, the cannon fire? The screams?"

"There is little we can do from here. Our only option is to press forward, remain one step ahead of our adversaries, and hope our crew manages the same." Again, he smiled at  his crew member. "Apparently, unbeknown to me, my friend Thomas bestowed a wealth of knowledge upon me just for this task." His smile faded, and his eyes moved rapidly, as if he was following some unseen flying insect. "That's it. Wealth. That rune is the symbol for wealth."

Buc's joyful revelation was once again interrupted by the distant sound of a feather-ruffling scream. It seemed to echo throughout the walls of the cavern river as if the river itself was passing on a message to any who dared challenge it. Buc stroked the feathers of his chin.

The screams, he thought, *the timing is too gathered. Too close together to be another attempt.* His face dropped as he came to a dreadful realization. *Multiple boats?* His stomach tightened into a powerful twisted knot. "Rojo is doubling down," he muttered aloud.

"Sir?"

Buc turned his gaze to his crewmate, still engaged in thought. "Rojo is playing a sick and dangerous game with his crew. "He spoke quickly, and his breathing increased, reflecting his rising anger. "There are three paths. You send three boats." Buc grit his beak. "The crewman on the boat that hears two screams is on the right river." Buc sneered. "Instructed, no doubt, to return and reacquire Rojo."

"But—" Pugwald paused as his own thoughts sent his feathers into a ruffle "—that means he be sending his crew to almost certain…" Again, he paused.

"Death," said Buc, completing the pelican's statement.

"Aye," whispered Pugwald.

"Mister Pugwald," muttered Buc.

"Sir?"

"You may spit now."

Pugwald spit and spun in one of his elaborate superstitious exhibitions, rubbing his clover and his beads, and tossing salt over his shoulder once again.

"Fowl like Rojo consider their crew expendable." The thought ruffled Buc's feathers. "They are nothing but shields to protect him from the real danger." He inhaled deeply. "Danger he so carefully avoids."

"What does it mean for us, sir?"

"It means, Mister Pugwald, now it is time to move with haste, for time is no longer our ally."

Buc pointed in the direction of the rune symbol marked 'Wealth' and Pugwald began to row.

Chapter 25

The Stench rocked and swayed in a fog of smoke and gunpowder as Robert and Chumlee led the battle against Rojo's crew. Wood splinters filled the air as another round of cannon fire hit the Stench's port side.

"Keep firing!" shouted Chumlee, ordering the crew to press on against the relentless attack from the Corazón del Mar.

Robert looked toward the cove then back toward the battle at hand. In a fight of firepower, the Stench was no match for the Corazón, and he knew it. "Master Chumlee!" called out Robert. "We need to bring her alongside."

"What? Are you daft, old man?" replied Chumlee, eyes wide and furious.

"No, mate," explained Robert. "At close range, her cannons be useless. They not dare fire at such close range for fear of backlash. Aye, we may be less than twelve score of men, but we stand a far better chance in close proximity than at a distance."

Chumlee's eyes went wider as he realized that Robert's words held truth. He dashed across the deck to the capstan, which controlled the anchor, and began to raise it. Marley and Twitch rushed to his aid, making the task of lifting the heavy steel anchor just a tad easier for the burly quartermaster. As the anchor rose out of the water, Twitch secured it, watching Chumlee sprint back across the deck and up to the helm. Upon arrival, he turned the wheel sharply.

"Prepare to be boarded!" he shouted.

"Every fowl to the ready!" shouted Robert. "Gather your swords and pistols and fight for your measly lives!" His loud, bellowing laugh left an eerie feeling on the deck as the Stench moved closer to the Corazón del Mar.

"You there! Turducken!" he shouted toward Twitch. "Gather the woman, the children and Mister Ayg below and tuck them in the captain's quarters for safe keeping."

"Aye sir!" shouted Twitch, on the move immediately.

Twitch hurried down the stairs as another round of cannon fire from the Corazón rattled the walls. "Miss Esmerelda!" he called. "Miss Ava!"

Ava popped her head out from the far end of the deck, hidden in the darkness. The little bird obviously had gotten used to battle cries and rumbles of cannon fire. "Mister Twitch? What is it?" she quickly asked.

"Mister Robert has asked me to escort you all to the captain's quarters for safe keeping." Twitch spoke in hurried tones, sensing the urgency.

"Are we not safer here?" she asked as air exploded with wooden splinters, the result of a cannon ball breaking through the outer hull of their deck. They all hit the deck as bits and pieces of the Stench were showered down upon them.

There was no need for Twitch to answer; Esmerelda, who had followed behind Ava, quickly gathered the children together as Twitch assisted her in carrying Mister Ayg.

"Hurry. Do not wait for us. Go. Go," shouted Esmerelda.

Twitch pulled a hammock from the wall and created a make-shift stretcher for him and Esmerelda to carry the ailing Mister Ayg. As they carefully wrapped him in the canvas, they dealt with the sticky ooze that covered the cracks where Ayg's wings and feet previously protruded. They slowly climbed the stairs one at a time, paying close attention to the precious cargo they carried in their hands. As they reached the last step, in the midst of smoke and embers, they heard a one-word shout from Master Chumlee. "Incoming!"

They ducked down to the decking as close as they could as another cannon ripped through the railing and upper deck, sending shrapnel and splinters of wood flying about. As the rain of wooden debris subsided, they resumed their task of delivering Mister Ayg to the captain's quarters.

Edward held the door and fanned away the smoke and dust with his feathers as the two entered. Aside from loose items being scattered about, and a small indent in the port wall, the captain's quarters was in relatively good condition. Twitch, still carrying half of Ayg's stretcher, looked at the damaged wall, hoping it would hold fast to more cannon fire.

Ava created a nest of pillows and blankets on the floor on which to lay Mister Ayg. "Place him here," she said softly.

The ship jostled and the sound of grappling hooks could be heard as they hit the deck railing. Loud shouts from angry pirates filled the air. They had broadsided Rojo's ship and were being boarded.

As Esmerelda opened the hammock carrying Ayg, her mouth fell open and she hissed in shock.

Fear flashed across the others' faces as they too gazed upon Mister Ayg—and the large, wooden splinter running through his shell.

Chapter 26

Once again, it became clear that Buc had made the right decision regarding which river the duo should travel. He could not help repeatedly thanking Thomas in his mind for the lessons he so patiently gave him. Perhaps if Thomas told him what the lessons were for, Buc would have been more eager to learn. But telling a young chick the lessons are meant to prepare him for a future treasure hunt is not the best way to keep a young one's attention.

The river reset in dim silence. Gone were all the drips and drops of water. The air was humid and warm, and the once crystal clear, turquoise-blue water had now been replaced with sandy sediment making the waters murky and unremarkable. The sides of the cavern walls were smooth and glasslike. The cavern shook, this time more violently than the last. Buc peered overboard through the murky water to see the faint glow of magma emanate from the river floor. It seemed the closer they inched toward the final test, the more peculiar the river became.

As Pugwald guided the longboat through the cavern and around the next bend, the air rang with the feather-curling scream of another sacrificed sailor. Rojo had made it to the second river.

Pugwald stood up in panic.

"Steady, Mister Pugwald." Buc tried to comfort his crewman. "By Lucky's rules, we should prepare for another before too long."

Pugwald sat back down and continued to row along the curve in the river. Ahead of their longboat sat the next and final river test. The markers for this trio of rivers were again different from the last. They were not simple boulders with moss covered carvings; they were smoothly carved rectangular stones with no symbols upon them at all. Nothing upon the rock indicated a difference between each river as in the tests before. Instinctively, Pugwald backed them off as they reviewed the options before them.

"Downright faceless, Captain," cried Pugwald.

"Perhaps," replied Buc as he studied the stones. Was this part of the test? He looked up at the large stalactites hanging from the cavern ceiling. He listened carefully hearing a clap of thunder rumbling in the distance mixed with the occasional roar of cannon fire. Retrieving his compass, he attempted to determine whether the test was one of navigation. The compass needle spun erratically before finally resting still. But it did not point north. It pointed to the nearest marker. *Is this the answer?* Buc thought. He moved his arm toward the direction of the second marker and the needle jumped. It now pointed toward the other marker. Buc stared at the marker in front of him. He grasped one of his coat buttons and snapped it off. Gently, he tossed it toward the marker in front of him, and it stuck to it.

"Loadstones," he muttered.

"Sir?"

Buc smiled. "Fill a path with loadstones and even a seasoned sailor will lose their way." He turned toward his pelican crewman. "Something an old friend told me." Buc pointed to the stone in front of them. "These markers are loadstones. Magnetic in nature. They wreak havoc on a fowl's compass." He showed the compass to Pugwald as the needle danced around, confused, and bewildered as he was.

"Longfeather is toying with us." Buc remarked. Buc pocketed his compass. "Bring us closer, Mister Pugwald." Pugwald slowly maneuvered the boat, bringing them within an arm's reach of the first marker. As the boat touched the shore, Buc reached out and placed his hand on the magnetic marker. He slid it up and down the face of the marker, feeling the occasional grooves and bumps that made the seemly smooth marker rough.

One by one, they moved to each marker and Buc gave each the same attention, slowly stroking and patting each of the stones in order to discover their secret meaning. Each was carved in the same manner. Each had grooves and bumps on its face. Each seemed no different to the last.

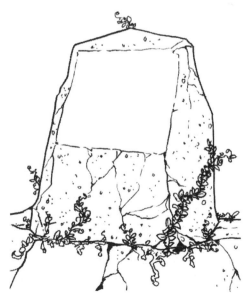

Disappointed, Buc sat down at the bow of the longboat, staring at the marker before him. "Perhaps we are too late," he wondered aloud. "Perhaps time has wiped clean the message intended for us."

Pugwald placed his oar in the boat and stood up. "I'll go, Captain."

Buc remained seated, turning in place to face Pugwald. "What?" he asked.

"I'll go," repeated Pugwald. "Permit me to take the boat down one path. If I survive, I shall return for you."

Buc slowly shook his head. "And if you do not return?"

Pugwald swallowed, forced himself to stand straight, and tried to hide his lucky clover from Buc's sight. "Then you will know at least one path that is wrong."

Just as Pugwald tried to hide his lucky clover, Buc tried to hide a prideful smile. "Completely and utterly unacceptable, Mister Pugwald," he replied.

"But sir—"

"Mister Pugwald"—Buc allowed his smile to show through—"as much as I appreciate your generous offer, I must insist…" He paused. "You are not expendable."

Pugwald slowly sat back down.

Buc returned to face his stone adversaries before him. "These, Mister Pugwald, are just another test for us to conquer—" he eyed Pugwald "—together."

Pugwald smiled and let out a small sigh of relief.

"Now, if you would be so kind as to back us off and take us back to the first stone marker, we shall redouble our efforts to solve this ponderous riddle."

Pugwald lifted the oars from within the boat and prepared to lower them into the water. Another river-rippling scream funneled throughout the system of caverns. Pugwald jolted and the oars slapped the water hard. He looked back toward his captain.

"We knew it would come, Mister Pugwald. It was only a matter of time." Buc turned back toward the marker and his gaze widened. "What do we have here?"

The surface of the stone had changed. Dark lines appeared at the base of the third marker. Buc leaned forward and rubbed his hand across the transformed area. He looked back at his open palm, now moist with water.

"Sorry, sir, I must have splashed the stone when the oars hit the water."

Buc's cheeks hurt as his smile widened. "Splash the stones, Mister Pugwald. Splash away!" Buc reached into the water and began to splash the third stone. As the water ran across the face of the stone, the grooves and bumps began to fill, revealing additional darkened lines and areas. Slowly, an image began to appear on the face of the stone.

Buc and Pugwald stopped splashing as they gazed at the fresh image on the stone.

"That not be possible, Captain," proclaimed Pugwald, clutching his lucky clover, "not possible at all."

Buc too was at a loss for words. His perplexed gaze examined the design on the stone, not fully understanding its meaning or, in fact, how it came to be.

"Obviously possible, Mister Pugwald, though one would think it improbable," he muttered.

Upon the surface of the third stone was a replica of Buc's flag. The flag given to him by his aunt on the day of sailing. The flag that stood tall as the Fowl Stench battled the governor's own Triumph. The flag which now waved on the mast of his ship doing battle with Rojo's pirates. The skull and cross feathers.

Buc didn't wait for Pugwald to row over to the other stones. He began splashing the stones with water to reveal what they had hidden on them. As water sprinkled about, the second stone revealed its design to be the same flag. Again, the two splashed at the first marker; this time Pugwald used an oar to gain distance on the spray.

As the splashing subsided, Buc sat down once again at the bow of the ship, systematically looking over each stone.

"But they are all the same, Captain," cried Pugwald.

Buc looked at the third marker then back to the first. He looked over at the second marker then back to the third. Pugwald tried to keep up with his head movements to determine what he was attempting to do. Buc's head continued to snap back and forth to each stone.

"No, Mister Pugwald," barked Buc with excitement, "they are most certainly not the same."

"Sir?"

"Look here." Buc enthusiastically pointed at the second marker with giddy excitement. "These feathers are not the same as those." He shifted his focus to the third stone marker. "The skull here, it is shorter than the other two." He turned to face Pugwald, the excitement of a schoolchild filling his eyes. "The flag IS the test."

"I don't understand."

"She knew," mumbled Buc, realizing that his aunt knew whose flag it was. He smiled inwardly. "Found it in a marketplace." He thought back to when she first presented the flag. No. The flag was not a bargain to be had amidst the fabrics and fruits of the Port Royal Market. The flag was the banner that flew high upon the pirate vessel known as the Fortunada. The ship was captained by his father, Lucky Longfeather.

Buc turned his attention back to the flags and again smiled. "You crafty devil," he said.

"Sir?"

Buc turned toward Pugwald. "That is the flag of Lucky Longfeather. That is why it is on the markers."

Again, he turned back toward the split in the cavern river. "Only a fowl who knew the flag intimately would recognize the real flag." He closed his eyes again, revisiting the time he first laid eyes on the flag. He thought it was a magnificent representation of what it meant to be a pirate. Slowly, he opened his eyes and pointed to the second marker.

He didn't need to make a sound as Pugwald began to row down the final river, and, with luck, to the treasure it held.

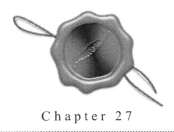

Chapter 27

Esmerelda hesitated to remove the piece of wood piercing Ayg's spotted, and discolored shell. She and the twins called to Ayg, but he did not respond. Not a shake, nor a wobble. She worried removing it could cause additional harm to his injuries, but in the same turn, leaving it could be causing additional harm as well. She examined the large splinter of wood from every possible angle, and finally decided it had to be removed. With him not responding to their questions, and his cracks all covered, there was no telling what could be happening inside his shell. She grabbed the far end of it and slowly removed it. Inch by inch, the shard of wood came out. "Oh my!" gasped Ava. As the last inch of wood was removed, it became visible that it was covered with blood.

The fighting outside grew louder, and Twitch did not hesitate to join the battle. Despite the injury to Ayg, Twitch knew he was in capable hands. He swallowed his fear, ready to fight for his crew. "I'm off," he said as he sprinted out the cabin door, closing it behind him.

Esmerelda touched the blood at the end of the splinter. Then, to the others' surprise, she flicked her forked reptilian tongue at the wood.

"Eww," Edward murmured, watching Esmerelda tongue lapping at the blood.

"No ewww. Dat's good." She wiped her fingers on her dress. "De blood is warm. De taste is fresh." She looked toward Ayg. "Dat means he still wit' us."

The hole made by the splinter was now covered with the same slimy residue that covered Ayg's other cracks. It prevented Esmerelda from seeing inside the shell and verifying that her thoughts were correct and that Ayg was, in fact, alive. Ava grabbed a few more water-soaked rags and placed them on Ayg's shell as the room lit up with the intimidating glow from the lightning outside.

The flash of lightning made visible to Edward a shadowy figure looming outside the cabin door. He watched as one of Rojo's thugs attempted to open the locked door. He looked about the scattered items on the floor of the cabin in search of something to use as a weapon. A weapon was what he found. He considered himself lucky that the captain had additional swords stored in his cabin. Struggling as he was, with two hands, he lifted the sword high as the door busted open. The lock on the door crumbled as its wooden casing gave way to the force of the intruder.

Edward leapt back as the thug approached, sword at the ready. The goon swiped hard at Edward. Metal hit metal as the force of the thug's blow easily knocked Edward's sword down.

"Edward, no!" shouted Esmerelda.

The goon backhanded Edward across the head, knocking the small fowl down and across the floor.

Esmerelda dropped the hood on her cloak and snarled in anger at Rojo's hooligan. His faced crinkled as he cringed at her hideous sight.

Esmerelda lunged at the distracted thug, madly swiping her clawed hands, tearing her target's clothes, and drawing first blood.

Rojo's thug shoved Esmerelda backward and drew his sword.

Esmerelda regained what composure she could, growled madly, and lunged once again at the thug. He raised his sword and stabbed her straight though her scaly, reptilian chest.

She let out a long, loud hiss at her attacker before grabbing her chest and falling backward to the cold, hard deck.

"Esmerelda!" screamed Ava, running to her side.

"Heave way, child, as I end this monster," demanded the thug.

Ava threw herself in front of Esmerelda. "No. Leave her alone. She's no monster. You're the monster!"

The thug grabbed at Ava and started dragging her out of the way. He gasped in pain as cold steel came down on his arm. Edward stood tall, holding the sword in his hand. "Get away from them!" he shouted.

Rojo's goon grasped his arm then tightened his grip on his sword. "Do not think being a child will stop me from killing you!" he grunted. As he approached Edward, he stopped, as a glass jar made contact with his face, shattering and splattering his face with a warm liquid.

It didn't take long for the liquid to penetrate his feathers and seep into his skin. As his face slowly dripped with a red liquid, he began to scream in pain.

Ava looked at the shattered remains of bottle she threw into the face of her brother's attacker. It was one of Esmerelda's spice bottles. The crudely written label read, "Hot peppa' oil."

Rojo's thug screamed, holding his face in pain. He stumbled backward through the broken doors of the captain's cabin and out onto the deck.

"Oy!" came a loud, bellowing voice from outside.

The injured thug turned to come face to fist with the Stench's own quartermaster, Chumlee. The blow knocked him across the deck and he fell unconscious on the hard wood below.

Ava and Edward crouched next to Esmerelda as she clutched her chest. As Ava reached out to her, Esmerelda began to shake violently. The twins backed away from her and quickly hid behind Chumlee.

Esmerelda's arms thrashed outward, her claws tearing into the wooden floor of the captain's quarters. Her pain was visible as she hissed and snarled loudly, foaming at the mouth. Chumlee held tightly the handle of his sword while the children hid behind him, occasionally peeking out from the sides. The vile woman thrashed from side to side, her tail whipping about in a mad frenzy. She dug her reptilian claws deep into her face and began tearing at her own scale-covered flesh. Shrieks of pain filled the room as she began to glow. Chumlee and the children shielded their eyes from the intense light.

The glow turned into a green flame, covering her entire body. Her clothes burst into flames and her green, scaly skin followed. The intensity of the flame was too great for the three observers to see Esmerelda any longer. The flame extinguished in a large flash, leaving her curled up on the cold, hardwood floor, a bright white glow still remaining.

As the glow subsided, the three lowered their wings from their eyes. Blinking away the dancing spots of light, they saw that Esmerelda was gone. In place of the green, reptilian hideous woman sat a beautiful, crystal-white-feathered hen.

"Sweet mother of pearl," muttered Chumlee.

The hen held her feathered hands over her face, feeling its shape and texture. Realizing her face was no longer distorted and covered in reptilian scales she stretched out and looked at her long, beautiful, white-feathered wings. She slowly stood up and saw for herself that she was no longer the hideous, grizzly beast she once was.

Ava slowly approached her. The little fowl's eyes were kind and filled with a newfound sense of hope. Her tiny, blue eyes fluttered as she realized she had seen this woman before. Edward rushed to his sister's side as Ava gently removed the locket carefully concealed under her shirt. She opened it and gazed at the locket portrait inside then back toward Esmerelda.

Ava's eyes widened. Since they were left at the orphanage, she had always dreamed that her mother was alive. She prayed that her mother was out in the world, desperately searching for her and her brother. Her tiny beak trembled as she managed to force out a single word, a word she had not spoken in a very long time. "Mama?"

Esmerelda knelt down and spread her wings wide. "Hello, my precious little ones," she said softly. Tears ran down the side of her face as she gazed upon her children for the first time in a long time with her real eyes.

Edward and Ava ran to her and she clutched her two children as close to her heart as possible.

Edward could not believe it, but it was true. Esmerelda was the woman in his sister's locket. Esmerelda was their mother.

Chumlee was shocked and confused. "She be your mother?" With a nod from Ava, Chumlee quickly realized why Buc had allowed the children to stay onboard only after he had seen the contents of her locket. *"He knew all along."* He thought. "Son of a finch.", he swore under his breath, realizing what a crafty fowl his captain truly was.

His secret praise for his captain was quickly abated by the familiar scream of Mister Twitch, as he ran past the cabin door followed closely by one of Rojo's crew. Chumlee pulled his sword from its sheath and turned to rejoin the battle.

"Wait!" shouted Esmerelda. She looked around the cabin floor and located the sword her son Edward had used. Picking it up, she tightened her grip around the handle.

Chumlee was perplexed. "I never known you to take up arms before," he stated.

Esmerelda looked at her two children and back to the powerful quartermaster. "I never had dis much to fight for."

Ava ran to her mother. "No!" she cried out, tears forming in the corner of her eyes. "We won't lose you again."

Edward joined his sister in embracing their mother.

Esmerelda comforted her children as best she could. "If Rojo succeeds, then we all lose." She mussed up Edward's feathered head. "I will not lose you this time without a fight." She knelt down and kissed her children. "You must protect Mister Ayg. He is in your charge now. Captain Buc is dependin' on us." She paused. "He's dependin' on you to look over him."

Once again, Twitch ran past the cabin door, this time in the opposite direction.

Esmerelda stood up and nodded to Chumlee.

The burly quartermaster opened the door as Twitch once again ran by. Chumlee reached out and grabbed his pursuer by the back of his shirt and slammed him to the ground.

He exited the cabin followed by Esmerelda who, before closing the doors, gave her children one last instruction.

"Bar the door."

Chapter 28

Captain Buc and Pugwald continued down the last river having solved the final puzzle left by the pirate Lucky Longfeather. The air grew warmer and the cavern walls grew tighter. The high ceiling that had seemed out of reach now hung low, barely over their heads. They continued on, occasionally avoiding large stalactites and stalagmites like the teeth of a mythological dragon protecting its treasure. Buc wondered what kind of a bird would follow Rojo and lay down his life knowingly on a dangerous path like the river tests. Crew are meant to follow orders and he hoped, if the time came, his crew would follow orders as expected. He let an inner smile seep through as he realized it's not the crew, it's the captain. Crew will follow orders, but only the captain can determine the plenitude of danger. Rojo purposely sent those men to their deaths. That was an act Buc could never see himself doing. He looked at his crew member sitting across from him in the longboat.

"Mister Pugwald," he called out, "allow me to take the oars for a spell."

Pugwald looked at the oars in his hands and back toward his captain nervously. "Have I done something wrong, Captain?" he asked, worried.

"No, Mister Pugwald." Buc chuckled. "I merely desire to give you a bit of a rest." He gestured for the oars, and Pugwald hesitantly handed them over.

Pugwald looked at his empty hands and awkwardly folded his wings. He switched left over right then right over left in desperate need of finding comfort. He reached down and placed his axe in his lap, holding its handle tightly.

"Relax, Mister Pugwald," Buc said, taking long strides on the oars.

"Sorry Captain," apologized Pugwald. "My father always said, 'Idle hands do the devil's work.'"

Buc snorted and chuckled. "If by chance the devil shall appear, I promise to relinquish the oars to your care."

Through his red beard, Pugwald forced a smile as he tightened his grip once more.

"Might I inquire as to the axe?" asked Buc.

Pugwald looked down at his axe then back at his captain. "Sir?"

"The axe. Why choose it over the lengthy sharpened steel of a saber or cutlass?"

Pugwald ran his feathered hand across the blade of his axe' "'Twas my father's," he replied. A sense of family and pride filled his eyes as he looked back toward Buc. "He too was visually impaired," he explained, pointing to his eyepatch. "He said, 'Swing an axe and you be bound to hit somethin.'"

The boat rocked with Buc's heartfelt laughter, reminiscent of his childhood, "Too true, Mister Pugwald, too true."

Pugwald smiled, loosening his grip upon his axe. "And your sword, Captain? Where did you acquire it?" he asked.

Buc look at the hilt of his sword. "As I was told by my uncle, Mister Pugwald, this sword has been in our family for a very—" his voice trailed off "—long—" the space between words was filled with cold emptiness "—time."

Buc, realizing that Lucky Longfeather was now part of his family, a simple heirloom would no longer be a common trinket. He thought back to the stories of Longfeather and his sword Tempest. Tempest was the sword that freed a thousand slaves and plundered a thousand treasures the legends stated. *This could not be Tempest?* Buc shook the thought from his mind, but still continued to ponder the concept of family.

His Uncle was doing battle on the Stench, as Ayg, although in name only, his brother lies sickly amidst a raging battle. He wondered *"Should I have not left the ship?"* Once again, he shook the thought from his mind. Perhaps it was the musty, sulphur ridden air, but Buc's mind was ricocheting from thought to thought. *You must live with the decisions you make.* Thomas' words rang true today as they did back in the day when he first heard them. But he knew there was no changing his mind or turning back. He was off the edge of the map now.

As he continued to row, Buc wondered if perhaps the real Tempest lie among the rest of Longfeather's treasure, the rage of the sea surrounded by the plunder of a thousand vessels. The answer, he knew, would have to wait until they stood squarely on the same ground as the treasure itself.

Chapter 29

The deck of the Fowl Stench was a veritable battlefield, with Rojo's men outnumbering the crew of the Stench. Chumlee could not help noticing that Rojo's men were just waiting on the deck of the Corazón. Their only movement happened when one of their crew was knocked out or injured. Rojo's crew outnumbered the Stench two to one. Their plan was simple. Tire out the crew; take the ship.

Lightning crackled across the dark, stormy sky, sending a shiver down Twitch's spine. The rain fell hard on the turducken as he glanced over at the Corazón Del Mar; the crew members simply sat and watched, as he, Chumlee, and the remaining crew of the Fowl Stench continued to press on in midst of battle.

Chumlee slammed his closed fist into the skull of an approaching goon, knocking him unconscious and to the deck. "We need to put an end to this!" he shouted. He looked about the deck.

"Where be Robert?" he asked.

Twitch didn't hear his quartermaster's question and ducked as the sky exploded in a bellowing rumble of thunder. Lightning illuminated the sky making the heavy rain more visible.

From his crouched position, he eyed a harpoon tucked along the decking. He looked up toward the main sail and the mast that held it. Perhaps it was the tingle of static electricity coursing through his veins, but Twitch was hatching a plan. He stood fast and grabbed the closest coil of rope. "Master Chumlee, can you throw a harpoon?" he asked.

"What?" shouted Chumlee, fighting off two attackers.

"Can you throw a harpoon?" asked Twitch once again, emphasizing each word.

Chumlee punched the closest attacker in the face then kicked the second in the gut.

"Since before I could walk." He forced one of the attackers in a head lock and continued to punch him in the face. "What are you getting at, freak?" he said, releasing his exhausted opponent.

Twitch tied the end of the wet rope to the harpoon and handed it to Chumlee, "When I give the word, throw this at their mast!" he shouted.

"You don't give me orders, freak!" replied Chumlee, raging with anger, intending to lash out at the turducken. Lightning lit the sky and in an instant Chumlee understood the turducken's plan. "Aye!" he shouted, taking the harpoon from Twitch. "This'd better work, freak!"

Twitch didn't hesitate, he let Chumlee's warning roll off him like water off his own back. Grasping the rope tight, and letting it out as he moved, he began to climb the rigging of the main mast. The wind raged, and the weight of the water-soaked rope made it difficult to climb.

Esmerelda watched as Twitch slipped on the rigging, falling several rows. With the wind whipping him about like the Stench's own flag, Twitch held tightly to the rigging with one feathered hand while clutching the coil of rope in the other. He looked below at his crewmates as they fought off their own obstacles on deck. Esmerelda elbowed her attacker in the beak, throwing him off guard. In his dazed state, he was no match for her dragging him to and over the railing. Chumlee fought three attackers, and Twitch watched as he took a blow to his head from one of them. Chumlee fell to the deck and fought desperately as the three goons beat on him relentlessly.

Twitch tightened his grip and looked up at the top of the tall, wooden mast. A sense of determination cascaded over him. He looked down once again and saw Chumlee make progress with his attackers. This was the boost he needed to motivate himself. Twitch climbed, faster and harder than before. He reached further, scaling the rigging at double speed. Within the last reach of the highest point, Twitch yelled down toward Chumlee. "Now, Master Chumlee! Now!"

6 Below him, Chumlee, still fighting off two attackers, used the harpoon itself to dispatch them. Holding the harpoon tightly in his hand, Chumlee did not hear the cries of Twitch warning him of an attacker approaching from behind. Chumlee eyed the mast of the Corazón Del Mar and inhaled deeply. As the goon snuck up behind him, Chumlee pulled back swiftly, elbowing the goon in the face. His arm recoiled, hurling the harpoon forward and straight into the mast of the enemy ship.

He looked down at the goon at his feet then back up toward Twitch.

Twitch stood atop the Fowl Stench, holding the soaking wet rope in one hand, balancing himself as he stretched up toward the sky. Seconds seemed like hours as the storm raged but nothing happened. He closed his eyes, took a deep breath. "Seize the day," he mumbled. Stretching upward once again, he screamed. His loud, awkward scream was overpowered by an even louder echoing clap of massive thunder. Lighting leapt across the sky and arced downward only slightly toward Twitch.

A single branch of lightning continued to descend, splitting itself, as if it desired to reach out and hold the turducken's trembling hand. The sky exploded. Mister Twitch ignited in a glow of electrified air. The enormous blast of electricity travelled down the wet rope. Moisture turned to steam as the powerful surge moved swiftly across the railing toward the metal harpoon. The wooden mast exploded under the relentless force of the electrical energy. The sound of cracking and splitting of wood filled the air and the main sail mast of the Corazón Del Mar came crashing down, dragging much of the ship's rigging with it. The sail burst into flames and bits of flaming rope and wood fell to the deck.

Twitch, smoldering in the darkness, fell limp, losing his grip on the rigging he was clinging to so tightly. He fell downward rapidly toward the deck of the Fowl Stench. With his last bit of strength, he opened his eyes to see the swirling smoke and grey sky above him as his body came to a jolting stop. Chumlee was balanced carefully on his knees, holding the turducken in his arms, having caught him only moments before the potential wooden impact. He gently laid Twitch on the deck, extinguished a small smoldering feather from his head, and summoned Esmerelda.

She ran to his side. "I shall take it from here, Master Chumlee."

Chumlee quickly rose to his feet, his full focus now trained back toward the crew of the Corazón Del Mar. Rojo's crew was shuffling across their deck, scrambling to avoid falling, burning debris. Chumlee was quickly joined by Marley and the rest of the crew of the Stench. Each member had their pistol drawn and their cutlass at the ready, pointed at the crew of the smoking ship.

The Corazón crew began to assemble, pointing their pistols as well. Lead was about to fly when a loud thud of metal-on-wood intervened. Mister Merryweather, former soldier of the governor, current crew member of the Corazón, threw his pistol to the deck. His action was soon after mimicked by the rest of his crew.

Chumlee smiled wickedly. His smile widened as Twitch approached, hobbling, and still smoldering. Chumlee smacked him with a friendly gesture on the back. "You did good, Mister Twitch. You did good." Smoke continued to emanate from the turducken's charred body.

Twitch stammered. "You … you called me Twitch."

Chumlee didn't say reply; he let his smile speak for him.

Twitch approached the railing of the ship and across the water, the crew of the Corazón stepped back. One crew member fainted, and others looked on in fear.

Chumlee raised an eyebrow, intrigued that after his epic display, the crew feared Twitch. Fear was a pirate's greatest ally.

He was about to laugh when a scream came bellowing from the captain's cabin. Quickly, Chumlee handed Twitch his pistol and drew his sword. "Watch them," he said, pointing to the crew of the Corazón.

Chumlee and Esmerelda darted to the cabin where the children's scream came from. At the entrance, Chumlee struggled to open the door, but it wouldn't budge, still barred from the inside as Esmerelda instructed. From inside the cabin, the sound of crashing glass and cracking wood filled the room. Chumlee took a step back, prepared to break down the door when it opened wide. Ava and Edward darted out of the room, directly into the arms of their mother.

Chumlee, prepared to attack whatever lay ahead, stopped dead in his tracks. He dropped his cutlass, stumbled backwards, and fell lifeless to his knees.

"Sweet mother of pearl!"

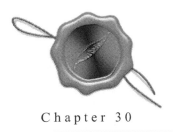

Chapter 30

Buc and Pugwald continued down the ever-narrowing cavern river, still uncertain as to what might lie ahead. Despite the mystery awaiting them, Buc could not help but reflect on his life. His head ached as he relived moments from his past, wondering how much of it had been pre-planned. Knowing his father was Lucky Longfeather justified his childhood yearn for adventure. Knowing his father died protecting him and his mother from Rojo made him angry. He thought back to Thomas and all the lessons, all the stories he read to the eager young chick. His mind ricocheted as he began to worry about how he would react if he were to come beak to beak with Rojo.

"Sir!" cried Pugwald, pointing beyond the captain's sight. "It seems we have reached an impasse."

Buc looked up to see the end of the river. The river's end was not a dead-end cavern wall but a lush jungle oasis. He was curious as to how the plants could grow within the dark cavern. Somewhere they had to be getting sunlight. He held his lantern high, curious if the roots travelled upward to a higher point in the cavern.

As their longboat touched the water's edge, the silent oasis presented a disturbing feeling of danger. Overgrown vines hung low from the trees as if they were trying to prevent visitors from seeing what lay ahead. Barely visible through the thick foliage and dense, humid air was a wall of solid stone blocks. The two sailors exited the longboat and began to make their way to the stone construct. The sticky air made vines and leaves stick to their clothing, almost tugging at them, pulling them back and away from potential danger.

The wall was a magnificent fabrication. A handcrafted wall guarding one of the greatest treasures any fowl could ever dream of. Buc glared at the wall, knowing all too well it could also be a trap. He ran his feathered hand over the closest blocks of stone, quickly realizing the blocks were not at all the same. Some of the stones were not composed of rock but made of a curious form of glass. Buc wiped one of the dingy glass blocks with his sleeve, removing the condensation and years of caked on mold. Walking along the wall, he noticed several more glass blocks. Gently gliding his fingers over one of them, they came to rest on a series of small holes cut deep into the glass. He pulled his torch closer to the glass block allowing him to see several grooves cut inside them. The strange carvings on the inside of the glass blocks gave the wall a more mysterious nature.

"Sir!" shouted Pugwald.

With his shout, the air filled with a high-pitched ringing. Pugwald pointed to a large, horizontal stone set at what would seem to be the

heart of the construct. The stone was covered in black dots. Painted on with tar to preserve them, the line of dots varied in height to one another, yet still seemed grouped together with purpose.

"What do we have here?" said Buc. Again, a melodic ringing sound filled the damp jungle air. "Did you hear that?" he asked, bewildered at the source of the annoyance.

"That sound?" asked Pugwald. "Aye. What is it?"

Buc held a finger to his beak to silence Pugwald. He waited and listed for the sound to fade. Once the the shrill sound concluded, he had a realization. "The sound appears to only take place when we speak," he whispered. He waited until he realized his whispers did not initiate the ringing sound.

Pugwald looked confused.

"It seems the louder the voice the louder the ringing," explained Buc in a hushed tone as he continued to examine the strange wall. He took several steps back and noticed a large series of intricate patterns of blocks at the top of the wall. Above them was a vast pile of rocks and debris, held in place by the rocks and vines below it. He closely examined the wall, taking careful note of the glass blocks and their resting locations. Tracing the spaces between the rocks with his fingers, he ran his feathers over the variety of both large and small. Each was held in place by even smaller rocks, vines, and green, flourishing moss. He flicked one of the glass blocks and the air once again filled with ringing.

He smiled. "I wish my uncle were here," he said softly.

"Why?" asked Pugwald. "Is he a good whisperer?"

"No, Mister Pugwald." Buc chuckled softly. "This is an engineering dream." He looked up at the wall. "And he loves puzzles."

"I do not understand, sir," replied Pugwald, now holding his lucky clover and beads in his shaking hands.

"By all accounts, anyone trying to gain access would think to break the glass blocks and let the wall crumble," he explained.

"Right," said Pugwald, placing his trinkets in his pocket and grabbing his axe.

"Hold fast!" snapped Buc in a hushed tone. "No need for that."

"Sir?"

"If you break the glass blocks, the stones above it will fall—a reaction that may bring the rocks and debris above down upon us and the entrance," explained Buc. "That would seal the cavern and the treasure would be lost behind a mountain of stone and earth."

"So, if we cannot break our way in, how do we get through this wall?" asked Pugwald, once again trading his axe for a clover.

"Those questionable dots must hold the answer." Buc looked over the black dots carefully painted on the stone. The distance between each dot was the same, yet some were higher or lower than others. *All the prior tests had something to do with Longfeather,* he thought. He touched the first dot and traced an imaginary line to each of the dots hoping a shape would trigger in his mind. He was missing something. Each test was solved by something he had learned from his friend Thomas. Thomas must have taught him something about these black dots.

As Buc stared at the dotted puzzle before him, Pugwald was performing an experiment of his own. He gently tapped one of the glass blocks and a familiar ringing sound echoed all about the two birds. He proceeded to tap another one, and again another ringing sound filled the air.

Buc's head snapped round. "Tap that block again," he instructed Pugwald. Pugwald tapped the block. "And the other now?" asked Buc.

Pugwald tapped the other glass block. Both times the ringing sound occurred but with a slight difference.

"That first block made a higher pitched sound than the second," he said aloud, causing the blocks to sing once again.

Buc looked at the black dots on the wall then stepped back and looked at all the glass blocks. After taking a quick look, he stepped forward to the black dot pattern and began tapping each one. As he tapped a dot, he hummed a sound, and whispered, "They're notes, mate." Buc looked inquisitively at the block wall and again took several steps backward. *Music.*

He closed his eyes, took in a deep breath through his nostrils, and began to sing aloud. "With the wind in our feathers, we all flock together, Yo, ho! Is a pirate so lucky!"

The air vibrated with high pitched resonance, as if song birds were reaching for their highest note possible. Two blocks of glass at the far end of the wall shattered and several stone blocks above it slid down, flipped, and shifted with the rustling sound of grinding sand. Pugwald jumped back and quickly moved behind his captain.

"On our way we set sail," Buc continued, "with the wind at our tail. Yo, ho! Is a pirate so lucky!" The lower notes caused another set of glass block to resonate and shatter. Vines tugged and snapped. Stone blocks slid into new placements, and slowly Buc could see an opening starting to form. He looked up at the large pile of debris and stone above the opening. It remained perfectly in place. The shattered glass and moving blocks did not affect the support system that was in place to prevent the landslide.

"All the loot and the swag, shove it all in our bags. Yo, ho! Is a pirate so lucky! We take what we can, that was always the plan. Yo, ho! Is a pirate so lucky. Yo, ho! Is a pirate so lucky!" Buc sang the final verse of the pirate shanty he had been singing since he was a small chick sitting in Thomas' bookshop. Dust and sand filled the air as blocks flipped and tumbled while others slid down into new positions. Vines seemed to come to life, gently affecting the order of the stone blocks. It was as if an enormous puzzle came to life and began to move under its own free will. When the dust settled, the wall had reformed itself into a new shape, and this new shape was a doorway.

Chapter 31

With the entrance to the cavern now revealed, Buc unexplainably hesitated. The darkness ahead of the two pirates seemed infinite and unforgiving, and the dimly lit jungle refused to share any light with the cavern before them. Buc could not help but wonder what lay ahead of them. Was it the true treasure of his father, the pirate, Lucky Longfeather? Did his father really die at Kismet Key, or would Buc find his father's corpse clinging tightly to a goblet of gold, his skull adorned with a jewel encrusted crown? His thoughts rolled back to the stories he had read about Longfeather's triumphs over the greedy individuals who used and tortured innocents to gain their wealth. He continued to gaze deep into the blackness as if it were a doorway to his past and his future. Was this to be the end of Thomas' story of Longfeather? Was the truth of his demise about to be revealed? Was this the final resting place of his father? Buc's focus on the darkened cave was cut short by the radiating heat of a flickering torch, held by Pugwald.

Inside the cavern, Buc realized the immense magnitude of the quest he had undertaken. As the captain of a merchant vessel, he knew what a fully stocked ship's hull looked like. He could calculate the amount of merchandise and cargo he could carry in a single voyage down to the last weighted bead. Even the largest of galleons had limits to the amount of cargo they could carry. But no single galleon, not even the Fortunada, could have carried the treasure overpowering his sight. At first glance, Buc calculated that the treasure currently visible by the light of his torch could burst the hulls of over a hundred galleons. At his feet, loose pieces of eight lay scattered about, pieces of gold and silver possibly touched by his own father. He knelt down and touched the gold coin closest to him. A sense of pride flowed through him. A feeling of accomplishment.

Pugwald stepped into the cave, his beak wide open and his gullet fluttering.

Buc stood upright and turned back toward his crewmate. "We're gonna need a bigger boat." A prideful smirk crossed his face.

Pugwald swallowed hard. "We'll be needing a fleet of ships for this haul."

The two-fowl ventured deeper into the cavern, mesmerized by the sheer magnitude of the treasure. Nowhere in history was it ever written that Longfeather amassed such wealth. Chests of gold coin, statues, and trinkets from all around the world flowed over the damp, musty cave floor. Gems and jewels shimmered in the glowing light. Buc reached out and touched a gold candlestick that had become encased in a stalagmite growing out of the cavern floor. Indeed, the treasure had been here a long, long time. Torches and lanterns were left behind, no doubt by either Longfeather or his crew. As Pugwald and Buc lit them, drips of water continued to fall on top of the stalagmites, covering them in a milky fluid flowing off the stalactites above them. The majestic awe of the treasure was interrupted by the sound of rattling coins. The floor seemed to shimmer in the torchlight as a small tremor shook the cavern. As the cavern settled, Buc refocused his gaze beyond the gold and jewels. He waved his torch about, looking around the cavern for possible skeletal remains. But none could be found. There was no indication his father's resting place was anywhere other than Kismet Key.

Buc turned toward Pugwald, who had helped himself to a crown and string of pearls. "We have a problem," he said.

Pugwald slowly removed the crown from his head and placed it on a nearby pile of gold. "Sir?"

"Rojo," muttered Buc.

Pugwald flinched. "Aye sir. We have to be prepared for when he arrives."

Buc's brow fell hard, and his eyes became slits of anger. "He's already here." He fixed his eyes beyond Pugwald.

Pugwald turned to see Rojo standing at the entrance to the cavern behind one of his crew. His crewman's face locked in surprise as he looked down at Rojo's blade sticking through his body. Slowly the blade retracted, and the crew member fell to the ground.

Rojo wiped his blade clean on the shirt of his fallen crew as Buc released his own sword from its sheath. "I'm mighty proud of you, boy," said Rojo. "I knew you were cunning, but this…" He spread his wings wide. "This is a monumental accomplishment."

"How so?" asked Buc, careful of Rojo's every move.

"I had to sacrifice six fowl to find the right path, and you—you did it with one lone, lame duck." Rojo moved slowly, inching his way closer to Buc's position in the cave.

"I am no duck. I be a pelican," barked Pugwald, feeling the need to correct the Spaniard.

Rojo chuckled. "As if it matters." His head wobbled as his insult flew.

"Enough!" snapped Buc. "Pugwald is as brave as any pirate on my crew. But I don't expect a beastly fowl like you to understand bravery or honor."

Rojo's eyes widened as he turned to point to his fallen crew member. "That?" He snorted. "One less bird to share the treasure with, lad." He then pointed his sword toward Pugwald. "You might be well to do the same to that one."

"You are mincing words, Rojo," said Buc. "The treasure of Lucky Longfeather was always meant to be shared with the likes of Mister Pugwald here. Not with the likes of you."

Rojo's beak curled and his eyes constricted. "This treasure was meant for someone exactly like me," he commanded. "It was meant for someone to use to change the world, to make the world a better place."

"A better place for you, not for those who actually need a better world," replied Buc.

"Helping the weak and pathetic will not make the world a better place. Longfeather was a fool."

"Do not speak ill of my father again!" shouted Buc; anger filled his lungs as he pointed his saber at Rojo.

Tremors filled the cavern, treasure clattered and clanged in response to the vibrations. Unlike before, the quaking did not subside quickly. Buc looked toward the entrance to the cave and saw the rocks from the trap above beginning to fall.

"Mister Pugwald," he ordered, not breaking eye contact with Rojo, "make haste to the exit. Get clear of this cavern. Fly through and true."

"Sir?"

"You heard me, Mister Pugwald. If this goes south, I want you nowhere near it."

"Sir, I shan't leave you," insisted Pugwald, holding his axe high, loyal as any English knight.

Buc broke his steady gaze to turn to his crewmate. "Remember what I told you. You are not expendable." Sincerity filled his voice, showing his appreciation for loyalty. Buc returned his gaze toward Rojo. "Return to the Stench at once, Mister Pugwald, that is an order," he called.

The cavern shook once again, mightier than before. Stones continued to fall at the entrance and stalactites along the ceiling of the cavern began to give way and break up. Pieces of calcified stone fell from the ceiling above.

Pugwald took flight and began heading down the path they entered, now covered in coins and gems shaken lose from their resting place. He was struck by a falling rock from above, planting him face first into the treasure on the floor beneath him. Before Buc could question his well-being, Pugwald used his wings to gain speed and ran out the entrance of the cave, taking flight once clear of danger.

Another strong tremor shook the cavern. Cracks in the floor began to appear, giving way to the bright orange glow of molten lava. The rocks protecting the entrance from thieves gave way, and heaps of stone and earth fell, sealing the entrance, with the two birds inside.

Dust and powder filled the cavern air. Jets of steam, rising upward from the cavern floor, moved the particles through the air.

Buc took several steps forward toward Rojo, his footing complicated by the uneven treasure-covered floor. As Rojo approached, Buc swung at him. His blow would have ended any untrained swordsman, but Rojo was no amateur. Buc's sword was easily blocked and deflected by Rojo. The clash of metal rang out  throughout the cavern, resonating off the walls. Buc leapt backwards, avoiding a jab from Rojo. The coin-covered floor caused Buc to slide across its surface as if he was floating on ice. Rojo followed him, hoping the sharpened steel dance had not ended.

"Perhaps you should have practiced your footwork more," said Rojo, swiping again at Buc.

Buc knew Rojo was the more expert swordsman, but it didn't matter — Buc was determined to defend his father's honor.

Buc flinched back and returned the action as his sword hissed through the air and clanged against Rojo's. He kicked up some coin at Rojo and used his reaction time to gain better footing. He stood tall atop a rock formation, above Rojo, gaining the higher ground.

Rojo swung at Buc's feet, missing as Buc leapt up and over Rojo. Buc landed firmly, surprising even himself. Rojo swiped at Buc's back, catching him off guard and tearing through his coat, drawing first blood. Buc, still reeling from the pain, swung around fast, the tip of his blade making contact with Rojo's cheek.

Rojo stumbled back across the coined-covered floor. He touched his feathered fingers to his face and gazed upon the blood Buc had drawn. Enraged, he surged forward and attacked Buc. His attack was blocked, but Rojo pressed on, swiping, and swinging wildly.

Buc stumbled back, trying to regain his footing while continuing to block Rojo's vigilant attack. The metallic song continued to ring throughout the cavern. Buc stabbed forward at Rojo who parried and expertly disarmed Buc.

Buc stared deep into Rojo's eyes, wondering if the Spaniard had it within him to strike him down. The robin's brow overshadowed his eyes, giving no indication of mercy or generosity. Buc watched as Rojo prepared to make his final move. As Rojo's blade began to swing, Buc closed his eyes tight and then—nothing.

Is this it? Buc wondered. *Has death taken me? Is there no pain?* He opened one eye to see Rojo's sword stopped mid swing by another sword.

Standing hilt to hilt with Rojo was Buc's uncle.

"Robert," Rojo sneered, "so nice of you to join us."

Robert levied and pushed Rojo off and away. "Get away from my son, you parasite-encrusted vulture!" he growled with unrelenting fury. Rojo, as well as Buc, stared at Robert in blind confusion.

Robert soaked in the wicked pleasure from Rojo's confusion, the veins in his forehead pulsating with ferocity. "You failed to realize one thing those many years ago at Kismet Key when you killed my brother." said Robert. He pointed his sword directly at Rojo. "You killed the wrong Longfeather." He took on an attacker's stance, "I am Lucky Longfeather!"

The color rushed from Rojo's face as Robert continued, "And I will pluck every feather from your hide and roast your body in public before I allow you to lay another feather on my son."

Rojo stumbled backwards, his eyes wide in rejection. "No. Not possible." His arms grew heavy and fell to his side as he dropped his sword.

"But it is." Robert stood rigid and strong. His hand tightened around the grip of his sword. "The riches you have been seeking all these many years belongs to me! Captain Lucky Longfeather."

Rojo continued to stammer backwards, tumbling into a pile of treasure; a rush of disbelief surged through his body.

Robert turned toward Buc. Slowly, Buc rose to his feet, dazed, and confused by the newfound knowledge.

"How?" shouted Rojo, regaining his stance.

Robert, still looking upon the shocked face of Buc, turned back to Rojo. "The tale is simple. When you attacked my village, Good Thomas and I were standing right here, amidst the treasure of a thousand plunders." His words fell heavy on Rojo's ears. "On our return, we found the village desolated, our loved ones murdered, and a Spanish flag sailing away in the distance."

Rojo grew tense. The thought of being tricked by a simpleton pirate irritated him.

"I spent the next few years wallowing in self-pity. I had lost everything I held dear. I travelled from village to village and drowned my sorrows from tavern to tavern."

A lump seemed to rise in his throat as he continued his tale. "I held the wealth most men would kill for, and yet I was as empty as a shucked oyster. It was not long before I fell into utter disarray, spending my days and nights drunk on cider, under the unrealized care of the tavern's barmaid."

Rojo's beak trembled as did the cavern floor beneath the trio.

"Until one night the barmaid told me of whispering about town. Tales of a Spaniard claiming to be searching for the family of the only survivor of Kismet Key"—his spine tightened, and face crumbled in anger— "a small chick." He hardened the grip on his sword. "In all my years on Kismet Key there only be one child ever hatched upon its shores." He looked back toward Buc, then returned his gaze toward Rojo, "My son." Robert glared intensely. "I will tell you this"—he pointed the tip of his sword—" telling others that you sailed to Kismet

Key with intentions of aid and assistance was low, even for you. But stealing my only son and then pawning him off like an unwanted cob makes you nothing less than a monster."

"I had my reasons," grumbled Rojo, reaching for his sword.

"I was sure you did. That be the moment when the barmaid and I hatched our plan to pose as relatives. We sent the word out. Lies spread from the belly of a tavern."

"No. My sources... "

"Your sources were deceived by ME!" he shouted, his voice echoing throughout the cavern as more stones fell. "We spread the tale. We laid the breadcrumb trail that led you to our door." Another tremor shook the ground beneath their feet. Fissures opened, and the smell of sulfur mixed with steam shot upward. Through newly formed cracks, the glow of hot molten magma radiated outward.

"Enough of this!" shouted Rojo, steadying his footing. "I was prepared to kill one Longfeather for this treasure; I have no reservations about killing another."

"I have been looking forward to this day for a very long time, Rojo."

Rojo moved forward toward Robert, recklessly. Robert backed off, stopping only when Rojo was in striking distance. Metal clashed as the two swordsmen danced what would be a final battle. Robert swiped at Rojo, the swoosh of the blade cutting the air in front of Rojo as he tucked back.

The two birds stood at the ready. "You fight with the recklessness of a child, Rojo."

"And you fight like an old bird, Robert—" he peered at him smugly "—or do you prefer 'Lucky'?" Rojo then jabbed forward, his blade blocked by Robert. The two birds closed in, their hot breath only overpowered by the steam filling the cavern.

"There's something else you don't know, Rojo," huffed Robert, his face almost touching Rojo's as their swords remained locked.

"What might that be?" asked Rojo, his brow raised inquisitively.

Robert swung his clenched fist into Rojo's face, cracking his beak in the process. The blow unlocked the two pirates, separating them and creating space between them. "Not a thing," said Robert. "Just a distraction so I could bash you." He turned to Buc. "Been waiting a long time for that, I have."

Spinning one hundred and eighty degrees, Robert lashed out at Rojo chest, hoping to end the battle once and for all. The sound of his steel blade colliding with Rojo's chest armor echoed off the cavern walls. What would have been a final blow was deflected and rendered inert.

Rojo laughed aloud, beating his chest plate like an angered gorilla. "Made by the finest craftsmen in all of Spain," he touted.

Robert's face crumpled as the cavern shook violently once again. New cracks formed in the cavern floor, revealing more exit routes for the molten lava. Robert smiled as he leapt to his right, landing directly over a newly formed crack. The heat emanated from the opening, blackening many of his feathers. Robert, resisting the heat, lunged his sword into the crack then quickly heaved it outward. His sword, now engulfed in molten lava, glowed vibrantly. Quickly, he stepped closer to Rojo and swiped wide from left to right. Lava splashed forward landing on Rojo's front chest plate, scalding several feathers in the process.

As the lava began to eat through the Spanish metal, Rojo frantically began to remove his armor. He pulled the armor over his head, carefully trying to prevent the melting parts from touching him. Throwing his armor aside, he heard Robert laugh.

The laughter subsided as Robert saw his own lava covered sword begin to melt. This time Rojo laughed as Robert tossed his melted sword to the ground.

"Uncle!" shouted Buc.

Robert turned to see Buc tossing his sword in the air. The same sword his uncle had once told him had always been in the family.

Robert took three steps back and easily caught the sword by the hilt. He turned the sword and felt its weight in his hand.

His fixation on his sword was quickly broken as Rojo approached Robert with a downward thrust. Robert blocked the blade and was thrown backward by the force of the Spaniard's blow.

He struggled to regain his footing as Rojo swung relentlessly and wildly at Robert. Knowing he was backed into a corner, Robert kicked at Rojo's leg, causing his footing to let loose as he fell over. Robert stood up and regained his stance.

Rojo regained his own footing and moved swiftly toward Robert, swinging wildly once again. The two were beak to beak, trading blows until suddenly Robert's eyes went wide. He looked down to see Rojo's knife stuck into his chest.

Robert stepped backward, as Rojo retracted the blood-stained knife from his chest.

"No!" shouted Buc, his voice echoing through the cavern. Rocks fell, and thunder could be heard rumbling beyond the stone walls.

Buc ran to catch Robert as he began to stumble backward and off his feet. "I have you, Father." Buc's voice fluttered.

"Father," whispered Robert, the corners of his mouth slowly curling to form a smile. "I have waited a lifetime to hear you call me Father."

"Lie still." Buc tore cloth from Robert's shirt and pressed it on the wound. Robert flinched as the pain shot through his body.

"That was my favorite shirt," said Robert, making Buc smile.

"Buc"—he looked deep into his son's eyes— "everything I did was to protect you."

"Father, there is no need for me to forgive you. I am everything I am today because of you. And now I know why I am as I am. In my veins flows the blood of my father, Lucky Longfeather. The fever that has burned within me for adventure is all because of you."

Robert smiled, but it faded quickly. "You must end this, Buc. Countless others will suffer the same fate as Kismet Key if that devil lays claim to this treasure."

Buc's chest heaved, and he felt as if every muscle in his body was on fire. A surge of anger and determination filled his heart.

❼ He looked down with empathy at his father. "Barnacle Bob, you shall live. That be an order from your captain." He smiled gingerly as he rose confidently to his feet.

Buc reached for his sword. He pushed his emotional cargo down deep and stood tall.

"Rojo!" he called out, his voice filled with years of compressed anger. "This ends now."

Rojo, plundering through the vast treasure, dropped the jeweled goblet he was admiring and turned to face the angry fowl. "There be no need for us to fight, boy."

Buc's face flushed red with anger. The ground shook violently beneath his feet as if the cave itself sensed the resentment growing within.

"Look around you, lad. Enough wealth for a dozen lifetimes." His voice went somber. "Help me transport this bounty to my ship. Together we can share the future of Port Royal, son."

Buc gritted his beak as Rojo's words cut him deep to his core, deeper within than any sword could possibly reach. His face was twisted with fury as he lifted his cutlass and pointed its glistening blade directly at Rojo. "I am not your son. I was NEVER your son. I am the son of Captain Lucky Longfeather, and I swear by all the lost souls of Kismet Key, by all those who have suffered by the extent of your greed, that on this day I will end you."

Rojo swiped left and right with his sword, delirious with pleasure. "Brave words from a fowl who until recently was a merchant sailor. Do you think a few weeks at sea can turn you into a pirate?"

Rojo swiftly attacked Buc, losing his footing as the ground began to shake. Buc seized the opportunity, stretched out and lunged forward. His attack was swiftly blocked by Rojo.

"Ah, perhaps there is a pirate in you." Gold and silver coins flew about their boots as the two engaged in a blood-pumping battle. Steel on steel clattered and echoed through the cavern as new fissures opened, spewing hot steam into the air.

Rojo swung wildly at Buc, missing him. His momentum turned him about as he slid on the coin-covered cavern floor, giving Buc the opportunity to swipe at Rojo's back.

"Ahhhh," he cried out. Rojo spun back around and aggressively swiped and parried toward Buc. Buc expertly blocked Rojo's attempts, driven by a deep, unseen impulse. As Buc blocked the latest of Rojo's attacks, the Spaniard grabbed Buc's wrist and held it tightly. Sword against sword, he pulled Buc in close. "It seems luck is on your side, young Buc."

Buc flashed a quick, cunning smile, his eyes ever bright and alive. "No mate," he replied, "luck be in my blood." He shoved Rojo off and took a steady stance, blade ready to fight.

"Then it be time to spill that blood," barked Rojo, agitated and irritated.

The two birds locked in a metal-clashing battle. Stones fell, and fissures opened. Rojo began to swipe wildly at Buc, like a rabid animal attacking with no reason, but his moves were skillfully blocked as the ground began to shake once more.

Beneath their feet, the coins trembled as the unstable volcano began to roar to life. Cracks in the cavern floor began to open and emanate the bright orange glow of molten hot lava. Steam and lava spewed upward through the cracks, creating a visual spectacle of heat and mist. Above them, the cavern ceiling began to crumble. Pieces of rock and stone began plummeting downward. Robert, clutching his chest wound tightly, crawled, and pulled himself toward the outer walls for safety.

Rojo looked about the cave floor as piles of gold coins, jewels and shimmering trinkets began to tumble downward through the rifts in the floor, lost to the volcano's rivers of lava below, decades of treasure from around the world now lost forever. The cave shuddered once again. Rojo, off balance, dropped his sword, holding fast to nearby stalagmite for safety. He watched as Spanish gold coins, Egyptian statues, and Incan artifacts all plunged into the depths of the volcano's belly.

Rojo cried out in anger as he watched the great shimmering floor slowly disappear before his eyes. He turned to Buc; burning anger filled his bloodshot eyes. "End this now! There still be time to save the treasure." His head whipped around at the jingle of coin and clatter of trinkets as they toppled and spilled into newly formed breaches. "The treasure, Buc!" shouted Rojo. "Your adventure has always been about the treasure!" Hot, lung-burning steam filled the cavern and the odor of sulphur wafted about, mixing with the humid air.

Buc turned his gaze toward the side of the cavern. He looked upon the face of his father clutching his blood-soaked chest. Buc thought of all he had gone through in his life. All the times his uncle was there for him. All the crazy notions and ideas Buc would devise that his uncle would entertain. All the skinned knees, bruised eyes, and broken bones. The hurricanes he spent huddled in a corner, clinging to him for safety. The day the pair visited his birthplace, Kismet Key. He looked deep into the soulful eyes of a fowl who he could have always, easily, called his father, and he realized the truth of his journey.

Buc innocently turned toward Rojo. He sheathed his weapon and sighed deeply. "Rojo," he called out, "I have all the treasure I need."

Rojo roared aloud as the cave trembled and the ceiling continued to crumble above them.

"End this madness. Leave the treasure. Come with us. Save yourself." Buc cautiously extended his hand to Rojo. Deep in his heart, he hoped Rojo would choose his safety over the treasure and understand that life meant more than greed.

A deep frown creased Rojo's face. "I am Capitán Vientre Rojo!" he shouted. Rage filled his eyes as he retrieved his pistol from his belt, pointing the barrel at Buc. "There only be one way you shall leave this place." He cocked the pistol. "Over my dead body." The sound of the shot filled the cavern like a percussive symphony. Buc, failing to react in time, flinched as the lead ball grazed his left shoulder. The cavern shook violently, and the roof crackled and crumbled, finally giving way to its own weight. A large section of the cavern ceiling broke loose and plummeted downward. Rojo screamed as the massive stone impacted the cavern floor, crushing him under its enormous weight.

Light beams from above penetrated the stone-dust-filled air. Rain poured into the opening, creating a new thickness of sticky steam. Fiery jets of lava erupted from the cavern floor. Buc, clutching his shoulder, looked up at the large opening in the ceiling then back to where the large piece impacted. "Over your dead body you say? Agreed." Outside, a loud, ear-piercing screech penetrated the opening and echoed off the cavern walls. The floor of the cavern began to break up rapidly. Stalactites fell from the ceiling as their opposites crumbled to the floor below. The impact from the ceiling stone had set off a reaction, breaking the floor into chunks of rock now floating on an ever-growing lake of molten lava.

Buc leapt from stone to stone, struggling to maintain his balance in an attempt to reach his fallen father. Another loud screech filled the entire cavern. The volume of the screech compelled Buc to stop in his tracks and cover his ears. When it faded he continued to leap stones, eventually reaching his injured father.

"We must get out of here," he said, cradling his father in his arms.

Robert smiled at his son; his eyes twinkled in pride. "There only be two ways out of here now, son." He pointed up at the opening at the top of the cavern.

"And the other?" Buc asked, the heat causing sweat to drip into his eyes.

Robert just smiled at his son, perhaps for the last time.

Buc understood his meaning immediately.

"No. I refuse to leave you here to die!" he begged, continuing to hold his father in his feathered arms.

"There may be no other way, son," said Robert, his eyes welling up like an overflowing tub. "Save yourself, Buc."

"No. There must be another way." Again, the loud screech filled the air. A deep darkness moved across the cavern floor as Buc lifted his father to his feet. "We will do this together," he said.

The ground shook once again, and the floor where they stood broke off and began to drift out into the sea of lava. Embers danced about them as the treasure continued to fall into the lava flow. Streaks of gold and silver now mixed with the lava as the treasure melted, losing its forged shape.

As the two stood on their own tiny island in the midst of the growing flood of lava, Buc realized this could be the end. At their feet, the stone on which they stood began to crack. Robert looked at Buc. "I want you to know I have always been proud of you, boy."

Buc forced a smile, hiding his deep concern and worry.

❽ Once again, a dark shadow encompassed the cavern. Buc looked up at the opening above and saw a dark, winged figure approaching from the air.

The cavern filled with the sound of another glass-shattering screech. From above, the large bird dove into the cavern through the spacious opening.

As the stone on which Buc and Robert stood began to split, the large bird extended its powerful talons and plucked the two pirates off the stone. Spreading its massive wings, the bird climbed upward, ever higher, exiting through the same hole it entered. Buc watched below as the rest of the cavern floor disappeared into an orange pool of lava.

The air felt cool upon his feathers compared to the heat of the cavern below. He held his father tightly, just as his father held him for so many years. The mighty bird circled several times before Buc decided to question its motives.

"I would like to thank you, but I can say with all certainty I do not know who you might be." Buc was gracious, but cautious. He had no idea if this bird was friend or foe.

Buc fluttered as the large bird swiftly ducked its head under its body. Its brown, sparkling eyes were narrow, with one scarred from top to bottom. The mighty bird glared intensely at its two passengers detained tightly in its powerfully sharp talons and simply smiled.

It was a smile Buc had seen a million times before. A smile that warmed his heart and fed his thirst for adventure. A smile usually found drawn upon the shell of his best mate. "Ayg!" Buc shouted! "You hatched!"

Ayg let out a small, happy squawk.

Buc looked over his magnificent friend. No one living at Madame Hensworth's Orphanage could have imagined that the little egg, bobbing and stumbling through the halls, would emerge as such a majestic creature. His shimmering brown and gold feathers, accented by his stark, white head, made for a dazzling appearance. Ayg always had the heart of an eagle, and now he had the shape of one too.

Buc laughed loudly but his celebration was cut short by a cry of pain from Robert.

"Ayg, take us to the Stench, with haste," he called.

Ayg replied with another squawk and veered off toward the Fowl Stench.

Chapter 32

The dust and smoke had finally settled. The storm subsided, and the fanfare of thunder and cannon fire had come to an end. Scattered across the deck of the Fowl Stench lay fragments of wood and debris, a reminder of the recently enraged battle. In submission and kneeling on the battle torn wooden deck planks, was the crew of the Corázon Del Mar. Their surrender was now complete, and Master Chumlee stood triumphantly over them, sword, and pistol in hand. As he watched over his prisoners, the sky darkened, and a gust of wind filled the air as if an enchanted storm was about to wash over them.

Above the ship, the newly massive form of Mister Ayg hovered, flapping his mighty wings, creating the windy breeze. Flapping his newly found wings to maintain aloft, he gently lowered Captain Buc and the injured Robert to the deck below. Once placed safely on the deck, Ayg rose back into the air and perched himself on the nearby railing.

"Esmerelda!" called out Buc. "Esmerelda!" he shouted again, hoping she would be willing to look after Robert's wounds.

Esmerelda pushed her way through the crowded deck and approached Buc.

"Esmerelda?" he inquired. Her new form was a welcome, but unexpected sight to him. "It warms my bones to see you whole again, love." Buc lowered Robert, helping him lie down on the cold decking. "'Tis a knife wound."

Esmerelda wasted no time in tending to Robert. She tore at his shirt to reveal the wound.

"Again, with the tearing?" muttered Robert.

As Buc watched Esmerelda administer aid to Robert, Ava slowly approached him. "You knew?" she asked.

Buc, still kneeling, looked her deep in her grateful eyes and smiled, "From the very moment I saw the portrait in your locket," he said, gently touching the locket around her neck. "I know what it is like to be an orphan." He looked at Esmerelda. "I hoped bringing you together would somehow break the curse and return her to you, and you to her."

Ava looked at the locket then leapt at Buc. She wrapped her arms around him as tight as she could with a warm, thankful hug. She loosened her embrace and looked back at her brother.

Edward approached Buc hesitantly. He stared down at the decking, avoiding eye contact with Buc. "Do pirates hug?" he asked.

Again, Buc smiled. "This one does," he said, spreading his wings wide to welcome the young fowl into the shared embrace.

Edward rushed in and hugged Buc.

As the embrace broke off, Ava returned to Buc before he had the opportunity to stand. She leaned in and whispered in his ear, "Thank you for giving us back our mama."

Buc stood up and smiled. His smile faded upon the realization that he was under the watchful eye of not only his crew but the crew of the Corazón Del Mar. He tugged on his coat and cleared his throat.

Turning his attention back to Robert, he stared at his father's face as Esmerelda applied a clean dressing on the wound.

Esmerelda looked over at Buc with amazement. "The blade missed everything. He be in no present danger."

Robert looked up at Buc, "Well, they do call me Lucky."

"Yes, you are, Father," replied Buc.

"Father?" inquired Chumlee.

"Father?" asked Twitch.

Even Esmerelda looked baffled. "Father?"

Buc reached out and helped Robert to his feet. "Yes. Unbeknownst to me, my uncle is actually my father, and he is also the long-lost pirate known as Lucky Longfeather."

"Sweet mother of pearl," muttered Chumlee. "You could knock me down with a feather!"

"Hardly," replied Buc.

Whispers began among Rojo's crew. No doubt the name Lucky Longfeather still carried weight in this day and age. It was clear to Buc they were concerned about their own fate. At times like this, Buc would seek the council of his uncle. He thought about what Robert would say and how he would act in this situation.

Buc approached the crew of the Corazón. "Who speaks for your crew?" he asked.

"I, sir," shouted Mister Merryweather.

"Stand," ordered Buc in a demanding tone.

The well-built rooster, once a model of the Governor's favor, slowly rose to his feet. His once spotless uniform was now tattered and stained. His face covered in soot and ash.

"Your name, sailor?"

"Merryweather, sir," he answered, wiping a small trail of blood from his beak.

"Mister Merryweather, I hereby inform you that your captain has met his end." He proclaimed, "Your ship is mine and, as my prisoners, your lives are now forfeit."

Robert looked to his son with great concern, knowing that Buc's next move may prove critical in his own fate. He fought his instinct to intervein but decided to let the scene play out.

"Mister Merryweather, do you have the necessary tools and skills to repair that ship?" he asked, pointing to the critically injured Corazón Del Mar.

Merryweather looked at his crewmates then back to Buc. "Aye sir. I do believe we do."

Buc nodded then proceeded to order the birds. "On your feet, sailors." He barked orders like a seasoned military commander.

The crew slowly made it to their feet, the effect of the battle apparent on their faces. Some of them were wounded, others just exhausted from their own time at sea.

"Here me now!" shouted Buc. "Your debt to Rojo, if any, is paid in full. You are no longer bound to him or his ship." Buc, arms crossed behind his back, strolled along the deck as he spoke. "You are all hereby ordered to return to your ship, make all necessary repairs, and sail back to Port Royal. At my request, Mister Merryweather will command as acting captain."

The crew of the Corazón began to mutter among themselves, but no one seemed eager to move or speak aloud.

Buc's brow furled as he remained confounded by their lack of motivation.

"Did you not hear me? You are all free fowl," he explained. "You are no longer bound."

The deck erupted in cheers and celebratory crowing. Fowl who had seemed beaten and worn down found a new sense of hope. Their merriment was accompanied by Mister Marley's guitar, playing a festive tune. Several sailors began to dance in place, while others fell to their knees, their faces filled with joyful tears.

As the crew of the Corazón began to make their way to their damaged vessel, Chumlee approached his captain, "Is it true?" he asked.

"Aye mate, Rojo is dead," replied Buc.

"No, Buc." Chumlee dropped the formality with his captain. "I be referring to the nature about your father. Is Robert really Lucky Longfeather?" he asked.

The history between Chumlee and Buc seemed to fade away for a moment. Buc saw Chumlee as the friend he had always hoped he was. He placed his feathery hand on his friend's shoulder. "He is indeed. Believe me, mate, I assure you, no one was more amazed than I." Buc pondered. "Well, perhaps Rojo." The two birds laughed aloud. All those years, the pirate Buc had grown to respect and admire was right under his beak. All the advice given to him, all the lessons, came from the very pirate Buc had read about as a chick.

Edward approached Buc. "Captain, sir, if he truly be Lucky Longfeather then he knew where the treasure lay all along?"

The deck went completely silent, with only the sound of the wind and waves filling the space between the crew.

The young fowl struck an intriguing chord. Buc looked at his father, wondering why a father would put his only child through all that they had been through. "The wee lad is right, and logic is sound, Father," explained Buc. "If you knew where the treasure lay then why force us to go through all those trials to find it?" He looked deep into his father's eyes, hoping to see the answer before it was spoken.

"It was your task, set forth by Good Thomas. It seemed proper to allow you to take the helm," replied Robert.

Buc scratched his chin. "I find it hard to believe you would put your only child in harm's way. Why would you risk never having the opportunity to tell me the truth?"

Robert smiled at his son. "I had faith you would survive." His reassuring smile didn't seem to falter Buc's concern. "All those lessons, and stories from Thomas were meant to prepare you." Robert's smile widened, "This …", he spread his wings wide, "has always been your destiny, son."

Robert chuckled and placed his gray feathered hand on Buc's shoulder. "Yer' whole life you be wantin' one thing. That one thing be the driving wind behind all your actions. It be flowing through your veins since birth. Thomas gave you the one thing you been craving. An adventure."

"But what if …", Buc was quickly interrupted by his father, "No sense worrying about what might have been. If you spend ya' life worryin' about the past, yer' gonna miss yer future."

Buc cocked his head, "Now you just be quoting your own self."

Robert laughed out loud, and the deck too erupted in laughter and cheers. His father was right. Buc had sought adventure his whole life. The same type of adventures his childhood hero, Lucky Longfeather, experienced. It all made sense now. His uncle's knowledge of pirating. The mysterious dealings with the cart handler in Tortuga. The reason why he didn't go ashore at Falcon Island. The answers became plentiful. No matter if he was called Uncle, Robert, Lucky or Father, they were all one and the same. They were all the oil that fueled the fire stoking Buc's sense of adventure.

"Aye!" shouted Buc. "An adventure we got, right, Mister Pugwald?" He looked about for the pelican but did not see him on deck. "Mister Pugwald?" he called out again, but there was no answer.

"Mister Chumlee"—Buc's voice was laced with worry and utter concern— "where be Mister Pugwald?"

Chumlee stood silent, his face expressionless. "We thought he was with you, on the island."

Buc felt cold as the fate of one of his crew set in. He looked back toward the lava covered island, watching it smolder and disappear into the steaming sea. The heaviness in his chest made it difficult to breathe, as if all the air had been sucked out of the world. In his heart, he had hoped Pugwald's departure from the cavern would save him from Rojo's treachery. A wave of regret and sorrow fell over him as he bowed his head. Pugwald deserved better.

The rest of the crew followed suit and bowed their heads in respect for their fallen shipmate.

"Rest in peace, Mister Pugwald." Buc sighed deeply as he searched for the proper words. "You were a brave, yet superstitious bird." He twisted toward Chumlee. "He spat in my boat." Buc turned back and continued respectfully, "You put your superstitions behind you to perform your duties. You offered to lay down your life in service of your captain and crew. For that, I say—"

Buc's statement was cut short by a loud thump behind him, as if a sack of flour were tossed down on the deck. He turned around to see the rear end of Mister Pugwald sticking up in the air, with a full belly-flopped face plant on the deck.

Buc approached the exhausted pelican. "Mister Pugwald, you have interrupted a spectacular service in your honor. What do you have to say for yourself?"

Pugwald strained to speak. He opened his mouth and the contents of his outstretched gullet spilled across the deck. Coins of gold and silver, rare gems, diamonds, rubies, emeralds, and pearls covered the surface of the Stench's wooden deck.

Buc gazed upon the sparkling treasure now sprawled out across the damp, wooden deck of his ship. He looked back toward the exhausted pelican. "Apology accepted, mate." Pugwald managed a weak salute before he fell flat on the deck, once again.

Chumlee approached the sapped out and wasted pelican. "Mister Pugwald!" he shouted. His loud bellow forced the last bit of Pugwald's strength to the surface. He rose and struggled to stand with as much dignity as he could possibly muster. "You be a frightful site, Mister Pugwald! Your appearance is lacking. You must have mistaken this ship for a roosting hall!" Chumlee's anger-filled shouting continued.

Pugwald attempted to address his appearance, struggling to tame wild feathers and wrinkled fabric.

Chumlee leaned in close to the bone-weary bird. "Mister Pugwald, I know not how long you plan to be part of this here crew, but I tell you this. At the first chance we make port in a town that could pass as semi-civilized—" he paused as Pugwald swallowed hard "—I will drag you from this ship to the closest tavern and buy you a tankard of their finest cider."

Pugwald looked at the quartermaster with his one good eye and blinked rapidly. "Sir?"

Chumlee burst out with a blustering laugh as he slapped Pugwald on the back, throwing him stumbling forward. The rest of the crew rang out in laughter until Chumlee lashed out once again. "What are you all looking at? Stow this treasure and clear the deck, ya spineless buzzards!"

The crew did not hesitate to start gathering the scattered treasure. If there was one task given to them by their burly quartermaster that they did not mind fulfilling, it was this one. They gathered gold and silver coins, often admiring them before tossing them into empty chests. Young Edward forwent the coins and selectively gathered the rare gems and jewels. His sister, disregarding the quartermaster's orders, stood off to the side, talking to Robert. She then ran to Mister Twitch and whispered in his ear. Twitch sprang up and blinked rapidly. A small clap of thunder made him pause and take in a steady breath.

As the crew collected their bounty, Buc strolled over to the railing where Mister Ayg sat perched. Ayg cooed as he approached. Buc reached up and stroked the large, feathery head of his oldest and dearest friend. "You saved my life, Ayg." Buc chuckled. "You saved my father's life."

Ayg let out a squawk in agreement. "You look like no other eagle I have ever seen, my friend," said Buc, admiring his friend's size and the strange feather protruding from his head. He smiled. "Will you ever cease to amaze me?"

Ayg ran his feathered hand over his head, forcing the odd feather down. It held for mere moments then popped back up once again.

"It's over mate." Buc said, thinking about how Rojo had filled his life with deception and falsehoods. From his visits to the orphanage, to his final words which sealed his doom. Everything Rojo did was to perpetually trick Buc into trusting him. Poor Thomas gave his life so that Buc would learn the truth. It was over.

Robert bellied up to the two birds. "Well, Captain Buc, a bigger success no captain could ever have asked for."

Buc took in a deep cleansing breath and looked at his crew. A dysfunctional flock of birds if there ever was one, yet, loyal and filled to the beak with fortitude. He watched as they scurried to collect, and marvel at the treasure they now possessed. As he continued to look out across the deck, his eye followed the ship's mast to his flag, the symbol of his family waving in the ocean breeze.

He smiled, *"This is where I was meant to be. "*, he thought. *"This is my place in the world."*

He turned to his father, "Aye. I do believe you are correct," he replied eloquently.

"So, what say you for our next move?" asked Robert. "Perhaps we rendezvous with your stepmother."

Buc's head jerked upward. "Stepmother?" With all the excitement, Buc had forgotten about his aunt. "Father, she's not…"

"No," added Robert quickly, "I am sorry to say your real mother was at home with you, at Kismet Key that dismal day."

"Oh," replied Buc, somewhat disappointed.

"Fanny, well, she be the tavern maid I spoke of. That pretty bird cared for me in my time of desperation," explained Robert. "We fell in love." He looked at his son's hopeful eyes. "She be no replacement for your mother, but she has always cared for you as if you were her very own."

Buc forced a smile across his face, torn between gratitude and loss. It wasn't difficult to draw in the similarities between the barmaid that changed Robert's life, and the one that changed Buc's.

"So," added Robert, "there be a small pirate commune settled on the island of New Providence."

Buc gazed downward at his feet. On the deck lay a solitary stone, missed by the crew as they collected their bounty. It was a perfectly cut emerald. He bent down, picking up the stone, admiring it closely. Looking deep within its pristine green hue, he could see his own reflection, in which he saw the pirate he had always dreamed of being. "That sounds exemplary, Father," he said. "But first…" He held the emerald up so the sun light could penetrate the green glass beauty. "I have a debt to repay."

Perhaps it was the beautiful weather of the day, or just a port full of newly arrived trading vessels, but The Wooden Stork was bustling with new salty faces. As the music played and the patrons laughed and drank their cares away, the tavern's barmaid Penny circled her way around tables and chairs to gather yet another tray of drinks.

She stopped at the bar, placing her tray before old Gus, the former owner, and her newest employee at the tavern. As he promised, Gus sold The Wooden Stork to her. The circumstances as to how she was able to raise the money so quickly eluded him, but he was happy to be a mere cog within the inner workings of the tavern.

As she waited for drinks to be poured, she reached down the neckline of her blouse and retrieved a pendant attached to a shimmering gold chain. She held up the perfectly cut emerald and smiled. With the tray refilled, she put back her pendant, and returned to her duties.

Placing the tray on a nearby table, she dispensed drinks swiftly to the thirsty fowl seated before her. "You lads new in town?" she asked.

"Aye!" shouted the tall, skinny heron. "Been at sea over a year!" He guzzled down his pint in a few short gulps, slamming the mug back on the table. "So, lassie," he began, "what bit of juicy blather can you share with us about this here unimpressive town?"

Penny smiled and leaned hard on the table before her. "Have any of you lads heard the legend of Buc Buccaneer?"

The End

Epilogue

The rain fell hard upon the crew and deck of the Fowl Stench. The heavy raindrops created a symphony of drums as they fell onto the ship's wooden deck. With the wind in her sails, the Stench sailed on, bobbing and weaving through the night touched waters of the Indian Ocean. Dark clouds seemed to follow them as they pressed on, determined to arrive at their destination in time for the next solstice. Perched on deck, Mister Ayg held his massive wing over his captain, shielding him from the falling rain.

"Mister Ayg, I hold a good feeling about this," Buc said with a smile, "There are answers to be found, and I am a fowl of my word."

Ayg responded in agreement with a powerful squawk.

"We are merely a day's journey away, my friend," replied Buc as he paused to sniff the air. He continued to sniff, turning about as he did so. Something was off. It was not the crisp, humid scent of rain he was detecting. Lifting his wing, he took a whiff of the underwing of his coat. His eyebrows rose. Although a bit rancid, it was not the odor he was detecting. He glanced upward at Ayg's wing. Quickly, he stepped into the rain and out from under its protective cover. "Mister Ayg, you seem to be smoldering."

Ayg lowered his wing, and it was apparent that something was wrong. Billows of smoke were emanating from the large bird's wing. The tips of his feathers began to glow brightly like the end of freshly lit tinder. Unaffected by the pouring rain, wing tips burned, and embers now danced around him.

Ayg looked at his wing and stared intently at his feathers, now glowing bright and discharging stronger puffs of smoke and steam. His condition worsened as it quickly spread to the rest of his feathers.

Buc's face fell as his concern for Ayg increased.

Ayg shrieked in fear as his feathers ignited into a violent blaze, encompassing him in a fiery ball of orange, blue and green flames.

Buc removed his coat and began thrashing it against Ayg's body, but the flames would not dissipate. He looked at his coat, unscathed by the flames. He looked up at his friend, now engulfed in flames, and panic set in. Despite the fact that the hard-falling rain seemed incapable of extinguishing the flames, he reached for a rain-filled bucket. As he slung back to throw the water on Ayg, the flames vanished, and Ayg was gone.

The bucket crashed to the deck, and Buc fell to his knees in front of the pile of ash that, until moments ago, was his best mate. *This cannot be how our story ends,* thought Buc. The crew of the Stench began to gather around their captain and stared on in disbelief. He reached out to touch the ashes that were once his life-long brother, and the pile of ash began to stir.

Quickly rising to his feet, he stumbled as the ash began to give way to a new shape.

Rising from the ashes was a large, dingy shell. Clumps of water-soaked ash slid off as the shell continued to rise.

Buc's eyes widened as he watched a complete egg poke through the muddy, rain-soaked ashes. He slowly approached it, reaching out with his feathered hand, and stopped as the egg began to move.

As he sprang back, he witnessed a wing break through the left side of the shell. With equal shock he watched as another wing broke through the right side of the shell and began to stretch outward.

Worry left Buc's face, and was quickly replaced with a cunning grin. Glancing over his right shoulder, he called out to his crew, "Someone fetch me a stick of coal!"

Made in the USA
Columbia, SC
03 February 2019